THE 9TH WITNESS

A Josie Bates Thriller

The Witness Series

REBECCA FORSTER

The 9th Witness
A JOSIE BATES THRILLER

By
REBECCA FORSTER

The 9th Witness
Copyright © Rebecca Forster, 2024
All rights reserved

Though certain elements of this novel were suggested by actual events, it is a
work of fiction. All characters, whether central or peripheral, are purely
products of the author's imagination, as are their actions, motivations,
thoughts, and conversations, and neither the characters nor the situations were
invented for them are intended to depict real people.

To the man who found the
things that belonged to me,
and brought them back
when he didn't have to.

Thanks To

Doctor Eliot Rosenkranz and Linda Dobie, VP of Legal Affairs at Torrance Memorial Medical Center. When **The 9ᵗʰ Witness** *was nothing more than a spark of an idea, these amazing people gave me counsel and inspiration. While the story did not follow the path I expected, the information they shared was not wasted. I was awed by their knowledge, willingness to imagine, and above all their generosity.*

Thank you also to Jenny, Bruce, Jiver, Glenn, and so many other who cheer me on.

Author's Note

I am fanatically curious about human nature. I wonder why some people step up to the plate in a time of need, and others turn their back. A hero fascinates me; a coward does not surprise me. That was why I was intrigued when I heard the story of a man who was named executor of a woman's estate despite not knowing her. He accepted the job and was led on an incredible journey of discovery. While there is no legal obligation for the designated person to honor such a request, an exceptional person like Josie Bates would step up to the plate. **The 9th Witness** is a story about a stranger, a choice, and, above all, integrity.

CHAPTER 1

EMERYVILLE, CALIFORNIA
BACKLASH TECHNOLOGIES
SEVEN YEARS EARLIER

A week before Christmas, things were happening in Emeryville.

First, the temp agency called Lily Daye. She had almost despaired of having a minimally happy holiday, but a position had become available, and she was urgently needed at Backlash Technologies. Technically, it wasn't Lily who was needed. The company simply wanted anyone who could take dictation, and this close to Christmas, few were eager to work.

After assuring the agency that she could do the job, Lily put on her good blue suit—her only suit—shined her shoes, and splurged on an Uber. The driver—a young man who appeared to be half asleep—deposited Lily in front of a building that looked like a carpet warehouse. The interior was a different story. The office of Backlash Technologies was a sleek sweep of stone floors and concrete walls. Both were studded with bright outcroppings of metal that took the place of walls and partitioned the area into work spaces.

A very young, very thin woman sporting very short green hair took Lily in hand. She seemed offended by Lily's attire, which was only fair since Lily took a bit of offense at hers too. The torn jeans were bad enough, but her t-shirt was emblazoned with a message that invited everyone in the world to go do something obscene to themselves. She also had a nose ring. All of this was, in Lily's estimation, terribly unprofessional. Of course, Lily didn't let her expression betray her thoughts. You never knew who was who these days, and this person might just be the boss of everything.

"You'll be there." The green-haired girl pointed to a desk just before she turned and indicated a closed door made of brushed metal. "And that is Jimmy's office. Jimmy is the CEO of Backlash and he is a certifiable genius. You need to transcribe everything he says verbatim. For history. We're making history here."

"How's that?" Lily asked.

"I don't know exactly. Only Jimmy knows," she said. "We all just do our part, and Jimmy personally puts it all together. It's finished now. It's shipping out today."

The green-haired girl paused. She gave Lily the once over again and shook her head.

"I can't even believe they're letting you in on it. Don't take that personally. It's just you're a newbie. Not even vetted. The rest of us have been here since the beginning. I was the first."

"Isn't there someone here who could take dictation then?" Lily asked this without considering the possibility that she was talking her way out of a job.

"Maybe Jimmy doesn't want us connecting the information we have with something he says. Who knows? I don't ask."

As she talked, the girl took an electronic pad off her desk and pushed it into Lily's hands. Lily had never seen anything quite like it, but she was familiar with the very long document she saw on the screen.

"That's an NDA. Non-disclosure agreement," the girl said. "You can't talk about anything you hear or see. Not a word. Ever."

For fear of offending, Lily did not say that she knew what an NDA was. Her silence miffed the girl.

"Just sign it. I've been here five years, and I wouldn't even know what was worth disclosing."

The girl leaned close, noted the signature line wasn't showing, and used her finger to scroll up, sighing with annoyance as she did so. She said, "Use your finger to write your name."

"Will I get a copy?" Lily asked. "I like paper."

"I'll send it to your email."

"I don't have an email," Lily said.

The girl rolled her eyes. "I'll print you a copy."

Lily signed.

The girl tapped the screen.

Somewhere in the cavernous space a printer was spitting out Lily's copy. Lily was sorry she annoyed the girl, but it was important to have standards. Paper was a reliable communication trail. Recordings could be manipulated. It was much harder to pull any shenanigans when there was an original paper document.

"Let's go. He's waiting."

"I am faster with paper and pen." Lily raised the tablet ever so slightly in a vain effort to give it back.

"You use that now. Not a word missed. If you can't handle it, say so."

Knowing the battle was lost, Lily was determined to win the war. She liked this place. The space was clean and manageable. Even the green-haired girl was acceptable. Lily could be happy here if left to do her work, so she said, "I'm fine."

"When you're done come back and plug this into that

unit." She pointed at Lily's temporary desk and the giant screen that sat atop it. "There's a cable in the top drawer. The data will dump, then go back over it and clean it up. You know, punctuation and stuff. Then you save it to the desktop file labeled *Distant2*. Don't take this home." She poked at the tablet. "Leave it on my desk when you're done." She pointed to her desk.

The green-haired girl liked to point.

"Okay," Lily said.

But it wasn't okay.

Electronics made her nervous. Being self-aware, Lily knew she needed a way to hedge her bet so that she could capture every word the man said. While she tried to figure out how to do that, she bought some time.

"What do you do here? I mean in general. It would be helpful to have some sort of context, so I will have a better understanding of what I'm hearing," Lily said. "I want to do a good job."

"We make stuff that's going to end war," the girl said. "Jimmy's a visionary. That's why you need to be so precise. Do you understand? We're all going to be part of friggin' history."

"Yes," Lily said.

The girl leaned in again. This time Lily smelled dope. She put a finger to her nose, but nicely as if she were scratching an itch.

"I mean, do you really understand?" the girl said. "Can you do it? The last one couldn't keep up with Jimmy. He sent her right out of the office."

Lily nodded, still trying to figure out a way to ensure that she would be able to do a good job, but the girl was so intense that Lily was struggling to think and listen at the same time.

"Yes, I can, but why do you even need me? Why doesn't he just talk into this?" Lily held up the pad. The girl smirked as if Lily had asked the dumbest question ever.

"He could do that easy, but Jimmy thinks better when there is a human being in the room. He's big on human beings," she said. "Any problems with the keyboard?"

Lily looked at the screen. It was smaller than an iPad and glowed purple when it went to sleep. There were a number of function keys that were unfamiliar to her, but the actual pad upon which she would type appeared standard. It was curious, though, that the keys seemed raised like a real keyboard. She assumed this was an optical illusion, but it was a comforting one.

"They retract when you're done," the girl said, as if reading Lily's mind. "Okay, that's it. You better get in there. He has to be at the train station in forty-five minutes because he wants to personally see to loading the crate. The hardware is very delicate. I heard it took two days just to make sure the crate and packing were strong enough in case something happened. In case it fell off the loader or something."

"You know what it does, don't you?"

Lily lowered her voice appropriately. This girl liked to talk. She liked to feel important. Lily knew how to ingratiate herself to someone like that. For the first time, the girl softened. The corners of her lips tipped up. Lily was pleased to find that she had read her correctly. The girl lowered her voice too.

"I've never seen it, but I heard from one of the coders that it can stop incoming nuclear warheads by pushing one button. They call the thing *Distant2*. I love that name."

"Was there a *Distant1*?" Lily asked.

"Yes, but nobody talks about that. Something went wrong and it almost put Jimmy out of business," she said. "But this time Jimmy did the final check and programming himself. Jimmy will turn over a special code when it's delivered. Only him and some general will know it. Once that code's activated, then *Distant2* will be—"

It was at that moment, just before the girl could tell Lily

what it would be, that a light flickered on the desk. The girl with the green hair—whose name Lily still didn't know—stood up real straight. She had very small breasts. They poked at her t-shirt instead of filling it out.

"Showtime," she said.

Lily, still unsure of how she would be able to pull this off, opened her mouth to beg for a minute more. Then the green-haired girl gave her the opening she was looking for.

"Take off your jacket," she said. "This isn't a mortuary."

Lily hurried to the desk in the corner, put her purse on the chair, and peeled off her jacket. She pretended to be particular about draping it over the back of the chair. The green-haired girl rolled her eyes, turned away, and went for the brushed-metal door. That was all the time Lily needed. She opened her purse, took out her phone, switched it to record, and slipped it into her skirt pocket. Lily reached the girl a second before she looked over her shoulder. The girl seemed disappointed that she wouldn't be able to snap at Lily again. Lily smiled. She gave her a solemn nod, and put her hand on the wall. She touched something Lily could not see. The door opened slowly.

"Good luck."

The green-haired girl walked away, and Lily stepped across the threshold into Jimmy-the-genius's office.

IT WAS A COCOON OF A PLACE, spun by a silkworm. Neither warm nor cold, dark nor light, it was bathed in a soft yellow glow, the origins of which Lily could not detect. The silence was profoundly peaceful. In the far corner, there was an upholstered gray flannel sofa. It was curved in the shape of a giant bean. The rectangular coffee table in front of it was carved from a polished white stone. A matching gray chair with deep cushions was positioned in front of a long, wide desk that was made of concrete. On the desk were three large computer screens that pulsed and scrolled with images and text Lily could not see. She only saw the changing colors: green and red and white.

"Come."

A tenor voice called to her. Lily wanted to laugh. The girl was wrong. Jimmy was no god. Everyone knew that God was a baritone. She moved forward, aiming for the deep-cushioned chair. It wasn't until she was standing in front of it that she saw him. Jimmy sat like a wise man on a mountain. He was framed by computer screens not cave walls, and he was the most beautiful man Lily Daye had ever seen.

Dark haired, dark eyed, his narrow face was defined by high cheekbones sloping into a soft jaw. His nose was high and royal. His mouth was wide, but narrow lipped. Lily had never met an Egyptian or a king, but she had seen a plaster cast of Tutankhamen at the museum. That's what this man looked like.

A boy.

A man.

Yes, a god.

Still, for a god, Lily thought him a bit unkempt. His long wavy hair was in need of brushing. His t-shirt was plain and stretched at the neck. His jacket had seen better days. It hung loose and looked more like a sweater than a blazer. Brushing his hair, putting him in a suit and tie, would negate the artistry of his appearance, so Lily decided he was perfect as he was.

He smiled warmly and gestured toward the chair.

Lily smiled back and sat down.

Her weight triggered something. A small platform popped up and unfolded like a tray table on an airplane. Lily tried not to show her surprise. She put the tablet on it. With this and the raised keys on the screen, she would be able to type quite comfortably. Knowing the phone in her pocket was recording meant the margin for error was nil.

"Let's begin," Jimmy said.

He leaned back in his chair, tented his fingers, and raised his eyes as if he were considering some profound text written in the dark above him. Lily focused on the tablet, waiting for him to speak. Just when she thought to peek at him to see if something was wrong, he began. Jimmy, the man who would save the world, talked and talked. He did not take a breath as the words flowed.

"...fulfilling our contractual obligation to deliver the device to Houston on December 19 barring any unforeseen circumstances including, but not limited to, acts of God. Full ownership of the device will be transferred to your representative at the station at that time. The technology will remain proprietary to Backlash Technologies. I will arrive in Houston on December twenty to oversee the hardware installation and testing of *Distant2* including programming of the Data Analysis Expressions. Per our agreement, these expressions will be recalibrated and put into force at the five-year mark to update as necessary, giving consideration to hard and software developments worldwide. It has been a pleasure taking this journey with you. Together we have made history; together we will protect this great country. Peace."

Jimmy fell silent as he ended the long litany of language that Lily did not understand.

Lily's fingers remained poised over the keyboard in anticipation of something more. When he still didn't speak, she raised her eyes and looked through the tunnel created by the computer screens. Jimmy was looking at her as if he had forgotten she was there. But Lily was wrong. He had not forgotten. Indeed, he was studying her. Lily was uncomfortable under such scrutiny.

"Is that all?" she said.

Jimmy smiled, and he didn't look Egyptian anymore. The slow widening of his lips and the subsequent softness around the eyes made him look a little more like Peter Pan if Peter Pan had messy dark hair and wore an old t-shirt.

Like a cat stretching in the sun, lazy, in no hurry to do anything, Jimmy said, "For now, but maybe later. Will you be available later?"

"Yes," Lily answered. "Of course. As long as you need me."

"That's fine then."

Lily moved, and the little tray table snapped down, startling her. She lost her grip on the tablet. As it tumbled to the floor, she swooped down, twisting at quite an unnatural angle, managing to catch it before any damage was done. Flustered, righting herself, she glanced at Jimmy to see if she had upset him. He seemed amused in a very kind way. Her blush deepened and she chuckled a little, pushing her hair back and patting her bun as she stood up.

"I'll get to this right away," she said.

Lily was almost at the door when he said, "I'm Jimmy."

Lily's head swiveled. Her brow beetled. Then she turned fully and took a few steps toward the desk. She stopped when he became visible. She could only see half of him now, and from that angle he wasn't as attractive as she originally thought. Perhaps, though, her perception of his physical being was now marred by this odd introduction. It was wrong-noted. She was put off because it felt as if he were toying with her. Lily did not like games. Wouldn't he know that she had been told his name? If he didn't assume that, wouldn't he have introduced himself the moment she appeared? In the normal course of business, one of those scenarios was a given. Then again, this wasn't normal business, and it took her a minute to figure out that this was personal. Now when the color rose to her cheeks, it burned. If Lily was right, her future at Backlash

Technologies would be quite different from the one she had imagined, and that might not be such a bad thing.

"I'm Lily," she said.

"Lovely."

"No, Lily," she said again.

"Lovely," he said. "Yes, Lovely."

Lily was smitten. Before she could smile or turn her head in a fetching manner, the metal door slid back and a woman walked past Lily without so much as a by-your-leave. She was not so much a woman as a girl. Plain of face behind her large glasses, she had mousey brown hair and was dressed in a manner that suggested she was color blind.

"Mary Margaret," Jimmy said.

Lily smiled because he didn't say her name in the same way he had said *Lovely*. In fact, his greeting indicated that he was somewhat displeased to see this person. She didn't seem to notice.

"We have to talk about the code, Jimmy, it…"

And that's all Lily heard. Clearly Jimmy had important work to do, so Lily went back to her desk to start her transcription.

CHAPTER 2

HERMOSA BEACH
PRESENT DAY

It was four-thirty in the morning, cold and dark, when Josie Bates, annoyed by her restless night, got out of bed.

She had dreamed, which was unusual. She couldn't remember the dreams, but they had kept her half asleep or half awake. She had no idea which it was, but both options were unacceptable. Her muscles jolted as if to give chase to the ghosts sailing through her brain; her lips opened as if to call to them. She did neither. The night seemed to go on forever.

When she finally woke, Josie lay in bed trying to figure out the cause of her restlessness. The possibilities were endless. The patio lighting was on the fritz. The young woman she was representing for trespassing had upped the ante when she dumped a dead cat into her neighbor's pool. And there was Faye. She was retiring, moving out of state to be closer to her daughter and selling the firm. Faye wanted Josie to buy it, but Josie wasn't ready for a sea change.

Not yet.

Not after everything that had happened.

Not when her life was in flux.

Hannah was gone to Oregon to attend an artist's retreat, Billy had shipped off on a trawler, and Archer–part-time PI, part-time photographer, full-time husband–had accepted a gig to photograph a rich guy while he shot big game in Africa. Both Josie and Archer knew the trip wasn't about photography as much as it was about healing. Josie's miscarriage had put them both off their game.

No wonder she dreamed and her sleep was fitful. No wonder she wasn't ready to take over Baxter & Baxter. No wonder she wanted to lie in bed staring at the ceiling. Disappointed that she was even considering such a thing, Josie got up.

Leaving the bed unmade, she pulled on her joggers and tied her trainers; she added a vest and watch-cap because the December mornings were freezing at the beach. She glanced at Archer's side of the bed. It was untouched. Josie hoped he was sleeping better in his fancy tent in Africa than she was at home.

Josie walked through the silent house ignoring the sadness that made her heart feel as if it were floating in molasses. She missed her humans, but this morning she missed Max the Dog, her beautiful German Shepherd, even more. He had been there to greet her, run the beach with her, and protect her from the moment she found him abandoned near the pier. He had grown old with her, watched over Hannah when she came into Josie's life, protected and loved everyone Josie loved. Now he was gone. Perhaps she missed Max so much because he was the only one who would never come back.

At four forty-five Josie left the house without bothering to lock the door.

By five thirty she had run two and a half miles past the Hermosa pier before turning around and heading home. She ran through the December drizzle on the deserted beach vaguely aware of a lone cyclist on The Strand and a man walking with his head down, his hands buried deep in his jacket pockets. They both looked lonely. Josie hoped that she didn't look like those men because she wasn't like them. Alone was different from lonely.

She was fine.

She was healthy.

And then she wasn't.

As she closed in on the pier intending to slalom through the pilings, Josie faltered. She lost her rhythm, her stride, and her purpose in one explosive moment.

An electric pulse sparked and pricked at her legs, making her muscles dance and nerves feel like live wires. The tingling jumped to her hands, shocking her as it ran up her arms. She snapped her hands at the wrist, trying to warm them. Suddenly cold to the bone despite the sweat that had gathered between her breasts and at her temple under her watch cap, Josie shivered.

Her mouth was dry and her heart was pounding, but not in a good way. It pressed hard against her chest as if its singular purpose was to push through flesh and bone and leap from her body. If her heart had a voice, it would be screaming.

Listen to me! Listen!

She would scream back, *Archer. Help me.*

Josie stumbled, and her breath came short. She fell against one of the pilings. Palms out, she leaned into it and pressed her cheek tight against the cold concrete. Her legs gave out, and she sunk onto the wet ground. On her hands and knees, Josie hung her head and tried to focus on breathing. It was hard because her mind was suddenly a chaotic kaleidoscope of images: people who hated her, loved her, those she had saved, and those she hadn't.

The baby.

Hannah.

Archer.

She closed her eyes, trying to stop the spinning in her head and the panic gripping her body. Josie dug her fingers into the wet sand. The waves broke like cannon fire, aggressive and graceless, forcing the water ashore. It swirled around her hands and knees; water so cold it could freeze her to death if the panic didn't kill her first.

Archer.

Needing to get away from the water, Josie began to crawl, pacing herself to the rhythm of her shallow, labored breathing. She moved an inch; she took a breath. Two inches more; a breath. A foot; a breath and then two. Off the hard, wet sand, away from the freezing sea water, Josie lay herself down and rolled onto her back. As quickly as it had come upon her, the panic receded. Her hand trembled. Her foot flexed. She took one more breath, and this time it went as deep as her gut. Just like that, it was over.

"Well, damn," she muttered.

She blinked. She turned her head so that she was looking at the sun rising over the horizon, painting Hermosa gray and pink. It was winter and that great orb was too far away to provide any warmth. Like the aftermath of an earthquake, Josie waited for the psychic aftershock. When that didn't happen, she got herself up, dusted herself off, took her watch cap off, and pushed her hand through her short hair to shake out the sand.

Then she started for home.

Josie walked past the bronze statue of the surfer perpetually riding the crest of his wave. Pier Avenue was empty. She went past Burt's by the Beach. Through the big window, she saw Burt taking chairs off the tables and arranging them just so. Soon he would fire up the grill. In another hour his staff would arrive to serve the early morning customers. The place would be busy and happy. At that moment, though, it looked like a

Hopper painting: an isolated man, illuminated by a harsh, flat light, the last man standing in a dark, lonely world. He hadn't turned off the string of pale blue Christmas lights framing the big front window. For some reason that made the scene lonelier still.

Burt would have let her in if she stopped, but Josie didn't. Instead, she went to the low wall separating the bicycle path and the beach, crawled over it, and went home.

Hers was a walking street, closed to traffic and home to ten houses, five on each side of the narrow road. At one end was the beach, at the other Hermosa Boulevard. Traffic was moving, but it wasn't as heavy as it would be in an hour. Mrs. Johnson's shades were open, the widow's signal that she was still alive and kicking. Josie was grateful for small favors. She wouldn't be of much use to anyone in need of help at the moment.

Josie opened the door to her house. When it was closed and locked, she put her back against it and tried to regroup. The air inside felt heavy, the drapes were shut, and the doors to Hannah's room and Archer's study were closed. It had been a very long time since her house was empty. She used to love her aloneness. Now it made her want to cry, a thing she never did.

Pushing off, Josie went to the bathroom, stripped off her running clothes, and shivered in the chill. Her body didn't feel like her own. She stepped under the water. It was scalding hot, and yet it wasn't hot enough to thaw her. Putting her hands against the tiled wall, Josie bent her head and let the water course down her back.

Five minutes later, her phone rang. She scrambled for it, grabbing a towel, wrapping it around herself, and leaving a trail of water as she rushed to the living room. By the time she got there, the ringing had stopped and the message light was on. She pressed playback and listened to Archer's voice saying he loved her, camp was moving, and he would call again when he could.

I miss you, Jo.

"I miss you, too," she said, even though he couldn't hear her.

Josie went back to the bathroom, renewed. Whatever had happened on the beach wasn't forgotten, but Archer's voice had put it in its place. Like Archer being so far away, the panic was a thing of the moment. He would return; Josie would make sure the panic didn't.

Josie shut off the shower, dressed, and walked to Burt's. By the time she got there, three tables were filled and Burt was still on his own. He lifted his chin to greet Josie but kept his eyes on the woman whose order he was taking. Josie settled in at the counter. He hustled past her to the coffee machine, filled a cup, twirled around, and put it in front of her.

"What'll it be, Josie?"

"Eggs. Toast."

"You got it. Susan's late, but I'll put you on the fast track."

They both laughed and he headed for the kitchen. For a man with a game leg, he could move with surprising grace. Josie checked her E-mail, setting it aside when Burt brought her eggs. Just as he promised that her toast was on the way, Josie's phone vibrated.

She held it up and mouthed, "Archer."

"Give him my best."

Burt went back to the kitchen, and Josie put the phone to her ear.

"Hey," Josie said.

"Josie Bates?"

The man's voice on the other end of the line was unfamiliar. Josie sat up straighter and swiveled toward the picture window.

"Yes?"

"This is Chief Miller at the PVPD…"

Josie listened. She nodded.

Burt was back with the toast, but when he looked at her, something in her expression gave him pause. He waited until she finished the call, and asked, "Everything okay, Josie?"

"Lily Daye is dead."

"That sucks." Burt refilled her coffee and put the toast in front of her. "Who is she?"

Josie picked up a piece of toast and shook her head.

"Beats me, Burt."

CHAPTER 3

Teddy Harper wasn't singing.

Neither was Henry Ross.

Their lips were moving, but the choir director could tell that whatever was coming out of their mouths wasn't even close to the lyrics of "Jingle Bells." He couldn't blame them. Teddy was eight, and Henry, the youngest of the group, was six. Singing Christmas carols for commuters wasn't half as interesting as a train lingering on the tracks making big sounds while crates were loaded onto the flatbeds.

The director would rather be watching the cargo lift, too, because he knew something important was being loaded. One of the crates in particular caught his attention. It was the size of an outhouse. Sturdy and unmarked, it had a car all to itself. Three railroad men worked on the lashings under the watchful eye of a short man with long wavy dark hair. When he was given a thumbs-up by the supervisor on the flatbed, the man with the dark hair waved the crew down before climbing onto the car. The director's hands waved more slowly as he paced his rag-tag choir because he was curious about the dark-haired man who lingered over the knots and ropes on the back side. The man tugged at the lashings and frowned. He looked vaguely familiar. He went for the ropes again and—

"Henry, stop!" Teddy Harper wailed.

The director whipped around to see Henry picking his nose with an energy that should have been put into shaking the bells he'd been assigned to ring.

"Henry," he said, a gentle reprimand in his tone.

All six children stopped singing. They looked at the director and then at Henry. The boy was surprised to be the center of attention. The girls giggled. The boys made faces and pantomimed wiping boogers on each other.

The director took a few steps, leaned down, and put a big hand on Henry's bird-boned shoulder.

Henry turned his giant hazel eyes up, his finger still embedded in a nostril.

The man whispered, "Henry, if you stop doing that and sing for just a little while longer, I will give you a very, very big surprise. Do you think you can do that?"

Henry nodded. The finger didn't move.

The director took Henry's little wrist and tugged on it. The finger moved. The older man put Henry's arm by his side and then took his place in front of his choir. He winked at his daughter, Melissa. She winked back with both eyes. The man smiled and the radiance of it lit up every little face. Two commuters paused to look as they got on the train, and they smiled too.

"Ready, angels? Ready to sing for God and all these people who have to go to work?"

Heads nodded with great energy. The director threw his shoulders back. The children mimicked him. They stood like soldiers with their little chests stuck out and their spindly arms and legs locked in place. He raised his hands, his chin, his eyebrows.

" 'Silent Night.' "

Gracefully, slowly, he moved his arms. The children had no idea what tempo was, but they knew when to sing. The director's heart swelled as he listened to their little voices, pure and untrained. He was a true believer and knew that God was listening. In fact, he was positive that God was especially watching out for this little crew because each one of them was a perfect example of His grace and goodness. These children were God's special angels.

When they were done with their song, The director motioned for the children to gather 'round.

"Because you did so well, we are all going on the train," he said. "You are going to ride with the engineer all the way to Martinez. You'll sing for the people there, and your parents are going to be there too."

The children broke into cheers. They jumped up and down. The director stood and herded them up the steps and into the engine. The engineer warned them not to touch anything, and then he sounded the whistle twice.

The children giggled and gasped with delight. The director almost clapped his hands. This was the best day ever. This was something the children would remember for the rest of their sweet little lives.

The director would never forget this day either because suddenly he remembered exactly who that dark haired man was.

CHAPTER 4

HERMOSA BEACH
PRESENT DAY

The sign on the narrow strip of lawn between the sidewalk and the two-story clapboard house was made from driftwood. The capital letters carved into the face of it spelled out Baxter & Baxter. Faye and her husband married, opened a law practice, and raised their daughter in that house. After her husband passed away, Faye continued to practice law. Eventually her daughter married and moved two states away. When Josie came to Hermosa Beach, Faye gave her a job and friendship just when she needed both in the worst way. Now Faye was bowing out of the bar, and she wanted Josie to continue on alone.

Today Josie paused to look at the sign and made one decision. If—and that was a big if—she bought Faye's practice, she wouldn't change anything. Baxter & Baxter had been part of the fabric of Hermosa Beach for forty years, and Josie wasn't above trading on the good will and affection the small city had for Faye. But buying Faye out wasn't top of mind as Josie took the three wide steps that led to the wrap-around porch. She opened the front door, blew in with an errant gust of wind, unwrapped her scarf, and unbuttoned her jacket.

"Hey, Ms. Bates."

The girl behind the desk smiled. Her name was Angela. She only came in three days a week since Faye was winding down her client roster and Josie didn't have much on her docket.

"How's it going?" Josie said.

"Okay." Angela shrugged as if to say that was an understatement. "I finished that filing and transcribed Mr. Carlson's deposition. It's on your desk."

Josie picked up her messages and glanced at Faye's office. The door was closed.

"Faye's not here?"

"She's in a meeting," Angela said.

"When she's done, would you ask her to come down?" Josie said.

"Sure."

Angela went back to work. Josie headed down a hallway that had originally led to three bedrooms and a kitchen. One of those rooms was now Josie's office, another, just off the kitchen, was a break room, and a third passed for a conference room. The latter was underused because the problems handled by Baxter & Baxter seldom warranted meetings of more than two.

Josie took off her jacket, tossed her bag on the small couch, sat down at her desk, and took a look at her calendar. There were no appearances scheduled. Tomorrow there were two, and Wednesday she had a full deposition for a client who left the scene of an accident, a case that could actually go to trial if the plaintiff had their way. After that, the world would start to shut down even though the holidays were two weeks away. With nothing pressing, before Josie could fire up her computer and do a little research into Lily Daye, Faye knocked and simultaneously stepped into Josie's office.

"I'm glad you're here," Faye said.

She smiled at Josie even as she motioned to someone behind her. Before Josie could say a word, her office was filled to bursting with sound, motion, and good cheer.

"Josie Bates! How fabulous is this? Last I saw you, you were in court giving Judge Jensen a whole shit-load piece of your mind. What was that? Like ten years ago. God, what did you do to your hair? You look like a boy. Still, pretty damn cute though."

Before she could blink, Josie was enveloped in a bear hug, pulled against a broad chest owned by a man five inches taller than she and all of him clad in a silk suit that cost more than Josie's car.

Rusty Gates, the man who had franchised the practice of law like it was McDonalds, was larger than life. If he wasn't pitching his firm on commercials, gigantic images of him were smiling down from billboards sprouting up beside the California freeways. If you missed him in the general universe, Rusty had a podcast, vlog, and a top-notch social media team to remind you he was there for you in your time of legal need. The only place you didn't see Rusty Gates was in a bona fide courtroom. Josie didn't watch television, she kept her eyes on the road when she drove, and basically did a fine job of evading Rusty—until now.

"Good grief. You just never know what's going to wash up on the beach." Josie extricated herself from his embrace and smiled. It wasn't that she disliked Rusty; it was just a little of him went a long way.

"I guess you two know each other," Faye said.

"We go way back. Law school, actually," Josie said, her smile full and genuine. Everyone loved Rusty except those who hated his guts. Seeing him lifted her spirits.

"Yep, we were something back then."

Rusty's voice boomed, his face broadened with his smile, his eyes sparkled. The man was made for television and should have been an actor. Then again, maybe he was an actor. His promises of multi-million-dollar settlements were most often scripted works of fiction.

He leaned toward Josie as if to take her into his confidence only to swing his head back to include Faye in their tête-à-tête. When that head of his swiveled, Josie saw that he had sprayed something on it in an attempt to cover up a small bald spot. He shouldn't have bothered. Not only did the cover-up not match his hair, but the effort was a waste of time. He could have been bald as a billiard ball, short as a munchkin, and every lawyer in L.A. would still want to be him. Rusty was wealthy, had style, and didn't work twenty-hour days or answer to anyone. He even managed to peel the legal onion in a way that kept him from stinking to high heaven of grift.

His glance at Faye was perfunctory. When he came back at Josie, he took her hands and pulled her arms wide, admiring how the little girl had grown.

"And look where we are now. Fighting for the little guy. Warriors, Bates. That's what we are."

"The only time you fight for the little guy is when you're sure the settlement is big enough to make it worth your while." Josie looked past him to Faye. "Check the till after you show this guy out."

Rusty dropped Josie's hands. In one stride he was beside Faye, his arm around her. The man had never met a woman he didn't like or felt free to touch. He was, after all, just good old Rusty. Harmless—unless he was on the job.

"Sorry, Bates. Can't chat," he said. "This little lady and I've got some business to attend to."

Rusty gave Faye's shoulders an energetic squeeze.

"Someday, Rusty," Faye said, "you're going to get your

head handed to you on a platter by a woman who doesn't think you're cute."

"You can sell tickets when that day comes." He gave her one more jiggle before he let her go. "All I'm asking is forty percent of the take."

"Since I'm old enough to be your mother, I don't think you have to worry about me being that woman." Faye knew Rusty could exhaust them both with his banter, so she cut him off before he took another breath. "Rusty is looking at Baxter & Baxter as a possible acquisition."

Josie's gut lurched and her smile faded.

"I didn't know you acquired, Rusty. I thought you franchised your business."

"I've got franchises in fourteen states. It's getting tough to keep 'em all on message. I do what I can, but I can't be in the studio shooting commercials four days a week only to find out that the franchisees don't know how to follow up on the 'Rusty Gates' rhythm. Know what I mean? You can't teach an understudy to be a star," Rusty said. "Then you've got state-by-state regulation, and it's just damn tiring. Anyway, I'm going to let that simmer for a while and acquire a few key firms that are already established. I'll help out with infrastructure and how to market. I'll be hands off. Various size firms, different specialties, under the umbrella of Rusty Gates, Inc. It's going to be a win-win for everyone."

Rusty shot his cuffs. His links were gold and fashioned with his initials. His initials were also embroidered on the pristine white cotton, but the font was too big, the shirt collar too long, the tie too wide. Everything about Rusty was oversized. Josie could imagine what would happen to Baxter & Baxter if he ran the shop.

"I didn't realize you'd gone public with the news that you were selling, Faye."

"I didn't officially, but Rusty has his ways."

25

Josie couldn't argue with that. Rusty Gates either had an uncanny sixth sense or big ears. Either way, he was always the first to exploit an opportunity or a tragedy. The man was a shameless opportunist.

"Don't worry, Josie," Rusty said. "Faye told me you've got first right of refusal. But frankly, I don't see you being the administrative type. You were hands on when you were in the big leagues, and from the looks of your press, you still are. That kind of defense law takes a lot of time, lots of focus. But you and me together?" He gave her a wink. "That would be a winning team. I'd even put you in the commercials. The way we look together..." Rusty turned to Faye. "Don't you think she'd look great on TV?"

He waved his hand Josie's way and the pavé diamonds on his signet ring glinted. Faye put a hand on his arm and with the other indicated the door.

"Before you start booking studio time, there's a lot to consider for both of us. If we go ahead with a deal, I'll leave it to you and Josie to duke it out about casting."

"Right you are, Faye. Let's take a look at the rest of the place, and I'll be on my way." Rusty passed Faye, but before he disappeared for good, he stuck his head back into Josie's office. "Heard you got married, Bates."

Josie held up her hand and showed him her plain gold band.

"Breaks my heart." Clearly, he was not heartbroken. "He's a lucky man."

"That's what he says," Josie answered. "But I think it's the other way around."

Rusty gave her a final wave and he was gone, but Josie begged for a minute of Faye's time before she left, too.

Faye begged back, "Give me another twenty minutes to wrap up with Rusty, and then I'll—"

"Just a quick question," Josie said. "Does the name Lily Daye mean anything to you? Spelled d-a-y-e."

"Context?"

"Palos Verdes PD called this morning. They did a wellness check and found a woman dead."

"And they called you about a woman you don't know?" Faye asked. When Josie balked, Faye pressed her. "Come on. I haven't got all day, Josie. How come you hit the jackpot?"

"She named me as executor of her estate," Josie said.

Faye's head wagged in dismay. Clearly, she did not find the situation intriguing. She glanced after Rusty, then back at Josie. Finally, she said, "Stay put."

Josie heard Faye ask Rusty Gates for a minute; she heard Rusty say he would show himself around. In the next minute, Faye was back, perched on the edge of Josie's sofa, speaking without preamble.

"The PVPD called you, gave you this bit of news, and you said what exactly?"

"I haven't said anything yet," Josie said.

"Then let me tell you what you should have said. The word would have been *no*."

For a second, it seemed that Faye's pique was going to continue. Then her face softened and her eyes met Josie's.

"Sorry. Sorry." She waved her hands a little. "I was about to go postal on you, and that wouldn't be right. Still, something like this is my business, and I think I should at least put in my two cents. I've been to hell and back with you ten times over when you pick up one of your more challenging cases. I always had a stake in the outcome because you're not just my colleague, you're my friend. Truth be told, you are like family. That's why I'm going to be frank.

"You and Archer are going through a tough time. Hannah and Billy are away. Most important, you lost a baby and you're grieving."

"That doesn't mean I haven't been performing," Josie said.

"Performance is muscle memory for you," Faye said, clearly frustrated. "What's roiling you is so deep inside that you can't even figure out where it's coming from. I get it. When Frank died, I thought I was on target with everything, too. I wasn't, and when I crashed, I crashed big time. You need to get your act together before you try to deal with a stranger's problems."

"But there has to be a reason she—"

"Of course, there's some reason, but for you this little mystery is nothing more than a shiny thing," Faye said. "Ignore it. You have decisions to make. Maybe you want to try again for a baby. Maybe you want to save this firm from Rusty Gates. Talk to Archer and Hannah. Talk to Rusty if you've got the energy and a couple of hours to spare, but for god's sake don't ignore your real life to chase after the problems of a stranger. I can't wait much longer for you to rebound."

"I'm not asking you to wait," Josie said.

"Your indecisiveness speaks for itself, Josie."

Faye's words were a lament. She clasped her hands and rested her arms on her knees as she collected her thoughts. When she looked up, her expression left no doubt that, as much as she cared for Josie, she was committed to her own affairs.

"That man down the hall wants to reshape this firm, and that makes me sad. I want you to decide your future, and selfishly I want you to choose to protect this practice. I guess I'm just arrogant enough to think that there will actually be a legacy when I'm gone, and I would like to see it in good hands. In the end, though, it doesn't matter what happens because I won't be here. The question is, where will you be?"

When Josie had no answer, Faye stood up, smoothed her dress, and touched the scarf at her neck. Instead of leaving the office in search of Rusty, Faye walked over to Josie, put a hand on her shoulder, leaned down, and kissed the top of her head.

"I love you like a daughter, Josie," she said. "Make your apologies to the PD. Walk away from whatever this thing is because no good can come of it. Either this lady was crazy and pulled your name out of a hat or…"

Faye pulled in her bottom lip. Her head tipped. There were blanks to be filled in, but Faye just shook her head.

"Or what, Faye?"

"Or you do know this woman and when you find out who she is, you may not like it."

Josie snorted and smiled, but there was no humor in either gesture.

"My past coming back to haunt me?"

"Don't make light," Faye said. "You've put your life on the line for people you didn't know before. You have a savior complex, Josie."

"I help when it's warranted," Josie objected, but Faye didn't listen.

"One day you're going to need saving. Who'll be there for you when that happens? Archer? Hannah? Billy? Me? What if we're not the right people for the fight? What if we get hurt in the fray?" Faye waited a beat and then asked, "Why tempt fate? Really. Why?"

When Josie had no answer, Faye started to leave, but when she got to the door, she turned around and put her hand on the jamb, laughed sadly, and gave it a pat.

"I didn't mean to go off," she said. "Eventually I will miss the chaos you bring. Right now, I just miss you. I want the old Josie, the one that doesn't stare into space, the one that doesn't rub her arms like she's cold all the time. You think I don't notice, but I do. Don't make me worry anymore. I'm too old for this, and you should know better."

Josie nodded because she didn't have the voice for what needed to be said. Words of affection didn't come easily to her. For Josie, actions spoke louder and Faye always understood. The older woman inclined her head. Rusty was waiting.

"If that one makes me a good offer, I'm going to take it," Faye said. "Maybe that will scare you into beating him to the punch and buying the shingle."

Faye gave the door frame a rap and was gone. Josie heard her apologizing to Rusty as she walked down the hall. The man said something that was followed by a boisterous laugh, the opening of a door, and then silence.

Josie sat for no more than a minute before she picked up her phone with the intention of following up with opposing counsel for the upcoming deposition. She never made the call. Instead, Josie got up, put her jacket on, and picked up her bag.

While Faye and Rusty Gates went out the back door, Josie walked out the front.

CHAPTER 5

EMERYVILLE
A STRIP MALL PARKING LOT
SEVEN YEARS EARLIER

Mary Margaret Watkins was not the most attractive girl in the world, but she was smart. Not just smart as a whip, not just a smart cookie, but really smart. Sadly, she was also really dumb. Dumb as in she didn't understand that calling out body odor was best done in a whisper. Dumb as in not understanding that when a group of coworkers left for lunch, she should not trail behind them, sit at their table, and stare at them instead of waiting for an invitation to join in. Mary Margaret was so dumb that she didn't even understand that such an invitation would never be forthcoming. It didn't matter if Mary Margaret was socially inept, though, because her colleagues still admired her.

Some speculated that she was a superior alien being, while others believed she was AI powered by a super-duper program. Give Mary Margaret a problem to solve, a challenge that intimidated others, and she would stay on task until the chore was done. She also recognized a superior mind when it presented itself. She believed Jimmy had such a mind.

Jimmy appreciated the compliment but he knew her assessment was flawed. Yes, he was intelligent enough to have a vision, to attract an amazing number of investors willing to gamble on that vision, but what made him brilliant was his understanding of human nature and his lack of ethical boundaries. Recognizing that Mary Margaret worshiped him, Jimmy was happy to use her and her brain to his advantage. He made her his special assistant on the *Distant2* project, the innovative defense system he believed would deter all warheads. He, Jimmy, would be responsible for ending the threat of nuclear war. He, Jimmy, would be more revered than the jackasses who built the damn bomb in the first place. Yet as the project neared completion, Mary Margaret became annoying with her nitpicking. Worse, she had come very close to exposing Jimmy for what he was—selfish. He was not as brilliant as he appeared and he was arrogant to a fault. The only thing that stopped this from happening was Jimmy himself.

Mary Margaret didn't know that Jimmy was aware of everything in his universe including the shortcomings of *Distant2*. She also didn't know that Jimmy had formulated a brilliant and secret work around.

So, there he was, king and castle, knight and bishop on the chessboard of his making. What Jimmy was not, and never would be, was a pawn. Therefore, when Mary Margaret scooted toward him like the privileged queen with her concerns about *Distant2*, when she threatened to expose his Achilles heel, Jimmy took action. Because she was stupid in her own way, Mary Margaret didn't recognize his deft moves and her attention was easily diverted. He pointed her elsewhere, to a project critical to his plan for *Distant2*.

Mary Margaret embraced that project with all the zeal of a blood-sucking tick.

Now there she was, standing next to the fruit of her labors, the definitive car of the future and the future beyond that. The value of this car was in a battery that required one charge at half-life to retain its power. Range would be counted in thousands, not hundreds, of miles.

In the last three months she had worked tirelessly on the project because Jimmy wouldn't budge from the deadline. He had sworn her to secrecy. She in turn promised to die before divulging any information about the battery. To further protect the project, she and Jimmy had personally embedded the amazingly small battery into Mary Margaret's very own car the night before.

Now it was the moment of truth. Jimmy had programed the course to test the car's responsiveness in all situations—uneven surfaces, pedestrian crossings, water hazards, heavy traffic, open driving, and so much more.

Mary Margaret wished he was there with her, but she understood that *Distant2* took priority. As she waited in the car for Jimmy to log on, she wondered what he had done about her suggestions for *Distant2*. Mary Margaret didn't wonder very long because things started happening.

Right on time, the ignition started. Mary Margaret's eyes swept across the large screen that showed a detailed map of the area. Data would accumulate with each response to terrain change—stop, hesitation, acceleration, turn. There was a clock in the corner of the screen ticking off the four and a half minutes before the start of her journey. Mary Margaret fastened her seat belt. It was extremely tight and became tighter still as she tried to adjust it. As she was making note of this glitch, Jimmy hailed her.

"How are you doing, Mary Margaret?"

"The seat belt is tight, Jimmy," she said. "It's never been tight."

"I made a little adjustment. I'm sorry. I just want to hedge my bet," he said. "We'll cut you out when you're finished if we have to."

Jimmy chuckled. So did Mary Margaret. He gave her a moment and then began to enter the code. Mary Margaret watched the screen, punching in confirmation when he made the request to do so. She hesitated once.

"Did you change the timing on three, Jimmy?"

"It's only a little tweak to make things more precise," he said. "You may confirm."

Mary Margaret took a minute. She didn't like confirming when she didn't know what the change entailed. Still, she didn't want to upset him again like she had when she brought up the Data Analysis Expression regarding *Distant2*, so she followed procedure.

When he was done, Jimmy said, "Are you ready, Mary Margaret?"

"I am," she replied.

"I'll have you in my sights from beginning to end. I promise."

Mary Margaret glanced at the clock. Thirty seconds before the car engaged. She wanted to use those seconds to the best advantage, so she said, "Jimmy, did you ship *Distant2* or are you going to—"

"Focus, Mary Margaret," Jimmy barked.

Startled by the sound and harshness of his voice, Mary Margaret pulled against the seat belt and almost choked herself. Then again, who could blame him? He was responsible for everything that came out of Backlash Technologies. His reputation and fortune were on the line. The pressure must be unbearable.

The clock ticked the last second to the hour and Mary Margaret remained silent.

Finally, Jimmy spoke to the car. "Drive the route."

The car began to move.

"Goodbye, Mary Margaret," Jimmy said.

"Goodbye, Jimmy," she answered.

CHAPTER 6

PALOS VERDES, CALIFORNIA
PRESENT DAY

Josie drove south on Sepulveda Boulevard, unfazed by the traffic crawl through Hermosa Beach. She lingered at red lights, gave right-of-way at crosswalks, and slowed behind the cyclists. She passed miles of small restaurants, salons, and bars that were housed in storefronts pushed together like a strip of Lego blocks before Sepulveda became Pacific Coast Highway for a bit. She veered right at Redondo Beach's King Harbor and onto Catalina Avenue.

Catalina Avenue, a wide boulevard that ran through Torrance and Redondo Beach, would eventually land her on Palos Verdes Boulevard where she would wind her way up the hill into the city of Palos Verdes Estates. She whizzed past the Redondo Post Office, a strip mall, a large storage facility, and high-rise apartment buildings. She considered cutting over to the Esplanade that ran along the ocean but decided the distraction wouldn't be wise. Instead, while she drove, Josie did as much due diligence as she could regarding Lily Daye.

She talked to her car, running Lily Daye's name through her search engine and listened as it identified sixteen women and a spa by that name. None of the women lived in the South Bay, and the spa was out of business. Josie put in a call to Hannah on the off chance the woman might have crossed her path, but she got voice mail. Josie left a message. Josie considered that Lily Daye might be a vendor—a hairdresser, cleaning service, or gardener that she had employed at one time—but she couldn't identify her in any context. She left a message for Archer asking the same question she had of Hannah. Billy was out at sea, and if he were the link, she would have to wait to find out.

Thirty-five minutes after she left Hermosa, Josie crossed into Palos Verdes Estates—one of five cities on a peninsula that few people outside the South Bay knew existed. That was good news for Palos Verdes where the hills were green with open land, and forests of eucalyptus perfumed the air. A body could hike the trails or ride a horse over the hills to the bluffs that looked out over the craggy coastline to Catalina Island. Nature shared her space with modest red-roofed homes on narrow streets at the foot of the hills and mansions on top. Palos Verdes Estates was the epitome of a bedroom community, and at two in the afternoon, it appeared to still be asleep.

At Malaga Cove, Josie merged left and came to a four-way stop. The white washed Spanish-style buildings nestled behind brick arches, ringing a decent sized parking lot, was Palos Verde's idea of an office park. The space housed real estate offices, family counselors, a small law firm, and a neighborhood grocery. There was a fancy little restaurant in a half-hidden courtyard where ladies lunched under yellow umbrellas. The centerpiece of it all was a three-tiered marble fountain where Neptune lorded over fish and sea nymphs, all of which spewed never-ending streams of water into deep basins. The place reeked of money, privilege, and contentment. When it was her turn to go, Josie made a left, a right, and another right as she pulled into a small parking lot across the street from the main complex. This one served the city offices of Palos Verdes Estates.

She got out of the car, took the stairs down to the lower level, opened the door to the Palos Verdes PD, walked up to a small, bullet-proof window, and spoke to the young female officer.

"Josie Bates for Chief Miller."

⊏⊐

"HOPE you didn't have to come far."

Chief Miller personally escorted Josie to his office. He motioned to a chair while he went to perch on the edge of his desk.

"Hermosa," she said.

"Good. Good. Glad it wasn't a hardship. Can I get you coffee?"

Josie declined.

Chief Miller was pushing sixty. He had the easy-going smile of a self-assured man, one who would rise to any occasion if the energy was warranted. She pegged him for a cop who had served his time on some big city streets, wasn't quite ready to retire, and preferred to finish his career alive and in one piece. A job in Palos Verdes Estates would check all the boxes. Crime was close to nil, and the department was appreciated, respected, and well-funded.

"I'll be honest, I thought twice about coming," Josie said.

"Understandable given the circumstances. So let me bring you up to speed, and we can go from there," he said. "We received a request for a wellness check day before yesterday. Came in at three-oh-one in the afternoon asking us to look in on the resident of one of the cottages over on the Vanderhaven estate."

"Isn't the estate in Rancho Palos Verdes? That would be the county sheriff, right?"

"A lot of people think we service the entire peninsula. Common mistake. That being said, we have a good rapport with the sheriff and gave them a heads up. They were happy for us to take it off their hands. We had the time, and an expedient wellness check is in everyone's best interest."

Miller reached behind him, picked up a manilla envelope, and handed it to Josie as he went on. "We found an unresponsive female, approximately thirty-five to forty years of age in the bedroom of a free-standing structure on the estate. Her name was Lily Daye. She's been in residence for three years. There are five rentals on Mrs. Vanderhaven's property, but this was the only one occupied. Ms. Daye was fully clothed. My officers did not attempt to revive her since it was clear that she had been dead for a while. They called the M.E., and her remains were transported to the morgue. My officer stayed on site and secured the scene."

"Any sign of foul play?" Josie asked.

"Unless the M.E. finds something, I would say not. I think we're looking at an accidental O.D. or a suicide. There were no signs of forced entry. Nothing was disturbed—not that there was a lot to be disturbed." Chief Miller raised a finger indicating the envelope in Josie's hand. "My officer found that on the bedside table."

Josie turned it in her hand, noted that ICE—in case of emergency—had been written in small, neat printing on the upper right-hand corner. She asked, "Who called in the wellness check?"

"It was a man. I listened to the recording. I would guess he was youngish. He wasn't panicked, and he declined to give his name."

Chief Miller got off the desk and went around to his chair. He was in full uniform including a sidearm. When he sat, he crossed his arms on the top of the desk and used one finger to fiddle with a stress ball that she doubted he had need of.

"I assume you interfaced with the Vanderhavens. Was this woman involved with one of the family members?" Josie asked.

"As far as I know, there's no one to interact with except old Mrs. Vanderhaven," he said. "She was widowed a hundred years ago. She lives in the main house with a caregiver—a woman—so that takes her off the table regarding the phone call. That lady isn't married, and she said that the only man in the house who comes around is Mrs. Vanderhaven's son. He doesn't live there. Mrs. Vanderhaven doesn't believe her son had any interaction with Ms. Daye."

The chief picked up the stress ball, squeezed it once, and put it back on the desk.

"As for the call for a wellness check, it could have been the gardener," he said. "The caller didn't have an accent, so I'm going to rule out a migrant who was afraid to leave his name. It could have been a friend or a relative trying to get in touch with her. Maybe the lady had a job, and the guy calling was her boss. You know how it goes. It could have been her dry cleaner wanting her to pick up her laundry.

"Bottom line is this, even good people don't like to get involved with the cops. Whoever made the call probably figured he'd done the good citizen thing and went about his business. You're welcome to listen to it."

"I will if I move forward," Josie said.

"All the paperwork is in there. It's a neat little package," Chief Miller said.

Josie opened the envelope and peered inside. She saw a small book, a check register, and a piece of paper. She pulled out the paper, unfolded it, and gave a look. It was a simple will assigning Josie Bates as Lily Daye's executor. Two witnesses had signed the document, one of which was Mrs. Vanderhaven. The will directed all proceeds of Lily Daye's estate to be used for the benefit and welfare of Mr. Murray.

"Fabulous," she muttered.

It wasn't the work of an executor that dismayed Josie. She was familiar with such responsibilities. The point was, there were only two reasons anyone took on a job like this—you were hired to perform the duties or you accepted the designation as a labor of love. Josie had been executor of her father's estate; she was her mother's guardian. She and Archer were one another's designees. She had been hired by any number of elderly clients in Hermosa Beach and acted as their durable power of attorney or executor for a fee. This was different. This was annoying. This woman was inserting herself into Josie's life, and it was that presumption that bothered Josie.

"Guess this kind of puts you in a bind," Chief Miller said when he deemed that she had enough time to read over the document twice. Josie gave him a weary smile.

"Not really," she said. "I have no obligation here, Chief. Unless there is something you have to share that is more compelling, I'll have to decline."

"I hear you. Not a soul in the world would blame you for letting this lie," he said. "Still, it's kind of a shame. Sometimes there are things that happen on the job that kind of stick in your gut. Personally, I can't imagine how desperate this woman must have been to reach out to someone she didn't know—or one who doesn't remember her. It would be worse if she actually thought of you as a friend."

"But she didn't reach out," Josie said. "If she had, I could have helped her. The point isn't if…The point is…"

Josie's voice trailed off; her eyes wandered to the certificates on the wall behind the chief. She could share that it was a tough time for her, too, but you don't say things like that to strangers. And a lawyer certainly doesn't admit vulnerability to law enforcement. One never knew when such an admission could be used against them in a legal proceeding. And a woman didn't admit fear to a man unless that man was trusted. Most of the time a woman didn't admit fear and failure to herself. Maybe that's what happened to Lily Daye. She just couldn't bring herself to say the words.

I'm afraid.

I've failed.

Help me.

Josie tapped the envelope on the arm of the chair.

Her eyes went back to the chief's. His were gray, but not cold. He reminded her of Archer.

"Do you have anything else?" she asked. "A place of employment? Some other affiliation that could help me identify her?"

"I don't," he said. "And it's not up to me to investigate unless it's a crime scene."

"What about a call back number for the guy who reported her."

"He wanted to remain anonymous, so we'll honor that. If you are requesting that information in an official capacity, I'll check with the city attorney and let you know."

Chief Miller gave his stress ball a little flick, and it rolled toward a picture frame on his desk. He smiled.

"I know it's a tough call, Ms. Bates. People like us aren't used to turning our backs. Still, sometimes you gotta do it," he said. "We'll keep it open for a day or two and see if something comes our way. Maybe a next of kin. Then you're officially off the hook."

Josie stayed silent. If this was a matter of being let off a hook, she knew how to wiggle away. This was a matter of expediency and timing. Josie had no idea what this woman's financial commitments were or what her wishes would be because the directive Josie held in her hand was minimal.

Without a roadmap to show her the way, Josie would be second guessing every step. That was a lot of energy to expend on a stranger. Not that it would matter. Lily Daye would never know that Josie had refused her final request.

"If anyone comes forward, give them my number. This lady needs someone with some skin in the game." Josie held out the envelope. He waved it away.

"Hang on to it just in case," he said.

Josie stood up and put the envelope into her bag.

"I don't think I'll be changing my mind," she said.

"Your decision, of course." Chief Miller got up and put his hand out. "I can see why Ms. Daye might have landed on you. At least you did her the courtesy of showing up."

Josie offered a shadow of a smile. She knew there was a difference between showing up and a mere presence. Since she wasn't up for the debate, Josie took her leave.

In the parking lot, she got behind the wheel but didn't start the car. Instead, she contemplated the brick building, thinking about nothing in particular. A woman in pink sneakers and sweats hurried by. Her blonde hair was rich with caramel high-lights; her sneakers were pristine. She disappeared into city hall, came out moments later, and strolled toward the plaza. Josie watched her in the rearview mirror as she crossed the street.

In the pretty little hacienda-style center, real estate agents fielded calls from people who wanted to live in Palos Verdes where life moved slowly. The community was safe because of geography and Chief Miller. This was how all of life should be and seldom was. Josie knew all too well that looks could be deceiving. Doors in Palos Verdes were like closed doors in every other place on earth: what went on behind them was anyone's guess.

Case in point—the sad circumstance of Lily Daye.

If the woman had sought Josie out before she became

desperate, Josie would have said that life is nothing more than a game of dodge ball. Everyone takes a hit and sits on the sidelines before they get in the game again. Not Lily Daye, though. Lily must have taken a big hit, because she wanted out of the game permanently. Josie consoled herself with the fact that she couldn't have helped a woman liked that. She was only a lawyer, after all, and despair wasn't something she could mitigate.

Suddenly, Josie's fingers jumped. The palms of her hands tingled. She didn't know when she had gripped the steering wheel, but there were her hands, white-knuckled at ten and two. A current of electricity shot into her wrist.

"Oh, come on."

Pulling her right hand away from the wheel, she flexed her fingers. The day had moved on, and the panic attack on the beach should have been a one-off. The fact that Lily Daye's circumstances—her tragic aloneness—could be a trigger was a sure sign that Josie should walk away.

Starting her car, she threw it into gear and left Palos Verdes Estates, driving downhill a little faster than she had driven up. She needed to get back to the office and talk to Faye. There was a deposition to prepare for. The holiday was coming on fast. Josie couldn't be bothered by anything else.

And yet she was bothered by a sinister annoyance, a current of concern, a swelling wave of curiosity. What she felt was ephemeral and urgent, like being caught in an undertow and pulled into dangerously beautiful but uncharted waters.

She stopped at a traffic light, waiting for the signals at the intersection to give her permission to move forward. When Josie finally got the green light, she stepped on the gas. At the last minute, Josie swung her Jeep onto the on-ramp of the freeway and headed downtown to the morgue.

CHAPTER 7

EMERYVILLE
BACKLASH TECHNOLOGIES
SEVEN YEARS EARLIER

Jimmy came back from the train station just as Lily was stopped cold by a glitch in her transcription. She reached into her pocket for her phone to play back his dictation only to find her pocket empty.

Her breathing went shallow.

Her hands went cold.

Her heart slowed until she thought it might stop completely.

She looked over her desk, pushed her chair back, and searched the floor to no avail. Her phone was gone and there was only one conclusion Lily could come to—the phone was still in Jimmy's office, fallen out of her pocket when she tried to keep the tablet from dropping. If he found it, he would think she was an industrial spy at worst. At best, he would believe her incompetent. Either way Lily would be diminished in Jimmy's eyes. He would never call her *Lovely* again.

For a moment, she sat stone-still, calming herself as best she could. Lily patted the bun at the nape of her neck and touched the collar of her blouse. She dipped her head, slyly looking around to assess the situation.

The green-haired girl was at her desk, the door to the inner sanctum was closed. Hard as she tried, Lily could think of no excuse to gain re-entry into Jimmy's office. Even if she could, how would she search for her phone without him noticing? But then Lily's luck changed. The brushed metal door opened. The green-haired girl stood up, and Jimmy came out of his office.

He said, "I'll be home if you need me."

"Sure, Jimmy," the girl said.

He was almost to the front door when he caught sight of Lily and paused. She felt his eyes on her back but pretended to be engaged in work. The longer he looked, the harder her heart beat.

When she couldn't stand it a minute longer, when she decided facing the music was preferable to this torture, Lily turned to face him. Jimmy looked deep into her eyes, and she into his. Lily tipped her head, forgetting about the phone for a moment because she was stunned to find that he had changed.

His lips looked bigger, slack, and moist. He was shorter than she originally thought. Lily hadn't noticed his pallor in the shadowy office nor the exhaustion in his eyes. Perhaps these were just manifestations of his disappointment in her. Perhaps he was getting ready to call her out in front of the green-haired girl and regretted the chore. Then again, maybe she was imagining things because when Jimmy spoke, it was gently, and he was as he had first appeared.

"Don't work too hard, Lovely."

Lily's head bobbed with a staccato-like movement. The green-haired girl seemed displeased. Then again, after hours working in this place, Lily had pretty much come to the conclusion that the green-haired girl was always displeased.

When Jimmy, the god of Backlash Technologies, was gone, the green-haired girl left the room and Lily seized the day. She bolted for Jimmy's office, poking at the wall until something tripped and the door opened. Lily dashed inside and went for the deep-cushioned chair where she had sat to take dictation.

Her phone was not on the seat, underneath the chair, nor on the floor beside it. Lily pushed her hands between the cushions. She prayed. Perspiration gathered at her hairline. She needed to pee. Lily sobbed once and sank to her knees in despair. She put her head on the arm of the chair. Jimmy, she was sure, had found her phone and was, even now, planning how to deal with her. Perhaps he would call the police and have her arrested. Maybe he was contacting his lawyer.

It wouldn't matter that her intentions had been good, it only mattered that she had been sly and stealthy, and a miserable little cheat. Lily had told them she was up to the job, and the recording would prove she hadn't been. The temp agency would drop her. She might go to jail because she had signed an NDA.

But none of that would happen.

As Lily sat back on her heels and wiped her eyes, she saw it. Her phone had, indeed, fallen to the floor, landing so near to the chunky wooden foot of the chair that it almost seemed a part of it. Swiping it up, Lily held it to her breast with one hand, put her other hand on the arm of the chair, and pulled herself up.

Knowing that she was not home free until she was back at her desk, Lily peeked through the door, confirmed the outer office was still empty, and slipped out of Jimmy's office. She got to her chair just as the green-haired girl rushed in to answer her ringing phone. Lily sat back at her desk, slipping her phone under a stack of papers as she tried to compose herself. Behind her, the green-haired girl's voice brightened.

"Hey, Jimmy."

The girl listened. She listened for a very long while. She listened so long that Lily chanced a glance and saw that she had gone deathly still.

Lily turned full face when she heard her say, "Oh, my god. Oh, my god. Yes. Yes. I understand. Yes. Yes. I will. Everyone. I'll tell everyone. Whatever you need. Anything. Oh, my god."

The green-haired girl sank onto her chair. Her elbow was on her desk, cradling her head in her upturned palm. She put down the phone. The minutes ticked by, and she didn't move. Lily got up and took a few steps her way.

"Are you all right?" Lily said.

The girl's skin was now tinged the same color as her hair and she seemed very young, unsure of herself, out of her element. When she finally looked at Lily, her lips moved, but she didn't say anything. Then she stopped trying to talk and started to cry.

Clearly, the girl with the green hair was not all right.

CHAPTER 8

LOS ANGELES
THE MEDICAL EXAMINER
PRESENT DAY

Death was not Josie's favorite neighbor. He had knocked on her door one too many times. Death had taken her child, and a part of her died too. The doctor had consoled her saying that her baby wasn't viable. Archer, ashen and shaken, put up a good front and concurred. Intellectually she knew this to be the truth; emotionally she would not accept that. What was lost was their baby. Death had taken it.

Death should have taken her mother, for she was not truly living. Death had come for her father too soon. Each time someone Josie loved opened the door to Him, part of her was taken to the grave, too. Perhaps that was how some people really died, in pieces.

Those who had gone before her would be disappointed if she used them as an excuse not to live, so Josie pulled up her big girl pants and headed for the medical examiner's office. She had never been there before, but Josie knew that the only thing in this building was Death.

Once inside, Josie stated her business. The receptionist called up Lily Daye's case number and told Josie to take a seat. Before she was settled in the waiting room, a man came to fetch her. He was large, middle aged, and retired military. It was in his bearing and his attitude. He stood at attention while he held the door, called her name crisply, and ushered her through without apology for the smell of formaldehyde and decay that hit her flat and hard.

"She's with Doctor Jordan," he said.

Since that was his idea of small talk, Josie didn't push it as she followed him past administrative offices. In one, a beautiful woman with long dark hair labored over her computer. Josie wondered what attracted a woman like that to a place like this. In another, there was a large desk that was home to a whole lot of framed pictures and a statue of a skeleton with an eyepatch and pirate's hat. None of the offices had windows.

Josie and her escort turned into a long hall only to stop short in front of a freight elevator. Josie's escort pushed the button. They waited. Him with his hands clasped in front of him, Josie hanging on to the strap of her bag as she gave him a side-eye.

"Marine?" she asked.

"Yes, ma'am," he answered and then looked her over. "PD?"

"Nope. Lawyer."

"Are you with the good guys or the bad guys?"

"Don't know yet," she said and he laughed.

"I'll say good guys."

"Thanks."

"No problem."

The elevator doors opened. When he pushed the button

inside, there was only one way to go and that was down. They dropped two floors to the basement.

When the doors opened again, her escort took the lead, simultaneously giving a curt warning. "Watch on your right."

Josie swerved, missing a gurney that had been pushed up against the wall. The corpse atop it was naked, but that was okay. The dead don't feel the cold, nor could they blush, so there was no need to cover the body. Josie knew what she was looking at—a man from the streets, his age impossible to determine. In life he had been strong and powerful. His black hair, a glorious mass of dreadlocks, was shot with silver. His dark skin was now ashen. His torso was raised, one arm was thrown out as if he were hailing a cab or fending off a blow. Both his knees were bent, his heels digging into the gurney. The corpse was strangely beautiful, and the expression on his face fascinated Josie. He did not look fearful, nor did he seem to have died in pain. Rather, he looked surprised. Funny that a man who lived the way he did had not expected Death; strange that Josie who had all the comforts the world could provide did.

"The lion king," the man said when he noticed her interest. "They found him down on skid row. He was a handsome guy, wasn't he? I bet he served. Lot of vets are homeless."

Josie smiled a little. He spoke the truth of both--the shame that veterans dropped through society's cracks and that the man was exceedingly handsome. She could only imagine the figure he cut among the homeless, the drug addled, the lost souls of skid row. The child he once was, the young soldier he had been, the old man who had been dealt a bad hand, were all gone. Without the soul, the body was simply a curiosity.

"There's an odd kind of beauty around here sometimes," the man said.

"I'll give you that," Josie answered, and they were off again. "Any chance his people will find him?"

The man she walked with shook his head.

"He's been on the streets a long time. If he was going to be scooped up by someone who cared, it would have been long before we found him. I was just going to put him away when they called me to fetch you."

He opened a door that had a glass window embedded with chicken wire.

"Here you go. Dr. Jordan is in the third room on the right."

THE AIR in this part of the building was frigid and the lighting stark, but that wasn't why a shiver ran through Josie. Concept and curiosity had suddenly taken a sharp turn into form and substance. The remains of Lily Daye were laid out on a long and wide metal table that was raised high to facilitate the doctor's work.

Her breasts were flattened, legs slightly spread, and her arms were by her sides. Lily's stomach was concave, the gases from her passing having been released as her gut was mined. In life, Lily stood five-five at best. She wasn't heavy, nor was she thin. Her shoulders were broad but her bones were delicate. Josie's first impression was that Lily Daye was a person you could walk past ten times a day and not notice. Unfortunately, the one thing that might jog Josie's memory was unavailable to her. Lily Daye's face had been peeled away, leaving bare the top half of her skull. Josie opened the door to the room just as Dr. Jordan reached for an instrument. He paused, smiled, and waved her in.

"Do I need a mask?" she asked.

He raised the protective plastic guard over his face. "Naw. You can't catch anything and you sure can't make her sick," he said. "I only use this because you never know what might squirt up. Are you here to get her to where she belongs?"

"No, not really."

52

Josie approached the table. The doctor put his fists on his hips. They both looked at Lily.

"Too bad. We've got a full house. Stacked to the ceiling. If we can move someone out to a mortuary, it's a good day." His shoulders rotated to loosen his muscles, and he smiled at Josie. "So, what can I do you for?"

"I just wanted to get a look at her," Josie said

Josie told her story. Doctor Jordan kept one hand on Lily Daye's arm as if to include her in the conversation.

"You're kind of the exception to the rule. I see stuff that comes in with the body—letters to loved ones, people to contact—one in a hundred respond. It makes me damn grateful for my family. At least I think they'd come for me."

Dr. Jordan chuckled. His laugh was the only thing contagious, and Josie was sorry he had no one to share it with during the course of the day. She also had no doubt his family would come for him in the same way Archer, Hannah, and Billy had her back. He took a deep breath.

"So, you want to take a look?"

"I do," Josie said.

"Okee-dokey." He snapped his face shield down and gestured with one finger, twirling it as if he were stirring coffee. "You might want to turn around. Otherwise, you'll get all caught up in the process. Outsiders can find it a little freaky when I put a face back."

"Freakier than seeing her without one?"

"Point taken? Still..."

Josie did as he suggested. When she turned back again, Dr. Jordan had Lily's skin tucked as tightly as it could be without suturing it in place. He had lifted her scalp so that her hair framed her face. Josie noted it was clean, light brown, and of no discernable style. Her first impression was of a nice-looking woman, albeit a dead one.

She moved closer to the table.

"Usually, I wouldn't go through all this," Doctor Jordan said, "but she had a bruise on her cheek and temple. I wanted to make sure there was no blunt-force trauma. And there were some puncture marks on her arm that looked like…"

Josie was half listening. His voice trailed away as he turned to see to his instruments leaving Josie to view Lily Daye.

No older than forty, no younger than thirty, her eyes were closed, her cheeks sunken, her mouth shriveled and her face not quite centered, yet Josie could see that she had been pleasant looking and well kept, but without affectation. There were no highlights in her light brown hair, no tattoos on her body, and her ears were not pierced. Josie thought her skin must have been beautiful in life. She glanced at Lily's wrists and her ankles and ring finger. There was no line of demarcation to indicate that she spent time outside.

"What color were her eyes?"

Doctor Jordan looked over his shoulder, his eyes lighting first on the body and then on Josie.

"Light Brown."

"Her teeth?"

"Well cared for," he said. "Two caps. Some old fillings. I'm surprised they held up as well as they did. I don't think they were done here in the States."

"Did you find anything in her stomach?"

"Not much," he said. "The pills of course. A lot of pills. If she ate, it was long before she died."

"What about alcohol?" Josie asked.

"Can't tell you on that one. I'll get the blood work back in a week or so, fingers crossed."

Dr. Jordan moved back and stood at the foot of the table. Josie's eyes went from Lily's head to her toes. Despite the doctor's worry, Josie's stomach did not churn, and she would not have nightmares after viewing Lily Daye, naked and in pieces. The things that gave Josie nightmares were memories of being chained in a cement building in the Santa Monica Mountains, of cowering with her mother in a bunker in Hawaii while being stalked by a killer. No, what tortured Josie Bates, was the horror of what the living visited upon the living.

"So, do you know her?" Doctor Jordan asked.

"No, I don't. I wish I did."

The first admission made Josie sad; the second surprised her. It would have been nice to have felt some attachment or at least experienced a flicker of recognition. Either of these things would have made it easier for Josie on so many levels.

"Did they bring anything in with her?" Josie asked. "A purse? A wallet?"

"Nope. Just her. I've got her stuff, though." He walked to a locker and pulled out a large plastic bag that was labeled with the date and time of her arrival. "I had to cut off her shirt because of the rigor. Her skirt I got off okay. Still, it's kind of a mess. I don't think you really want to pull any of it out, if you know what I mean. No shoes. No stockings. Her underwear is pretty basic. No frills. The bra is the same."

He tried to give Josie the bag. She raised a hand.

"I don't want to take anything just now. I'm not sure how this is going to play out," she said. "How long will you hold her?"

"Well, she's got a name. That's more than most. We can list her on the website. In theory, we'll try to find her next of kin but..." He raised his shoulders in a sign of vague apology. The morgue held in excess of two hundred bodies. Like with all government bureaucracy, there weren't enough live bodies to deal with the overflow of dead ones.

"And if no one shows up?"

"We'll cremate her in about two weeks—after Christmas certainly— but we hold the cremains for three years. If nothing happens after that, there's a communal grave in Boyle

Heights. It's actually kind of nice. Volunteers do a whole cere-mony." He pointed at Lily's remains. "You done?"

"Yes. Thanks."

"I'll patch her up really nice before I put her away. Just in case we do find family. I want them to look as good as possible. You're welcome to stay if you're curious about the process."

"No, thanks," she said. "I appreciate the time. Who do I tell if I'm going to have her moved to a mortuary?"

"The mortuary will take care of all that. Doesn't matter where we're transporting, they all know how to do it. You'll have to work out the cost with them though."

"Of course," she said. "When can I get a death certificate?"

"Leave your information at the front desk. We'll let you know. I should have the paperwork done day after tomorrow. Blood work is a little iffy. Maybe I'll get it by the end of the week at the latest."

Josie took one more look at the corpse, which not long ago was a living, breathing woman, one with enough determination to point to Josie as her representative. She wanted to make sure Mr. Murray was well taken care of after her death. Lily Daye wanted to set her life right after she had left the earth, and she wanted Josie Bates to see to it.

"It's a shame," Josie said, more to herself than Dr. Jordan.

"There's a lot of shame in this world."

It was an off-handed comment. Dr. Jordan had long ago given up worrying about shame no matter what sense of the word was being referenced. He snapped down his face guard and leaned over Lily. Josie heard the pop of the needle punc-turing skin as he began to stitch Lily's face in place. She hoped he centered it. She hoped he could make her mouth softer so it didn't look as if she were girding for another of life's devas-tating blows.

By the time Josie got back to her car, she had forgotten

what Lily Daye looked like, but she would remember her visit to the morgue for hours because the smell of death clung to her. Josie thought Lily would cling to her, too, if she didn't see to her estate. The woman's need and desperation wouldn't be washed away with a scented soap if Josie turned her back. If Josie was going to do any good at all, she had to know the extent of Lily Daye's estate. She took out the items in the envelope Chief Miller had given her. She checked the little book, a savings account record, the check register, and glanced again at the will. By the looks of her accounts and the simplicity of the will, it appeared that Lily had left little on this earth. She hoped the beneficiary wasn't expecting a windfall; she hoped there was no next of kin who would contest the seemingly modest estate. It wouldn't be worth their time or hers.

Josie put the envelope back in her bag as she formulated a basic plan that would be both expedient and professional. Her first thought was to file a level one probate, passing assets by affidavit and bypassing the courts completely. Then all she had to do was find Mr. Murray, make the transfer, perhaps get some insight on what Lily's last wishes might be, have her cremated or interred if no next of kin could be found, and she would be done with this.

On the other hand, it might be better to file a level two probate. Then again, maybe it would be best to wait until she had seen the rest of what Lily Daye left behind her before any decision was made. You just never knew what valuable thing someone might have squirreled away that would be a game changer.

CHAPTER 9

EMERYVILLE
JIMMY'S CONDO
SEVEN YEARS EARLIER

Jimmy was home, sitting in a room that looked quite like his Backlash office except there were no big computer screens. At home, he worked on a laptop.

He had a drink. Whiskey on the rocks with a splash of water.

He had a blunt.

He had his thoughts for company. They weren't as dark as he had expected, thank God. There would be a lot to do in the next few weeks. Now he just had to wait for the wheels to start turning. It was going to be tough to get through, but shit happened. Sacrifices had to be made for extraordinary gains. Fate and karma were real. It was what it was.

Jimmy giggled. That was all he could come up with, and it would all work. He didn't want to be too scripted. Jimmy took a toke. He took a drink. He nodded off. The day was done, and tomorrow he would move on.

Death was a terrible thing. Mourning was worse. Needy people were uncomfortable to be around.

Unless you were Lily Daye. She was born to handle tragedy. He knew the minute he laid eyes on her that she would be important to him. It was in the way she held herself tight, her perfect posture, her rigid spine, the mouth that seemed clamped shut instead of closed. Jimmy didn't know what she had dealt with in her life, but it didn't matter. He needed her to deal with what life had sent him. It was Fate. Karma. What a day.

He took one more toke and then another. When he was done, he got out of his chair, and headed back to the office because this day wasn't quite done.

⊏━━⊐

WHEN NEWS of the train accident reached Backlash Technologies, when first reports indicated that Mary Margaret had been killed, that there was additional loss of life, that the force of the collision had toppled the crate that held *Distant2*, that it would be weeks before Jimmy could retrieve the device and determine if it had been damaged, the employees of Backlash Technologies gathered in the large room near the green-haired girl's desk.

Lily did not know any of these people, but her kindness and control were appreciated. They acquiesced to her steady authority. She brought coffee. She listened to people lament Mary Margaret's passing as if she had been a friend. Lily suggested they call home to reassure their loved ones that they were okay. She was a patient listener as they speculated why Mary Margaret would be on the track at all.

Jimmy arrived at the office, red-eyed, with grief—they assumed—struggling to keep on his feet. He put his arms around his employees one by one and spoke to them in his soft, low voice. He told them about the secret battery, and Mary Margaret's obsession with it. He told them he had worried about her because she seemed out of sorts and overworked. She was too eager to test it. She was angry with him when he urged patience. He took their faces in his hands and laid his brow against theirs as if to cosmically heal their shock and pain.

When he came to Lily, he put his arms around her and pulled her close. Closer, she thought, than anyone else. When he held her face in his hands, he looked deep into her eyes before their brows met. Lily was shaking when he let her go. This was as close to rapture as she had ever experienced.

Then he disappeared into his office. Lily continued to serve coffee. One by one, the engineers and the computer people wandered away. They packed their things and left until it was only Lily sitting outside Jimmy's office.

After a while, she thought it would be better if she left too. She went to the door of Jimmy's office, put her hand on the wall, and considered what she was about to do. Then she did it. She pressed the hidden button, the door opened, and she walked inside.

Jimmy did not acknowledge her, nor did he berate her because he was intent on watching a television. Like so many things in this place, she had not seen the screen because it had been hidden inside the walls, appearing with the push of a button, disappearing the same way.

Lily walked over to the desk and stood beside his chair. Together they watched the coverage of the accident, the worst in the history of the railroad, the announcer said. They confirmed eight dead, many injured. First responders were on the scene. The cameras moved closer.

Lily gasped.

Jimmy's eyes clicked her way, but Lily didn't notice. Her shock was too great. Lily knew what she was looking at under six of those white sheets; she knew by the length and width of the bundles. She tried to swallow but her throat was closed. Not that it mattered. There was nothing to swallow but sorrow, and that never went down easy. She was transported to a time when she was a different Lily, but she fought against the memory. The great emotion bubbling and boiling inside her kept her upright. Then, as if he understood what she was feeling, Jimmy took her hand in a way no man ever had. Gentle and firm. He held tight. The anger and fury inside her receded. Soon the memories faded too. She was Lily Daye, a woman of sublime control and understanding of her path in life. A woman who did what was needed, when it was needed.

Jimmy kept his eyes on the screen when he said, "I need you to stay with me, Lovely. Will you do that?"

"Yes," she said.

Together they watched the television and listened to the commentary about so many lives cut horrifically, inexplicably short. As she listened, Lily thought only of Jimmy and his need for her.

Focus was how the memories stayed buried.

For good.

Forever.

CHAPTER 10

THE FIRST WITNESS
THE LANDLORD

Josie spent a restless night after her visit to the morgue. First, she dreamed of a woman whose name she couldn't remember, whose face and figure remained elusive. This lady kept asking Josie if she had time for coffee. She also had a cat.

The next dreams were of her mother, alone in a lovely room overlooking a tropical forest. She saw her mother's face and her smile. Sadly, she didn't seem to be smiling at Josie. She was smiling at someone who stood behind Josie. Hard as she tried, Josie could not turn around to see who that person was.

Josie dreamed of a beach, but not Hermosa Beach. The sand was white and the breeze gentle. There wasn't a cloud on the horizon. There were no berms, no waves, no rock formations, nothing to identify which part of the world she was dreaming about.

None of Josie's dreams had a through line. They were simply there, lying in her mind like an oil slick atop the ocean —slippery and impossible to dive through or rise above without a thin layer coating her body, covering her eyes, clogging her ears.

When she woke, the dreams disintegrated, leaving nothing more than a residue of annoyance that was easily washed away by a hot shower. The calendar was busy, made more so by the extra work created by a dead woman.

She went to the office and cleared her desk of impending matters. Faye was not in, a small grace because Josie already knew her colleague's opinion on the matter of Lily Daye. Now, it was after two in the afternoon, and for the second time in as many days, Josie was driving from her home in Hermosa Beach to the Palos Verdes Peninsula.

On the way, she called Chief Miller, advising him that she would be handling the matter of Lily Daye. He in turn advised that the responding officer had taken a box of items from the cottage and she could pick it up anytime.

The box would have to wait because even though she was on Palos Verdes Drive, she was headed in the opposite direction of the police department in Palos Verdes Estates. Her destination was Rancho Palos Verdes and the Vanderhaven estate, the place not quite in Chief Miller's jurisdiction, the place where Lily Daye lived and died, a place that was just a little bit of a mystery to everyone in the South Bay.

Just before Portuguese Bend, where Palos Verdes Drive gave way to a roller-coaster ride of asphalt and concrete buckled by the unstable earth as it made a run for the bluffs, Josie saw the entrance to the estate.

Half hidden at the foot of a hill, her turn was late, sharp, and fast. The Jeep swerved before coming to a hockey stop on a short drive that was a mosaic of packed dirt, broken black top, and gravel. She eased the car forward to straighten it out and got her first look at the legendary place.

Once magnificent wrought-iron gates guarded the entrance. Ten feet tall, the iron rods were thick and fashioned into gold tipped spears. Woven between them was a metal grapevine that created a *V* when the gate was closed. Flecks of gold leaf still clung to the now weathered and black metal scroll.

Josie drove toward it looking for a call box. She found it on a post half buried in thick brush, a pink bougainvillea vine lying across it. She opened her car door and got out to move the vine away. The box was rusted and dirty. She pushed the button, got back in her car, and waited.

Beyond the gate, the long drive was a glorious carpet of Spanish pavers, each footprint as big as a closet. This was flanked by rows of towering Italian cypress. Life-sized marble statues were interspersed between the trees. The hacienda couldn't be seen from the drive, which spoke to the vastness of the land holding in a state where a regular homeowner was lucky to get a patch of grass.

When it became clear the call box was not working, Josie phoned up to the house. It was picked up on the first ring.

"Josie Bates for Mrs. Vanderhaven. The call box isn't working. Can you open the gate?"

"Sorry, I should have told you yesterday," the woman said. "You need to roll it back. Right side only. You can leave it open while you're up here, but close it when you go."

The woman hung up. Josie got out of the car. The gravel crunched under her feet. When she got to the gate, Josie saw that only the right side sat properly on its track. She rolled it back far enough for her Jeep to pass, dusted off her hands, got back in the car, and drove into Palos Verdes' past.

THE VANDERHAVEN FAMILY developed the Palos Verdes Peninsula in the 1920s, envisioning it as a mirror image of Malaga, Spain. The family's first order of business had been to build themselves a hacienda, white walled and roofed in red-tile. The pictures of the estate did not do it justice.

The hacienda was a two-story structure flanked by one-story wings. At one time, the acres of land had been well tended, plotted with sculpted gardens that now struggled to survive. Josie noted the bones of a rose garden, an octagon of boxwood hedges overgrown with weeds. There were paths through the woods of eucalyptus and pine. The drive had turned into a half-moon of raked gravel, and that's where Josie stopped. She got out, took her bag, and left her jacket.

It was warmer on this part of the hill, bright and sunny. The air was so still Josie heard birds singing. A bee brushed past her. She took off her sunglasses as she walked to the front door. The tile was chipped on the first step up to the verandah. Cobwebs coated the immense chandelier over the entry. Paint had peeled off the wooden frames of the tall leaded windows. The front door looked like it had been taken from a Spanish cathedral. It was beautiful but in desperate need of a strip and stain. There was no doorbell, so Josie lifted the huge brass knocker and let it fall.

The door opened before the last echo sounded.

A large woman in a pink top and khaki pedal pushers presented herself. She wore thick soled, wide-strapped white sandals. Her hair was short and thinning. In a nod to some fashion, a pink barrette held her bangs away from a face that was a cascade of fleshy ruts from brow to jaw. Her nose was small, her lips cupid-like, and her expression that of a woman who would be unmoved by a nuclear explosion.

"Mrs. Vanderhaven?" Josie asked.

"Hardly," she said. "I'm the caregiver, Fran."

She stepped back, opening the door wider, closing it tight as a coffin lid as soon as Josie crossed the threshold.

CHAPTER 11

EMERYVILLE GRAVEYARD
CHRISTMAS EVE
SEVEN YEARS EARLIER

Lily Daye stood beside the open grave.

Her black dress, stockings, and shoes were all new. She had considered purchasing a hat, but thought that would be a bit much since she did not know Mary Margaret. A knit cap, though, would have been welcome because the day was cold and blustery.

Lily stood next to Jimmy. He swayed into her now and again as if remaining upright was proving difficult. This was understandable because the last two weeks had been hell. It was clear that the train crash had taken more than just lives; Backlash Technologies was also DOA.

Distant2 had been rendered useless, whether by the impact of the wreck or the toppling of the crate was yet to be determined. The snowball of consequences began to roll, picking up speed with every passing day. The insurance company would not issue payment until an investigation was complete.

The military would not issue the monies due upon delivery since the device had not been delivered. Backlash attorneys argued that once *Distant2* was packaged and on the train, the contract had been fulfilled and ownership transferred.

Employees fled, peeling off one by one as they saw the writing on the wall. Lily became more important to Jimmy by the day. Lily thought this was the best job she ever had. Over the course of the week, though, she had come to realize it wasn't the demise of his company that made Jimmy skittish and sick, it was this day, Mary Margaret's funeral. Facing her family. His guilt made him ill. Lily knew this even though Jimmy didn't speak of it directly. She could almost read his thoughts:

If it hadn't been for the project...

Perhaps there was another solution...

I didn't mean to let it get so far...

It seems so unreal...

All this was sad, of course. There was no way Jimmy could have known what was going to happen that fateful day —not that anyone really knew what happened. The investigations would take a very long time, but everyone had their theories.

Whatever the truth was, Jimmy would carry his perceived guilt for a long while. Then something would happen. That guilt would be gone. He would stop asking questions that had no answers. Lily knew how it would go because It had happened to her.

His shoulder touched hers. She looked his way, but he was looking at Mary Margaret's coffin. It was being lowered into the ground. Lily looked away. She no longer looked at coffins being lowered. Instead, she stared into the distance thinking how lovely the great sweep of lawn was, how pleasing it was that all the headstones were uniform, spaced properly and upright. Her eyes wandered to Mary Margaret's mother and brother. Rosary beads passed through their fingers as they had since the beginning of the service.

Mary Margaret's mother was tall and plain, as was her brother. Lily tried to decide if there was a resemblance to the dead girl. Their interaction had been so brief, that all Lily could come up with was that the daughter was much shorter than the mother.

When the coffin was settled and the priest offered his last blessing, it was time to leave Mary Margaret to her rest. Jimmy moved beside Lily. His shoulders went up and down, then around as if he would like to shrug out of his jacket. Finally, he stepped forward and took the mother's hand in both of his. She looked at him as if this gesture was unwelcome.

"Your daughter gave so much for the company," he said. "You will never fully appreciate her contribution."

Mary Margaret's mother answered, "She liked her work."

"If I had known she was depressed, I would have never let her in that car." Jimmy shook his head. "Suicide. A horrible thing. She must have been in a great deal of pain."

Lily looked at Jimmy, openly and with surprise. She may not remember what Mary Margaret looked like specifically, but the woman who had passed her in Jimmy's office had been confident and self-assured. She had left his office the same way. Lily wondered what made Jimmy say such a thing. Mary Margaret deliberately killed herself? Lily thought not. More than likely she had thought she knew more than Jimmy. He said that he had warned her the car was not ready. Or Lily thought he said something like that. Still, it wasn't Lily's place to intervene. She had nothing to add in any event.

"May God forgive her if it was," the mother said.

The brother stopped massaging his rosary beads. It was obvious he didn't think much of Jimmy either.

"It could have been the car," the brother said. "If it was the car, then it would be your fault."

"It could have been so many things," Jimmy murmured. Lily heard the words *investigation* and *time*. Then Jimmy clearly said, "I will miss her. We will all miss her."

"Yes," the mother answered.

That's when the brother put his arm around her shoulders. They wanted to leave, but Jimmy didn't read the room. He still held the woman's hand.

"Did she tell you anything about her work?" Jimmy said. "If it was something at work that caused her concern, I would like to know. Any little thing she shared with you."

The mother shook her head and took back her hand. She was not comfortable being touched. That surprised Lily who had come to deeply love this man's touch in a very short time. In fact, Lily loved all of him because he had chosen her for comfort instead of turning away from her. No one had ever chosen her in that way before.

Jimmy stepped back. He and Lily watched the mother and brother walk away. Alone at the graveside, they were at a loss for what to do.

Finally, Lily said, "It was a nice service."

"Yes," Jimmy answered.

"There's a lot to do. I never finished the transcription from the first day, I—"

Jimmy turned to face her. His attention was so intense that Lily found herself unable to complete her thought. He was seeing her as no one else ever had. He understood her without knowing her history. Lily felt as if his heart and hers were one. He took her by the shoulders, not roughly, not to pull her into him, but to hold her in place, so that she understood that was where she belonged.

"Aren't you a wonderful soul," he said. "There are other things that matter now. There is a lot ahead of us. Are you strong enough? Shall we do it together, Lovely?"

When Lily nodded, Jimmy kissed her. She was both electrified and at peace; she was giddy and grounded. She did not kiss him back because she wanted time to consider the ramifications of such a thing. She had a job. With Jimmy. Did his kiss mean she had a life with him?

Wouldn't that be amazing after all this time?

Tragedy had brought her such despair in the past, and now tragedy was giving her happiness, purpose, and a future.

How about that.

CHAPTER 12

THE VANDERHAVEN ESTATE
PRESENT DAY

The interior of the home was heavily silent in the way a big house can be when those who exist inside the walls have stopped living. Like the outside, the once exquisite interior was shabby. The grand staircase was worn down the center, the tiles on the risers were marred, and some were missing. A large round table was dwarfed by the size of the foyer and the height of the ceilings. The beautiful carved trestle still shone, but the top of the table was scratched and gouged. A huge glass vase on top of it held a riot of dead flowers.

"She won't let me throw them away," Fran said when she saw Josie looking. "Mrs. V. thinks they look pretty."

"I can see it." Josie inclined her head, giving the arrangement a bit more consideration.

"They're dead. They make a mess."

Fran sighed. Josie smiled. The woman was right. Dead things made a mess. Reference Lily Daye. When Fran the caregiver moved, Josie did too.

"Word of warning. Mrs. Vanderhaven's a pistol, so get ready."

They went through a dining room where there was a table that could seat twelve. The formal living room could host thirty. The rugs in each room were stunning, but like everything else, they had seen better days.

The kitchen was large and home to a restaurant-worthy stove and fridge. A cereal bowl and spoon had been left on the counter next to a tray of prescription pill bottles and a container of MiraLAX.

And then there was Alice Greely Vanderhaven, sitting in a room just off the kitchen.

Josie couldn't help but think of her own mother when she looked at the old lady. Two women whose worlds had shrunk to near oblivion—Josie's mother because her mind had been wiped of any memory by a vicious government experiment, and Alice Vanderhaven because she had outlived her peers. Both women lived with their caregivers—Josie's mother in a condo in Hawaii, and Mrs. Vanderhaven in one room of a once elegant home. Both were locked away from the world in their own way, and Josie couldn't decide which was the crueler fate.

A big-screen television flickered. Flip-book images of smiling, shocked, disappointed, elated faces created a collage of people trying to figure out the right price for whatever prize the game show host dangled in front of them. The sound was low, making the pantomimes seem stranger still. A sofa was backed up to the French doors. The drapes were open, and through the glass, Josie could see a garden of fruit trees. There were two upholstered easy chairs in front of the television, each with a table beside it. On one was knitting interrupted, and on the other were three pill bottles, a tall plastic-lidded cup with a flexible-straw, and a small box of tissues. The old lady sat in the chair closest to the window. She had the TV remote in a stranglehold. Her eyes darted to Fran, then to Josie, and back to the caregiver. They were the eyes of a snake.

"Where have you been? You're not supposed to leave me alone. I'm going to call the agency. I want a new girl. Do you hear me? I'm going to get a new girl."

"I know Mrs. V. You already called. They're going to send someone new tomorrow, and I'll be out of your hair."

Fran gave Josie a wink. There was no *new girl* waiting in the wings; no phone call had been made. Josie admired the white lie. This was Fran giving power to a woman who controlled nothing. When Josie stepped up, Fran made the introductions.

"This is the lady who called yesterday, remember? Her name is Josie Bates. She's a lawyer."

"Of course, I remember. I'm no fool." Mrs. Vanderhaven sniffed and looked Josie up and down.

"You're a giant. What are you, seven feet tall?"

"Six," Josie said.

"Well, sit down, so I don't have to look up."

Alice Greely Vanderhaven pointed to the sofa, and Josie did as she was told. The leather upholstery was cracked and soft from years of wear. Josie rested her hand on the rolled arm and felt history under her fingertips. It would have been interesting to sit with Alice Vanderhaven and learn about the past, but the woman had a different idea of hospitality.

"I guess you need something to drink," she said. "You, girl. You. Get her something to drink."

Mrs. Vanderhaven waggled a finger at her caregiver. Her skin was as translucent as a jellyfish, her fingers twigs, and her joints gnarled and twisted. She wore a wedding ring, the underside wrapped with yarn to keep it from falling off.

Fran was already back in her chair, knitting in hand, footrest in place. She counted stitches and asked, "Do you want something to drink?"

"I'm good, thanks." Josie noted that Fran hadn't made any effort to get out of her chair.

"Mrs. Vanderhaven," Josie said, "I won't take up too much of your time, but I wanted to ask you for—"

"Save your breath. I don't give money for anyone or anything. Last one who asked for money got five thousand dollars, and I got a stupid t-shirt. I complained, so they sent back the check, but I got 'em. I kept the shirt."

Josie started to assure the woman she was not there for money, but Alice Greely Vanderhaven was on a roll.

"My husband would have given away the whole kit and kaboodle if I didn't watch him. He was a Vanderhaven, you know. Good bunch, but soft touches those folks. We have a boy. He's a Vanderhaven, but not a real one. Got too much of the Greely in him. I'm not even sure I like my boy. He's a mean son-of-a-bitch, that one—"

"I'm not here for money," Josie said. "I want to ask you about—"

"History! Lord save me. You're one of those? You want to write a damn book about the place? You're wasting your time. It's been done—"

"I want to ask you about Lily Daye," Josie said.

That stopped the woman cold, but her motor was just idling. It revved a second later.

"Lily? Lily Daye? I don't like her. Never did," the old woman said. "Mousey little thing, that one. Well, not so little. But not big. I don't like fat people. I don't like mousey people. That one was trouble for sure. Arrogant. I don't trust people who won't give you the time of day."

"How do you mean?" Josie asked.

"She never showed the proper gratitude. Everyone wants to live here. It's Casa Alicia, for god's sake. My husband named this house after me. Alice is my name. My husband was a romantic. Fine looking man. Good in the sack. Sometimes those two things don't go together, but my husband was perfect."

For a moment the old lady's face softened, but a long-dead husband didn't have a tight hold on her anymore. In the next minute, Alice Vanderhaven was leaning forward, using the pointer finger of one hand like she was trying to drill through the arm of her chair and shaking the remote at Josie with the other as if she could turn her off.

"All these years, and Lily Daye just stays in that house. Curtains pulled. The place looks like a crypt. She didn't even put out a potted plant. Sometimes she walks around out there. I can see her from my bedroom. She walks around. Then she goes behind the cottage. Then in front. Then behind. I can't see her then. She stays in that place, and I never know what she's doing in there."

"You must have spoken to her in three years," Josie said.

"You'd think she'd give me a wave. You'd think she'd holler up a thank you or some such. She lives in heaven, and I never raised her rent, and she can't be bothered with a thank you."

"Well, she must have come to see you at least once." Josie took Lily Daye's will out of her bag, stood up, and showed it to Alice Greely Vanderhaven. "I believe this is your signature as witness to Ms. Daye's will."

Josie moved closer so the woman could see clearly. Alice Vanderhaven looked it over, and then zeroed in on her signature.

"It's dated three years ago," Josie said. "Do you remember that?"

"I must have done it. That's my name, isn't it?" Josie's eyes flitted to the caregiver. She didn't seem to be listening so she asked the old woman: "Do you know the other person?"

Josie pointed to the second signature. Alice shook her head, and then looked at Fran.

"Maybe it was her."

Josie showed the document to Fran. If Alice Vanderhaven didn't know the name of her caregiver, there might be a question as to the validity of this will. Not because the second signature was invalid, but because Mrs. Vanderhaven might not be considered competent. Still, the will was dated years ago. Even Josie wasn't the same person she had been three years ago.

"That's the girl before me. I'm not sure what agency she came from," Fran said.

Josie back-stepped to the sofa, and put away the paper as she sat down.

"Did Lily have friends visit?" Josie asked.

"Twice I saw a man," Mrs. Vanderhaven said. "I tell you I didn't cotton to that. Didn't like strange men on the property. Then again, they never bothered me, so I guess I can't complain."

"Did you see the man who visited her?" Josie asked this of Fran. "Can you describe him?"

Fran shook her head and put a finger to her temple, then her eyes and mouthed the word *imagination*. Josie didn't buy that. She had dealt with enough elderly clients to know that there was always some truth in what they said. She also knew that caregivers could be dismissive, not because they weren't concerned but because their job was exhausting and they saved their energy for real problems.

"I saw him clear enough," Mrs. Vanderhaven insisted. "Not much of a man. Kind of scrawny, I think. I saw you, too. Trying to make out like I'm cuckoo, tapping your head like that."

Fran kept knitting, unapologetic even though there was a slight coloring high in her cheeks. She had been called on the carpet by the old lady and was on notice.

"Okay, Mrs. V. You saw a guy out there," Fran said. "But I think the lady in the cottage just liked to be alone. I only saw her a few times. She looked… I guess she looked like a woman who put one foot in front of another to make her way." Fran paused, her knitting dropping into her lap. "Yeah, she looked kind of worn out and resigned to it all. Funny that she would give up like that. Wonder what happened to her?"

The caregiver's take on the situation surprised Josie a bit, and shamed her a bit more. She hadn't really considered that there was a catalyst. Josie had been curious only about who Lily was in relation to her, Josie Bates, the lawyer. Perhaps the human being in Josie should be asking what pushed Lily Daye over the edge, whether her death was accidental or intentional, whether a decision had been made to take those pills in those quantities.

"Lily Daye was no artist either." Mrs. Vanderhaven raised her voice, not happy to be left out of the conversation. "That's who was supposed to be in those cottages."

"Do you know what she did for a living?" Josie asked.

"I don't know. She was just there. The artists always were about, doing things. They always left something. Lily Daye did nothing."

"Mrs. Vanderhaven, I'm here because I'm the executor of Lily Daye's estate." The old woman looked blankly at Josie. "You do know that Ms. Daye is deceased, don't you?"

"Did I know that?" Alice turned toward Fran.

"Yes. I told you when the police came to check on her."

"So she's dead?" Alice's small eyes widened, not in shock but with excitement. This was something interesting in a life that had long ago ceased to be.

"Yes, she is," Josie reiterated.

"Well, I'm sorry. It's never good to be dead, but it happens."

Alice didn't appear to be curious at how this turn of events came to be. There were plans to be made. Her future looked bright.

"I'm going to get some senior citizens in those cottages now. People who'll be grateful to live in this place. Maybe we'll play cards. Maybe we'll have a book club."

Alice twirled her wedding band. She looked through the window, neck craning as if she could see all the people who would soon come to keep her company. But there were no people; just trees and plants growing around the patio outside the French doors.

"The cottages were my husband's idea." She looked Josie's way. "People applied to live here you know. We had them to dinner. Those were lively affairs. Franklin and I walked out every night to see what they were all making—paintings, sculpture. We were young, but they were always younger. We had so many paintings and statues. Oh, and the man who worked with glass. He was handsome. He made the vase in the front hall. Beautiful. Franklin had them pay with one piece of their art. It's all around here. You'll see it."

Alice's mind wandered, then the cloud came, and her wrinkled brow darkened again.

"Once Franklin let a writer live here. The book he was writing was crap. I tried to read it. My husband never admitted it was a mistake to have that writer here, but he kept that piece of trash book to remind himself never to do it again."

She laughed and then she sighed.

"We could have made a lot of money if he rented to real people with real jobs. Starving artists. That's what my husband called them. Con artists I said. Freeloaders. Left all that junk behind."

"That was a long time ago, Mrs. Vanderhaven." Fran knit one and purled two as she spoke. "Lily was the only one out there for as long as I've been here. She wasn't an artist."

"She wasn't anything…"

The old woman's voice trailed off. A squirrel had paused in front of the window, and Alice liked him better than she liked

Josie. When she reached for her cup of water, Fran was up faster than Josie thought possible, helping her steady the cup. When Alice was done sipping her water, Fran sat back down and picked up her knitting.

"She must have been something. She paid her rent every month, same time," Fran said. "You saw those checks. I brought them in with the mail."

Fran settled back in her chair, tilted her head, counted her stitches, and spoke to Josie. "I didn't even know Lily was there until I'd been working here almost a year and saw a rent check."

"I thought you said you saw the check every month?" Josie said.

"Only after her son stopped coming by so often. Once he figured I wasn't going to steal Alice blind, he let me collect the mail."

"Got it," Josie said. "Mrs. Vanderhaven, I'm trying to find a next of kin for Ms. Daye. Could I see the rental agreement or the tenant questionnaire?"

"I don't know about that. Brian might know about that. My son's been taking care of things the last few years."

"How can I get ahold of him?"

"You want to live here?" Mrs. Vanderhaven perked up. "I like the way you look. You'd be fine."

"No, thank you," Josie said.

"I'll tell him you need to talk to him." Fran said. "Just so you know, the apple and the tree. He's not a charmer."

"Was he here when the police came? Do you think he called in the wellness check?"

"Who died? Did Lily die?" Mrs. Vanderhaven started, and that neck of hers craned again, and this time her attention went to Josie.

"Yes. Remember?" Fran said. "You were napping when the

police came to check on her. They called, so I knew they were coming."

Mrs. Vanderhaven was satisfied with that. She clicked the remote and the game show was replaced with *Matlock*. Law shows amused Josie. She wished she could wrap up her client's problems in an hour, but this was going on half a day now that she'd been chasing down information on Lily Daye. Matlock would be disappointed in her.

"Thank you for your time, Mrs. Vanderhaven," Josie said. She got up and put a card on the table next to Fran. "Her son can reach me here."

"I'll let him know when I see him."

Fran put her knitting on the side table, lowered the footrest on her chair, and pushed herself up. She put her hand on Alice Vanderhaven's arm and squeezed. The old woman looked at her.

"I'm going to see this lady out, Mrs. V. When I come back, you're going to take your medicine, and then you're going down for a nap. Does that sound like a plan?"

Alice Greely Vanderhaven waved her off and went back to watching the nearly silent television. Josie followed Fran. They paused in the kitchen.

"Sorry about all that," she said. "I figured you should talk to her because this is her place, but, honestly, she just gets notions in her head that aren't quite reality. Lily was okay. She didn't cause trouble. It could be that she was just antisocial, but I think she was scared of her own shadow. Who knows what troubles people have these days? If I'd known she was thinking about hurting herself, I would have stopped her."

"I'm sure you would have."

Josie smiled politely. Experience told her that intentions seldom translate to action, especially when a situation called for heroics. The question of what Fran would have done was moot.

"I saw her down by the gate a couple of times, looking out like she was waiting for someone. As soon as she saw me, she went back to her place."

Fran opened a drawer and took out a set of keys. She handed them to Josie.

"Since the cops sent you, and it sounds like Lily needs some help right now, I figure it's okay to give you these."

"Do you want to check with her son first?" Josie asked.

"If he didn't care enough to call me back when I told him it was about Lily and it was important, I doubt he's going to care that you're looking through her stuff. You're the executor after all." Fran was on the move again. "I don't know if it means anything, but he's been pissed off at Lily for a while now. She wouldn't let him into the cottage."

"Why did he want to go in?" Josie asked.

Fran shrugged. "Who knows. He's been running around this place for a couple months looking at everything. Maybe he's finally going to do some renovations. The place could use it."

Fran walked to the front door with her and onto the porch. She pointed west.

"I'd walk you down to her cottage, but I have to keep Mrs. V. on schedule," she said. "Go past the rose garden. After that it's just wild, trees and such. Stick to the path. It's the first cottage, the one with blue pavers going up to the front door."

Josie palmed the keys and started off, but Fran had one more thing to say.

"Mrs. V.'s got binoculars upstairs in her bedroom. I used to think she was birdwatching, but maybe she was spying on Lily. Just thought I'd mention it. You never know."

"You never know about most things," Josie said.

"Ain't that the truth."

Fran was chuckling as she went back to her charge, and Josie started for the cottage. She passed the ruins of a formal garden, pentagons and squares of untended boxwoods and bushes. There was a patch of succulents and cactus. Those thrived with the neglect and had grown to immense proportions. At one time there had been an herb garden; now there was only a rosemary bush, woody and fragrant.

Soon Josie found herself in a stand of towering eucalyptus —thirty, forty, fifty feet high. There were dozens of them in the throes of nature's strip tease, the white skin of the trunks revealed by graceful ribbons of peeling brown bark. Leaves cushioned the ground, drifting like snow this time of year. Fallen branches lay here and another there. One particularly large limb had been cut into pieces, and Josie coveted the firewood.

High above, the tree leaves shivered with a breeze Josie did not feel. Two squirrels played hide and seek, running across the ground, bounding up the trees, launching themselves back to the earth again. She came upon a metal structure and veered off the path to check it out. The metal was tortured and twisted. To Josie's eye, there was no recognizable shape or purpose. Still, the time with Hannah had taught her to appreciate the effort of expression and craft.

Josie circled it and then stopped in front of the partially buried stone. She swept the leaves aside with her foot, exposing the artist's name and the title of the work crudely carved into the marker. The thing was called *Heaven*. Josie hoped the artist didn't have an inside track because *Heaven* did not look hospitable.

Josie went back to the path, and moments later she saw two things—an incredible view of Catalina Island and the blue pavers leading to Lily Daye's cottage.

The structure was a simple rectangle of white-washed stucco. Unlike Casa Alicia, the door was hollow-core and cheap. The window on the left was large, which made sense since an artist needed light. The window to the right was small and narrow. There was no porch, no potted plants, no brass knocker, no doorbell.

Josie looked at the keys Fran had given her. One for a standard lock, the other for a padlock. Josie put the larger key in the lock, turned the knob, and went inside to meet Lily Daye.

CHAPTER 13

EMERYVILLE
SIX YEARS EARLIER

It was a new year, and so much had changed.

One by one, the employees of Backlash Technologies disappeared until it was just Lily and the green-haired girl. The girl's name was Zack, and her pronouns were Xi/Xem. Lily found this silly, but like the offensive t-shirt, it was not Lily's place to comment. She felt bad when Zack was let go. Not only had she been Jimmy's first employee, but she harbored a true undying admiration for him. She cried as she left the offices for the last time.

Then it was just Lily. Lily and Jimmy. Together they would close down the company and deal with the aftermath of the train wreck that had taken so much more than Mary Margaret's life and *Distant2's* promise.

The engineers and programmers were gone because the grand project that would have ensured years of work was no more. The world would not be safe from nuclear annihilation because the hardware was irreparable and Jimmy refused to hand over the final codes. If the hardware no longer existed, there was no need for the Digital Analysis Expression. He did not want anyone trying to recreate what he, Jimmy, had envisioned. Not only that, he believed in Karma. The universe was telling him *Distant2* must be laid to rest.

That is what Jimmy told everyone.

The military didn't believe in Karma. Having paid the first installment entitled the government to the plans and programming per their contract. Jimmy refused to give them anything, including the monies they had already paid.

That's when all the planets circling Backlash Technologies imploded—tech, military, government, finance.

Everyone got angry except Jimmy. He was Zen. As well he should be.

His personal fortune had been protected by a cadre of accountants, and he had Lily as a devoted buffer. She saw to the unthreading of investor agreements, disposition of classified documents from the military, lawsuits and counter lawsuits that would determine who would ultimately be responsible for the loss of life, goods, and money. There should have been ten Lilys to see to all this, but there was only one. She greatly feared that she would make a mistake or overlook a critical piece of information that would create even more devastating problems for Jimmy.

When she suggested this, he took her face in his hands, called her Lovely, and swore she was the only one he trusted. She believed him and worked harder than she had ever worked in her life. It was soon clear that she was indispensable. So here they were, the two of them working side-by-side day and night six months into the new year. By the looks of things, they would be together for the next six years, or six decades, before all this was done. Here was the way things stood—

Jimmy's investors had lost millions, but that was the least of his problems.

Jimmy's insurance on *Distant2* was held in abeyance until liability was established.

Jimmy sued the railroad, citing the fact that the engineer had allowed children to be in the engine cab, distracting him, breaching safety protocol.

The railroad denied any misdeeds and countersued. They argued that they had no liability in the damage of *Distant2* because Jimmy had been the last to examine the lashings and had not let their representative do the final inspection.

The court had been petitioned to order railroad representatives access to *Distant2* which was now housed in a facility paid for by Backlash. Jimmy had it partially disassembled before that order was served, making their inspection a waste of time. They petitioned the courts once more to force Jimmy to put it back together. The petition was denied.

The car Mary Margaret had been driving was also housed there after having been thoroughly inspected by the Federal Transportation Commission.

Backlash and Jimmy were named in seven wrongful death suits, given that Mary Margaret was his employee and/or the car she was driving was untested in a controlled arena before embarking on a public test.

The railroad filed a similar suit.

Mary Margaret's family sued everyone for wrongful death. The good news was, the family was waffling since the company that held Mary Margaret's life insurance policy would pay a handsome settlement after they finished their investigation. That, the family thought, might be better than a litigation that could drag on for years and possibly net them nothing.

Backlash/Jimmy countersued everyone.

Once, when they were working late into the night and Lily was exhausted, she said, "I wish we knew if Mary Margaret did something to the car. I mean, did she want to die? I wish we could know if the engineer was distracted by those people. I wish…"

Lily never finished her wishing. She sat up straighter and touched her hair. It was time for a second wind. Wishing accomplished nothing. If it did, she wouldn't be where she was now. She would be home, with her family. She gave up. She said, "I guess we'll never know."

She looked at Jimmy through the corridor created by his big computer screens. Lily looked at him the same way that she had on her first day. But he looked back in a different way. He looked at her as if he were deciding what to do with her.

He said, "We never will know." His Cheshire-cat smile widened. "Would you like to see my house?"

CHAPTER 14

THE VANDERHAVEN ESTATE
THE COTTAGE
PRESENT DAY

Josie gagged. She huffed and dry heaved. She pushed out the bad air and pulled in the good as she put distance between her and the cottage. When she reached the end of the walk that led to Lily's house, Josie planted her hands on her hips and lifted her head. She closed her eyes, deepened her breathing, and drew in the scent of eucalyptus. Finally, Josie shook her head and wiped the back of her hand across her mouth.

The last thing she expected when she walked into that place was the smell—stale cigarette smoke, depression, desperation...death. Especially death's last goodbye, loss of bodily function. The smell was an assault not only on Josie's senses, but on her sensibilities. It was a wake-up call that this situation was serious. A woman was dead and god only knew how long she had been gone before she was found. If the cottage was a clue, then it had been a while before the wellness check was called. Josie knew it wasn't up to the cops or the paramedics to clean up after an event like this, but at least they could have opened a window.

What made the situation worse was that it was a beautiful crisp December day. The sun was shining. The ocean was sapphire. The sky was a robin's-egg blue. Lily Daye should have been alive to see it. At that moment Josie understood she hadn't seen Lily Daye in the morgue. Josie had seen the woman's remains. The thing that made her a human was long gone.

From the moment Chief Miller had contacted her, Josie had been curious, annoyed, bemused, and surprised by the situation presented to her; what she had not been was serious. She was sorry to have been flippant, regretful to have sleep-walked through the process until now, shamed to have packaged all this as a curiosity and not recognized the reality that Lily Daye's outreach had been her last scream for help. The will she had authored was proof that her cry hadn't been answered.

Put me to rest.

I have no one else.

Josie took a tissue from her bag, collected a few eucalyptus leaves, snapped a piece of rosemary off a rangy bush, and made a sachet. Holding it close to her nose, she entered the cottage again.

⸻

THE COTTAGE WAS BUILT in two sections—a large front room divided into three distinct spaces and a door to a hallway that she assumed led to the bedrooms.

In the living area, a small couch was placed against the wall just to the right of the door and beneath the smaller of the two windows. The sofa was covered in a cheap, nubby, stain-resistant brown plaid fabric. A throw pillow of the same fabric was tucked into one corner. There was a ladderback chair, and neither that nor the couch was visitor friendly. Lily's coffee table was made of pressboard.

On the wall opposite the couch was a wooden crate with a mid-sized television on top. There were no markings on the box, and the television was unremarkable. Above it, two pictures hung on the wall at a height that seemed to suggest they had been placed there by someone else who had real furniture. One picture hung slightly askew. Upon closer inspection, she thought they could even have been greeting cards that someone had stuck in a frame. One was a watercolor of butterflies, the other of birds. Both were faded. One looked padded as if someone had been too lazy to take out another picture that was already in the frame.

The 'dining room' was defined by a small table and two metal chairs set neatly against it. One chair faced the blank wall and the other the kitchen even though there was a window with a priceless view a quarter turn away.

The table was spotless. Glass salt and pepper shakers were placed on either side of an empty plastic napkin holder. The salt was almost empty, the pepper was not. Lily Daye, it seemed, did not care for pepper as she dined alone facing a blank wall.

Josie opened the window and let in the ocean air before continuing on to the kitchen, a linoleumed space behind the counter. It was three feet wide, five feet long, and defined by the single counter against the wall that was clean and bare. A sad picture of Lily Daye was emerging. The woman spent her time staring at things—blank walls, small televisions, empty counters. She filled her time cleaning. She did all these things alone, occupying the cottage space, leaving no footprint in the world. She was not a neighbor nor a friend to Mrs. Vander-haven or anyone else, it seemed.

Lily Daye was a sleepwalker—her heart beat through the night, her eyes opened every morning, her lips remained closed because there was no one to talk to. Josie couldn't help but wonder why her life was like that. More importantly, what prompted her to end that life? Crushing loneliness? A challenge she wasn't ready to face? A broken love affair or the fact that she had given up trying to find anyone to care if she lived or died? Josie doubted it was any of those things. More than likely, an orderly woman like Lily simply wanted to wrap things up. She had, after all, left the world long before she took those pills.

Josie touched the small stove with the three gas burners. There was no dishwasher. The Frigidaire was round-topped and vintage. A small blue rug had been placed in front of the sink. A red towel hung from the oven door handle. Two spots of color in a gray world.

"Come on, Lily. Give me a hint."

Josie hunkered down and opened the cabinet under the sink. She found bleach, cleanser, a pair of rubber gloves, glass cleaner, and three dry-as-a-bone sponges.

Josie stood up and opened the trio of drawers to the left. The silverware in the top one was dollar-store fare, one step up from plastic. Five forks, two knives, and two spoons.

In the next drawer there was a wooden spoon, a ladle, two hot pads, and a small sieve.

There was nothing in the bottom drawer, but crumbs embedded in the corners indicated that it had been used for bread storage. Who was to say these were Lily's bread crumbs, though, and not one of the starving artists that had come before?

Josie opened the cabinets above the sink in quick succession. There was a coffee maker, a pot, and a pan in cabinet one. Cabinet two held two white dinner plates, three soup bowls, and an orange plastic storage container. Then Josie opened the third cabinet and smiled.

"Now we're talking."

Josie got the teacups and saucers out of the cabinet, setting them down on the counter, only to pick up the cups in turn. They were colorful, gold rimmed delicate China cups. One commemorated Prince Charles's wedding to Diana and the other Prince William's marriage to Kate Middleton. They were a dime a dozen in English tourist shops. Maybe Lily Daye was a romantic or a traveler. Perhaps she was English. Or she had a friend who sent her these cups. Finding a friend would make this all so much easier, especially if the friend was named Mr. Murray.

Josie put the cups back, closed that cabinet, and opened the narrow pantry. Lily had two cans of soup, a tin of pineapple chunks, a box of pasta, and English tea in a painted tin. Josie picked up the tea. On the bottom was a sticker with the name of a shop. She opened the refrigerator. It was empty save for small jars of condiments and two tiny bottles of vodka, the kind you would get on an airplane.

Finished in the kitchen, Josie went back through the living area, pausing in the doorway that led to the back of the house. There were three doors off the hall. Two were closed, and one was open. Josie could see a rumpled bed through the open door. Not quite ready to tackle the place where Lily had died, Josie decided to start with the room behind the first closed door. Turning the knob, she pushed it open, but it was loose on its hinges, and she lost her grip. It hit the wall, and bounced back at her. Josie put out a hand, and stopped it before it closed again. Slowly, she pushed it all the way open.

The room was smaller than a standard eight by ten bedroom, but not by much. There was a high rectangular window on one wall and a closet on another. A long folding table and chair had been placed in the center of the room. More folding tables were pushed up against the longest, windowless wall, but what Josie really found interesting were the body parts covering every inch of those tables.

CHAPTER 15

EMERYVILLE
JIMMY'S HOUSE
FIVE YEARS EARLIER

Jimmy's bedroom needed picking up. In Lily's room the bed
was made. She had also cleaned her bathroom and the kitchen,
although there wasn't much to clean in the kitchen. Jimmy
liked to drink, and he liked to smoke weed. The first time she
visited Jimmy at his home, he had done these things. He drank,
got high, ate stuff out of bags, held her hand and fell asleep.
Lily didn't quite know what to make of it. Not that she was a
prude; it had just been so long since she relaxed, and she
couldn't quite remember how it was done.

An only child of a quiet couple, Lily had gone to school
and then to work and never quite found her footing. There had
been three men in her life. One was abusive, one she loved
dearly but it ended sadly, and the third she had simply gone
with, not giving it much thought. When that ended, Lily picked
herself up and decided to go it alone. She took jobs where she
could get them and made her way from one coast to the other.

Then she had seen Jimmy and fallen head over heels. She didn't know if it was a good or bad idea to get involved with him, but Lily knew it was her last chance to live, and so she gave it a whirl.

Lily moved in with Jimmy three months after that first night. She had nothing of note to bring with her except her tea cups. Jimmy laughed at those, but it was a sweet laugh. He said such sentiments suited her. They slept together now and again, because that was the way he wanted it. Lily said she preferred that too. It wouldn't have been good to comment on his *abilities* in the bedroom, no man liked that. Besides, Lily was there for a different kind of intimacy. She was there to dream with him; she was there to serve him. Lily Daye felt appreciated. She felt seen.

The problems emanating from the train crash multiplied, but at night, Jimmy shared his plans for a new company. He told her investors were lined up. It was only a matter of time and they would be back in business.

They.

That was the word he used. Lily thought she couldn't be more in love. She lived in a beautiful home with a man she admired. She was cherished. She wasn't a wife, but she was a partner. One morning he sat down at the table, his robe falling open. Lily kept her eyes on his because they were beautiful, and his body was not.

He took her hand and said, "Lovely, I need you to do something for me."

CHAPTER 16

THE VANDERHAVEN ESTATE
THE COTTAGE
PRESENT DAY

A mountain of legs and arms were stacked on the floor by the table. Torsos were thrown into one corner of the room and heads into another. Glassy round eyes and narrow black lips were stitched into perpetual smiles on those heads. Tails and ears were scattered across the tabletops, and stuffing erupted from every fuzzy appendage. If all these pieces were assembled, Josie guessed there would be at least fifty large brown teddy bears. Only one was finished, and that bad boy sat atop the table in the corner, lording it over his disassembled buddies.

Josie walked in. She touched one of the heads, and it toppled to the ground, taking two more with it. She kicked one back under the table and was immediately sorry. She had the oddest urge to apologize. Instead, she opened the closet. There was no place to hang clothes because someone had shelved it top to bottom. On one shelf were clear vases, the sort that came with a basic floral arrangement. They were all labeled with specific dates. She picked up another and one more. The dates were the same; the years differed.

Josie closed the door and looked over her shoulder. An identical vase holding a dead bouquet had been placed next to the big teddy bear. Dried flower petals littered the table top, and the water was cloudy with scum.

Behind the bear and the flowers was a cheap frame leaning against the wall. Josie picked it up and looked at the collage of pictures of children and one adult. Some were on photo paper, others ripped from newsprint, and still other images were Xeroxed on yellowing paper. A picture of two small boys had been tucked in the outer frame. The boys were sitting on a stoop. Josie could see the edge of a car. She turned the frame over, noting the faded writing on the back. Written in pencil on the slightly corrugated cardboard, the names were hard to make out. When Josie turned the frame again, she pulled the loose picture out of the frame. On the back of that was a date and two names, Andy and Patrick. The picture was almost twenty years old.

Josie put the frame back where she had found it and considered what it meant. Lily might have been a teacher or a nanny. She might have been married and some of these children were hers. Then again, Lily Daye could just as easily be a crazy lady. Lonely people collected animals, pretended dolls were children, created families out of whole cloth. They were the frayed ends of the loosely woven fabric of society, easily unraveled until they were nothing more than kinked useless threads heaped in a little corner of the world.

Josie picked up a teddy bear arm.

A leg.

She swept away a torso so that she could sit on the chair at Lily Daye's worktable.

She touched the things the woman had touched—an ear, a button nose, a curved and threaded needle. She sat in Lily's silent house piecing together a chubby-tummied body, two stout legs, two arms, and a head. She positioned two little ears on either side of the bear's head. When she was done, Josie found herself quite pleased, and that's when her fingers jumped and her chest tightened. She jerked and her knee hit the table. The teddy bear fell, its head rolling away.

Josie clenched her teeth. She propped her elbow on the table, clasped her hands, and rested her head against her fists. She kept her eyes open. She stared at the table, thinking, thinking, thinking about Lily. Thinking about Lily so that she wouldn't think about the anxiety rising inside her, that useless, ridiculous, inexplicable panic.

Lily Daye made teddy bears.

She could probably make ten teddy bears a day if she stitched quickly. Each one would look at her with the same frozen smile, the same unseeing eyes and hold out short fluffy little arms that could not bend to give her a hug. She would stitch lips that could never speak. Lily spent her time not with people, but with bits and pieces of toys, princess tea cups, and dead flowers.

How sad, Lily Daye.

Josie would not be Lily Daye.

She would rather die than be Lily Daye.

Startled by that thought, Josie dropped her hands, retrieved the bear head and put it on the table. It seemed to be asking where Lily was.

"You don't want to know," Josie said.

She turned it face down, got up, and closed the door when she left the room.

⊏⊐

THE ROOM behind door number two was smaller than the first one, and it was equally as interesting. Two walls were covered with cheap bookshelves. A third was host to an old armoire of no particular artistry, its doors missing, shelves added. The centerpiece was a desk with two large computer screens and a high-back chair. The computer terminal was under the desk and would have pressed against Lily's right knee, the two-drawer filing cabinet against the left. Josie roamed the perimeter of the room, pulling out a three-ring binder here, looking in a basket there. In the binders, plastic sleeves held floppy disks; thumb drives filled the baskets. There were external hard drives lining one shelf. All were labeled with names and numbers that meant nothing to Josie. In the armoire, there were accordion folders with neat paper files.

Because this was a reconnaissance mission and not a deep dive, Josie passed by all this quickly.

When she got to the desk, she opened the file drawers and took a picture. She sat in the chair and hitched it closer to the desk, found the switch, and fired up the computer. One of the screens lit up blue. There was a lighter blue circle where the user could put a picture of themself. Lily had chosen not to do that. Josie was prompted for a password that she didn't have. She shut the computer down. She would call George Handle and get him out here to hack into Lily's system.

Josie got up and pushed the chair back under the desk thinking she had learned a few more things about Lily. She was smart and she worked to make ends meet. Josie was about to leave when something caught her eye. She pulled the chair away from the desk again and took a closer look. Far back under the well she saw a briefcase and an open box filled with envelopes. She pulled them both out.

In the box there were letters, magazines, and catalogues. Josie rifled through the envelopes noting past due notices and bills. Some were addressed to aliases. Lily Kensington. Lillabeth Horner. Ms. Lily Daye.

Josie opened the briefcase, saw that there were papers and

bound reports inside. There was plenty of room, so she dumped the box contents inside, closed it up, and took the briefcase with her. Josie put it down by the hallway door and went to Lily's bedroom.

There, Josie lingered in the doorway. Like the other rooms, this one was serviceable with a full bed and one bedside table. There was an ashtray with two cigarette butts on the table along with three pill bottles and a bottle of whiskey. The pill bottles were empty and had been put in a neat row. The whiskey was half empty and sealed. The indentation where Lily's body had lain was still in evidence; the stains on the white spread were now the color of dried mud. Josie pulled her sachet out of her pocket, but the scent was gone, so she went into the small bathroom to search for something to mask the smell.

The bathroom was small and charming with its vintage pink and sea green tile laid in a diamond pattern on the floor, sink top, and shower stall. Under the sink, Josie found cleanser and a sponge, but no air freshener. In the drawer, there was a hairbrush, a toothbrush, floss, and basic drugstore make-up. Josie tried to imagine how the woman in the morgue would have looked with make-up, walking down the street, perhaps passing Josie on Pier Avenue, smiling at her in a shop, sitting across from her at Burt's. She would look presentable, even pretty. But if she had been in any of these places, Josie had not taken note.

She opened the mirrored medicine cabinet above the sink and counted twenty prescription bottles for sleep aids and anti-depressants. Once again, Josie took pictures, so she would have a record of the pharmacy and prescribing doctors.

Back in the bedroom, she checked out the cigarette butts, the bottle of booze, and the pill bottle. The pills were gone. There was no lipstick on the butts and no glass by the bedside. Josie went to the bureau against the wall and opened the drawers. Underwear, bras, a sweater or two. Another drawer held socks and stockings. Josie went to the closet and rolled open the door. Blouses, pants, a dress. Size ten. Lily's shoes were size seven. There was a garment bag. Josie unzipped it and found five suits, tailored and made of fine wool. Lily didn't wear those to stitch teddy bears, but she could have worn them at a corporate job, one that required knowledge of computers.

Josie closed the closet, went to the bedside table and looked in the single drawer in the hopes of finding a wallet, a health card, or an address book. She came up empty handed, so she opened the high window. She would be back to go over the place with a fine-tooth comb, but the day was getting on and she was tired.

Picking up the briefcase on her way out, Josie realized that any trace of annoyance had been replaced with an energy she hadn't felt in a long while. She had purpose. She would get Lily Daye out of the morgue, find Mr. Murray, and settle this small estate because it was the right thing to do.

In the living room, Josie took one more look around, all the while prioritizing her next steps. Just as she reached for the door, it slammed open, sending her reeling. She fell over the rolled arm of the sofa, losing her hold on the briefcase as she hit the floor hard. Before she could get to her feet, a big man filled the doorway. He was only a silhouette, backlit by the mid-afternoon sun. Josie opened her mouth, but before she could speak, he roared at her.

"Who in the hell are you?"

CHAPTER 17

EMERYVILLE
FIVE YEARS EARLIER

Within a year of the accident, it was determined that Mary Margaret's corporate life insurance would not pay out until fault had been assigned. If she took her own life, or caused her life to be taken intentionally, then her insurance was moot.

Hoping to salvage something out of Mary Margaret's death, her mother doubled-down on all her lawsuits—Backlash Technologies, Jimmy, and the railroad in that order. She also sued the city of Emeryville for not having appropriate signage at the crossing where her daughter died. She sued every manufacturer whose parts were used to create the battery in the car her daughter was driving.

The military refused to pay Backlash for *Distant2* because, while it had been completed and loaded for shipping, they had not taken possession of the device in full. The external housing had been sent on ahead along with the programing, but without the DAX code and the internal workings that were on the train that day, they considered the contract breached.

Jimmy's lawyers argued that everything had been included in the shipping container which had left his possession on time. He was due the final payment and the military could then take the matter up with the railroad.

The families of the other victims—seven in all—had lawyered up and each were suing a) the railroad, b) the engineer's estate, c) Jimmy, d) the choir director of the church that the families had attended at one time.

The railroad sued Backlash and Jimmy.

Jimmy countersued.

On and on it went in a marvelous maelstrom of pain, grief, retribution, business as usual, slander, defense of reputation, and, above all, greed.

Jimmy had known what was coming. He understood that the years of litigation would demand an inordinate amount of his time. He also understood that he was not of a temperament to oversee all the moving parts. When, in the first heady throes of their affair, he asked Lily for a favor, she was thrilled. Yes, yes, yes. She would keep all the legal matters straight, interface with the lawyers, go to court, report to him in the most efficient way possible. He gave her complete authority over everything, and he paid her handsomely. They were partners in every sense of the word.

Yet, when he asked her to destroy all the Backlash files including and especially those pertaining to *Distant2*, Lily balked. She was sure that once Jimmy recovered from the shock of what had happened, he would want to reconstruct his work on *Distant2* and the car battery. Both were projects destined to change the world, and Lily wanted to protect his legacy.

Soon it was evident that Lily would not have to struggle with her indecision regarding Jimmy's request anytime soon. She simply didn't have time to deal with the old files. The years got away from them both. As Jimmy's surrogate, Lily was buried under the crush of the responsibilities. Jimmy focused on rebuilding a new company.

Considering the disaster that had been Backlash, Lily thought Jimmy would be a pariah, but nothing was further from the truth. Angel investors threw money at him. She was happy, of course, and grateful because he was generous. She would have preferred they married and shared both the good and the bad of his situation, but he was not one to be pushed.

So Lily Daye went about the tasks she was assigned. She felt alive for a good long while. She monitored the newsworthy litigation of the major players as well as the actions taken against the minor ones. The litigation was spread across the country, and many of the court cases did not merit even a column inch or a mention on social media.

One day as Lily sat in a Los Angeles courtroom waiting to monitor another round of motions, the world suddenly went dark. Lily found herself exhausted and depressed, tired of courtrooms, lawyers, life, and, yes, even Jimmy. He did not call her Lovely anymore. He did not call her anything really. She reported to him like an employee; he listened like the boss. They slept in separate rooms. Sometimes he didn't come home for dinner. Sometimes Lily didn't see him before she left for meetings.

Lily was not overly surprised that she was feeling blue. She had experienced this before. Back then her depression had been all-encompassing. This time Lily was functioning, but felt as if there would be no end to this dull road littered with more courtrooms, more time typing her reports, more loneliness in a house with a man who needed her desperately, but in all the wrong ways.

She thought to talk to Jimmy, but in her heart of hearts, Lily knew he was not wired to understand that her emotional state was critical to her work as well as her life. Jimmy lived in his head; her heart was unimportant. No, talking to Jimmy would be a last resort. She would see a doctor. A doctor would give her something to get her back on track. Then she would decide if she really wanted to jeopardize her relationship and her work by speaking to Jimmy.

When the judge raised his voice, Lily snapped out of it. She recrossed her legs. She smoothed the skirt on her dress. It was a lovely dress, one of many. Jimmy wanted her to look right when she represented him. She took that to mean he wanted her to look pretty. She wished she felt pretty; she wished she felt right.

Lily squared her shoulders and tipped up her chin, forcing herself to be in the moment. The lawyer for Mary Margaret's family was once again inundating the court with motions for one thing or another; the lawyer for the company that manufactured the battery casing counter attacked with motions of its own.

All Lily heard was a string of consonants and syllables. She had become adept at peeling away the nonsense of the law and found most arguments to be meaningless gibberish. Today was worse than others. Even the judge seemed bored. In the next few moments, Lily's shoulders rounded, her chest caved, her chin fell. Her body was heavy, and it exhausted her to watch the lawyers standing up, sitting down, standing up again. Talking and talking and talking. Fingers pointing, eyes darting to computer screens, clerks rustling through stacks of papers. The American flag. The gold seal of the court that was just a piece of wood painted gold.

It all meant nothing.

People were dead because of an accident. She refused to believe anyone would intentionally cause those lives to be taken and certainly not so many at once. If anyone was responsible, it was Mary Margaret, and you couldn't get blood out of a corpse. Not to mention, Lily had a very hard time believing Mary Margaret would have killed herself in such a public way. Lily had recognized a fellow misfit when she saw one.

Lily wanted to stand up, raise her hand, and suggest to the lawyers that they move on. She would tell the court that Jimmy had lots of money and could afford to give everyone some. She could write them all checks. Right now, though, Lily just wanted to beg the judge to stop this because it was painful to her in ways the court, and Jimmy, could never understand.

But Lily did nothing.

The lawyers finished. One of them nodded her way as he hurried to another hearing. Lily didn't nod back. She should know his name, but she couldn't remember. Nor could Lily find the energy to move. Her spirit was lost inside her body and she was too low to go looking for it. Lily Daye stared at the judge. She noted that his black robe was frayed. Maybe the search for justice had worn thin with his years on the bench, and the robes were a manifestation of his spirit.

He took a drink of water.

The short Hispanic woman who was the judge's clerk stood beside him, but faced the courtroom. She announced that another problem, another injustice, another ridiculously convoluted problem would be heard by the court and the raggedy judge. Lily watched it all, knowing the truth of the matter. They would all die and no one would remember any of this.

Then things changed— at least for Lily.

A woman passed by her, pushing through the bar with a confident step.

Lily blinked. She raised her head, watching closely as the tall woman took her place behind the table assigned to the plaintiff's attorney.

She was beautiful, but unaware of her beauty. She was strong and carried her strength with grace. She was sure of herself, unafraid of the judge or the man who represented her adversary.

Lily watched even though there was no reason for her to do so. Slowly, it dawned on her why this woman was of interest. It was because she was more alive than anyone in the room. She had purpose. The woman was not just in the moment, she *was* the moment. Lily was inspired. No. That was wrong. Lily was comforted.

In the next moment, the judge put his water aside, the Hispanic clerk took her seat, and the two attorneys turned their attention to the bench.

The woman said, "Josie Bates for the plaintiff, Your Honor."

CHAPTER 18

THE VANDERHAVEN ESTATE
PRESENT DAY

Josie righted herself as she kept an eye on the large angry man standing in the doorway of Lily Daye's cottage.

"Josie Bates. I'm an attorney." She picked herself up and dusted herself off. "Who are you?"

"It smells like shit in here."

Ignoring her question, he turned his back on her and stormed away. Josie picked up the briefcase and went outside. She locked the door before joining the man at the end of the walkway.

He had not been pleasant looking at first sight, and he was no better up close. They stood eye-to-eye. While tall, he was not fit. His butt was flat, his belly large, his shirt too big and his jeans too small. Oddly, he wore lace-up oxfords. At one time they had been quality, but now they were scuffed and worn at the heel.

Josie inclined her head to indicate she was ready to talk.

He stopped pacing, covered his face with his hands, and

then drew his palms down to calm himself. The face he revealed was as sad as his body—weathered, worn, and fleshy. Puffy bags made his small angry eyes look smaller still. She thought of Archer, a man of the same age who was toned, fit, and slow to anger. Archer took on the world clear-eyed and strong. Archer won a fight with one well-placed punch. This guy was a bully, a high school football player gone to seed, a man who would flail until he landed enough blows to bloody his opponent.

"What were you doing in there?" he said, lacking the courage to look her in the eye.

"As I said, I'm an attorney. Specifically, I'm Lily Daye's attorney," she said. "Now, why don't you tell me who you are?"

The man snorted. "Attorney. Friggin' attorney. Look, I've got attorneys too, and I'm done talking. I want her out now. You tell her to get her butt off this property. Is that understood?"

"What I understood is that this property belonged to Mrs. Vanderhaven," Josie said.

"I'm Brian Vanderhaven, her son," he said. "And I don't answer to you. You answer to me."

"Well, that's not exactly true," Josie said. "I've spoken to your mother. She knows I'm here and she knows—"

"She doesn't know nothing," the man said.

"I understood she owned the property," Josie said.

"And if you talked to her, you probably figured out she's not exactly sharp. I run things around here."

"Really?"

Josie gave him a look he didn't like.

"Yeah, really."

He mocked her and seemed quite pleased with himself. Josie noted his wedding ring. She prayed he didn't have children.

"I'll have to confirm that with Mrs. Vanderhaven," Josie

said. "If you'll give me your contact information, I'm happy to keep you in the loop on matters regarding my client if your mother agrees."

"I better be the only one in the loop."

He dug in his pocket and came up with a card. The man was a real estate agent. They were a dime a dozen in the South Bay. Josie knew the ones who were at the top of the game, and this guy wasn't even on the bench.

"It's my understanding that Ms. Daye has paid her rent, that she does not present an annoyance. Therefore, you have no legal reason to evict her," she said, stringing him along, wanting to hear more about the threat of eviction.

"I don't need to give her a reason, and I did everything by the book. I gave her notice three months ago that she'd have to find a new place by the first of the year. That's more than enough notice. That means you've got five days before I toss everything on the street."

"I'm afraid that's not going to happen. Ms. Day passed away and until the estate—"

"What the hell? The broad is dead? Like *dead*?"

"Yes, like dead," Josie said. "I'm the executor of her estate. I believe your mother's caregiver called you to advise you of the situation. You didn't return her call."

"I figured it was something stupid," he said.

Listening to him, Josie pondered the question of nature versus nurture. She had the strange feeling the man Brian Vanderhaven became was the result of both his parents' obsession with the artists who once lived on the estate and some throwback Neanderthal gene.

"What happened to her?"

"The coroner hasn't ruled yet, but it could be suicide…" Just to see his reaction Josie added, "Or possibly foul play."

"Foul—" He sputtered, his eyes widening before they narrowed once more as he understood the implication. "Don't you look at me like that. I wanted her gone, but I wouldn't waste my time killing her."

He took a few steps away, raised his head, and then swung it back Josie's way. She could almost see a lightbulb go on.

"You know what? This works out great. You're the executor. You pack her stuff up. Let's say by January fifteenth. I'll give you that. A grace period. We'll call it even," he said. "I don't want my mother involved. I don't want her putting up a fuss."

"Your mother wasn't stressed by the news of my client's death, so why would she be upset by the disposition of her property?"

"I don't know what stresses my mother. I don't know who she likes and who she doesn't. She's delusional. My mother still thinks the Vanderhavens still own the Peninsula."

That big head of his swung again. Josie sympathized with a son dealing with an elderly mother, a son at the end of his rope. What she couldn't abide was the disdain she heard in his voice, the disgust his body language communicated for the woman who bore him.

"She doesn't know that we're scraping the bottom of the barrel." He pulled a thumb toward the cottage. "That bitch was getting this place for a song. My mom thinks we should be grateful that we have a renter. My mom is an idiot, and I'm trying to salvage what I can. Now one part of the problem is gone, and I've got to take care of the rest of my problems. There's stuff in there that belongs to the Vanderhavens. If you're not going to help, then just get out of my way."

"You're going to have to wait for the police to give the go ahead, and they have to wait to get the coroner's report. While you're waiting, you may want to check with your attorney on renter rights laws," Josie said. "There are also laws against elder abuse, Mr. Vanderhaven. I wouldn't want you to buy yourself more problems if, for instance, your mother hasn't had the appropriate psychological and physical assessments to prove that she is unable to make decisions about her legally owned property. Unless I'm misunderstanding your intent."

Josie looked him straight in the eye. He blinked once and then twice. She doubted he had ever met a woman who didn't turn tail when he was in a mood—not because they were afraid of him, but because it wasn't worth their time to quibble. She wondered if Lily Daye had seen this face, heard these words, been given her marching orders in person.

As the silence deepened, Brian Vanderhaven faltered. His lips went slack; behind those eyes there was confusion. It was one thing to intimidate Lily Daye or a sick old woman, quite another to try to railroad Josie. He moved back a step, understanding that he was outgunned.

That was a start.

Josie mirrored him.

"I only ask whether you've taken the proper steps, Mr. Vanderhaven, because it seems that there is a great deal of animosity on your part not only toward your mother but also my client. Of course, I'll have to note this with Chief Miller at the Palos Verdes Police Department. Right now, we don't have anything definitive on Ms. Daye's cause of death."

Brian Vanderhaven's head pulled back, disappearing his thick neck.

"I don't like the game you're playing." Brian Vanderhaven waved a fat finger at her. "You're trying to scare me into thinking the cops think she was murdered. You're trying to set me and my mom up for a law suit, aren't you? You're going to say we were negligent and didn't keep that idiot safe. I know how you work. Threaten a law suit and settle. Even if you're suing on behalf of the estate that means you get a bigger cut. Nice. Real nice."

He shook his head and laughed without humor. "You're tangling with the wrong guy. That chick was weird. She took herself out, no question. What did she do? Slit her wrists. Women like her—"

"She's dead, sir," Josie said, her voice flat. "That's enough."

"Okay. Okay," he said. "Do what you can. As fast as you can."

"I will wrap this up as soon as legally possible," Josie said. "But if I have to go to court to protect Ms. Daye's property, I will. That would take time—"

"A threat? Again? A threat?"

"I'm simply suggesting that you tell the next renter the property might not be ready by the fifteenth."

"There isn't another renter," Brian said. "There's a buyer, and I have a window. I'll do whatever it takes to close this deal. Do you understand?"

"A buyer for the cottage?"

"For the whole friggin' property," he said.

"Your mother didn't mention the estate was on the market."

"I'm taking care of it," he said. "And I would suggest you don't mention it to my mother."

"I see." Josie paused, looking at him longer than he was comfortable. "It would help me expedite things if I had the rental agreement or an emergency contact for Ms. Daye."

"My mother didn't have her fill out an application. She lived out here like a mushroom."

"Do you live on the property?"

"No, but I didn't need to be here every day to know what went on."

Exasperated and angry, Brian Vanderhaven whipped out his cell phone. He held it high to record her.

"What's your name?" he said.

Josie told him and clearly recited the Baxter & Baxter number.

"Your attorney will confirm that I am within the law when

I say that I will not be moving any faster than circumstances dictate. You will have to advise your buyers," she said.

Because this man was getting on her nerves, Josie fired a wild shot that hit its mark.

"Where will your mother be living when this place is sold? Will she be living with you or going to a nursing home?"

"Screw you."

He turned around and started to walk away, but Josie wasn't done.

"Mr. Vanderhaven," Josie said. "The police have a recording of the call for a wellness check. Did you make that call?"

In response, Brian Vanderhaven raised both hands and shot his middle fingers into the air.

Josie snorted with a sound close to amusement, but not quite. The estate was worth a fortune, and that shed a whole new light on both Lily Daye's and Alice Vanderhaven's circumstances. Josie had no doubt that man would kick them both to the curb for less than what this property was worth.

Josie watched the path long after Brian Vanderhaven disappeared for no other reason than it was pleasant to stand outside. Forty feet above her, the deceptively delicate branches of the eucalyptus trees swayed in the winter breeze. The air was so fresh, the silence so complete, it would be easy to live in this cottage like a mushroom, hunkered down, existing, sheltered, working on a computer and sewing big teddy bears. From the outside, Lily Daye might seem eccentric; from the inside, she would see her situation as safe. For some reason, she had removed herself from the world, but when the world landed on her doorstep wanting something that overwhelmed her, all Lily could do was check out.

Then Josie laughed, chuckling until the sound grew to a full-fledged hoot.

Lord, she was a sucker, romanticizing a woman who had

landed hard in her life without so much as a how-do-you-do. It was actually funny that without talking to anyone, Lily Daye had made Brian Vanderhaven and his mother angry, Fran the caregiver sympathetic, and Josie her champion.

Josie went back to the cottage, got the briefcase, and headed to her car. As she pocketed the keys to the cottage, she took note of the second, smaller one. It was there for a reason, so before she left the property, Josie decided to look around. It didn't take long to find the lock. It opened a padlock on a chain threaded through the handles of the double doors on an old garage behind the cottage. It was built when cars were long, gas was cheap, and families only had one vehicle. Given there was a direct path to it, Josie assumed it was meant to be used by the cottage tenant.

The double doors were weathered, solid, and heavy. The chain and lock securing them had been there a while, but the lock was in good working order and opened easily. Josie pulled the chain away and let it drop, took hold of one door and pulled. The ground was uneven so it only opened halfway.

Inside, it was shadowy, musty, dusty, but not abandoned. While the building was old, the boxes inside were not. Dusty though they were, they also were all neatly taped and labeled, and they shared the space with a blue Toyota. The car had been totaled; the driver side crushed. Still, there might be a registration inside, a receipt from the grocery, a letter from someone who knew Lily.

In the quiet, Josie heard her own breathing. Dust turned golden in the light that came through spaces between the old wood slats. From the amount of dirt on the car, she could tell it had been sitting for months, maybe years. Just as she reached for the door handle, Josie's skin pricked. This time she dismissed that feeling that something was amiss, and that was a mistake. She knew it the minute the thing came at her. It was fast and furious, a dark blur of flesh and bone. Josie screamed, threw up her arms, fell to the ground, and rolled under the car.

The last thing she saw was a set of fangs.

The last thing she felt was a hot spray of spittle.

The last thing she heard was the snarling and snapping of a demon that had been hiding in the dark.

CHAPTER 19

LOS ANGELES SUPERIOR COURT
FOUR YEARS EARLIER

Lily sat through the thirty minutes of motions on a case she knew nothing about. When the hearing was over, she went into the hall and waited for the woman who had identified herself as Josie Bates. Lily had been so impressed that she now lay in wait, approaching the attorney the minute she left the court-room. Her intent was to waylay her long enough to look her in the eye.

Lily was not disappointed. Josie Bates was attentive and professional. Lily was not a woman's woman—given Jimmy's behavior lately she wasn't sure she was anyone's woman these days—but Josie's attention changed all that. This woman faced her like an equal. Lily lied about needing an attorney. Josie inquired about her problem. Lily said she wasn't ready to talk about it, and took the card the attorney offered.

Josie Bates smiled and went on her way giving, Lily was sure, no more thought to the encounter. Lily, on the other hand, felt stronger for it. She had acted on her own and in her own best interest. It had been a long time since she'd done something that was not Jimmy's bidding.

Lily left Los Angeles feeling more grounded than she had in years. She would write her report of the trial that marked another win for Jimmy and a loss for Mary Margaret's family. It was funny how this trip to Los Angeles was the end of the road for them, but somehow a new beginning for Lily.

There were going to be changes when she got back to Emeryville. It was time for Jimmy and her to wrap up the past and figure out exactly what their future held. Lily would make sure that happened whether Jimmy liked it or not.

She put Josie Bates's card in her purse and headed for the airport.

CHAPTER 20

THE SECOND WITNESS
THE DOG

Even when the chain snapped and the animal howled, even when Josie was sure the restraint's radius did not allow the animal to reach her, Josie didn't move. She stayed under the car, her arms outstretched, her cheek on the cold packed dirt, her eyes trained on the space between earth and car as she watched for the paws of the prowling animal. She could hear him growling, rattling the chain as he paced, retreating into the dark shadows at the end of the garage, again and again testing the limits of his chain. Finally, Josie took a few deep breaths and shimmied backwards until she was out from under the car. She pushed up, and back-stepped to the garage door. Once there, Josie pushed the second door open to let in more light. When that was done, she stamped the ground to stop her knees from shaking, snapped her wrists and, when she was ready, inched toward the back of the garage.

The dog had retreated into the shadows. Josie could just make out his silhouette; she could feel him watching. When she was almost parallel to the front door of the car, Josie side-stepped toward the wall until she stood at a safe distance in a space where she could see the dog clearly. Her first thought was of Max, her second was of reincarnation.

Max, her companion for so many years, had been found on the beach looking at the horizon, a pink leash attached to his collar. Josie thought he had been abandoned. Now, seeing this animal, Josie thought that she might have been wrong all those years ago. Perhaps Max had been waiting for someone who intended to return but couldn't—a swimmer caught in an undertow, an old person who had wandered off down the beach and couldn't remember where the dog was left. Maybe this dog was waiting for Lily.

At that moment, though, Lily was an afterthought. It was the dog and Josie. He was alone, purposeful and focused. He was a German Shepherd like Max had been, but the differences were chilling.

Max had a fanciful leash that someone would hold; this one had a chain to hold it back. Max had been beautiful and strong; this animal was magnificent and mighty. He stood two hands taller than Max, his chest was broader, his coat more golden. His black markings were minimal, but strategically placed so that he looked dangerously majestic. His coal-colored eyes were deep and intelligent. Max would have killed for Josie as a last resort, this one would kill without question and upon command.

Josie took a step closer and saw that the chain was attached to a thick leather collar on one end, and secured to a spike in the ground on the other. There were two dishes in the space. Both were empty.

The questions running through Josie's head were obvious. Was this Lily Daye's dog? Brian Vanderhaven's? Why was it chained? How long since it had been fed? The answers were moot until she figured out how to rectify this situation. She could not leave the dog here. Mrs. Vanderhaven would be useless, and Brian Vanderhaven was not exactly compassionate.

Josie extended her hand palm down and took a step forward.

"Good. That's good."

She went one more step. The only thing that moved on the animal was a twitch of one ear.

"Come on. It's all good."

Josie took a third step. She stopped when she was close enough that he could get her scent and understand her intentions.

She was right about the scent and wrong about the dog's understanding. He lunged. She fell away. For a minute she just lay against the stack of boxes that had broken her fall.

"Okay then."

Josie straightened up, gave him one last look, left the garage, pulled out her phone, and did what she had to do. She stared out across the sea to Catalina Island as she waited, thinking how strange it was that only fate could change the course of events if you were abandoned.

The dog could have died in there. Lily Daye did die in the cottage. For the dog, Fate was paying attention; for Lily, Fate had taken a breather. The bottom line was that being safe boiled down to luck and timing. You just had to hope that the right person came your way at the right time.

CHAPTER 21

EMERYVILLE
FOUR YEARS 340 DAYS EARLIER

Jimmy was not there when Lily got home from Los Angeles. His new venture was gaining steam. Nothing about people with money surprised Lily anymore. No matter what happened to him, Jimmy always had people wanting to give him money.

He would be gone at least two weeks, so Lily had the house to herself. She found it difficult to think of Jimmy's house as her home for two reasons. First, she lived here by default. Jimmy had not begged her to stay, professed his love, or made a commitment. They had simply come together—Lily in love, Jimmy in whatever passed for affection in his strange heart. Second, Lily didn't like using the word *home*. At one time she had had a real home, but it had been ripped from her by a tragedy much like the train wreck had taken Backlash from Jimmy. That wreck and Mary Margaret's car had flooded her with memories of another tragedy that had brought on her depression. Then it ruined Lily's life. This time, when it engulfed her, Lily was better prepared. Not having Jimmy around made it all easier to deal with.

The residual blues she had experienced in Los Angeles were taken care of with a little help from the white coats. Lily didn't care for the medication the first doctor prescribed, so she went to another. This one was satisfactory, and she very much liked the new pills. When the fog had lifted by half, Lily went to a third doctor with a vague complaint about her flagging energy and restless nights. After seeing the results of her blood work, he thought she needed a bit of a tweak, and gave her something that would put pep in her step and yet more pills that would let her rest comfortably.

Now Lily was laser-focused, knocking everything she touched out of the ballpark.

She had analyzed the activity on the last three major legal actions against Backlash and Jimmy personally. The reports she typed were exquisite. Jimmy would be so pleased. Amazingly, she had caught up with her work before the first week was out, so she decided it was time to tackle the old boxes of Backlash Technologies data.

All this time she had been proud that she had defied Jimmy and not destroyed the files for *Distant2* and the car battery. One day he would revisit those projects; one day he would thank her. That's what she thought. Given her complete control over Jimmy's business, and his assumption that she would do whatever he said, it had been easy to store the documents without his knowledge.

Now, though, Lily understood she had been wrong to do that. Backlash was Jimmy's legacy, not hers, and it was a legacy that pained him. Lily knew what it was like to be tortured by memories and failures. The lawyers had every bit of relevant information to the lawsuits, there probably wasn't anything important left, but she would go through it all just to make sure.

Dressed in her favorite pajamas, Lily worked long into the night, reviewing every document, checking every back-up drive. She lingered over internal memos that went on for pages because Jimmy dictated in stream of consciousness.

Lily found herself warmed by the memories—the chance call from a temp agency, Zack, the green-haired girl who had disliked Lily on sight, the tubby engineer who preferred tea to coffee, the little intern who was charged with backing up every hard drive in the place.

Lily dragged a box full of accordion files across the floor and sat down with a glass of wine to go through them. She pulled the first one out. The elastic that secured it had long ago given up the ghost. She smiled at the neat handwriting on the outside label, recognizing it as her own. Only she would have created hard files of everything.

She opened the folder and found her signed NDA, still valid for the work she was doing. She read over the printed version of the dictation she had been taking from Jimmy that first, fateful day. It was like paging through a yearbook. Sad memories, funny memories, memories of how inadequate she had been. She was a different woman back then, afraid of her shadow, afraid of Jimmy's greatness. Now she lived with him and knew the truth. Jimmy wasn't the god the green-haired girl purported him to be. He was brilliant—she gave him that—but his brilliance was in his people skills. The man could make anyone believe anything.

Now, Lily found herself smiling at the bloviated diatribe Jimmy had indulged in. Had she had more time before the news of the accident and Mary Margaret's death, Lily would have put that first meeting in the proper order. Then she turned the page, and the transcription stopped abruptly.

For a minute, Lily was befuddled. It was unlike her to be so careless. Then the memory came flooding back, embarrassing and humbling. Unsure of her rusty skills, she had recorded that first meeting with Jimmy and lost the phone in his office. Even now, sitting quietly, mistress of all she surveyed, handler of the great Jimmy's legal woes and bank accounts, Lily remembered the panic she felt upon discovering that her phone was gone.

She took a drink. She blessed her pills. Lily got up and went to her bedroom. Her business phone was on the table near where she had been working, but her old personal phone was in the drawer by the bedside. She kept it out of habit, out of sentiment, and because now and again she called home—or the place that used to be home. She owed Carolyn a call, though she much preferred the letters they wrote to one another. Lily had always preferred letters.

Lily found that old phone. The battery was dead as a doornail and for a second that annoyed her greatly. She had gotten used to everything working when she wanted it to work. She looked in the back of the drawer. Miraculously, she found the charger.

Back in the living room, Lily plugged it in. The screen lit up. Lily let it charge while she poured herself another glass of wine, ate a cookie, packed up some of the boxes. Finally, she settled herself on the floor again, her back up against the sofa, and saw that the phone was fifty percent charged. It would be amusing to see if the recording of Jimmy at that first meeting was still there, and, if it was, if it had picked up Jimmy's voice all those years ago.

Lily tapped the phone and there was her home screen. She scrolled, she tapped and clicked. A few minutes later she found what she was looking for. In the dark house, surrounded by the boxes of Backlash history, Lily laid her head back and listened to Jimmy's voice. Because she had been a distance from the desk, his voice sounded as if he were at the far end of a tunnel. Still, she could have made out what he said, she could have transcribed from this. She took another drink. Hadn't she been the smart one that first day?

Lily was listening, drowsing a little, when the recording ended. She took a deep breath, sat up and was about to erase it when she heard Jimmy's voice again. It was strong and clear, which meant he was closer to the chair where the phone had dropped.

Lily looked at the old phone. She held her breath. The next voice Lily heard was Mary Margaret's, and the next words Lily heard made her ill.

CHAPTER 22

THE VANDERHAVEN ESTATE
PRESENT DAY

The man locked the back of his truck and took a long look through the small barred windows before he turned to Josie.

"It's a good thing you didn't call the cops," he said. "That dog would be toast. Not that I would have blamed them if they had to get rough. He's something scary. Beautiful, but scary."

"You did a great job," Josie said. "Thanks."

"Not a problem. Do you know where I can find the owner?" he said. "I'll have to report them if they left that boy in there with no food and all chained up."

"I think he belonged to the woman who lived there." Josie motioned toward the cottage. "She passed away."

"Sorry to hear that," he said. "I guessed it had to be something big. I don't think our friend was meant to be chained too long anyway."

"Why would you think that?"

Josie and the man both glanced through the window. The dog ignored them.

"He's in good shape, well-cared for, you know. Usually, you put your dog in another room if someone comes over who doesn't like dogs. I'm thinking this guy scared the pants off most people, so that the lady kept him in the garage if she knew a visitor had issues. She probably did it for the visitor as much as for the dog. You wouldn't want to upset him. Otherwise, he's in good shape, so somebody loved him up."

Josie appreciated his point regarding visitors, that dog being "loved up" was almost amusing. Worshipped maybe. Catered to. But loved up? That's what you did with a lap dog. The man started for the front of the truck, so she went with him.

"Where will you take him?"

"He'll be over in San Pedro."

He opened the driver door, reached for the console, and came back with a card that looked like all city services cards. His was a little the worse for wear. There was a dirty smudge near his name. Josie's dad would have said this man was a *good fella*. He had great respect for the good fellas under his command. They were the ones who did what needed to be done, no fear, no fuss.

"I appreciate you coming so fast, George."

"I appreciate you waving me down. Hard to see this place," George said. "I was in the neighborhood, anyway. I picked that little one up on the bluffs. Poor guy's been knocked around some. It's sad. All these animals I gotta pick up."

He went inside the truck again. This time he had a receipt book when he came back to Josie. He wrote out a description of the dog and handed her the paper.

"Here you go," he said. "I know it's not your dog but you're the human that's standing here, so you're it."

"Not a problem."

Josie noted the time, date, description of the animal, and the contact information for the local animal control. George got into the truck, shut the door, and raised a hand in farewell. Josie walked to the back of the truck again and peered through the window as George got the engine going.

A tiny white dog was curled up asleep in a small cage, bare patches on its behind where he seemed to have a skin infection. There was a cut on its ear. Across from the little dog was one large cage. The German Shepherd sat at attention, staring straight ahead before turning his head toward her. Its dark eyes glittered in the gloomy interior. He was looking right at Josie as if to say he understood his indignity but wanted no pity.

Josie gave the truck a pat and stepped back thinking what an odd choice of pet for a woman who lived like a pauper. Dogs like this did not come cheap. Then again, maybe Lily had something to fear. That dog would not bite the hand that fed him, but it would bite off the hand raised against the person he protected.

Josie heard the engine catch. She saw George in silhouette turning his head to give his charges one last look. He must have seen Josie too because he raised his hand one more time before the truck started to move. The last Josie saw of the dog, his eyes were still trained on her—or perhaps the house behind her.

When George's truck had bounced across the uneven road and turned onto the main drive, Josie went back into the cottage. She rummaged through the kitchen looking for dog food, did a quick sweep of the front of the house, and finally found what she was looking for in the bedroom.

She had initially erred, opening only one side of the closet's sliding doors. When she slid the other one open, she found a dog bed and, on the shelf, a bag of food. Josie closed the door slowly, considering the questions this discovery brought to mind.

If Lily was in despair, wouldn't she have wanted the dog beside her as she left this world? He would be a comfort, her one loyal friend. If Lily Daye loved this dog, would she not have made arrangements for someone to come get him—and find her—once the deed was done?

Unsettled, Josie went through the house closing the windows. The property was remote, and anyone wanting to score would go for the treasures in the main house, but Lily's need for a guard dog and Josie's run-in with Brian Vanderhaven made her cautious.

Tired now, she retrieved the briefcase that had been left outside the door, walked through stand of eucalyptus and across the paths that ran through the neglected formal gardens of Casa Alicia.

When she had stored Lily's things in the back of her Jeep, Josie paused to look at the villa and found herself surprisingly angry. Mrs. Alice Greely Vanderhaven had nothing but complaints about a woman who was desperately alone. Brian Vanderhaven was a greedy bastard wanting to make a buck on both Lily's misery and his mother's. But mostly Josie was angry at herself for taking her own sweet time getting up here, for acting like this SOS from Lily Daye was some sort of lark. That was unforgivable. Then again, she was here now, so that had to count as amends.

Josie got in the Jeep and drove out of the Vanderhaven estate. If she hurried, she could be at the courthouse with time to spare, and fill out the forms to start the probate. She would make it level two, Small Estate Administration. That would take a little longer to settle, but given the computer equipment and the boxes in the garage, it might be that Lily's estate qualified. As she drove, Josie made a mental list of all the things she had to do. She didn't look in her rearview mirror. Casa Alicia was forgotten, and she was unaware that Brian Vanderhaven was watching.

When he was sure she was gone, he raised his voice loud enough so that the caregiver could hear him. "I'm leaving."

There was no answer. It wasn't that Fran and Mrs. Vander-haven hadn't heard him; it was just that they were hoping he actually did what he promised.

He opened the door and slammed it behind him for good measure. Instead of getting in his car, Brian Vanderhaven went back to the cottage where Lily Daye had died.

It was a wasted walk. Josie Bates had locked the place up tight and taken the only set of keys.

CHAPTER 23

HERMOSA BEACH
PRESENT DAY

Josie made it to the court, just under the wire. The paperwork was complete, and she was grateful she didn't have to go to downtown Los Angeles to file it. Hopefully the letters testamentary would be available in days and not weeks. From the car, she called a local mortuary and made arrangements for Lily to be transferred from the morgue. The M.E. was cutting the death certificates, and by the time she got home, Josie was feeling pretty good. She put Lily Daye's briefcase on the dining room table, changed into her sweats, one of Archer's t-shirts, and a hoodie. She ordered a pepperoni pizza.

Josie checked her messages.

Chief Miller's assistant had called to ask if Josie was coming for the items his officer had taken from Lily Daye's cottage. Josie returned the call, apologized for forgetting, and said she would try to make it during the week, but she was home for the evening.

There was a message from Faye asking her to put lunch with Rusty Gates on the calendar.

Hannah's call was the one she was sorry to have missed. Hannah did not know Lily Daye, the Oregon retreat was amazing, and she would see Josie soon.

Normally Josie would head for the beach to walk, sit on the sand and watch the sunset or stop into Burt's for a chat, but things weren't normal, so she passed. In a day, maybe two—or a year or two—Josie would get back to her routine. The strange panic would settle once Archer was with her, or Hannah, or all of them together again. Perhaps settling Lily Daye's problems would put her on an even keel. Then again, maybe Lily Daye's spirit had caused all this. Perhaps as she lay dying, it grabbed Josie by the throat to warn of the misery coming her way.

Since superstition wasn't her thing, Josie headed for the fridge in search of a beer. She found one in the back behind the mayonnaise, made a note to restock, closed the door with her heel, popped the top, and reminded herself to count her blessings. The beer was cold, a pizza was coming, Hannah and Archer would be home before she knew it, and eventually Billy would call from the port for a pick up.

Life was good.

There was work to be done.

JOSIE WROTE the notice to creditors, uploaded it to the local newspaper, and hedged her bet by placing it in the *Los Angeles Times* and the Orange County newspapers, too. After that, she settled down to see what was what with Lily's mail. When she finished, she was looking at three piles. The first included magazines, catalogues, and envelopes addressed to Occupant.

She tossed all of it, but not without wondering why a woman who lived so minimally subscribed to a home-and-garden magazine.

Unopened bills and second notices addressed to Lillian Daye, Lillabeth Horner, and Lily Kensington were in a second pile. Lily's electricity was about to be cut off, and a charge card had been sent to collections. She had prepaid rent on a storage unit in Redondo Beach, so Josie didn't have to worry about that for the time being. Money could be one cause of Lily Daye's despair. Perhaps the aliases pointed to her attempt to outrun her debts.

In the third pile, there were nine personal letters, all post-marked in the U.K., sent by a woman named Carolyn Barnes and addressed to Lillian Kensington. One had been sent to an address in Houston, Texas, four to an address in Emeryville, California, and four had been sent to the cottage in Palos Verdes.

Josie took a drink and then chose one of the personal letters at random. The writer was frugal, writing on onionskin paper to lighten the letter for overseas postage. The corner of the paper was decorated with a child's drawing of cats and dogs and hearts, but the handwriting was beautiful and measured. The message began with a cheeky "Hey girl" and was dated soon after Lily's move to the cottage.

I'm so glad you're settled with a job, but you're way too smart to be doing such a thing. Still, you know best. And you are handy with a needle. I assume you've put that man behind you, and your troubles are a thing of the past. You've nothing to be ashamed of. I swear you haven't, and I don't even know what it is that has you in a bloody knot! But I know you and your heart. Whatever pain there was in leaving was undeserved. And, no, no one has contacted me about you, so no worries. You tell me when you're ready, and I'll let folks know you are well.

In other news, little Georgie has grown so big you wouldn't know him.

I've enclosed a picture. Isn't he the handsome one! I've been to see Andy and Patrick. I just wanted you to know that I haven't forgotten. I even bring toys at Christmas. It's a small thing, I know, but, well...

I hope to see you soon, love. It's been too long. It's time to come home, don't you think?

Carolyn

The letter wasn't dated, but the postmark showed it had been sent eighteen months ago.

Another letter, sent eight months ago bore news of Carolyn's battle with a terrible cold, and her thanks for a letter that Lily had sent some time earlier, but she was worried about Lily. Now the silence was growing too long. Andy and Patrick were mentioned again. Carolyn begged Lily to write, or make an exception and let her call.

Josie would check the dates on the pill prescriptions to see if they coincided with the date on the letter. If Lily was battling depression, the silence would not be unusual. Sad, but not unusual.

In another letter sent to Emeryville, Carolyn gossiped about people they both knew, asked to hear about her new man, teased Lily about her immense responsibility, and the money she now made. Certainly, she was rich enough to afford a trip home for a bit. The letter was dated five years earlier.

Another one dated four years earlier: *You're working too hard. Such responsibility. Is it good for you, considering? Such work is horrible considering what happened to you. It's not the same, I know, but I worry it will bring up bad memories for you.*

Josie opened the last one. The postmark was only months ago.

Answer your damn phone. Please Lily, contact me. Letter. Pigeon. I don't care

The writer was by turns angry at a perceived game, concerned that something had happened to Lily, and confused, wondering if she herself, had done something to offend Lily. The bottom line—Lily was either cruel or in need. No matter what, she was silent.

Josie put all the letters back in their envelopes and then arranged them in chronological sequence, mulling over the progression of Lily's life as she now knew it.

Lily hadn't lived in Texas long.

She had been settled in Emeryville, had a good job, and a man in her life. She had money. She had responsibility.

And then Lily was alone with a job her friend felt was beneath her. She was also afraid or at least cautious as evidenced by Carolyn's reassurance that no one had been asking after her.

There were now three names of import to Josie's cause-- Carolyn Barnes, Patrick, and Andy. These people had to be family. From the way Carolyn wrote, all three must have loved Lily. Josie was sorry that she would be the bearer of such bad news when she found this woman.

Checking the clock, she did some quick calculations. It was three in the morning in England, not a great time to reach out and tell her that her friend—or relative—was dead in California. There was also the problem of communication. Josie didn't have time to write a nice letter back, inquiring about the relationship between the two women. She needed an email, a phone number, or even a Facebook page. Hopefully, there would be something in the briefcase to guide her. If not, Josie would have to do some digging. Not for the first time, she wished Archer were there. He was a master and would have had contact information in no time.

Josie fingered the bills, thought of the prescription bottles, considered all the letters. Clearly, Lily Daye's life was shutting down. Whatever worries and pressure she had, they were so great that not even the love of a good friend could get her through the dark times.

Josie sniffed. She blinked. She got up so fast that one of the letters fell on the floor. She swooped down to pick it up. Her fingers had turned stiff and cold. Her mind had wandered off the straight path of her legal duty and into the dark of her own personal theater. The show that waited to queue up was not one Josie wanted to watch.

Josie got her computer out of her office, came back to the dining room table and had just started her initial search for a woman named Carolyn Barnes when her phone rang. She smiled when she saw who it was.

"There you are," she said when she answered.

"How you doin', Jo?" Archer said.

"Good. I'm good."

Josie told a little white lie of omission, keeping the news of her panic attack to herself. She closed the computer, took her beer and said, "Hold on, babe."

Josie went to the patio, put her phone and beer on the table, lit the fireplace, sat on the sofa, and pulled a blanket over her knees. When she was settled, she picked up the phone again.

"I'm back," she said. "What time is it there?"

"Five in the morning," he said. "We slept in."

"Are you loving Africa?"

"The client's okay, and you can't knock the pay, so I guess it's all good," he said. "I'd like it better if you were here. We'd have a time of it, Jo."

"I know we would," she said. "Are you getting some good pictures?"

Josie put her head back and nestled the phone on the pillow next to her. Archer felt so darn close. She loved that man's voice. She loved that man.

"When I get home, I'm going to make you look at every one of them twice," he said. "Who would have thought an old cop would have an eye for beauty in something so brutal."

"I would," Josie said. "One of us has to have a soul."

"Yeah, like you don't." Archer chuckled, and for a minute Josie just listened to the sound of his breathing.

"So," she said. "Am I going to lose you to the rich and famous?"

"I'm thinking about it," he said. "My tent is fancier than my old apartment, and we've got a friggin' chef. The food is great."

"Then it's going to be hard on you when you get back unless I learn to cook."

"Why bother? We've got Burt's," Archer said. "This fancy camping bed is pretty cool, though. Why are sheets always cold, Jo?"

"Haven't got a clue, but I promise to warm your side when you get home."

"Won't be long. I need to come back."

Archer paused, and in her mind's eye Josie saw him as clear as day, lying on a camp bed, one arm behind his head, eyes closed as he spoke to her. If he were home, his other arm would be around her, and the night would get old as they talked. When the news of the day was shared, they would make love. Some things had changed, but that never would.

"I need you to come back," Josie said.

"Good to hear."

With that their love language was over. They weren't kids. They knew what they meant to each other, and he was curious about what occupied her while he was gone.

"So, What's the story on this woman you called me about?" Archer said.

"Well...."

Josie pulled her legs up so that she was sitting in the lotus position and put the phone on speaker. She told the story of Lily Daye in front of a warm fire under a clear Hermosa Beach night.

"I was just starting a search for this woman in England when you called."

"Did that car in the garage have a license plate?" Archer asked.

"I didn't notice," she said, and then told him about the encounter with the dog.

"Let me know if you find a plate. If she's an organ donor there might be a contact. I could try to run a full check from here, or I could call in a favor. I've got a good contact at the DMV."

Josie declined his offer with thanks.

"I've got enough moving parts that I'm bound to catch a break on one of them. I feel good she's in the mortuary. Between the lady writing letters, the pill prescriptions, and her bank account, I should be able to figure this out pretty quickly."

"And what happens if you don't find anyone, or no one is willing to get involved?"

"I'll take care of it," Josie said. "I'm not going to let her be buried like a pauper. She has a name. It should be on a headstone."

"I wish I was there to help," Archer said.

"I wish you were, too."

"You do realize that you don't have to do any of this, Jo," Archer said.

"So I've been told over and over. But I keep thinking about my mom. What if she reached out to someone and they turned their back? What if it was you or—" Before she could finish, the doorbell rang. "Hold on, babe. Pizza's here."

Josie went through the house, flipping on the lights now that it was dark, and opened the door. It wasn't a pizza delivery guy on her doorstep; it was a police officer.

"Ms. Bates?" he said.

"That's me."

"Chief Miller asked me to bring this to you." He had a box in both hands. He gave it to her with a warning. "It's heavy."

"No kidding."

"He told me to tell you that this was all they took when they secured the house at the Vanderhaven estate. He said you would know."

"I do. Thanks for making the trip."

Josie put the box on the table near the door, signed a receipt, and wished him a good night. She knew Chief Miller was simply passing his clutter on to Josie. Lily Daye was not his problem anymore. When she returned to the phone, she went for her garden shears as she spoke.

"No pizza, Archer. It was a cop making a house call. He brought me a box of stuff they took from Lily Daye's house."

"Gotta love small town PDs. Concierge service," Archer said. "It's odd that they would secure the scene of a suicide."

"Maybe it's a box of money, and I'll be able to bury Lily in style."

Josie scored the tape running down the middle of the box, pulled up the flaps, took out the crumpled butcher paper.

"What have you got, Jo?"

Archer's voice was tinny and far away, but Josie didn't pick up the phone. Instead, she reached into the box, raised her voice, and recited the inventory for him.

"A Glock 17. A box of 9-millimeter ammo. A Glock 44 and a box of .22 LR ammo." She pushed aside more paper. "A Sig Sauer P320 and one box of shotgun shells."

While she talked, Josie checked the weapons to make sure they weren't loaded. Chief Miller's officers would have tripled checked them, but she did it anyway.

Archer knew that too, but still he asked, "Are they clear, Jo?"

"Yep," she said. "Hold on, there's one more thing."

Josie took out the thing that had caught her eye—a water bottle, both ends sliced off, the interior stuffed with bunting. She held it in one hand and picked up the phone with the other so Archer could hear her clearly.

"Looks like Ms. Daye made herself a silencer."

CHAPTER 24

EMERYVILLE
FOUR YEARS, 355 DAYS EARLIER

It had been four days since Lily listened to the conversation that she inadvertently recorded in Jimmy's office during her first day of work at Backlash Technologies. She had listened and listened. Five, ten, fifty times to be sure that she understood what she was hearing.

With the shock of what had happened that day, and the ensuing snowball of grief and bad luck, this audio file had been forgotten. The train wreck had made any future work on *Distant2* a waste of time. But now...

Now...

Now Lily realized that the last years had been spent defending a man who did not deserve her love, her admiration, or her loyalty.

In the wee hours of the morning, Lily concluded that there could be no mistake. Mary Margaret's voice was clear as a bell. Jimmy's voice, a mumble for the first minute or so, had become clearer as the conversation went on. Lily surmised that he had left his chair, walked around his desk, and stopped when he was close to Mary Margaret. Neither knew the phone had been on the floor, much less that it was recording. Jimmy talked as Jimmy always did. Low, smooth, reassuring.

Why are you worried?

...I've taken care of it.

...A small glitch, Mary Margaret.

...Yes, yes, we retested.

...Just think of what you have to do now

...I've taken care of everything.

Everything is under my control

Given Mary Margaret's silence, Lily knew exactly what happened next. Jimmy took Mary Margaret's face in his hands, looked into her eyes, convinced her that her concerns were really of no concern at all, and sent her on her way.

Lies. All of it had been lies.

Lily would not have understood the implication of this conversation had she listened to this recording on that first, fateful day. She would have dutifully transcribed the necessary information and shut off this personal conversation. But years of working with the lawyers to defend Jimmy from families who had lost loved ones, to hold the railroad accountable for ruining his life's work, to stave off a tenacious military who demanded their money back, had educated her. She knew everything about Jimmy's business, and now she knew everything about Jimmy.

In the five days since Lily had unearthed this ancient information, she had not slept and had barely eaten. There was no time to do either. Instead, she spent the time compiling files and packing them in boxes. She double checked the hardware and software specs, the testing results, the sign offs, the chronology of Backlash Technologies.

143

When she was ready, Lily picked up her phone to call the head of their legal team and present him with the information. Lily never dialed. Those people worked for Jimmy; they wouldn't bite the hand that fed them. Instead, she picked up the hard copy of the NDA. She was legally bound to silence. She was also, she imagined, complicit in some way. She had had all this information at her fingertips for years. Logically, she knew that was silly. But Lily also knew that once the system got hold of a person, they were chewed up and spit out, left by the wayside, destroyed. That's what happened to Mary Margaret's family. That's what happened to the small businesses caught up in this nonsense. That's what had happened to Lily's own family years ago.

Fine. She knew how to play the game now. She would create her own justice.

She secured a place to live in a town she was sure Jimmy had never heard of. The place was remote, and yet not. It was isolated, and yet not. It was also close to a woman Lily believed she could trust if it came to that.

Lily called the storage facility in Emeryville and arranged to have the car towed. She called a service to collect the boxes of information she had prepared. When everything was arranged, when it was time for her to leave Jimmy's house forever, there were still a few things Lily had to do.

She packed her clothes and her teacups, the only things that truly belonged to her.

She contacted the bank.

Two days later, Lily was almost out the door, leaving for good, when she paused. There was one more thing to do. At her desk, she wrote a note. On her way to Jimmy's bedroom, Lily put the house keys on the coffee table in front of the bean-shaped sofa. It was strange how she once thought that these things were so innovative and beautiful. They were just a cold hunk of stone and a lazy bit of design. Just like the man who owned them, they were nothing special.

In the bedroom, Lily put her note on Jimmy's pillow. It read:

I know what you did.

With that, Lily Daye disappeared.

CHAPTER 25

TORRANCE COURTHOUSE
PRESENT DAY

Josie didn't have time for a run, she didn't stop at Burt's for coffee, she barely got a comb through her hair before she bolted out the door. She had overslept, and the best she could do was present herself to the court dressed in khaki pants, a blue blazer, a white shirt, and low-heeled pumps. She looked like a first-year law clerk, and she felt like crap: unsettled, tired, drawn, and bothered by the box of guns in her house.

It was, perhaps, understandable that she had missed the alarm, considering the last five days had been busy. In addition to her regular work load, Josie had placed more notices in the papers asking anyone who knew Lily Daye to contact her at Baxter & Baxter. Notices were posted on Craig's list and Facebook missing persons threads locally and nationally. She had Angela compose messages to put on X and directed her to do her best to get some traction since Josie had no idea how to manipulate the hashtags. A post was put on LinkedIn. Sadly, Josie had no picture to accompany the messages since it appeared Lily had no driver license. Still, she included what she knew of the woman: a general description, residences in Emeryville, Texas, and Palos Verdes.

She contacted the LAPD and the police departments in cities that ringed the South Bay to inquire as to whether the name Lily Daye had come across anyone's desk: a criminal transgression, a parking ticket, a call for a domestic problem. She prayed if anything was found it wouldn't be a warrant for Lily's arrest. That would complicate matters. On the other hand, that might answer the question of what plagued Lily Daye. All of this was a long shot. The LAPD was unwieldy, and the smaller towns didn't have the staff or the infrastructure to handle such inquiries quickly. More than likely, it would be the internet that provided the information she needed.

Josie put in calls to the doctors who prescribed Lily's pills. They had no record of an emergency contact and did not specifically remember Lily. That meant Lily doctor-hopped to get all those meds.

Josie contacted the ATF National Tracing Center to put in a trace request on Lily's guns but got nowhere. The request had to go through law enforcement, so Josie shot an email with the serial numbers and descriptions of Lily Daye's guns to Chief Miller requesting the PVPD follow-up with the Tracing Center.

Now any thought of Lily was pushed aside. Josie had hit her mark this morning just as her case was called. This court was run like a well-oiled machine, and the judge was not one to cross, so she was on her best behavior as she argued that the court could not convict her young client of trespassing since she had been a renter in the house, the month in question was still within the parameters of the rental agreement, and she still had possession of the key. It was the landlord who had changed the locks and held her client's belongings hostage. There were documented attempts by her client to arrange for the return of her property. That her client had put a dead cat in the land-lord's pool was categorically denied. Thankfully, Josie's client behaved. Only Josie knew that the reason for her contrition and her behavior was that her client was not drunk.

Charges were dismissed. The landlord was directed to return the girl's belongings; the defendant was directed to stay away from the house and the landlord. No damages were awarded and that was fine with Josie. Her client was thrilled and wanted to celebrate by taking Josie for a drink. It was ten o'clock in the morning, so Josie suggested she retrieve her things, pay the bill Josie would forward to her mother's house, and stay away from cats.

When that was done, Josie left the courthouse and made a beeline for Legal Grounds, a small coffee shop near the court. She ordered a very large coffee, settled herself at an outdoor table, and opened her tablet to resume the search for Lily Daye's friend, Carolyn Barnes. She didn't get far before two big hands landed on her shoulders, pushing down so hard that Josie could feel the edge of a heavy ring hit her collar bone

"How's my favorite barrister doing this a.m.?"

Rusty Gates gave her shoulders a squeeze before swinging himself onto a chair opposite her. First, he leaned over the small table and gave her a grin, and then he leaned back so the front legs of his chair lifted off the ground. Someone must have told him he looked charming doing stuff like that because he seemed to hold the pose in anticipation of her approval.

"Rusty, never do that again."

"Lighten up," he said. "You look like the day isn't going so good and it's not even lunch time. I'm here to help. Tell me what you need."

"I'm good, but thanks." Josie kept her eyes on her tablet. Clearly, Rusty had no intention of moving until she gave him attention, so she obliged. "What are you doing here anyway? I didn't think you handled the small stuff anymore."

"I'll tell you, Bates. I'm getting a little tired of being the poster boy for the firm. I'm feeling a little used. You know, like, say if you were known for your fine ass instead of your brilliant mind," he said. "But if you ever repeat that, I'll deny it."

"Don't know who I'd tell, Rusty," Josie said. "We don't run in the same circles anymore."

"We could." Josie thought he wiggled his eyebrows, but it was hard to tell behind his fancy sunglasses.

"You can't be serious about buying Faye out. You'd be bored and miserable."

"Probably," he said. "If I planned on actually working there."

The front legs of his chair hit the ground hard and he scooted his chair closer to the table, put his hands on top of it, and used one finger to punch at the dirty metal.

"That's why I've got a proposition. I buy the firm, you run it. I stay out of the picture for the day-to-day stuff unless it's something really juicy. I've been looking over the numbers and they're good, even with Faye winding down. Look, we'll set a billing floor. You meet it, I get my cut, and you take everything over and above. You're still salaried, but the bonus potential would be awesome, and you can still be a do-gooder since you seem to like it so much. I'll make sure you're the new face of justice in the South Bay. You'll be a rich woman. You see me once a year when I pop in to check the books."

Josie fingered her cardboard cup and considered the logo printed on it, a gavel smashing a hill of beans. Josie would love to dismiss Rusty's offer as a hill of beans, but she knew better than to underestimate the man. Beneath the Las Vegas bluster was a smart guy. The carrot he dangled was attractive. On the face, it was a well-thought-out plan that could mean a big pay day for Josie and still satisfy her professional aesthetic.

But money didn't mean much to Josie. She had made more than enough defending the rich and famous before she found out that she had a conscience. But the idea of order in her professional life was attractive these days. One foot in front of the other. Bill the hours. Do the paperwork. Bring home the bacon.

Lose your soul.

Maybe.

Maybe not.

"I didn't ask you to marry me, Bates," Rusty said. "What do you think?"

Rusty was the impatient sort, but then that's what made him successful. Get a client with a decent beef, threaten a prolonged court fight, settle for half of the demand, and move on to the next fifty clients. Wanting a just resolution to problems was a handicap in Rusty's world; it was the only thing that mattered in Josie's.

"It's an interesting proposition, Rusty," Josie said. "I'd need to hear more. Faye probably does too. It's her firm, after all."

"Don't wait too long. If you don't take it, I'll find someone else who will. Still, I'd rather it be you." Rusty pushed back his chair, stood up and looked at her with a curious mixture of amusement and admiration. "Why can't you be like other women, Bates? The bucks should have sealed the deal."

"What can I say? I'm a mystery." Josie said.

"That you are. I never would have pegged you for a bleeding heart, though. Faye told me about that dead gal. If it was anyone else but you, I'd figure you were on it because the estate has got deep pockets."

"I don't know what she's got yet," Josie said. "It wouldn't matter anyway."

"I still say it's a waste of time. There's no percentage," Rusty said.

Josie twisted her cup. She bit her bottom lip. When she looked up, the sun was behind Rusty, and he looked like he had a halo around his head.

"Wouldn't you be a little curious about her if she named you?" Josie asked.

"Only if I knew she could pay the tab. Once you figure out the cash flow, it doesn't matter what the funnel looks like," he said. "See you around, Bates."

"Yep, we've got lunch on the calendar," Josie said.

Rusty took a deep breath, and looked around as if he was master of all he surveyed. When he looked back down at Josie once more, his voice changed.

"I'd like to have you with me. I know there are markets where my brand of representation doesn't work and yours does. We could be a good team."

With that, he took his leave, sauntering off into a world of his own making. While they talked, Josie's coffee had gone cold, so she got a refill and went back to work. An hour later, her coffee was cold again but a couple of ducks were in a row.

When she was done, Josie took a minute to relax and watch the human traffic at Legal Grounds. Most had business before the courts, and Josie realized she would be hard-pressed to figure out which ones were there for traffic tickets, family law, civil cases, or criminal complaints. It was impossible to tell if most people were simply annoyed or ready to blow because their lives were on the verge of ruin.

She finished her coffee, closed up her computer, and put it in her briefcase. She retrieved a file and gave it a last-minute check. Everything was there. If she skipped lunch, that would mean she had a couple of hours to spare for Lily and one more chore could be checked off the list of executor duties.

It was going to be a good day after all.

CHAPTER 26

THE THIRD WITNESS
THE BANK

The young man behind the teller window paged through the little blue savings book and then picked up the check register that Josie had passed through to him.

"Wow, I don't think I've ever seen a savings book. Most people prefer online banking, Ms. Daye."

"I'm Ms. Daye's attorney." Josie said. "She is deceased. I'd like to transfer her funds and open an executor account."

"Got it."

He smiled and excused himself. He came back a few minutes later with the woman to whom he had given Lily's savings book, the check register, the EIN number Josie had set up for the estate, the letters testamentary, a copy of the will, and the death certificate.

The death certificate bothered Josie. While the pathologist had been thorough, cause of death was clear—an overdose of TCA (Tricyclic antidepressants), approximately 1500 milligrams and hypnotics, specifically Zolpidem, 30 milligrams, along with blood alcohol of .07. The alcohol was elevated but not deadly. It was the pills that did her in. Still, the manner of death was undetermined. The pathologist could not determine if Lily Daye committed suicide or was the victim of an accidental overdose. The bottom line was that Josie could bury Lily Daye without interest from an investigatory body, and she could open up an account for the estate, settle the woman's debts, and distribute funds to Mr. Murray. Hopefully, the woman in possession of all these documents, the one who introduced herself as Amelia Johnson, branch manager, would be able to steer Josie toward Lily's beneficiary.

Amelia Johnson thanked the teller, and made small talk about the weather and the holidays as she led Josie to the only private office in the bank. It was a corner space carved out by two glass walls. There was a porcelain Christmas elf on her desk. Her business cards were in its hands.

"I'm not sure this is the totality," Josie said, "but unless you tell me differently, Ms. Daye's funds seem to be minimal. If you have something else, great, I'd like to roll everything over into an executor account."

"Understood."

The manager sat down and opened a drawer. She retrieved a signature card, and put it on the desk in front of Josie.

"While I scan your paperwork for our files, I'll have you fill this out. I'll check on the activity and balances, and we should have you up and going with that account. It won't take long."

"I'd also like to know if there is a signator on either of these accounts," Josie said. "I'm looking for a next of kin or a beneficiary."

Ms. Johnson's head bobbed as she ran her finger down the spine of the blue book, and laid it flat.

"I have a feeling we're not going to find a beneficiary. It's not something we ask for when the account is opened. Not that we won't do it, but the customer has to ask," she said. "Still, you never know, so let's take a look and see what we've got."

The manager kept her eyes on the book as she worked on her computer. Her fingers flew, hitting more keys than were required for the account number alone. When she was done, Ms. Johnson took a minute to check her work. She handed the blue book back to Josie.

"The savings account has been closed for over a year, and that coincides with the updates. I see no additional signator nor a beneficiary. The money in that account was transferred into Ms. Daye's checking account." She executed a few more keystrokes, leaned toward the screen, and drew her finger down it. "The checking account hasn't been closed, but there hasn't been activity for about six weeks. Before that, though, there were regular deposits on the first and fifteenth of the month."

"Were those deposits electronic or by check?" Josie asked.

"There were deposits directly from Ms. Daye in varying amounts late last year ending in January of the new year. The checks came from a company called Jolly, Inc. There were also direct deposits from Flag Auto beginning at the end of January this year and continuing until six weeks ago."

Ms. Johnson took up a pen, wrote the address of Flag Auto and Jolly Inc. on a piece of paper and passed it to Josie. Jolly, Inc. was in New York, and Flag Auto was in town. While Ms. Johnson attended to the information on her computer, Josie did a quick search and found that Jolly, Inc. was a small toy company. She shot them a message, asking to be put in touch with legal counsel regarding a former employee who was now deceased. Ms. Johnson was back at her screen, energetically hitting keys, pausing, and finally she pushed away from the desk, got up, and said, "There is a cross reference here that I'd like to check out. While I run it down, would you like to access Ms. Daye's safe deposit box?"

LILY'S safe deposit box was one of a hundred little crypts lining the walls of the room accessible only through a steel gate. Hers was the smallest the bank offered, but Josie jumped to no conclusions. From the looks of Lily's cottage, it appeared she valued nothing. Then again, the existence of this box was not the first surprise Lily had left for Josie. There had been the guns, the silencer, the dog.

When asked for the key, Josie had initially thought she didn't have it. She found it in the bottom fold of the envelope Chief Miller had given her. Now the banker was turning both keys, sliding the narrow box out of its space, and walking to a cubicle where she left Josie alone with Lily Daye's treasures. Josie unlatched the box and lifted the lid.

She was disappointed.

There were no jewels or stacks of cash, no birth certificates, quit claim deeds, or passports under different names. Lily Daye, it appeared, was not a spy nor an international assassin.

What Josie did find was a bound notebook that appeared to be an engineering manual or some sort. The handwriting was precise, and Josie assumed it was Lily who wrote it; her artistic abilities, however, were lacking. The drawings that accompanied the text were juvenile at best.

Still, the level of the mathematical documentation pointed to an exceptionally intelligent person. If Lily Daye was that person, why did she work for a toy company and auto dealership? Maybe her decline was the most epic case of burnout ever. Or she was a woman so disappointed that her genius had not been recognized that she gave up.

Josie set aside the book in favor of a well-worn, unsealed number ten envelope. The flap was creased with use. Inside was a piece of torn newspaper. The picture showed a Porsche wrapped around a tree and a headline lamenting the deaths of two little boys, sons of the local grocer, who had been struck by the car driven by a rich man.

She put the envelope on top of the journal thinking these might be Lily's children.

Patrick and Andy had been referenced in Carolyn's letters. Perhaps Lily was the wife of the rich man who killed them. The victims could have been relatives, friends, or neighbors. In the extreme, Lily could have been the creepy neighborhood woman who was interested in tragedies. The only thing Josie could say with certainty was that this accident meant something to Lily Daye.

The last thing she found was a small velvet bag tied with a satin ribbon. Inside was a thumb drive wrapped in plain white paper and held in place by a rubber band. Josie unwrapped it and saw a list of numbers and acronyms. George was due out to look at Lily's computer; he would tell her what this was.

Josie closed the box. If Lily was an engineer or a mathematician, her reclusiveness might be normal to her, a woman more comfortable with numbers than people. If she had experienced personal trauma, retreating to the quiet of the Vanderhaven estate would be understandable. Lily could have worked remotely on her computers and perhaps taken up the teddy bear gig as some kind of therapy.

Josie pushed the call button, put the contents of Lily Daye's safe deposit box in her bag, and told Ms. Johnson the box would not be renewed. Once again, Josie was led back to the manager's office, and this time there was a man waiting for them.

"This is Stan Walford," Amelia said. "He handled Ms. Daye's account when she first came to us."

"Are there more accounts than I've seen?" Josie said as she shook his hand.

"Not at this bank," he said. "Ms. Daye first opened her account with a succession of large deposits. Those deposits weren't in excess of the federal banking regulations, but because they were substantial, we referred her to Merrill Lynch. She would have had no growth in a savings account."

He handed Josie a piece of paper.

"The manager's name is Janet Smith. Her contact information is there, along with the transfer information."

Josie looked at the paper, raised a brow, and asked, "Where did these funds come from?"

"A bank in Northern California. It came in three deposits over the course of that many days," Mr. Walford said. "For a total of—"

"Three million dollars," Josie said.

"I imagine there's been some activity since the transfer." Mr. Walford smiled. "I'm sure you'll find the account has grown."

"Great," Josie said. "That's just great."

CHAPTER 27

THE FOURTH WITNESS
THE EMPLOYER

"Michelle Drapeau."

The tall woman with shoulder length light brown hair and curtain bangs started talking somewhere between the Honda Passport and the all-electric Prologue. When she finished her introduction, she was standing in the middle of the showroom shaking Josie's hand.

"I'm the manager here, how can I help you?"

"Josie Bates. I'm an attorney at Baxter & Baxter in Hermosa."

"Good news, bad news, or do you want to buy a car?" the woman said. "If it's bad news, can you hang on to it until tomorrow? If it's good news, I could use some. If you want a car, we've got 'em."

"No car, no news. I'm looking for some information about one of your employees," Josie said.

"I can do that, too. How about we talk in my office? I have coffee."

Josie followed the woman through the showroom, admiring the cars and the ambiance.

"I've been by here a hundred times," Josie said. "It's a beautiful place."

"It's a family business, but right now I'm pretty much the only family running it." She smiled easily, obviously proud of her space. "My husband retired and spends his time surfing, but I'm not quite ready to make every day Sunday."

"I'm a few years out myself."

Josie told a little white lie. The word retirement was not in her vocabulary unless she could do it like Archer. He slid from Detective III, LAPD, into gigs of his own making. Now he split his *retirement* between hiring out as an investigator and making a few bucks indulging his passion for photography. His hours were flexible and the opportunities interesting. Josie would find it hard to give a hundred percent to clients if she was working part-time, and she doubted anyone would pay her to play volleyball on the beach.

Michelle stopped at a coffee machine and filled two cups. Josie waved away milk and sugar. The woman raised her cup indicating an office that looked much like the one at the bank except the three walls that were not glass were covered with flags.

"It looks like the United Nations," Josie said.

"Our name is Drapeau, but nobody can pronounce it. It's French for flag, ergo Flag Auto. Once people heard that they started giving us flags. At first it was cute, but then it was like breeding rabbits. They are everywhere." Michelle took the chair behind her desk, finished with any talk of flags. "So, what can I do for you?"

Josie sat down and laid it out for Michelle Drapeau. Lily Daye was dead, and as executor of her estate she was following up on any monies still due to the woman and information on next of kin or friends.

"First off, I'd say that qualifies as bad news for Lily. I just assumed she was headed for a better job when she left us. I don't have much on her, but what I've got is yours."

"How long did Lily work for you?"

"She was here a year, maybe a little less. She was very nice, very quiet. She was a good worker. I think she quit two months ago?" Michelle pulled a face. "We haven't filled her position yet. How did she die?"

"Might have been an accidental O.D. or suicide," Josie said.

"That's tough, but maybe not so surprising."

"What makes you say that?"

"No reason other than she never said anything personal. She was very…" Michelle paused as she searched for the right word. "Alert, is the word, I guess. I got the feeling Lily was waiting for a shoe to drop. Maybe that's me being dramatic, but someone who plays things that close to the vest has something they don't want you to know about."

Michelle waved her hand like she was erasing her comments. "Anyway, it's a shame. I hope it was an accident. I'd hate to think we ignored some warning sign and could have prevented it."

"What did she do for you?" Josie asked. "I'm assuming she wasn't a salesperson."

"Heavens no," Michelle said. "I hired her for customer service because she had a nice voice, but then one day Frank needed help in the parts department. She filled in and she was incredible. I think she had a photographic memory. Frank said she could lay her hands on anything in seconds. She rearranged the way we handled storage and ordering. She saved us a lot of money."

"Was there a problem when she was in customer service?"

"Not really a problem, but have you ever met someone who is like obsessive-compulsive? Well, Lily…"

Memories of Hannah as a young girl flashed through Josie's mind. Those early days were hard. Hannah, a teenager abused by her mother, wrongly accused of murder, was overcome with compulsions. That girl had braved every hardship known to man and then some. Compulsiveness and caution were the only things Hannah shared with Lily Daye because whatever misery Lily had known broke her. Josie put away thoughts of Hannah and attended to what Michelle was saying about Lily Daye.

"Anyway, this older gentleman wanted his windshield wipers replaced, but his car was out of warranty. He was just looking for a little commiseration, some hand holding. That wasn't Lily. She was by the book. Dot every *I* and cross every *T*. He was not happy, and I had to smooth things over. Sometimes you have to read the room, you know."

Michelle chuckled as if to underscore that this was not a talent Lily had. "I think it was the accent. Usually, English accents are kind of cool and charming, but she sounded like a nanny. Once we moved her, she was happy. It was all good. I was sorry when she quit."

"Can I see her application?" Josie said.

Michelle opened a drawer and rifled around, and handed the application to Josie.

"Lily didn't own a computer, so she filled out a paper form. I'm not even sure why I kept it considering I scanned it."

Josie put her cup on the edge of Michelle's desk, again struck by Lily's love of paper when she had a perfectly good computer at her house.

"She didn't fill out an emergency contact," Josie said.

"I guess she didn't want to." Michelle shrugged.

"Did you ever hear her mention family?"

"Nope."

Michelle finished her coffee, crumpled the cup, and put it in a trashcan at her feet.

"Any kickbacks on the Social Security number?" Josie asked.

Michelle shook her head. "The accountant would have flagged that immediately."

Josie put her fingers against her lips and thought for a minute. She asked, "Did Lily have any visitors? Did someone pick her up after work? Anything like that?"

"You really need to talk with Frank. He spent more time with her than anyone. Come on, I'll introduce you."

Michelle took her through the showroom and the service waiting room. Josie asked "Just out of curiosity, what was her pay grade?"

"Twenty an hour. She didn't try to negotiate, and she never seemed to worry about money," Michelle said.

This was no surprise. Lily didn't need to worry about money because she was sitting on a pile of it. Depression could account for her not touching it, or her spartan ways, but Josie did wonder why Lily wanted to make sure Mr. Murray thrived.

"You're not still carrying Lily on the books, are you?"

"No. She definitely quit," Michelle said. "She told Frank and he told me."

"Shouldn't she have told you?" Josie asked.

"In a perfect world, yeah." Michelle laughed. "I've had mechanics walk off the job at lunch, and we didn't figure out they weren't coming back for a week."

Josie caught the door that Michelle had pushed through and then followed her into a back room that was shadowy, gray, and chilly. To her left was a door that led to a repair bay. In front of her were rows and rows of shelving stacked with auto parts and tires. Chains hung on the walls and from the ceiling. The place smelled of hard rubber and grease.

"Frank? You here?"

Only seconds passed before the women heard a rustle, a clang, and the sound of heavy steps. Seconds more went by before they actually saw the big man emerge from the back of the cavernous room. He lumbered toward them, wiping his hands on a rag. He was so wide the clearance between the shelves was minimal, but he managed it with some grace. He had a big belly and a bigger smile. Josie was reminded of Lily's teddy bears. This man would qualify as big, safe, and cuddly.

"Hey boss?" His voice was surprisingly gentle. "This my new helper?"

"Sorry, you're still on your own." Michelle made the introductions. "She wants to ask you about Lily."

"Ah, Annie Oakley," the man said. "How's she doing?"

"Not great," Josie said. "She passed away."

The big man's smile faded. He dropped his chin, and he wagged his head as he turned away.

"Man. Aw, damn."

Michelle put a hand on his arm, gave him a squeeze and left them to it.

He sighed, tossed his rag onto a shelf, and showed Josie to his "office": two chairs in a corner, a radio on the shelf above the one that was clearly his, and a stack of auto and gun magazines with a tin on top.

"Does that still work?"

"It does." The smile he gave her was not as bright as the one he had greeted her with, but that was understandable. "Me and Lily listened to it all the time. She didn't like the new phones and stuff anymore than I did."

He looked around the storage room as if seeing it for the first time. Josie understood. Hearing that someone you knew had passed away suddenly put things a little off kilter. But Frank's unease was notable, sincere, and hard to hide. Lily, it seemed, was quite a good friend.

"Did the boss give you coffee?"

"She did, thanks."

He took up the tin, opened the top, and offered her a cookie. Josie declined.

"Lily loved these. I probably should throw them away now, but I kind of thought she'd come back and visit," he said. "That's why I kept them."

He put the top back on the tin, and the tin on the magazines. He looked at that tin a second longer than was necessary. He wouldn't throw those cookies away any time soon.

"What happened to Lily?"

The story of her involvement with Lily was getting tighter with each telling. While he listened, Frank at first leaned forward, clasped his hands, and let them dangle between his knees while she spoke. When Josie told him Lily still hadn't been claimed, he tipped his chair onto the back legs, his shirt pulling over his great stomach. His head fell back as if he was rolling back tears. The chair dropped and second later. Frank was alright and ready to talk.

"She wasn't the happiest person in the world, you understand, but suicide…" He sighed, clearly struggling with this bit of news. "I kind of knew she had things tough, but when we worked, she was happy. She was funny."

"I heard that she was reclusive and not very friendly," Josie said. "Or maybe I should say not social."

"Might just be me, but I thought she was funny. Lily had this dry humor, you know. Biting. English kind of funny."

"I haven't found a passport," Josie said. "But I did find some letters to Lily from a lady in England. Her name was Carolyn Barnes. Does that ring a bell?"

"Never heard that name," Frank shook his head. "I do know Lily's been in the States for a good long while. From what I pieced together, she married some guy in the service and came on over here with him."

"Did she mention his name? That would be really helpful. If I could find him."

"Nope. Didn't give him a name either. I don't think it lasted long. They lived somewhere like Texas maybe," he said. "Even if she did say it, a guy's name would go in one ear for me and out another."

"She got divorced and came here? Do you know if that's how it went?"

"Naw, she moved down here about three years ago," he said. "Before that she was up north. Not San Francisco, but close. She had a relationship, but she didn't want to talk about that one either. Man, just her thinking about it sent her into a tailspin. Never saw a woman get sad and mad all at the same time. She just pulled into this tight little package, and you couldn't get a thing out of her. Even cookies didn't help."

The man's countenance went dark. He lowered his voice even though there was no one to hear or care.

"And she was bitter. Like she'd been through hell and back. She was sorry she had let it slip and shut me down pretty fast when I brought it up again. I was just trying to give her a safe space, you know. Sometimes it's good to talk things out, but nothing could get her to open up. It must have been bad with that guy."

"I wonder why she mentioned it in the first place?" Josie said.

"That I can tell you," he said. "Some psychologist came on the radio and was talking about something that triggered her. I found her crying back there in the stacks near the batteries. Saddest thing I've ever seen. Women like Lily don't cry. Still, I guess no matter how tough you are, you still got a few tears to shed if the situation is right."

They sat in silence for a minute, lost in their own thoughts. Josie sat forward, forearms on her knees, looking at the floor, thinking. There was nothing to see but grease stains.

"What did you do?" she asked, sympathizing with both Lily and Frank in that situation.

"Nothing," he said. "When Lily was done, she came back and got to work. Anyway, she said something flip with that accent of hers, and I knew she was okay."

"Can you remember what the psychologist on the radio was talking about?"

"I was half listening. In and out with the job that day, so it wasn't anything that stood out in my mind."

"But she opened up to you about her relationship?"

Josie sat back and draped one arm over her chair so she could really look at him. He was nice looking, gentle, and sweet. He was the kind of man women loved, but didn't want.

"I wouldn't really call it opening up." He waggled his head a little bit; he shifted his bulk, more uncomfortable with the talk than the way he sat in the folding chair. "It wasn't bonding stuff, if you know what I mean. Not for her anyway. It was more of her making a statement. Something like, 'I was with a man I thought was perfect. He wasn't. He was evil.' Sounds stupid when I say it, but I remember when she said it. I hope he didn't hit her."

Frank shrugged and gave her a sheepish smile. Then he smiled.

"We had a good time, too, though. We talked about guns and hunting and such. I like to think I'm am expert of sorts, but Lily, she was the real deal. She won awards for marksmanship when she was a teenager. At least that's what she told me."

"How do you know she wasn't pulling your leg?" Josie asked.

"One of my pistols had a squib," he said, animated for the first time. "She took that thing home and brought it back the next day all fixed. She used to go to the Angeles Range way up in Sylmar. She brought back one of her targets. Man, that woman could shoot. Are you into guns?"

"Not really." Josie shook her head. She could handle one, but she didn't seek them out.

"Then it's hard to explain the satisfaction of being on a range, of knowing that you are in control of that kind of power. It's a skill and an art," he said. "Now, I don't know if that's what it was with Lily, but I do know she said the world dropped away when she was on that range. Guess no matter what you're doing, the world goes away if you do something well."

"Sylmar is out of her way if she was living here," Josie said.

"Yeah, but it's an outdoor range. I go to Montana to hunt but if I wanted some practice, I would want to be outside. You can use different weapons, scopes, and such when you're outside," he said. "I offered to go with Lily, 'cause we got along so good. She said no. Just like that. No. Then she got all Lily on me for a day or two and hardly said a word. She probably thought I was asking for a date, but I just wanted to go with someone who would appreciate what I got, you know? I like to show off a little, same as the next guy. I would have liked to go up against Lily."

He chuckled and Josie thought it was sad that he didn't have someone who appreciated him.

"How did Lily get there?"

"I never thought about it. Maybe she already had a friend, and that's why she didn't want to go with me." He pulled a face and Josie had a funny feeling he had worn that expression before where women were concerned. "She really was a mystery, that one. Sorry I'm not more help. I'm sad she's gone."

"You've been more help than you know," Josie said. "And I think you were the best friend she had."

"Really? His smile said he was pleased with the compliment. "That's nice to hear."

"Why did she quit working here, Frank?" Josie asked.

"I thought it was something I did, and that kept me up at night. But it wasn't."

"How do you know it wasn't?" Josie said.

"'Cause I called her a couple of weeks after she was gone. I thought about it before I did it. I didn't want to bother her, but I was worried. She said she appreciated that I was worried, and then she said the funniest thing. She said, 'Disappearing is something I do.'"

"You thought about her a lot after she left, didn't you?"

"I did, ma'am. I missed her." Frank laced his fingers together and put his hands on top of his head. He looked off into the distance. "Lily saw the world really clear and was kind of—I don't know—disappointed and accepting of it all at the same time. But when she looked at me, she really saw me. She talked to me, and she listened back. I think Lily was smarter and kinder than all of us."

He dropped his hands onto the arms of the chair, and looked Josie in the eye. "Something really sad happened to Lily, and I think she was too scared or too proud to ask for help. Or maybe it was my help she didn't want. But keeping to herself made her lonely and paranoid, and I guess she only saw one way out."

"Did you ever talk to her after your call?"

"A couple times," he said. "The last time there was no opening, you know, like for me to see what was going on. She wasn't engaged at all. She said it was a pleasure and hung up. Isn't that funny? A pleasure. I should have sat on her doorstep just so she knew someone was there for her."

"Frank, did you know where she lived?" Josie said.

"I did," he said.

"Did you ever go up there? On your own. Without her inviting you?"

"I did once, but she was ready for me," he said. "I don't know how she heard me coming, but she had a Glock on me by the time I got to the door."

"What did she do when she saw it was you."

"She said sorry." He mimicked an English accent. "When I said I was checking on her, she said she was fine and closed the door. She wasn't fine, but I went home and..."

His eyes were clouding again, so hazy Josie knew that a tear or two had been shed over Lily even before she died.

"Frank, did you call in a wellness check for Lily? Did you make that call and not leave your name?"

Josie put her fingertips on the arm of his chair. He looked at her hand and his head bobbed up and down. The back of his hand swiped across one eye. Josie touched his arm and gave it a quick squeeze.

"She was lucky to have you as a friend."

"Not lucky enough," he said. "I should have called sooner. I figured if she didn't know it was me who called it in, she wouldn't have anyone to be mad at when it turned out okay. It was stupid."

"No, it was kind," Josie said. "And I think Lily was happy here with you."

"Not happy enough."

He paused a beat and then scooted up in his chair a little. He splayed his legs and rested his forearms on his knees. Josie leaned in to hear what he had to say.

"There was one strange day. Lily was in the john." He pulled a thumb over his shoulder. "The john is right there, so it's hard to be really private.

"She was on her phone talking really loud, and I heard her say 'your fault' and 'you owe.' Then it was like she realized how loud she was, and after that I couldn't hear anything. She was all flushed when she came out, but she just went back to work. I wouldn't have wanted her to have a gun in her hand right then. She was cold, man."

"So that's it?" Josie said.

"Yep. Whatever it was it must have been important to get Lily to raise her voice."

Frank shifted on the small chair, rubbed his chin, and pushed up on his full cheeks as he gave that a second thought.

"You know, now that we're talking, I realize everything I got about Lily came in bits and pieces. Funny, how you think someone's your friend, but they're just someone you've passed some time with. Funny, that."

"As far as I can tell, you were Lily's only friend, so hold on to that."

"You're right." He slapped his thighs and the grin was back. "I'll think of the good stuff. She was pretty, she liked her work, and she let me talk her ear off about all the computer crap on cars these days. I liked cars when you could take 'em apart in your driveway and put 'em back together. Nowadays, somebody sitting in an airconditioned office somewhere can unlock your car, turn it on, turn it off just like that."

Frank snapped his fingers, a sign of disdain for the guys who took away all the fun in life.

"Yep, she didn't like technology any more than me. She said just because you can do something, doesn't mean you should."

Josie smiled as her phone began to vibrate. She pushed the message button and asked one more question.

"She never mentioned needing a lawyer, or me specifically, did she?"

He shook his head in the negative and said, "But you made some impression on her at some point. You might not remember, but she did."

"Did she mention a Mr. Murray?"

Frank shook his head again. Josie gathered her things. There wasn't much left to talk about.

"Thanks for the time. Thanks for everything."

"It might be too late, but if there is anything I can do, let me know." He stood up like a gentleman seeing a lady out of his parlor. "I'd like to know about a service, if you don't mind."

"I'll let you know," she said. "And don't beat yourself up. Making that call was a good thing."

"Not good enough," he said. "Poor Lily."

"I got her now," Josie said, and that satisfied him.

Before Josie was out the front door, before Frank was back in his man cave of car parts, she had one more question.

"The day you surprised Lily at her house, did she have a dog?"

"Not that I saw, but it would make sense," he said. "Maybe that's how she knew I was there."

"Maybe," she said and then told him goodbye.

Josie waved at Michelle Drapeau, left the dealership, and paused on the sidewalk to return that call she had sent to voice message.

"Ms. Smith? Josie Bates. I'm calling about one of your accounts. I'd like to confirm the balance."

Josie gave the woman at Merrill Lynch's offices Lily's account number. The woman was expecting Josie's call and had the number ready. Lily Daye's account had grown two hundred thousand dollars since its transfer.

Josie asked that the paperwork be emailed to her so that she could transfer the funds to the executor account.

There was one more stop to make before the end of the day because Josie had an epiphany while she was talking to Frank-the-parts-manager. She was almost sure she knew who Mr. Murray was.

CHAPTER 28

EMERYVILLE
PRESENT DAY

It had been a very long day for Jimmy.

Breakfast with the primary investor had turned into lunch because the man wanted to go back in time. Jimmy wanted to tell him that history not only sucked, it was useless to try to dig through its rubble. But this guy was richer than God and fixated on *Distant2* and the battery that had been part of Backlash Technologies.

But you made it once.
You can do it again.
Tell me what you need.
We'll resurrect…

Jimmy could only endure it.

His back hurt. He had gained weight. He was fat. He was smoking too much dope. He was drinking too much. He had run through four assistants in the last three years. They taxed him with their questions and updates. They groveled. Adoration was one thing; groveling quite another. Groveling was close and cloying; adoration was passive and distant.

Thankfully the problem of an assistant had been resolved. A trusted Backlash employee was back. One who adored him. One who moved in and simply lifted the responsibility off his shoulders like Lily had.

This one wasn't as smart as Lily, nor as tenacious, but she caused no problems, did as she was told, and was efficient. She was exactly who Jimmy needed and he was grateful.

Eventually the meeting with the investor ended with Jimmy's promise to think about the man's request and the man's promise of money. When he got home, Jimmy was hungry, so he had had food delivered. The burger tasted bad. When he tossed it aside, it hit the cardboard box that held his super-sized fries. The box fell over, the fries spread across the bedside table. Some fell on the floor.

He thought about picking the fries up, but instead he lay back and lit a joint. He held the hit deep in his lungs, stared at the bedroom ceiling for a while, and then he looked at his computer sitting beside him in the big bed. In a haze, he clicked to see who was writing him that time of night. He hoped it wasn't the money man. He was a bore. It wasn't, but it was a message about the money man's favorite topic: history.

Jimmy rolled over, snuffed out his joint and laid it in the ashtray. When he rolled back, he hoisted the computer onto his stomach and read the words that caused his heart to race.

Found her!

Jimmy clicked the URL that came after and up popped a Google Alert. He read it twice before he typed back a message of his own.

Thank you, Lovely.

CHAPTER 29

SAN PEDRO, CALIFORNIA
ANIMAL SHELTER

Josie walked between the cages, looking at each dog in turn. Some barked and turned circles looking for an out or a rescue; others were silent, staring as she passed by. A caramel-colored mutt cowered in the corner of one cage. Seeing him, Josie felt like doing the same in a show of solidarity. An animal shelter was no one's favorite place, but Josie knew it was a necessary evil. The lady she followed didn't even think about it. She was all business as she led Josie through the facility.

She walked with short, hurried steps, flicking out a hand one way and then the other as she called soothing words to the caged animals. It was the best she could do since she was the only one on duty. Finally, the woman came to a big door, opened it, and held it for Josie.

"He's in there."

"Thanks. I won't be long," Josie said.

"Take your time."

The woman went back to work, leaving Josie in a small

room that held six cages. One housed four puppies. There were mongrels in another four. In the sixth cage was Lily's dog, resting like a sphinx on a thin blanket. Josie didn't waste any sympathy on him because he was too proud to take it even if it were offered.

Instead, she walked over to the cage, made sure he was looking right at her and said, "Mr. Murray. Come on, Mr. Murray."

He didn't move and Josie's hopes went out the window. She had been so sure that this dog had been the thing Lily cared about most in the world. Josie tried again, and this time she did hold out her hand. She snapped her fingers, and this time his name was a command.

"Mr. Murray. Come."

Nothing.

Josie got down, balancing on the balls of her feet in front of the cage. The dog never took his eyes off her. Unlike Max who looked at her like a friend, this one's eyes appeared to acknowledge her as a fellow combatant.

"Okay, so you're not Mr. Murray," she said. "You would have been one rich dog if you were."

Tired of her posture, she put one knee down, raised the other and draped an arm over it. Her other hand was palm down on the clean, cold floor. The mongrels barked. One of the puppies whimpered. When one of the dogs yelped as if in pain, the Shepherd turned its head as if to make sure nothing was truly wrong before turning its attention back to Josie. Slowly, the Shepherd stood up, two hands taller than Max had been at his full height. In three steps, it was at the grill. He didn't try to push his snout through the wire, he didn't beg or cry.

"God, you are beautiful," Josie said as she shook her head. "I wish you could talk."

The dog turned its back on her, went to the far corner and

lay down on the blanket again. Josie got off the floor, and dusted off her slacks. There was nothing for her here. In fact, she was leaving with more questions about Lily than she had when she arrived.

Why have a dog that was built like a tank when you lived in a walled compound?

Why live like a pauper when you're sitting on millions?

Why the menial jobs? Or the computers? Or the guns?

Why didn't you recognize that you had friends in Carolyn and Frank?

Why are you dead?

Josie found the woman who had walked her in. She had a puppy in a tub and was giving it a good wash. He looked like a drowned rat but when he was dry, he would be a ball of fluff.

Josie leaned against the wall and asked, "Have you had the Shepherd checked for a chip?"

"I doubt it."

"Can I leave a request to have it done?" Josie said.

The puppy went onto a counter and she put a towel over it.

"I don't think it's going to happen for that one," she said, intent on the puppy. "They tagged him. I guess he had been aggressive and that's why we got the call to go get him. That room? That's where we put the unadoptables."

"Sorry?" Josie pushed off the wall and went close to the table. The woman had no choice but to stop what she was doing and look at her.

"We're not a no-kill facility," she said. "The Shepherd is going to be put down tomorrow."

CHAPTER 30

Over an hour later, the paperwork and interviews needed to adopt the Shepherd were complete.

In the normal course of events, Josie's home would be inspected, her loved ones interviewed, and her neighbors questioned before she would be allowed to take possession of the dog. In Los Angeles, it was as difficult to adopt a pet as it was a child, but he was on a kill list so the rules were bent.

Josie left with the massive dog tethered to a flimsy leash. He was neither curious about her, concerned with where they were going, nor grateful for the rescue. In fact, the dog walked with her as if he'd known she would come for him.

She opened the car door. He chose not to sit beside her and settled in the back so that he could look over her shoulder. Josie got in after him, shut the door, put the key in the ignition, and started the car. Before she released the emergency brake, she looked into the rearview mirror.

"You know I just saved your butt, right?"

Josie could have sworn the dog smirked. So did she as she threw the car into gear, and hand over hand, turned the car toward home. Forty-five minutes later, she had made a quick stop for pet supplies and was now parked on Hermosa Boulevard, two blocks from home.

Juggling her packages, her bag, and the dog, Josie walked him down the street at the pace he set. The dog noted everything: pedestrians, traffic lights, cars. He stopped at the sound of an electric bike, and went into high alert when a kid on a skateboard made a jump out of a side street. The Shepherd recovered just as fast.

When they turned onto her street and the beach was near, the dog sniffed the air and then the ground. He marked the territory, and so it went until they were through her front gate. Then Josie dropped the leash and let him explore the patio, the furniture, the small patch of grass outside her bedroom. By the time the front door was open, he was satisfied that his new surroundings were safe. He made the rounds inside, too as Josie put a towel on the kitchen floor and set up the dog's bowls. She filled one with water and the other with food. Finally, she took the brand-new rawhide bone, walked back to the living room, and held it out to the dog. He looked at it and then at her. He made no move to take it.

"You're going to be a barrel of laughs." Those ears twitched. Josie smiled. "At least you hear me."

She wiggled the bone. He craned his neck and walked toward her until he was close enough to smell it. Josie took off his leash and then used the rawhide as a lead, walking backward, enticing him into the kitchen. Josie put the bone near the food and water, and left him to decide if he was proud or hungry.

⊏⊐

WHEN JOSIE CAME BACK, the food was gone as was half the water. The rawhide bone was still untouched, and her new friend was politely waiting by the French doors to go out. He was a well-trained house guest.

Josie took an apple out of the fridge, her computer off the table, and opened the patio doors. The dog went to the grass while Josie lit the fireplace. It was another perfect Hermosa night: just enough chill and a little winter breeze to boot. She thought she heard *Jingle Bells* playing in the distance as she settled on the sofa. The Shepherd lay near the fireplace close to the low wall enclosing the patio.

His presence made Josie realize how much she had missed Max, and that served as a warning not to get too comfortable with this one. This dog would be part of the estate. If Mr. Murray wanted him, then off he would go

Josie put her computer on her lap, opened her email, and munched on her apple.

The first message was from Mrs. Westral inquiring about the status of her complaint against her neighbors. Josie wrote back assuring her that the neighbors would not be able to move their fence three feet into her property. The next one was from Faye confirming their upcoming meeting with Rusty Gates. Josie had it on the calendar, and would prefer not to think about it until the day of.

She set the computer aside and went back to the kitchen, threw away the apple core, filled a glass of water, and added ice. When she got back to the couch, Josie sensed something was different. It wasn't until she was back on the sofa that Josie realized *she* was different. For the first time in a long while she felt peaceful, as if everything was going to work out: her and Archer, Faye's retirement, Lily's estate. It was a lovely feeling and the dog seemed to have caught it. He now lay on the cool concrete halfway between the couch and fireplace, closer to Josie but not too close.

Josie picked up the computer and opened the message from the account manager at Merrill Lynch. Lily Daye's investment history was attached. The strategy was conservative and the returns impressive. Lily invested her three million dollars in pharmaceuticals, transportation, and oil. Notable by its absence were technology stocks.

Just as Josie clicked to look at the beneficiary instructions, she lifted her head, aware that there was a stirring of the air, and a new warmth that didn't come from the fire. It was the Shepherd and he was moving toward her.

Josie closed her computer, measuring every movement so she wouldn't spook him. She scooted down until her head rested against the couch pillow and closed her eyes. The dog advanced, one foot in front of the other, his head lowered. He stopped between the couch and the coffee table. Josie turned her head so that her chin rested on her shoulder. There was something intimate about it all. If he had been human and a man, this would have been the moment when they realized they meant something to one another.

The dog listed toward Josie. She touched him, putting her hand on his back, pressing her fingers in to his fur. When he accepted this, Josie's throat constricted. She closed her eyes against the tears that were forming.

She was filled with something indefinable, something that she had only known a handful of times. It was a deep sorrow. She had felt it with the death of her father, the discovery of her mother who now called another woman daughter.

It had overcome her when she had been left to die in a cement cell in the Santa Monica Mountains and she thought she would never see Hannah, Archer, and Billy again.

This feeling had clamped over her heart in the hospital when Archer climbed into her bed and held her after she lost the baby.

And, yes, she felt it when Max was gone.

It was a feeling between fear and loneliness, faith and hope. The dog understood because he had felt it in his lifetime, too.

Just because the world believed in your strength, that did not mean you were indestructible.

The Shepherd's snout nudged her computer. Josie let it slip off into the crook between her body and the sofa cushions. The dog rested his head on her stomach. He raised a paw and placed it on her chest near her heart.

That's how they stayed, the woman and the dog. The dog did not move when the cinders in the fireplace went cold. It was only when Josie quieted, done with her weeping, that he lay on the ground beside her and they both drifted off to sleep.

CHAPTER 31

At three twenty-four in the morning, the Shepherd raised his head.

Josie stirred.

The dog's muscles pulled tight.

Josie turned, half asleep. The couch was narrow and she rolled onto her back again.

The Shepherd made a sound, a low rumble deep in his chest.

Josie mumbled in protest.

The dog's growl blossomed, bubbling up from his gut, reaching his throat, growing in tenor until it sounded a tempered warning, and Josie woke. She mumbled words that would calm him as she shook off her sleep.

It was natural for him to be on edge. In the last week, he had been chained in a dirty garage, caged in an animal rescue, and who knew what before that. What caught his attention could be a neighbor's cat prowling, a bar-fly stumbling down The Strand trying to remember where he parked his car, a night swimmer hurrying home to get warm and dry. Every noise would be suspect until he assured himself it meant nothing.

Josie's touch did not reassure the dog, so she sat up and took hold of his collar. He sat up, too. He was agitated and quivering.

"Okay," she whispered. "Let's see what it is."

Slowly she scooted off the couch, holding him from behind, positioned so she could try to identify what he was seeing. No one was walking the dark -street, and the houses lining it were dark.

The patio lights weren't on because she had not intended to spend the night on the outside, but she could still see well enough given the neighbor's solar lights in the flower pots and the bright moon. Nothing moved. People were sleeping.

She put her free arm around the dog, and saw that he was looking inside the house at the hall light.

"I see it. It's fine. It's fine," she said.

Josie didn't remember turning it on, but she must have. It was winter and the dark came early. But the Shepherd was not satisfied. He strained against her hold, wanting her to open the door so he could check out the house even though she could see that nothing was amiss. The kitchen cupboards were closed, the front door shut, the furniture was in place.

As suddenly as the dog had become alert, he went stone still and silent, intent on that light. That's when she saw it: a long shadow cast on the hall wall.

The dog jerked forward, silent save for a succession of hot hard huffs. No match for him, Josie let go of his collar. He went to the French doors and pawed the glass. He fell back, waiting for her to open the door, keeping silent so as not to alert the intruder.

The shadow slid away into the bedroom.

Josie stayed low as she went for the door. Once there, she paused, waiting to see if the person showed themself. Her breath caught when the small light in the bedroom was turned on. A split second later whoever was in her bedroom headed for the hall. His shadow was deformed now, his head large and his body silhouette a squiggle.

Josie opened the patio door.

The Shepherd bounded through the house, snarling and snapping as he disappeared into the hallway. She heard a man cry out as she sprinted into the house, stopping only long enough to grab Lily Daye's Glock out of the box on the dining room table.

Her bedroom door slammed. The dog barked so loudly he sounded like ten hounds from hell. Knowing he had the hall covered, Josie ran onto the patio and positioned herself outside the bedroom doors, cutting off any escape.

The sheers were drawn, but she could see a man leaning against the door that led to the hall.

Raising one foot, she kicked at the French doors and screamed, "I've got a gun. Get down. On your knees. Hands on your head."

He turned at the sound of her voice, but instead of doing as he was told, the man rushed the French doors. Josie stepped back, cursing herself for not grabbing a clip. There was a chance she could make it back inside to get one, but in the next instant that window closed. The man grabbed the sheers, tangling in them as he tried to push them aside. His head was covered by the fabric, but his hands were free and he had ahold of the door handles.

"I said down!"

Josie screamed louder, but it did no good. The door flew open. Josie fell back, tightening her grip on the Glock, aware that lights were turning on behind her as people awakened to the commotion. Josie lowered her face, cheek against her shoulder as she looked down the sights. She prayed the mere existence of the gun would deter him.

It didn't.

Suddenly freed from the curtains, the man flipped on the outdoor lights, blinding her. Before she could clear her eyes, he lunged, knocked the gun aside, and enveloped her in his powerful arm, dragging her back toward the patio wall.

Hearing her cries, the dog headed for them, barking and barking as he launched through the patio door, skirted the sofa and came at them. Josie and the man hit the wall. She dropped the gun and he released her. They both went for it, but the man was stronger and faster. He pushed her out of the way. That's when Josie got a look at him and froze.

He paid her no mind as he grabbed the gun in one hand and her arm in the other. Swinging her behind him, he pointed the Glock at the Shepherd and roared, "What in the hell is that, Jo?"

———

IT WAS three thirty in the morning when the police arrived, summoned by the woman in the house directly across the way from Josie. They came with guns drawn, warning they would take the dog out if someone didn't subdue him, and Archer, too, if he didn't drop his weapon.

Archer dropped the gun and Josie corralled the dog. Although they were known to the Hermosa PD, the cops did their job and separated them for interviews.

Yes, that's my husband.

No there was no problem. She is my wife.

Yes, he surprised me. I didn't expect him back for a week.

Yes, I wanted to surprise her. I came home early from a business trip.

He didn't know about the dog.

I didn't know about the dog.

Sorry for the disturbance.

Sorry to bring you out.

When the police and the neighbors were satisfied, Josie and Archer were left alone. Josie let the Shepherd out of the bathroom and made the introductions. The dog accepted Josie's word that Archer belonged, but kept a cautious eye on him during their flurried conversation.

Why didn't you call?

Why were you outside? Where did the dog come from?

I'm so happy to see you.

Jesus, Jo, a gun?

I'm so happy to see you. It wasn't loaded.

Josie made eggs and bacon and toast because feeding Archer seemed like the right thing to do. She split her time between the stove and hugging him until finally, they were at the table.

"Really. Why didn't you let me know?" she said.

"I couldn't find a time. I was either in the air or running for the connection," he said. "And I thought it would be kind of romantic to surprise you."

"Thank you," she said, noting his exhaustion, loving him for the effort. "I missed you."

"Missed you, too, Jo." He put down his fork, put his elbow on the table and rested his chin on top of his fist. His eyes roamed over her face. "I'm thinking if we ever need time alone again, one of us should just go to the beach for a few hours and we'll call it a day."

"I could do that."

The beach was the last place she wanted to be, but now was not the time to tell him why though.

"Where did you get that one?" Archer motioned to the dog who still had a wary eye on him.

"He was at Lily Daye's place. I thought maybe he was the beneficiary named in her will, but he doesn't answer to *Mr. Murray.*"

"You're babysitting an asset?"

"And he was on the kill list," she said. "I couldn't leave him at the shelter."

Archer snorted and shook his head. "Another orphan. I swear Josie. What am I going to do with you?"

"I won't keep him if Mr. Murray wants him," she said. "I really thought he was Mr. Murray."

Archer held out a piece of toast and waggled it.

"Murray. Come on, Murray."

The dog stared, unimpressed with Archer's bribe.

Archer tried again. "Mr. M."

The dog remained stone still.

"Told you," Josie said.

"Doesn't hurt to try a few permutations." Archer finished off his toast, chewing slowly, still eyeing the dog. "Is he chipped?"

"I don't know. I'll get him to the vet when I have time. I hope he is."

Josie pushed her plate away. It really was an ungodly hour to eat. She crossed her arms on the table.

"What about you?" she said. "Is everything okay?"

"I just wanted to come home, babe. Simple as that." He reached for her, she reached back, and they entwined their fingers. "Do you mind?"

"Not in the least."

"Can you take the day off tomorrow?"

"You mean today?" Josie laughed. It was a sad little sound made as she answered in the negative. "I wish I could. I've got a meeting with Faye."

"She would understand."

"Not this time," Josie said. "This is important. She might have a buyer for the firm."

"And that means it's not you," Archer said.

"Are you disappointed?" Josie gave his hand a little shake.

"It's not my call, babe, and any advice I would give wouldn't be worth the paper it's printed on. I know you too well."

Archer sat back, releasing her, his hand sliding across the table and falling into his lap. A minute later, both hands were on his face and he gave it a good rub.

Then he looked at her again. "That's the last time I try to be romantic without checking your calendar."

Josie got up and went to him, took his hand, and gave it a tug. "Let me show you how much I appreciate the effort."

Archer got up. They left the food on the table, ignored his luggage, and paid no mind to the dog trailing behind them. When they got to the bedroom, they wished him goodnight and shut the door.

Climbing into bed, Josie took Archer in her arms, but when his eyes hooded and closed she rolled him onto his back, put her head on his chest. She listened to his heartbeat as he fell asleep. There would be time to show him how she felt, but this wasn't it.

When six o'clock came, Josie got out of bed and dressed for work. Archer didn't stir even when she covered his shoulders and closed the curtains. He would wake when his internal clock said it was time. He would wonder where he was for a minute, and then he would smell the scent of her shampoo, smile, and sleep again.

Before Josie left the room, though, she was caught by that strange feeling again, the warning shot before the panic. It passed as quickly as it had come and she knew why. Archer was home and the dog was there just outside the bedroom door.

Josie whispered good morning, and took him outside. When he was done with his business, she brought him back to the hallway, took his face in both hands and said, "Keep your eye on Archer. When he wakes up, try not to eat him."

The dog didn't exactly smile, but she was sure he understood.

By the time Josie got in the car, the warm glow of Archer's homecoming was fading. There was business to be done that had nothing to do with Lily Daye or her estate. Today was all about Faye Baxter, Rusty Gates, and the beginning of the end of Baxter & Baxter.

CHAPTER 32

Josie's side of the bed was cold when Archer woke up, which was unsurprising since it was almost noon. The real surprise was that he was awake at all. Considering the length of the flight and last night's welcome, Archer figured he should have been knocked out for a couple of days.

He rubbed his eyes, stretched, and turned his head. They never shut the bedroom door, but now it was closed tight and that meant their new roommate was on the other side. Since the last thing he wanted to was wrestle ninety pounds of dog before he had his coffee, Archer slid one arm over his eyes, sighed deeply, and slipped back into a snooze that was as deep as a mud puddle. An hour later, he got up determined to plow through his jet lag.

With a great heave and grunt, Archer righted himself. Palms down, he gripped the edge of the mattress, splayed his feet, and hung his head. His shoulders slumped. Finally, he gathered his wits, stood up, and opened the curtains an inch, flinching at the muted glare of the December sun before pushing back the curtains. The pretty little garden Josie had landscaped herself was still little and pretty, unchanged save for the massive Shepherd lying outside the French doors. Still, it was better than seeing a lion and African scrub.

Their eyes met, held, and the Shepherd sat up.

Archer snorted. They were making progress. The damn thing wasn't throwing himself against the door trying to get to him. Archer kept looking, waiting for the dog to flinch first or at least lose interest. The dog was a master at chicken, and the game wasn't even worth the time it took to play it, so Archer headed for the shower.

The dog was still there when he came out, dressed and awake for at least another few hours. By the time he left the bedroom and walked down the hall, the dog was back inside. Archer walked by him, eyed the dog's dishes, and saw that he had water and had been fed. He poured himself a coffee. One cup and he could feel his extremities. Halfway through his second cup he was full on awake, so Archer dumped his stuff in the washing machine, did the dishes from their meal the night before, and stashed his carry-on. He did a run through on his camera bag, noted he needed to clean his equipment after his time in the bush, and then found Josie's note saying she wouldn't be home until after five. She was also sorry there wasn't much in the fridge, and she loved him.

He was bummed she had to work the whole day, didn't really care about food, and loved her too. By three, Archer had finished his laundry, napped for an hour, checked his email, and thought of going to Burt's for a bite but decided to wait for Josie. The news on the television was depressing, and the classic movie channel was running silent films. Archer looked at the dog who was lying near the leather chair.

He said, "Want to go for a walk?"

He got nothing. Any other dog would be turning circles at the prospect, and it amused Archer that this one was above such behavior. Still, Archer would bet money the prospect of a walk was sounding pretty good to the big dog. Archer got up. So did the Shepherd. Archer closed the patio doors, collected his keys, and got Max's pink leash out of the closet.

"It may not be your color, but it's got a lot of good history," he said as he affixed it to the heavy cowhide collar. He stood back. The dog looked ridiculous.

"I think we gotta get you a new collar 'cause it's a sure bet Josie's not going to give up the leash."

The dog's head listed right and then left. Archer chuckled. They left the house and headed for the vet, an easy walk away. When they got there, Archer apologized for not having an appointment and asked if they had time to check for a chip. The receptionist oohed and aahed over the dog, and said how happy she was that they had found a new pet. She promised to get him in. Archer sat down, nodded at the woman who had a cat carrier in her lap, scrolled through his phone, and waited. By the end of the day, he hoped to have a name for this beast and maybe a history. At the very least, he wanted to be able to confirm that the last owner of this beast was Lily Daye

———

JOSIE AND FAYE let Rusty talk.

Not that they had a choice.

When Rusty Gates was on a roll, nothing could stop him. However, his soliloquys were a thing of beauty, and they had time blocked out, so it wasn't really a hardship. Rusty never paused or wasted a word. He looked at you like you were the only one who understood his problems, were intelligent enough to grasp his reasoning and sensitive enough to help him get where he wanted to go. No one interrupted an artist.

At lunch, Rusty entertained them with stories of his travels, his married life, and his years as a college football star. He asked Faye about her long-dead husband, her very alive daughter, and her grandchildren. He inquired about Hannah and Billy, having versed himself on the cases that resulted in Josie's ad hoc family.

When lunch was over, they got down to business, and now they were into the nitty-gritty of Rusty's buttoned-up presentation that outlined his plans for the expansion of Baxter & Baxter. He gave a clear analysis of Faye's practice's existing cash flow, expenditures, and income. His proposal allowed for pro bono work for any defense or representation Josie would pick up, but underscored that there would be an expenditure cap. This would be in direct correlation to the public relations value of the project.

For example, Rusty said, if Josie took on a particularly heart-wrenching case that maybe caught the attention of *People Magazine*, no expense would be spared on the matter. An indigent on the streets of Hermosa picked up for panhandling would not entitle her to support from the firm and she would be left to handle it with nothing more than her own time and wits.

Faye glanced at Josie, assuming that she was thinking about Hannah's trial too. The press had been all over it for months. A beautiful teenage girl accused of murdering a prominent judge was salacious enough. That he was her step-grandfather was the cherry on top. When Hannah's mother was convicted of the crime, the press continued to beat the story to death. Even a Parisian paper picked it up. By Rusty's paradigm, the firm would owe Josie money for the publicity that case garnered. Josie gave no indication that she was thinking about anything other than Rusty's plans and her future.

"If you're going to be as hands off as you say, Rusty, what's to keep me from doing exactly as I please?"

"I know you, Bates. You couldn't lie your way out of a

paper bag. You're not even good at fudging. Not to mention the fact that I have spies everywhere."

Now Faye laughed outright. Josie gave Faye a look and indulged in a chuckle. He was right on all counts. Josie fingered his proposal, her eyes skimming over the numbers.

"You're assuming seventy-percent personal injury work," Josie said. "We don't really specialize here. We take what comes through the door, what needs to be done."

"Personal injury is where the money's at," Rusty said.

"I don't want to be an ambulance chaser." Josie fiddle with her pen.

"Not to worry, the advertising will bring it in. We've been handling South Bay problems out of the Los Angeles office, so the move to local will be our selling point. Bus benches, billboards on Crenshaw, that digital monster in Lomita that they put near the freeway—that thing can be seen for miles. We'll put ads in the *Beach Reporter*, the *Daily Breeze*, *PV News*. PR of course for you, me, us. We'll blanket El Segundo and Lomita, too. Those are target rich areas. I think we'll do quantity in those cities."

"Are you profiling, Rusty?" Faye asked.

"Just talking about city density," he said and winked at her. "And maybe profiling a little."

His laugh was deep and hearty. Faye smiled. Josie was more uneasy with Faye's smile than Rusty's casual assessment about the potential marketplace.

"Look, half the appeal of acquiring Baxter & Baxter is that it underscores our pitch about the personal touch. The fact that your offices are in this house makes it look like a client will be coming home to tell their family their problems. We'll position Josie as the neighborhood lawyer with a heart—"

"Oh, for god's sake."

Josie rolled her eyes and shook her head. Rusty's bull was threatening to bury them all, so she got up and went for the coffee pot. She wasn't put off by Rusty's strategy, but she wasn't sure there was a place for her either. She poured a cup and then put her backside up against the credenza, leaving Rusty to engage the woman who held the keys to the kingdom.

Faye was at the head of the table, looking as she always looked: professional and, yes, approachable with her suit, pearls, and low-heeled shoes. Rusty looked as he always looked too: a three-thousand-dollar suit, his gold links and diamond pinky ring announcing who he was.

They belonged together. Both were handsomely dressed and well-coiffed, confident in the face they presented to the community. Faye considered every client a neighbor and handled the law like a warm apple pie—everyone deserved a slice. Rusty considered the application of the law a game show, something where winning was shiny, bright, and lucrative, losing was endured with a pat on the back from the handsome host. In this trio, Josie was the odd man out. She loved the law, but only when it was applied properly, and she loved her clients when they respected the law. But it was her real life —the beach and water and sunshine—that gave her energy to work for the people who needed her. She understood that a law firm needed to be solvent, but she didn't like the idea of driving her profession based on a bottom line.

Rusty pressed a key on his computer, and a mock-up of the billboards and print ads popped onto the screen. Josie shook her head again. She didn't think she could be surprised, but Rusty proved her wrong. He stood in such a way that his face overlapped the image of Josie on a layout. It was a strange little show of his absolute command of the way modern law was conducted: by image and sound bite.

"It works, Bates." Rusty moved aside and she got the full impact of billboard with a picture of her standing twenty feet tall, arms crossed, a look of competent compassion on her face.

"Where did you get that, Rusty? I've never worn a suit like that in my life."

"You have been in the suburbs too long," he said. "AI, Bates. You gotta trust me on this one."

"I do, that's the sad thing," she said. "You know your stuff; you don't know me."

"You can pull it off. Lord, woman, you on a billboard will stop traffic."

He threw out his hands inviting her to buy into his vision of stardom.

"That's exactly my point. I don't work that way," she said. "I'm not going to be on any billboard."

"Talk to her."

"No one 'talks' to Josie." Faye shrugged, knowing that wasn't quite the whole truth but it was close. "I have to agree it isn't her style, but she would be a fabulous face of the firm."

"Well, one of us is going to have to convince her, or we have a problem."

Rusty shut down the presentation. Josie's image disappeared. Rusty stepped up to the table and tented his fingers on the hard wood. The ringmaster was gone. No more dog and pony. It was time to get an answer.

"This is your decision, Faye," he said. "For the next ten years you'll be getting ten percent off the top for use of your name. I look at your books now and see a decent revenue stream, but if you want to assure a solid retirement, one that gives you a cushion for unforeseen circumstances, then this place needs to grow by thirty percent. The only way to do that is to refresh and reposition the firm."

He kept his eyes on her for a minute to underscore his point, but Faye didn't need convincing. She knew all about unforeseen circumstances. She had almost been buried by the debt incurred when her husband became ill and she still had to raise her daughter and keep the firm going.

While Rusty's empire would feed him a fortune until the day he died, Faye had this one shot to cash in big. When he was sure Faye was thinking hard about what he had said, Rusty looked over his shoulder at Josie. It was a cool move, as if he were talking to her as a courtesy because Faye wanted her in the loop.

"If that's going to happen without you—or with you in a secondary role—I can accept that. I'd rather we join forces, but I'll work the magic another way if I have to and leave you salaried. Whatever way you want it, Bates."

Rusty stood up so straight that he looked like a general taking charge of his troops. In that minute, Josie was reminded of the old days when they had squared off in a courtroom for clients that could buy and sell them both. Back then they fought for the bucks, the media, and the notoriety. He had been good; she had been just a little better. Still, things had changed. If the prize was money and not justice, her edge was gone and Rusty knew it.

"I think you're spectacular, Bates, but this is Southern California," he said, his voice softening as he told her what she already knew. "I can find twenty smart and gorgeous attorneys to take your place. They won't have the grounding in this community, but they'll put down roots soon enough. They won't have your pedigree, but they'll get there. If I do that and you decide to stay, there will be no special arrangements for your good-deed clients. I don't put resources into something that doesn't pay its own way, and that includes you."

Josie sipped her coffee, assessing Rusty but not challenging him. While he wasn't quite the devil himself, he was close. On the other hand, Faye was a saint. She always had Josie's back, even when they disagreed. More than once, Faye had put herself in jeopardy for Josie because they were colleagues, friends, and family. Rusty wanted none of that. The good news was that he was up-front about it and that was admirable. Faye was going to sell Baxter & Baxter no matter what, and it was up to Josie to decide what part she wanted to play.

One arm was crossed over her middle, her other crooked so that she could hold her mug upright. She put the warm white ceramic against her lips, hiding her smile, her gaze softening as she looked at Faye and weighed what she could live with. Faye moved forward in her chair. She was still the owner of Baxter & Baxter, and it was time to wrap things up so they could all go to their corners and think on it.

"Rusty, thank you. Your offer is clear. It is attractive. I'd like to—"

Before Faye could finish, Angela knocked on the door and simultaneously stuck her head through. She looked apologetic, even a little frantic.

"I'm so sorry to bother you, but there's a man out front who says he has to talk to Josie right now."

"Did you tell him I'm in a meeting?" Josie asked.

"I did, but he's—"

Before Josie could finish her sentence, Angela was moved aside. No one saw exactly how it was done, but the receptionist disappeared, and the door opened further to reveal a small man who brought with him a strange sense of unease. It wasn't just the way he looked with his unkempt hair and clothing or his pale skin and odd features, it was the tainted aura that rolled into the room with him. He was like one of those creatures who lived at the bottom of the ocean without light or sound, sustained by sucking in small things that floated by him.

He looked at the three people in the room, before settling on Josie.

"Josie Bates." This was not so much a question as it was a quiet command that she confirm herself.

Josie pushed away from the credenza. She lowered her arm and put her cup down. The man moved his head and looked her over. His eyes were deep and dark and at first glance seemed attractive. On second glance Josie saw they were deep, dead, and yet somehow compelling. Josie wanted him to go away as much as she wanted him to state what business he had with her. She chose to satisfy the latter.

"I'm Josie Bates," she said.

He smiled and said, "Lovely."

CHAPTER 33

"Jimmy Burroughs. Backlash Technologies."

Rusty pushed past Josie, and took the small man's hand in both of his. He shook it heartily before taking it upon himself to make the introductions.

"This man is a visionary. His company, Backlash Technologies, was ahead of its time. It was the tech guru's tech company. Seriously cutting edge of—"

"That was a long time ago, and of no consequence now." Jimmy's hand slipped from Rusty's. He moved forward, forcing Rusty to fall back, a first for Rusty, Josie was sure. Still, if this guy was tech royalty, Rusty would fade into nothingness if it would get him a shot at the king's court.

"I'm here about Lily Daye, Josie," Jimmy Burroughs said.

Josie was thrown off by the use of her given name. It was a liberty not taken in a law office without invitation, and his tone was more suited to a spa than a place of business. Josie tamped down her pique knowing that it wasn't caused by this instant familiarity, but by her instant dislike of the man who assumed it.

"Yes. Of course," she said. "I'd almost given up finding someone who knew Ms. Daye."

"I knew her well."

"I'm glad to hear it." Josie gestured to Faye. "This is Faye Baxter."

The man murmured his own name in lieu of another greeting. Rusty hovered, sparking with his desire to be part of the conversation. Josie ignored him, Jimmy Burroughs had forgotten him, and Faye would be left to deal with him

"Why don't we go to my office?" Josie said, but Rusty was having none of it.

"We can sit down right here, Mr. Burroughs." Rusty pushed back into the conversation. "I'm Rusty Gates, and I think I speak for all of us when I say that everyone here at Baxter & Baxter would all be happy to help you in any way we can."

"I think not." The man did not do Rusty the courtesy of looking at him. "Josie and I will take care of this business easily. No need for you."

Josie swept her hand toward the door. He gave her a nod and went into the hall. Before Josie could follow him out, Rusty had hold of her. She shook him off.

"This is going to be a one-on-one, Rusty," she said, but that didn't stop him.

Rusty took her hand and pulled her back far enough so Jimmy Burroughs couldn't see them. He stuck his head into the hall.

"Angela, will you see Mr. Burroughs to Ms. Bates's office? She'll be right along." He was back at Josie. "You have no idea what just fell into your lap, Bates."

"None of this is any of your business, so back off," she said.

"But it could be my business," he said. "We are talking serious money. Big money. Whatever he wants, you take care of it. Show him what you got, and you could snag one of the biggest clients in the country. Word is he's getting funding for a new launch. There's a bigger picture to consider here."

"Just stop." Josie held up a hand. "This is about my pro bono client. You know, the kind that aren't worth your time unless there's press to be had? Besides, if this man is as important as you say, he's got an army of lawyers."

"Not like us," he said. "There are no lawyers like us."

"There is no us," Josie said.

"Not yet, there isn't." he said.

"See you later, Rusty."

Josie left him chuckling, suddenly full of the Christmas spirit. It wasn't visions of sugarplums dancing in his head. Rather, it was a plum, deep-pocketed, high-profile client that had just been placed under his professional tree.

When she opened the door to her office, Jimmy Burroughs was at her desk holding the picture of Archer that she kept near the phone, and that annoyed her. No matter how much money this guy had, she wouldn't be his lawyer. Like Rusty, he had no boundaries. Once he was gone, she'd wipe down the picture frame and the chair she offered him.

"GOOD NEWS."

Doctor Carl bounded out of the back office into the room where Archer and the Shepherd waited. The man had taken care of Max, and in all those years Archer had never seen him walk. He leapt, he scurried, and today he bounded like one of the puppies he cared for. Archer loved the guy, and Doctor Carl loved animals. He gave the Shepherd a good rub before sitting beside Archer.

"Our buddy here is double chipped," Doctor Carl said. "This beautiful guy was most recently tagged by Pets of PV."

"The group who does adoptions at the street fair?" Archer said.

"One and the same. I called over to Cheryl Anderson, the lady who runs the program, and she remembers this one very well. He wasn't your run of the mill rescue. A lot of people thought he was scary and passed." Doctor Carl pushed a shock of blond hair off his forehead and considered the dog. "I can see it."

"You're preaching to the choir, Doc," Archer said. "Does your friend know who adopted him?"

"She does because she handled it herself. It was a woman. She put her name down as L. Daye. She remembered the lady because it was a surprising choice. Cheryl thought a small dog would have suited her better."

"Then I'd guess she wasn't looking for a pet," Archer said.

"Not with this guy. He is pedigree all the way, isn't he? I'd love to know his history."

The doctor petted the top of the Shepherd's head. The dog seemed to endure his touch, but it was an act. He was a dog. No matter how tough he was, a sign of affection from a worthy human was appreciated.

"Was the second chip put in by the woman who adopted him?" Archer asked.

"Nope, that one was older and registered to Frank Kaplan. Here's the number."

"Thanks," Archer said. "Mind if I make the call here?"

"Be my guest. I've got a few things to do in the back. I'll be another half hour before I close up."

When he was gone, Archer dialed the number he had been given. A woman answered on the third ring. Her name was Judith. She was Frank Kaplan's daughter, and Archer was lucky to have gotten ahold of her. She was at her father's house getting it ready to sell and shut down all his services including his phone. Frank Kaplan, military cop, and K-9 trainer, had died six months earlier.

The Shepherd was the only animal in his care when he passed suddenly. Judith lived in another state and was overwhelmed when it happened. She passed the dog onto a friend who she imagined passed him to the rescue in Palos Verdes. She tried to find something that indicated who he was being trained for, but couldn't find a thing in her dad's records. Sadly, she didn't know anything about the animal, not even his name.

Archer thanked her for corroborating what he had suspected. He told her that her dad must have been a heck of a trainer because the dog was great. When he was done with the call, Archer said his thanks to Doctor Carl and took his leave.

He and the dog walked the long way home, going down Pier Avenue to The Strand. The bronze statue of the surfer on his wave was festooned with a Santa hat, the bars and restaurants were serving drinks with holly in them, and the gift shops had shirts festooned with surfing Santas on the rounders outside their stores. Archer stopped more than once to say hello to someone he knew. Everyone admired the dog; all were happy that Josie had found a good companion and laughed when Archer asked if he counted. Merry Christmas and Happy Holidays were thrown like confetti, and Archer thought there was something to the song that told the world it was good to be home for Christmas.

Once they were at the house, Archer grabbed a beer, set up his computer intending to cull the photos he had taken in Africa, and then he closed it down again. Instead of working, he took the remote and settled on the couch. The dog lay down next to him. While Archer clicked through the channels, his other hand scratched the dog's head. When he drew it down to his neck, his hand bumped up against the heavy collar.

"That's gotta be uncomfortable," Archer said.

He unbuckled the collar and tossed it onto the coffee table.

It was beautifully made, perfect for a guard dog, but too heavy for a pet. The dog rubbed against Archer's hand, happy to be free of it. Archer kicked off his shoes, arranged the pillows on the couch, and settled down hoping to find a good football game. The Shepherd lay down, giving Archer a clear view of the screen. Archer, though, wasn't paying attention to what was on the television. Instead, he was looking at the dog's collar and the characters burned into the leather interior. Rolling over, he picked it up, took a better look, and smiled.

He couldn't wait for Josie to get home.

CHAPTER 34

Josie listened to Jimmy Burroughs wax poetic about himself, his brilliance, and his business. Within five minutes, Josie was more than ready for the punch line, but he was blissfully unaware. He talked in the same way a long slow wave rolls toward the shore, the kind of wave that looks like it will never crest. Then, just when you least expect it, that wave rises up close to shore and smashes itself down with a brutal force. God help anyone who is in the water when that happens.

Josie decided it was time to get out of the water.

"Mr. Burroughs," she said. "I appreciate the biography, but my concern is Lily Daye's estate. If you could address your relationship with her specifically, that would be great."

"But all of it is intertwined, you see," Jimmy said. "Lily was my rock when tragedy hit Backlash Technology. I'd only known her that one day, and yet she was the one who just took control of everything. That's the thing you should know about her. She is—was—very smart, very…"

"Controlling?"

"No, no, that is not the word I would use. She was loyal. Perhaps to a fault, but there it is. Loyal as the day is long. I left

The 9th Witness

both my business and personal interests in her hands. You see, I am a visionary; I deal in concepts. I needed Lily to oversee the daily grind because she was exceptional with that sort of thing."

"I heard she had a talent for organization," Josie said.

"I thought you said you never met anyone who knew her." Jimmy Burroughs's tone didn't change, but Josie thought a wave of suspicion was getting ready to rise up and crash on her beach.

"I spoke to people she worked with," Josie said.

"Of course. She would work. She would have to work. I didn't know. We've been estranged for some time," he said. "I'm surprised she didn't use me as a reference."

"She didn't do the kind of work that needed a background check," Josie said. "When she worked for you, what exactly were her duties?"

"She had been brought in as a temporary worker. But there was an accident that embroiled Backlash in multiple lawsuits across the country. The company folded. I had to let everyone go. Lily stayed. She helped me through the initial stages of my shock, and I realized she was a very special human being. I would not have been able to recover. I would not have been able to move forward had it not been for Lily."

He smiled the smile that director who lived inside his head had cued; he sighed as if thinking fine thoughts of the now dead Lily. Or maybe he was thinking about his once-thriving business.

"You should also know that we had a personal relationship. Yes, you should know that. We lived together for many years."

While she listened, Josie opened a file on her desk. Jimmy Burroughs scooted up to the edge of his chair.

"Is that something about me? Something Lily left? If so, I would like to see it."

Josie looked through her lashes at Jimmy Burroughs. He

207

would be a funny little man if she didn't know his history. Now that she did, Josie determined he was a troll, a man controlling the narrative all the while assuming she was too stupid or too impressed to understand what he was doing.

"No, Mr. Burroughs, this isn't about you. In fact, it's fairly reasonable to assume that had I known you existed, I would have been in touch."

Josie looked him straight in the eye and realized that his eyes were his best feature. Perfectly positioned on his face, clear and dark brown, beautifully defined by dark lashes. She held his gaze thinking she detected a twitch of annoyance, but then his wide lips turned up and his gaze softened.

"Of course. That's logical. That's how Lily would have thought. Yes, it's no surprise Lily named you to settle her affairs. I think you're quite like Lily, aren't you?"

"I don't know about that, but I am curious as to how she might have made that decision," Josie said.

"I wouldn't know, Josie," he said. "I wish I did."

"I ask because if Lily was your right-hand, then she must have had access to some of the best lawyers in the country."

"I can only speculate that she saw something in you that made her feel safe. Yes, I suppose that's the word. She was quick to assign her affection and loyalty. She was also quick to withdraw it," he said. "I wasn't aware that was a possibility. When it happened, I was surprised. It was distressing when she left me."

"I see," Josie said. "I'm sorry."

She referred to the file she had opened. "Perhaps you know Carolyn Barnes. She lives in the U.K.? I have some letters she sent to Lily. Did Lily ever mention her?"

"No. I didn't pry into her private life," he said.

"But you lived together." Josie pressed him, wanting to be convinced that he and Lily did, indeed, have a personal relationship.

"We did, but I don't know this woman you're asking about." He put a period on her line of inquiry.

"Then I'll keep looking." Josie looked down as if referring to her notes again, but only because it seemed to make him nervous.

"Since you were lovers, I'm assuming she at least told you where she was born and something about her parents or siblings."

Up her eyes went again. His were no longer soft and understanding. He was not happy that she continued to pursue this line of questioning.

"As I said, I didn't pry into Lily's personal affairs."

Josie closed the files and crossed her arms on her desk. Unimpressed with his narcissism, sincerely confused by the picture he was painting.

"Mr. Burroughs, I am not prying either, but I have a duty to my client to settle her estate according to her wishes. I cannot simply take your word for a relationship. She has left a substantial estate. All of it is to be used benefit a Mr.—"

"Ours was an unconventional relationship, and, truly, Josie, it has no bearing on what I'm here for."

Jimmy Burroughs's heels tapped the floor. He trembled with impatience. His fingers curled, closed, and opened again.

"Exactly what are you here for, Mr. Burroughs?"

"I'm here about her estate, of course. We lived together. I believe that makes me her common-law husband. Her estate would go to me no matter what she wrote down. I can arrange to have her things…moved…disposed of…"

His voice trailed off. His wide lips pulled together in an expression of impatience. His head tipped up so that his eyes went to the ceiling. His arms rested on the chair, and he brought his hands together in front of him so that his fingers made a tent. His attempt to look contemplative and authoritative fell short. With his long hair and a belly protruding just over his belt, he looked tiresome. While she had no doubt Jimmy Burroughs had standing in the tech community, to her he was just a man who was taking up her time. Before the day was out, she would know everything fit to print about him; before the week was out, Archer would find out things about Jimmy Burroughs that he didn't want anyone to know.

"Mr. Burroughs, California does not recognize common-law marriages," she said.

His demeanor changed in the time it took his hands to drop and his eyes to focus on Josie. She saw the truth in his eyes. He was not a dreamer; he was not a geek lost in the world of algorithms. This man was a strategist and tactician who held his troops back until he saw the size of the opposing army.

"Is that true?"

"Yes, it is," Josie said. "The good news is that, while Lily's estate does not transfer to you, it also has no claim on your holdings. Given your profession, I think this is something to be celebrated. I assume that patents and stock ownership will not be in play since you weren't married."

Josie flipped her pen between two fingers. Burroughs made no effort to hide his displeasure, but what there was of it was muted.

"That is good," he said. "Sometimes things in life get messy. That's why I valued Lily so much. She was able to deal with messes."

"That doesn't mean, of course, that I won't need to look into the time you lived and worked together," Josie said. "It's my duty to administer her estate, and that would include confirming the estate is not owed anything like royalties, back pay, property in common, that kind of thing."

"No is the answer to all of that," he said. "I don't understand why this needs to be so difficult. I want what you want: to be done with Lily's business. I thought you would be grateful to have someone who cared enough to come forward."

Josie suppressed a smile. If this was how Jimmy Burroughs showed he cared, she would hate to see him when he didn't.

"Again, I have Lily's wishes to consider, and her wishes—"

"It shouldn't matter what Lily wished. She is dead. She has things that belong to me."

Jimmy Burroughs sat up in his chair, his agitation on full display. He didn't look Josie in the eye any longer. His voice had taken on an edge, and Josie felt a snapping of her nerves and a constriction in her throat. The man was triggering.

She recrossed her legs and cleared her throat when she figured out that this feeling was not about her at all, it was about Lily. Jimmy Burroughs had not asked about the woman he said lived with him, that he relied upon, that he cared for. He didn't ask how she died, where her body was, nor did he show any sign of sorrow.

"Mr. Burroughs, Lily left a will, and since the estate is substantial and you are not named in that document, the courts must ascertain your standing if you wish to pursue the matter."

Jimmy Burroughs allowed his lips to undulate briefly in something that passed as his rendition of a beatific smile. He shook back his hair like a hooker on a first date.

"Oh, dear, You're talking about money. I do not want any money. What I want has no monetary value, so you should not worry about running afoul of Lily's wishes." Jimmy said. "Lily took records from my business. I have no idea why she would do that. They were of no use to her, but I want them back, Josie. I want them now."

Josie waited a beat. She relished the moment as he fidgeted under her gaze. She liked the expression on his face when she said, "That's not going to happen, Mr. Burroughs. I have to inventory her estate and determine the worth of everything. If need be, I will have experts review her computer and any documents that I find so that I can determine their worth, origin, and ownership.

"I'll ask you for a list of what you're looking for. Please be as specific as possible. Then, if there is any question or disagreement, I'll ask the court to determine what is yours and what belongs to the estate."

"That is absurd," Jimmy said. "Lily had nothing before she came to me. One suit. A studio apartment. She was a ridiculous, introverted shell of a woman. It was me who gave her purpose. I made her over so that she was presentable. I gave her any authority she had. She was nothing before me or after me. I am the heir. I am her common-law husband."

He was half out of his chair, turning ugly with his anger. He had forgotten—or was not accepting of—what Josie had told him. What he didn't know was that his anger, his mere presence, gave Josie the insight to Lily Daye that she was looking for. Lily was a desperate, sad, lonely woman ripe for manipulation. She was probably fooled by his attention, then enslaved by what she perceived to be his need. At some point she either found the strength to break away or she was thrown out. One thing didn't add up though, and that was the money. Women controlled by men like this usually gave everything and took nothing.

Now it was Josie who leaned forward. She picked up a pen and put the point of it against a notepad. It was a posture that drew a line in the sand.

"Mr. Burroughs, as I have stated, common-law marriages are not recognized in California. You have no rights." Taken aback, Jimmy Burroughs sat down again.

That's when Josie asked, "Do you know Mr. Murray?"

HERMOSA AVENUE DAZZLED with Christmas lights. People were everywhere, and the holiday spirit was palpable, but Josie's little street was quiet and dark save for the lights coming from inside the homes.

Not that there wasn't a nod to the holidays. Mrs. Jenkins had a beautiful wreath hanging on her door and a small Christmas tree centered in her front window. The man at the end of the street had draped a lei of Christmas lights and tinsel around the old surfboard he kept on his front patio, but the lights weren't plugged in. Josie hadn't so much as tacked evergreens to her gate because Hannah would be home soon and she would decorate.

Josie put her keys on the entry table, smelled dinner cooking. The dog came to greet her, and she ruffled the fur at his neck. Giving him a final pat, Josie went to find Archer. He was in the kitchen, sleeves rolled up, sautéing onions. He noticed her when he reached for a box of mushrooms.

"I didn't hear you come in."

"Some watchdog we've got here." Josie pretended to scowl at the dog, then smiled at Archer. "If I was a bad guy, I'd have you dead to rights."

"Yeah, but I bet you wouldn't hurt me until I finished cooking dinner."

"Smells great." She took off her jacket, tossed it on a dining room chair, and put her arms around him. "I'm starving."

"Good. Mushrooms, onions, steaks and potatoes."

"Great, an all-American man's meal," Josie said.

"You got that right." Archer added the mushrooms to the pan. "I dreamed about this in my African tent. Wildebeest just didn't cut it. I've got a glass of wine for you, already poured."

Josie kissed his cheek, spotted the wine, and sat at the kitchen island while he cooked. "Hard day?" he said.

"Strange day," she answered.

"Eat first, then tell me all about it." He opened the oven door and took out two baked potatoes. "While you're waiting, there's a present for you. Check out the coffee table."

While Archer dished out the food, Josie went to the living room.

"I don't see it," she said.

"The collar. Take a look at the inside," Archer said.

Josie picked up the heavy collar and thought maybe Archer was playing some sort of joke, but then she saw the burned leather inside and started to laugh. Archer left the stove and watched as it dawned Josie what she was looking at.

"It's a sign, Jo. Sort of makes you believe in heaven."

"This is amazing. He has a name." Josie balanced on the balls of her feet and held her hand out to the Shepherd. "*DAX*. Is that you? *DAX*?"

The dog barked and she hugged him. Max had surely taken pity on her and sent his brother her way.

"Dax," she said again.

Five minutes later, Archer called her to dinner. Over the meal, he told her about the dog, the K-9 training, and the journey Dax had taken to reach Lily Daye.

Josie told him about Jimmy Burroughs and his insistence that he be given all of the paperwork in Lily's house. They speculated about everything: why a woman would want to be with a man like Burroughs, why Lily left, why she had so much money but never used it, and especially, why she chose Dax for a pet. Josie concluded that Lily Daye was fearful and speculated that it was Jimmy Burroughs she feared.

Archer played devil's advocate, pointing out that men like Burroughs were seldom physical. When it was very late, the dishes were done, and the dog had been taken out for the night, they went to bed. It was there, when it was dark, that Josie told Archer about her panic attack.

He told her she was only human.

She said prove it.

He reached for the tank top she wore to bed and proceeded to do just that.

CHAPTER 35

Jimmy Burroughs took an Uber back to his fancy hotel in Manhattan Beach. He did not tip the driver because it did not occur to him to do so. People served Jimmy; he accepted their service. It was as simple as that.

He walked into the hotel and took the elevator up to his suite without noticing that he had cut in front of a woman trying to corral three children. Reaching his floor, he snapped at a maid who was returning to her cart to retrieve towels. He opened the door to his suite and slammed it behind him once he was inside.

The woman sitting in the large common room at the table that was meant to be a work station was startled. She had never seen him slam a door, heard him raise his voice, or move with such speed. Jimmy had always been more of a glider or a slider, kind of teleporting from one place to another. Even when Backlash was in the first throes of turmoil, his life's work destroyed, Mary Margaret dead, law suits flying, he was Zen. That's what she had always admired about him.

She had definitely never seen him take a candy bar, strip

away the paper, drop it on the floor, and stuff half a chocolate bar in his mouth at one time. When he spoke, he spit shards of chocolate and drooled caramel.

"Well, that didn't exactly go as planned, I'll tell you that."

Jimmy announced this like he was center stage and the house was full. He was off again, going past her into his bedroom as he chomped on the rest of the candy bar. She heard him open a drawer and root around. The drawer slammed again and when he came back, he threw himself on the sofa and lit a joint. He had not said hello to her, nor did he offer her a hit, much less a joint of her own. She would have liked one or the other or maybe all three because she was feeling a little tense, given that this situation was new to her despite their history. Of course, she understood why he might be upset. Lily was dead, and they had meant something to one another. Lily had things that he would like to get back, which was not unusual in a breakup. Jimmy had admitted all this made him sad, but what made him angry could only be that he had not gotten what he wanted from the lawyer he went to see.

As he stewed, she got up and poured him a drink. She poured herself one too even though she didn't really like bourbon. She handed it to him, but didn't dare sit beside him on the couch. Someday they might be close like that, but today was not the day. He took the drink and started talking to her mid-thought.

"What difference would it make to that lawyer if she gave me those friggin' files? She should be happy anyone showed up at all for Lily. Damn bitch."

That startled the woman. *Damn bitch?* Lily might have been sad and confused, but a damn bitch? The woman took a big drink of her bourbon. Jimmy didn't notice her surprise. He didn't retract his words. He wasn't done. She took another drink. Sometimes it was hard to know when Jimmy was done.

"Wouldn't you be happy if someone offered to take crap off your hands? I know I would be. Stupid woman. She won't even know what she's looking at."

The woman sitting across from Jimmy made noises. She commiserated. She tried to make things right. "It's old news, Jimmy. I mean, what use is it now?"

"Well, aren't you just missing the point." He snarled at her and that made her feel so small. "There is still litigation pending. She could have something critical. Think about it. She was angry with me when she left. Who knows how long she'd been angry? What if she withheld something that could help me or hurt me or whatever? The lawyers would never know. I would, but I have to see what she has to know that, now wouldn't I?"

He raised his heels and used them to pound the sofa cushion like a child throwing a tantrum.

"Damn Lily. I gave her everything. She spoke for me. She was me. And she did this? For what? For what? To hurt me, that's what. Everything she had I gave her. Everything."

He inhaled hard. His last sentence was a croak as he tried to speak and hold in the smoke at the same time. The woman made a sound like breaking wind, but it came from her mouth, and her lips flapped a little. She took a long drink and swallowed her sudden epiphany.

This was about Jimmy's ego. The world was a rough place for regular people, but for a genius, it was hell when the outside world poked at their bubble. Funny that it was Lily who had wreaked such havoc. The woman was actually very nice; she took things to heart. She was incredibly sensitive, but she was a mouse. Or at least she had been until she screwed Jimmy the way she had. The woman understood why it happened; she simply didn't agree with how it went down.

Then again, she may be wrong about Lily. Maybe she really was the strong one. After all, she thought of herself as a badass, and yet here she was, no life of her own, worried about a pothead with big plans, putting her life on hold because she was sure this time Jimmy was going to knock it out of the ball park with his new company and take her with him. Bottom line, she and Lily were different but the same; they both loved Jimmy, warts and all. The good news was, Lily was dead. That left the field wide open.

"What's the problem with the lawyer?" The woman got comfortable on the big stuffed hotel chair.

"Lily made a will." Jimmy coughed. His next remarks were snide. "She left everything to 'benefit Mr. Murray'. That attorney is taking it literally. Everything, not just money. I didn't even know about the money. But, yeah, she wants to go over every scrap of paper to make sure 'Mr. Murray' gets what's due him. Crap."

"Mr. Murray? Just *Mr. Murray?*" The woman said.

"Yes. Mr. Murray."

She snorted and took another swig. Jimmy looked at her as if to say, "Lame." They both knew that was a ridiculous bequest. Nothing could truly benefit Mr. Murray.

"That lawyer's like Lily. She wanted details. Did we live together? Who were her friends? Who's this person? Name things you want." Another toke. "Yeah, my day sucked. Mr. Friggin' Murray."

"I'm sorry," the woman said.

Jimmy's head rolled on the stiff couch pillow. He was miserable, yes, but he was getting mellow. He didn't care if she was sorry. Sorry was a wasted emotion. He never indulged in sorry.

His joint had gone out. He snapped his fingers, closed his eyes, and waited. The woman got up, picked up the matches, and lit one. Jimmy smelled the sulfur and heard the sizzle. He put the blunt to his lips. She put the flame to the tip. He inhaled. A moment later, Jimmy Burroughs rolled off the couch and stood up. He walked across the room and pulled back the curtains. He seemed quite taken with the moon hanging in the sky; only it really was the sun setting.

The woman relaxed, thinking about nothing, while Jimmy's mind wandered over the lay of the board in front of him. He was still King. The queen had been taken out, but a woman named Josie Bates filled the vacuum, determined to protect the queen's legacy at all costs.

What she didn't know, was that the legacy she was protecting was not Lily's. It was his. Damn Josie Bates. Damn the law.

On the other hand, Jimmy had been protected by that law for three years. Lily, for all her smarts, was neutralized by it, specifically her signature on a nondisclosure agreement.

She believed the NDA to be binding in perpetuity when, in fact, she could have invoked any number of legal premises to break it. Silly girl. So odd. Such a perfectionist. Righteous. A broken soul. An underdog looking after other underdogs, and that one little piece of paper kept her in line.

"I need another drink." Jimmy said, his voice once again hushed and low.

The woman was on her feet, pouring him another drink in a fresh glass. She waited until he had drunk half of it before she said, "Ralph Balm called. They're ready to ink the deal. Another one hundred million to move you forward."

She spoke brightly, excited because this news made it feel like old times. She loved success for Jimmy. His eyes closed, and he smiled remembering the look on Josie Bates's face when he said he wasn't interested in the money Lily had taken. She was too dense to know that money meant nothing to him because he would always have it. People believed that he would make them rich in the future, so they threw money at him in the present.

Silly them.

Still, there were a few things that could do him in, and Jimmy thought Lily had them. He could never be sure until Josie Bates got out of the way. She didn't even know what she was fighting for, and yet she stood with her shield up, ready to do battle for Lily.

Silly woman.

Silly everyone.

Jimmy took a toke and a drink, only now realizing he had played the game badly. It had been a mistake not to inquire after how Lily died, or where she was, or if he could pay for any services for his once-lover. He had seen that in the lawyer's eyes when she spoke about Lily's body. Friggin' bleeding heart. He should have moved slowly, offering to help the lawyer go through Lily's things to explain what she was finding. Yes, he should have offered help.

As Jimmy Burroughs listened to the woman in the room talk about the new investors, he decided it was time to regroup. He needed to show the right face to the right people; he needed to watch his words; he needed to lead that lawyer to the right conclusion. Jimmy knew now that his mistake was in assuming that Josie Bates was just a small-town lawyer.

Happy now that he realized this was only a challenge and not a real threat, Jimmy Burroughs relaxed. It would be fun to best Josie Bates. Yes, it would be…

"Lovely."

At the sound of that mumbled word, the woman in the room with him blushed. It never occurred to her that Jimmy wasn't talking to her, the green-haired girl.

RUSTY GATES LIVED in a mansion where he hosted grand parties. He did this often because money was no problem, the affairs were tax deductible, and his guests always showed their gratitude one way or another. A Rusty Gates invitation meant you had made it. Lawyers, actors, politicians, judges, and journalists all came. They mingled, made contacts, and generally went home feeling as if they were Rusty's friend. If they were Rusty's friend, he would be there to help them if they ever ran afoul of the law.

Rusty didn't have the heart to tell them that *A*, he had no real friends, and *B*, should they need his help, it would cost them. That first point, though, wasn't technically true. Rusty had a real bro, in college, but the guy was drunk when he jumped into a churning ocean off a Mexican cliff during spring break. He died right before Rusty's eyes. Once he sobered up, Rusty mourned that guy, and came to the conclusion that sorrow took a lot of time and energy.

By the time he got to law school, Rusty had picked himself up, dusted himself off, and completed the process of reinvention. He was Rusty Gates, charming guy, good lawyer, great entrepreneur, mover and shaker. A man who didn't waste time on real friends.

The people he invited to his parties were the same, though none of them reached Rusty's level of all-around awesomeness. Still, each and every one of them was of use to Rusty. Luckily, he also liked most of the people who came to his awesome soirees.

Tonight, though, Rusty's grand house was empty. His third wife was away somewhere—Italy he thought—and he was glad for it. Much as he liked her, it could be exhausting having her underfoot, asking him what he thought of some new decoration or dress that she would feature on her Tik Tok channel. He admired her energy, her youth, and especially her boobs, but sometimes Rusty was his own best company. One day his wife would probably figure out that she wasn't adored and leave him. They had a prenup, but he'd be extra generous because he was that kind of guy.

Rusty changed out of his work clothes. He threw on a robe, letting the boys swing free and easy because the housekeeper was gone, too. He walked barefoot down the long staircase, across the cold marble floor in the entryway, over the cozy carpet in the TV room, and into the cavernous kitchen. Rusty grabbed himself a handful of peanuts and sauntered outside into the rather cool December night. He dropped the robe and got into the pool au naturel. He swam a little, but mostly he bobbed around because there was nothing like the feel of cool water on your junk.

Eventually, Rusty floated on his back and stared at the sky. For a while he didn't think about anything. This ability to tune out was a blessing in both his work and his private life. More than that, it kept him from savaging himself when his professional behavior was questionable. Thankfully, he could turn his big brain back on just as quickly, and find himself refreshed by his psychic catnap. By the time he had floated from one end of the pool to the other, he was riding his thoughts like a cowboy on a stallion.

Faye Baxter, he was sure, was going to accept his offer to buy her little firm. He had wanted it before, but then he desired it because Josie Bates was part of the deal. Now he lusted after that firm because Josie brought with her a connection to Jimmy Burroughs, late of Backlash Technologies.

Rusty had kicked himself all those years ago for missing out on the train wreck that brought Burroughs down. There had been enough personal injury gold for a hundred lawyers to mine, but Rusty had been too proud to chase down business; business came begging to him. Still, he should have made an exception for Backlash. Then again, maybe he had dodged a bullet. Backlash cases had been rolling around for years, and there hadn't been any precedent-setting settlements. Now, here he was in Burroughs's sphere and Rusty took that as a sign. The man was starting a new venture that could make Rusty a trillionaire if he played his cards right.

Rusty did a slow turn in the middle of the pool and connected the dots.

When he contacted Faye, Rusty thought it was because the universe was trying to tell him to slow down. That was so wrong. Fate had sent him to Baxter & Baxter knowing that would put him in the path of the greatest client a lawyer could ever hope to have. A client on the same level as Google and Facebook and Apple.

God bless the universe.

Rusty used his hands like flippers, propelling himself a few feet through the pristine water. He cut an exceptional figure: tall, handsome, naked and set aglow by the strategically place underwater lights.

He stopped paddling and floated some more, mulling over the vagaries of life. Some chick takes herself out and tags Bates to wrap up her mess. Bates, not even knowing who the woman is, decides to spend her own time out of the goodness of her heart. The executor fee probably wouldn't settle Rusty's cleaning bill, but Bates is cool with that. Then out of the blue, Jimmy Burroughs appears. Rusty chuckled. Not only did he appear, he appeared at a meeting that should have wrapped twenty minutes earlier.

Rusty rolled over, dived to the bottom of the pool, and touched the concrete like he had done when he was a kid at the community plunge. When he surfaced, he swam to the edge of the pool, pleased that he could still lift himself up and out of the water by the strength of his upper body instead of having to take the steps. As he dried off, Rusty thought it was like they were all right there with him: Bates, Baxter, and Burroughs. The only thing that bugged him was Josie shutting him down when he tried to get alongside the creepy little guy.

All Rusty needed was fifteen minutes, and she had shut him down.

Forty minutes after he arrived, Jimmy Burroughs left. When Rusty inquired about their meeting, the only thing Josie said was that she had taken care of the matter. She added that she didn't care much for Burroughs. When Rusty had inquired as to why, she said because he was presumptuous thinking she would just hand over Lily's things. She disliked arrogance.

That latter comment had been accompanied by a bold look at Rusty and that meant she was digging in. He would simply have to cool his heels and wait for her to come around—or not.

While he put on his robe, Rusty took pieces of conversations, observations, and knowledge about Burroughs and rearranged them to see if the puzzle looked any better. He checked out the new rose bed the gardener had labored over for weeks, and then walked back through the house, his gait slow, his mind running at full speed. It pinged between Josie and Burroughs. Baxter & Baxter was in there, too. Rusty flashed on his wife's boobs for a minute, but even that wasn't enough to distract him. He wanted an in with Burroughs. He just had to figure out who could open the door for him and what irresistible service he could offer once he got inside.

Rusty showered. He dried his hair. He checked around his eyes and decided the micro-needling was working. He donned boxers and a wife beater and got in his big bed, settling in, closing his eyes. He was a perfect picture of repose. Sadly, his mind kept churning.

Rolling over, Rusty grabbed his phone, looked through his contacts, and decided to call Tom Williamson. Tom was none too pleased to be awakened from a deep sleep at an ungodly hour, but he perked right up when he heard Rusty's voice. It was to Tom's advantage to help since it was well known that Rusty Gates made things happen. The fact that when things happened it most often benefitted Rusty only dawned on the people who helped him long after the fact. Tom gave Rusty what he had, and they both went to sleep happy.

In the morning, Rusty took the number Tom had given him, and hooked up with a woman who was flattered to be talking to *the* Rusty Gates. When he finished with that woman, he had everything he needed.

Not that he was surprised.

Things always worked out for Rusty.

CHAPTER 36

Archer was feeling good for two reasons: he finally had enough energy to show Josie how happy he was to be home, and she had enough energy to show him that she was pretty happy about that, too.

After that, he slept the sleep of the dead.

Dax had decided he would sleep outside the bedroom door. Neither Josie nor Archer tried to dissuade him. When he heard them stir, he walked into the bedroom, sat down, and waited patiently until they let him out. It was as if he had lived with them forever.

That morning, Josie dressed for a run, managed a mile on The Strand, avoided the shoreline and the pier, and came home happier than she'd been in a very long time. Archer had easily fallen into investigator mode. Now that he had the VIN number for the totaled car in Lily's garage, he contacted his friend at the DMV for a history. He would do a deep dive on Carolyn Barnes, and follow up with Chief Miller to see if he had anything on Lily Daye's guns. The most pressing matter was the inventory of hard goods in Lily Daye's cottage, and he had given Josie two options.

The first choice was to hire someone to move everything to a storage unit and satisfy the landlord who was still breathing down her neck about vacating the property. The second was onsite culling. This second option made the most sense. They would save storage expenses and not have to move Lily's things twice.

The money was another matter. No doubt Mr. Murray would want that immediately, but given the size of the bequest, the transfer couldn't be made without thorough vetting. The bigger problem was identifying the man. Neither of them had any doubt that as soon as they started going through Lily's things, they would find a history of, and a contact for, the beneficiary of the estate.

With Josie due in court, Archer and Dax headed to the Vanderhaven estate to take a good look at the car and start packing. Having been warned, Archer caught the turn without a problem, and took the back way up to the cottage. For a minute he just looked at the property. When he spoke, it was to Dax.

"Is it good to be home?"

The dog didn't answer. Clearly, he and Lily Daye had not bonded. Because the car was parked on a ridge, Archer had a clear view of Catalina Island in the distance. The midmorning sun was breaking through, lifting the curtain of haze to show a stunningly beautiful blue sea. The sunlight had reached inland far enough to dapple the grounds of the Vanderhaven estate as it shone through the tall trees.

The air was still, the smell of eucalyptus strong, and the cottage looked inviting. That was the saddest part of all of this. Lily Daye had killed herself inside that house despite the fact that she was living in paradise. Then again, if Lily was as private as Josie seemed to think, throwing herself off the bluffs to the rocks below would not have been an option.

Archer touched Dax's head and gave him a nod.

"Let's start slow. I vote for the cottage and not the garage."

Dax's eyebrows undulated and Archer took that to be a sign of agreement. He got an armful of boxes out of the back of his car, set them down near the door, and unlocked it. He opened it wide, picked up the boxes again, and went inside.

The first thing he thought was packing up was going to be a breeze. His second thought was that something wasn't right. The first clue was the broken glass on the floor near the open back door, and the second was Dax growling as he slunk toward the back of the cottage.

JOSIE PASSED through the metal detector in record time. Torrance was a small town compared to L.A., and its court was easily accessible. No parking problems, no lines to get through security. Josie was headed to probate for the hearing as prescribed by law. Her position as executor would be confirmed, and she would be out of there within the hour, heading back up the hill to help Archer pack up Lily Daye's worldly goods.

She hit Department Twenty, Judge Justine Alby presiding, with five minutes to spare. Disposition of another estate was being called. Josie sat on one of the wooden benches, her brief-case on her lap, and zoned out. The courtroom was empty save for the attorney who was speaking, the judge, and the judge's clerk. Less than ten minutes later, Josie heard Judge Alby wrap up the matters of estate number 4389288. Paperwork was passed back and forth between clerk and bench. The first attorney went on his way, and Josie took her place. The judge wished her good morning; Josie gave it right back.

"Ms. Bates, we are here on the matter of the disposition of the estate of Lily Daye, case number 5674439. You have filed for a Small Estate Administration resulting in the issuance of

Letters Testamentary. I also note that the coroner has provided death certificates. Today is your formal hearing, do you have other business before the court?"

"I do, Your Honor…"

Josie paused when the judge's eyes flicked over her shoulder toward the door as someone came into the courtroom. When the judge was satisfied the newcomers were settled, Josie continued.

"Judge, my initial determination is that the estate of Lily Daye, a single woman residing on the property of 256 Palos Verdes Drive North, Rancho Palos Verdes, Unit 3, was a level two application. Since the filing of that paperwork, I have discovered that the estate has surpassed the limitations of a Small Estate Administration, and I would like to…"

Again, Josie paused. This time the clerk was walking the perimeter of the room to talk to someone who had approached. Josie gave her a passing glance as she walked back toward the bench and handed a piece of paper to the judge. Justine Alby lowered her readers, slid her eyes over the paper, and then looked at Josie again as she set aside her glasses.

"Sorry, Ms. Bates. Continue."

"I would like to revise my application to a level three. I have been advised that the decedent was in possession of a wealth account. Her initial investment was three million dollars. Current balance on that account is three-million-two-hundred-thousand dollars and fifty-six cents."

"Is there a beneficiary?"

"There is, Your Honor. A Mr. Murray has been designated as recipient for all estate assets. I have not completed an inventory to date, but I have a man out there now beginning the process. We will report back to the court when we determine the value of her physical holdings. My initial assessment is that there is nothing that would add to the wealth account in any significant way, but I would like to confirm that. Ms. Daye also had a checking account. The balance was modest and has been rolled into an executor account. I will ask the court to allow settlement of the estate debt from the Merrill Lynch account before distribution to Mr. Murray."

"The court will allow that and will set a hearing for—" Judge Alby consulted her calendar, mentioned a date six months hence, confirmed with her clerk, and then spoke to Josie. "We have that hearing on the calendar, Ms. Bates. At that time, I will expect you to present the court with an itemized account of the full estate."

"Not a problem." Josie reached for her briefcase, but the judge wasn't finished with her.

"We're not done, Ms. Bates," Judge Alby said. "There is a challenge to the estate that was filed this morning."

"A challenge?"

"Per the requirement listed in your public notice, the challenge is to be made at this hearing in person. At this point, I would like to hear from Mr. James Burroughs."

Josie's head dipped. She looked over her shoulder to see Jimmy Burroughs sitting in the courtroom like a messy little Buddha, his hands clasped over his soft tummy. He looked stoned. Not that Josie cared. It was the other guy that had her truly peeved.

His grin was a mile wide and his stride a yard long. As he reached for the bar, the diamonds from his cufflink and pinky ring winked at Josie.

"Morning everyone. Looking lovely, Your Honor." The judge smiled despite this breach of decorum. "Rusty Gates representing James Burroughs in a claim against the estate of Lily Daye."

DAX WAS ON HIS GUARD, but not in fight mode and that was a good sign. When he stopped in the hallway door, Archer did too. For a few seconds everything was quiet. The glass and the open back door had alerted him, but he was still assessing the situation and not finding it threatening. Just when Archer was about to reassure him that it had probably been a long-gone vagrant who caused the damage, a sound came from Lily's bedroom.

Archer took ahold of Dax's collar. His growling remained at a manageable level, the dog didn't strain against Archer's hold, so it was logical to assume that whoever was in the cottage was known to him. Perhaps not loved, but known.

Whoever was in Lily's bedroom didn't hear them coming, as evidenced by the fact that the man was headfirst in the closet, and it sounded like he was scraping the wall. The only thing Archer could see was a pair of jeans covering a flat butt and a pair of hard shoes that had seen better days. The broken glass, the open door, and those lace-up shoes were a dead give-away that the guy was not there to fix the plumbing.

Archer gave Dax's collar a shake.

The dog let out one perfectly terrifying bark and the guy in the closet collapsed to his knees. It took him a minute, but he managed to roll into the bedroom, dig in his heels, and propel himself across the floor until his back was against the wall.

Dax lunged, but it was half-hearted and meant only as a warning for the man to stay put. Archer was starting to like this dog a lot. He was a pro, gauging the threat, determining it to be minimal, and expending only enough energy to control the situation. That, or the dog had a sense of humor, and was teasing this man who looked like a bully and cringed like a coward.

"Friggin' dog. I thought she got rid of him. You keep hold of him." The man got to his feet. "Who are you?"

"Name's Archer. I work with Josie Bates. I was supposed to start on the inventory, so we can move things out."

"'Bout time," he said, his eyes avoiding Archer's.

"Did you break in?"

"I got in," he snarled. "That lawyer took the keys. I have the right."

"Brian Vanderhaven?" The man nodded. "You know you could have just called, and told us what you needed. That might have been easier."

"It's personal, okay?" His fleshy face contorting with displeasure, Brian looked at Dax. "Can we get out of here?"

Archer motioned for him to get up and then stood back to let him pass. Brian Vanderhaven waved him and Dax further back.

"She always put that dog away when I was here. I don't like dogs," he said as he walked down the hall.

"I don't think he's crazy about you either, so you're even."

Brian Vanderhaven gave Archer a dirty look and huffed his way through the living room and out the front door, without looking at the evidence of his break in. Archer took the time to close the back door and push the glass aside. When that was done, he left the dog and went to talk to Brian Vanderhaven. Archer didn't bother with pleasantries.

"Did you have a thing with Lily? Did she have something on you that you didn't want the wife to know about? Naughty pictures, a video?"

"That's rich. Did you ever see that broad?"

Brian Vanderhaven made a rough sound, ran the back of his hand across his mouth.

Archer hooked his thumbs in the pockets of his jeans and waited. His patience seemed to upset the man.

When he was upset enough, Archer said, "I can call the cops to figure this out, or you can tell me what you wanted in there. From my perspective, it looks like you were trying to steal from the dead. The estate could bring charges."

"Alright. Okay. Look, it's nothing bad. I want something that my mother thinks is in there, and I didn't want there to be any trouble during probate," he said. "I mean, I couldn't prove it is mine right off, but it is. I tried to get in when Lily was alive, but the bitch wouldn't let me through the door. I even asked nice. I don't know what she thought. Like I'd rape her or something."

"I doubt she was afraid of you," Archer said. thinking about the box of guns, the ammunition, the silencer. "I think she just didn't like you."

"Jesus, this is a lot of trouble for a renter," he said.

"Believe it or not, I agree with you," Archer said. "So, tell me what you're looking for. I'll run it by Ms. Bates, and ask her to expedite ownership if it's really not relevant to the estate."

Brian Vanderhaven did some lip gymnastics while he thought about Archer's proposal. That mouth of his tightened, pulled up left, then he shot out the lower lip. Finally, he said, "My mom and dad used to rent these cottages out to artists. Most of them didn't know what they were doing, but two of them got pretty big. Their stuff is valuable. My mom told me one of those guys supposedly left a painting in Lily's cottage. That's what I was looking for, a damn painting."

"Why didn't you just tell us?" Archer said.

"Because I know how this works. If it's valuable enough, it goes into probate, and we haggle about who owns it for a couple years. I get my lawyers, and we fight hard for another couple of more years. Screw it. I just wanted what belongs to my family."

"You could have saved yourself a whole lot of trouble, my man. Show me proof or describe it to my satisfaction, and it's yours when the inventory is done."

Brian Vanderhaven kicked at the blue paver. He stuck his

hands deep in his pockets. The petulant baby was gone, replaced by a middle-aged guy who was hand-over-hand just about at the end of his rope.

"All I've got is my mom and she's half batty. I was hoping there was something to find, and I also knew I didn't have any authentication," Brian said. "Look, I got major debt. My business is going down the tubes. I got a buyer for this whole damn place. That buyer's on a schedule. I tried to get Lily out, but she knew that I couldn't force her out. Then she kills herself, and that lawyer locks me out of the place. You could have just moved her shit, I could find the picture, we'd be square. Can't you just do that?"

Archer had to admit the man was in a spot. Still, he wasn't going to help out just because he had finally asked nicely.

"I can do what I told you I can do. Any artwork I find, I'll document it, but it's not my call legally. Ms. Bates will advise on that. Talk to your mom. If it can be predated to Ms. Daye's occupancy, that should be all you need," Archer said. "I wouldn't hold out a lot of hope, though. You've seen the place. There's not much in it."

"Yeah, well, my mom says it could be anywhere—painted on a wall, hidden in a cupboard. The people who lived here were strange."

Archer nodded. Who was he to say about artists? The only one he knew was Hannah, and she was as normal as they came if you liked the adventurous sort who would die for the people she cared about.

"Let's call it a draw for now," Archer said. "I'll keep an eye out and you stay out of the cottage until we remove everything, If not, I'll have to get the cops involved."

Brian Vanderhaven grumbled his agreement. He kicked at the dirt. He looked at the cottage like a gambler who was sure if he could just put one more quarter in the machine, he would be good to go. Before Brian Vanderhaven left, though, Archer had one more question.

"Just out of curiosity, do you know when Ms. Daye got the dog?"

"Maybe my mom does or Fran. I wasn't here enough. I just started coming around to check things out when the buyer got serious," he said. "Please, get that stuff out of the cottage fast."

That was it. Brian Vanderhaven walked away, Archer turned toward the house and then turned back. He called out to the man.

"You didn't kill Ms. Daye, did you?"

"Naw, man."

"I didn't think so," Archer said.

When Brian Vanderhaven disappeared into the wood, Archer went to the car, got more boxes, and brought them into the cottage. He cleaned up the glass, used one of the boxes to tape over the broken window, and was packing up teddy bear parts when his phone rang.

He almost didn't answer it.

He was glad he did.

CHAPTER 37

"Mr. Burroughs lived with Ms. Daye for almost five years. During that time, Ms. Daye enjoyed unprecedented access to Mr. Burroughs's business. While she was designated his administrative assistant, Ms. Daye acted as a partner in the company with full decision-making power over all of Backlash Technology business. This meant that she was the point man, if you will, on all legal and financial affairs for the company."

Rusty gestured toward the bench.

"If Your Honor will refer to the exhibits in front of you, we have an overview outlining the demise of Backlash Technologies. Should you need additional information, we will be happy to provide it. The accident referred to resulted in extensive litigation from which the company and Mr. Burroughs personally had to be defended. Exhibit three is the list of the four legal firms representing Backlash Technologies, and Mr. Burroughs himself, in these actions. These firms have provided us with notarized affidavits that it was Ms. Daye whom they interfaced with, Ms. Daye who authorized their fees, and Ms. Daye who interfaced with Mr. Burroughs.

"That is to say, Ms. Daye was an employee of Backlash

Technologies and therefore not the owner of any files, monies, or records belonging to the company. Ms. Daye was also not a wife to Mr. Burroughs and, therefore, is not due any of his personal belongings."

Rusty swiveled so that he could smile at Josie briefly before turning the full wattage on the judge.

"We will, of course, be providing additional affidavits from employees of the company stating that Mr. Burroughs put a great deal of professional trust in Ms. Daye only to be betrayed when she left him without notice, taking with her company funds and Jimmy Burroughs's personal papers. Dates alone on these items should prove our point because many will predate Ms. Daye's employment and personal relationship with Mr. Burroughs. Everything after that date, would be considered an extension of the original documents."

"Your Honor," Josie said. "This is highly irregular."

"Not irregular in the least, judge," Rusty said. "The hearing date was set by the court and publicized by Ms. Bates herself. Per that announcement, anyone with a claim against the estate was directed to appear in person, in this court, on this date. We are here. We are contesting the estate."

"I did not mean the proceedings were irregular. I meant the representation is irregular," Josie shot back. "Mr. Burroughs came to my office yesterday, advised me that he had a personal relationship with Ms. Daye, and that he believed she had certain items belonging to him. I advised him that I had not done an inventory. I further advised him that, once that was done, once I could corroborate his relationship and he could identify the items in question, we would meet again to discuss the proper disposition of said items to which he was laying claim. He did not mention that he was concerned with such a plan, nor did he indicate that anything in Ms. Daye's estate was proprietary to any lawsuit or to his company. In short, Mr. Gates's appearance is redundant and without merit. The matter was settled."

Rusty interrupted, energized by Josie's outrage.

"The meeting between Ms. Bates and Mr. Burroughs was hardly long enough to allow for a full disclosure of the long relationship between Mr. Burroughs and Ms. Daye or the—"

Josie raised her voice and talked over him. "And it is suspect that Mr. Gates is even associated with this hearing, given that he met Mr. Burroughs, who was in my office to discuss Ms. Daye's estate," Josie said. "Until then, he had no interest in the matter of Ms. Daye's estate, nor had he any interaction with Mr. Burroughs. I would be curious as to why Mr. Gates is suddenly counsel for a man who has four firms that employ an army of atto—"

"Not relevant, Your Honor." Rusty raised the hand with the pinky ring as he objected.

Josie bridled. She hated that ring, she hated that he was amused by any of this.

"Your Honor," she said, "we are in a shadowy area of ethics at the very least. Mr. Gates was at the offices of Baxter & Baxter to discuss the acquisition of the firm. In essence, he is representing a man who is posing a legal challenge to a client of the firm. A conflict of interest, Your Honor."

"Mr. Gates," Judge Alby said. "Is this true?"

"Judge, Faye Baxter, the owner of the firm, and I are in preliminary discussions. Nothing is set in stone. My inquiries could be characterized as a fishing expedition."

"Mr. Gates is the one serious about catching a fish," Josie said. "We met for over three hours, during which time he made a solid offer for the firm and outlined my involvement including renumeration and marketing."

"Due diligence, Your Honor, nothing more. Rusty Gates is prepared for every contingency," Rusty said. "While I hate to point out a colleague's misinformation, I must tell you, Judge, that the possible acquisition of Baxter & Baxter has no bearing on this matter because the estate of Lily Daye is not represented by the firm. This is a private matter being handled outside of the firm's business."

Judge Alby gave Josie a look, inviting a response.

"While technically true, Your Honor, I would argue that there is professional decorum to be upheld here."

"And I would argue that an attorney's first obligation is to his—or her—client," Rusty said. "Ms. Daye's estate is Ms. Bates's concern; Mr. Burroughs's claim is mine. It seems pretty straightforward to me unless I'm missing something."

"He's right, Ms. Bates," the judge said. "So, Mr. Gates, let's hear what your client is looking for."

"Only what belongs to him, Your Honor," Rusty said. "Ms. Daye removed items from the home they shared and from storage units he paid for that were specific to Mr. Burroughs's business. While she had incredible leeway in representing him, she did not have ownership over these files. Ms. Daye is also in possession of a car that belongs to Backlash Technology and therefore Mr. Burroughs."

"Your Honor, the only car in Ms. Daye's possession is one which is no longer operable," Josie said.

"Then there should be no problem returning it to Mr. Burroughs if you are stating that there is no monetary value."

"For what purpose?" Josie asked.

"That is up to Mr. Burroughs," Rusty said.

Josie's jaw clenched as she tried to control her rising ire. She wasn't annoyed because a claim was being brought, but rather because of who was bringing it. Rusty Gates's hutzpah was beyond the pale. Representing Jimmy Burroughs successfully would put a pretty penny in Rusty's pocket; scooping him up as a client before the deal was done for the firm meant that neither Faye nor Josie would benefit.

"Mr. Burroughs is not mentioned in the will, Your Honor.

An inventory is being conducted as we speak. If there are records of Mr. Burroughs's business that Ms. Daye had in her possession, I have no problem returning them after determining that they are of no monetary value. However, I have a will duly witnessed directing all monies be turned over to the beneficiary of the estate, and that is not Mr. Burroughs."

Judge Alby looked at her notes.

"The wealth account amounts to three-million-two-hundred thousand dollars and change. Is that correct?"

"That is correct, Your Honor."

"Right now," Rusty said, "Mr. Burroughs is only asking for correspondence, plans, memos and any other record of proprietary information that is relevant to any and all of his business concerns. We will stipulate that these are valuable papers, but they are valuable only to Mr. Burroughs."

Josie turned her head, reacting to the slight hesitation in his voice. Only someone who had once been like Rusty would have noticed. Smooth as he was, he couldn't hide the fact that news of a substantial amount of money in Lily Daye's estate was a surprise. Before she could even smile, Rusty turned on the proverbial dime.

"I think there is a lot to consider, judge," he said. "Not the least of which is the question of whether or not Ms. Daye's will is even valid."

"On what grounds would you question this, Mr. Gates? Probate has already certified it."

"The question arises because of the age of one of the witnesses. I would like a cognitive test for the lady in question."

"Your Honor, this is ridiculous. I have vetted Mrs. Vanderhaven. The court has ruled on the will. Mr. Gates is overreaching."

"I am only looking out for the best interest of my client, Judge." Rusty raised a finger, begging the court's indulgence. "There is also the question of Ms. Daye's mental state. While

Ms. Daye lived with Mr. Burroughs, she was under a doctor's care for depression and other mental issues. We will need a hearing to vet her physicians. I believe Ms. Bates is in possession of that information."

Josie rolled her eyes, realizing now that she had built the roadblocks Rusty was using to stop her. She had told him about Mrs. Vanderhaven. She had mentioned her empathy for Lily, a woman depressed and alone. Now he was using it all against her. Lord, what would happen if he bought Baxter & Baxter and she had a problem? He'd throw her under the bus and then get behind the wheel and run her over.

"Judge, if taking antidepressants made Ms. Daye incompetent, then half of the state is incompetent," Josie said. "I might even suggest that counsel be looked at because his disorder is equally concerning. Narcissism leads the sufferer to believe he should dictate how the world turns."

"Mr. Burroughs has also raised other concerns, Your Honor." Rusty spoke over her. His toe was on that dime again. In a few short minutes, he had assessed his new information, put it in its proper place, and reformed his argument. "He did not wish to bring this to light because he still harbors love and respect for Ms. Daye. But Ms. Bates is misguided to think she is protecting Lily Daye's estate. Mr. Burroughs is willing to overlook quite a bit—including the funds in Ms. Daye's account—if his files are returned. If not, we will have no choice but to start legal proceedings not only to recover those files, but also any money."

"On what basis would you have to lay claim to Lily Daye's accounts?" Josie said.

Rusty's shoulders lifted, and he held his palms heavenward as if he were reluctant to speak, but speak he did.

"Because, Your Honor, Lily Daye was an embezzler."

"FOR GOD'S SAKE, Rusty. Have you lost your mind? Some guy walks into the office, you get all star-struck, and now you're taking his word that my dead woman was a felon?"

Josie and Rusty walked side by side, cutting glorious figures. People gave them wide berth as they stormed through the courthouse and out the door headed to the parking lot. There was heat coming off them, and no one wanted to be burned by the back draft. Actually, the flames were coming out of Josie's ears. Rusty's head was high, his stride long and loose.

"Wipe that smile off your face," Josie said as she pulled over to stand in the shade of a tree.

"Sorry, can't help it. That was fun," Rusty said. "You gotta hand it to me, Bates. I did a great job. Damn, Jimmy Burroughs is a catch."

"He's not a catch. You're a friggin' shark and you swallowed him whole. You're going to feed on him for as long as you can," she said.

"Lighten up. We're not talking about some rube. This is Jimmy Burroughs, he's brilliant. He—"

"I don't care what he did, has done, or will do. I don't care how much money he has or how much press he'll generate. I care about settling this damn estate. Another two weeks, and it would have been done. Burroughs could have dealt with Mr. Murray, and Lily Daye could rest in peace."

Josie paced to the edge of the shade, turned, paused, and took a deep breath. She transferred her briefcase to her other hand so she could flex her fingers. Those fingers hurt and her chest was tight. She swiveled back and looked at him. She knew what he was, but that didn't keep her from being disappointed.

"Damn it, Rusty. Is this what you call non-interference?"

"I didn't say there wouldn't be exceptions."

Rusty leaned back against the tree trunk. He held his briefcase in front of him with both hands, his legs splayed, his head tilted just a little. He looked like a model, he thought like a general, but he had his moments of humanity, and this was one of them.

"You've changed for real, Bates," he said. "I didn't think it was possible. You were so damn good when you were at the top of your game. What happened?"

Josie shook her head. Her shoulders slumped, and the anger went out of her like a slow leak. It was replaced with a strange gratitude. No one had ever asked her that question. People had talked behind her back, they had speculated over drinks, but no one had ever asked that to her face. She owed Rusty the truth for that courtesy.

"I don't think I have," Josie said. "I still fight hard for my client, Rusty. But after what happened—after those kids were killed—I just couldn't muster the energy to advocate for people just because they were rich. That's all."

"No," he said. "It isn't."

He sighed, turned his head and seemed to find the traffic on the wide streets of a small town more interesting than he found Josie. She knew what he was thinking because she thought it too when she retreated to the South Bay and Baxter & Baxter. Rusty was feeling the soft world under his feet, and it made him uncomfortable. He needed the ground to be hard, moving and cracking so that he had to maneuver fast or be swallowed whole by one fissure or another. He needed to be electrified every minute so that he could stay sharp. She got it.

"Bates, you used to whip a jury into shape, take down a judge, exonerate a client, hold a press conference, and move on to the next thing before breakfast. You didn't mind that someone else had to clean up whatever mess you left behind. Watching you was a thing of beauty." He smiled at her and it was a lovely, genuine expression. "Don't get me wrong. You were still damn good in there, but you were emotional."

"I wasn't," Josie said.

"Then explain why you're digging in on this thing. Three million is pittance. Why should you care about those records? You've probably wasted a hundred hours of billable time working on this. If I had to guess, you're going to waive the executor fee."

He waited for an answer, but Josie stayed silent. Rusty snorted affectionately. It was that silence that proved him right.

"You're tough as ever, but damn if you haven't lost the edge. I'm sorry to see it."

"That isn't true," Josie said. "The problem is that you don't know me, and you never did. When we were working it, we were just bright shiny things. We got brighter and bigger with every case we won. When I realized that I didn't care how I won or whether I should win, I started to tarnish around the edges."

Josie let her head swing as she walked over to the tree. The trunk was big enough for the both of them. She put her back up to it. Rusty was one of the few people who stood inches taller than she did, but at that moment they were equally diminished by the truth.

"I know you know that, Rusty. I don't care how many suits and rings you put on, underneath, the moral rust is eating at you." His shrug, Josie thought, was agreement, so Josie kept at him. "I went a different way and you doubled down. Every client is a means to an end for you. It's that simple."

Josie gave it a beat. Her chin clicked down a notch and she lowered her lashes. This tree felt like a confessional, but the priest she was confessing to was as flawed as she.

"You know that last big case I handled, Rusty?"

"That was a beaut. That woman killed her husband outright and you got her off."

"I did," Josie said. "I was actually proud of finding that loophole. What did I care? Who knew if he was a bad guy or she was a bad woman? They chose each other, they played a game, and lost. But when she killed her children…when she asked me to…"

Josie's voice caught. She swallowed her shame before she started again. "When she took me to her house and I saw those little bodies…"

Josie rolled her shoulder on the tree trunk. Rusty hadn't moved an inch.

"She wanted me to do it again. Speak for her. Be ruthless for her even though I knew she was guilty. I couldn't do it; I wouldn't do it. And you want me to do the same thing now. You want me to hand it all over to the guy with the money."

She touched Rusty's arm. "Don't you ever wonder what happens when our job is done, Rusty? Don't you ever stay up at night and ask yourself if you did the right thing? Or if your client is guilty? Or if you're really the bad guy? Don't you?"

Rusty Gates turned and looked into Josie's big blue eyes and saw that the pain was still fresh despite all the penance she had done.

"If I'm doing it, it's the right thing." He pushed himself away from the tree, shot his cuffs, gave her that Rusty Gates smile and a pat on the shoulder. "Get over yourself, Bates. You'll be happier."

Dumfounded, Josie watched him go. He was a great lawyer, but so was she. He had mistaken her sincerity for weakness. That was his problem, and there was work to do. As she started for her car, her phone rang and she answered it.

"Hey," she said when she recognized Archer's number. "What's up?"

"The car came back with a hit," Archer said. "It doesn't belong to Lily Daye."

CHAPTER 38

THE FIFTH WITNESS
THE MOTHER

At seven in the morning, the airport was a mess, but Archer had no luggage and TSA priority, so he was through to his gate with ten minutes to spare. The flight was on time, an hour in duration, and pleasant enough since the middle seat between him and a girl taking selfies was empty.

San Francisco was equally frenetic, but he got his rental and was on the road by ten thirty heading to Sunnyvale, California, in Santa Clara county. Sunnyvale's claim to fame was food-processing plants in the early 1900s. In the thirties, it morphed into a U.S. dirigible base, and in the forties had a make-over as ground zero for Westinghouse Electric. Now, much like the rest of the Bay Area, it was home to tech firms. The city wasn't exactly sleepy, but it wasn't San Francisco, and many of the neighborhoods remained true to their blue-collar roots. Family homes, wide streets, nothing to write home about, but a great place to live.

Archer came armed with the address his buddy at the

DMV had given him. It had taken some digging since the car's registration had lapsed years ago. Archer said he owed him, his friend said no problem, and that was that.

Now Archer was parked at the curb in front of a blue two-story house in a neighborhood that was quiet save for one woman pushing a baby stroller at the end of the street. There was a plumbing truck parked mid-block. Every house was decorated for Christmas except the one he wanted. That one was well kept but that was all he could say about it. There were bushes in the beds but no flowers, one tree in the middle of the lawn, and no chairs on the porch inviting a visitor to take a load off. There was a Honda Hybrid in the driveway. It was spotlessly clean, and like the house, it was blue. He got to the door, rang the bell, and stepped back so that whoever came to look through the peephole could see him in full.

It was no more than thirty-seconds before he saw the tell-tale shading behind that tiny piece of glass indicating that someone was checking him out. Archer heard no dog bark or children cry. He did not see a cat jump onto the back of the floral sofa that was pushed up against the picture window, and the woman inside was taking her own sweet time making her mind up about whether to open the door. Archer knew it was a woman because a man opened the door to his house as he pleased, ready to take on any comers. His castle was his kingdom and looking through a pinhole of glass to see who was trying to breach the walls was a waste of time.

Another thirty seconds clicked by before she decided to give him the time of day. The door opened, but only so far. She kept the chain on. Archer could see a sliver of her: half a nose (long and narrow), a jaw (ditto), half a mouth (wide and taut), one eye behind wire-rim glasses (large and plain). She wore no make-up. Her hair was gray—short on the sides, long on top and sprayed into what passed for a pile of curls. The top of her body was encased in a shapeless blouse crafted of a flowery fabric. The bottom half of her was encased in blue pants, and on her feet were white sneakers.

Archer said, "Mary Margaret Watkins?"

———

Archer sat on a love seat covered in plastic. Mary Margaret Watkins's mother sat across from him on a larger couch that was also shrink-wrapped. She had offered tea after he explained why he had come calling; he had accepted. The woman had years of stories to tell but no one to share them with until now, so she didn't hold back. The coffee table between them was neatly stacked with plastic three-ring binders. There were twelve in all, four stacks of three, and each of them bristled with a rainbow of various sizes of Post-It Notes. It was an impressive display.

"Learning of the accident—the day my daughter died— was not as painful as what followed." Archer noticed that she uttered the word *accident* with disdain. "My daughter was vilified. Our lawyers did little to dissuade the courts of this characterization; our lawyers I now know were not top notch. Still, it wasn't their fault. The justice system is quite flawed, don't you think?"

"It can be," Archer said.

"Yes, well, in our case, justice was not served," she said. "It was the premise of fault that was flawed. It was suggested that Mary Margaret was depressed and that she intentionally drove her car onto those tracks, stopped her car, and waited for the train to hit her. Suicide by train. Of course, that was ridiculous."

She sniffed and tossed her head. Her helmet-hair didn't move.

"It was further suggested, in court, in public, that she did this out of unrequited love for Mr. Burroughs. That was the most ridiculous notion of all. Mary Margaret wasn't the kind of young woman to get involved in a purely emotional relationship. I would have known if that had happened. Even if, by some remote possibility, she had been so inclined, that nonsense would have been fleeting. She would have pulled herself out of it. That's what she did when a problem presented itself. She analyzed, regrouped, and adjusted. My daughter's mind worked differently than most women's. You know how they say someone has a big heart. That was not Mary Margaret. It was her mind that was big."

Mrs. Watkins sniffed again. Her bottom jaw moved back and forth and her breathing seemed to quicken. She had it all under control a second later.

"Not to mention, she was a Catholic. A Catholic does not commit suicide."

Mrs. Watkins's gaze wandered, settling on a spot just over Archer's shoulder where a portrait of the Watkins family hung on the wall. He had noticed it when he walked in and remembered it as garish, amateurish, and huge. Four people had sat for the portrait. Two he could identify: the long-gone Mary Margaret whose driver license photo he had seen, and Mrs. Watkins, who sat in front of him. Mary Margaret appeared to be twelve or thirteen, awkward and destined to be unattractive forever. Mrs. Watkins's younger self was interesting. It seemed that she was wearing the same outfit then as she wore now. Joining them, Archer assumed, was Mr. Watkins and their son. The son was a few years older than Mary Margaret, and took after the father. Long bodies, long faces, and sad eyes. Archer would describe the boy as being in an awkward stage, but he thought awkward might be destiny in the case of the Watkins family.

"Mrs. Watkins?"

It took a minute, but finally she did look at him and managed a thin smile. Awkward or not, the woman was a mother who had loved her child. Beauty was in the eye of the beholder, and Mary Margaret Watkins would be forever beautiful to her mother.

"I'm sorry. Of course, you wouldn't know anything about the subtleties," she said. "It was the lawyers who turned everything around. There were so many of them. Different lawyers for different companies, all of them with their own spin on who bore responsibility. In the end, all of them pointed a finger at my daughter. It was so easy and the worst was Backlash. They told the court so many vile things about my girl. They said she wanted to ruin Jimmy Burroughs because he wouldn't listen to her, because she wanted credit for that thing they were sending to the military. They said she was intellectually arrogant. Then they said she loved Jimmy Burroughs and wanted to ruin him because he didn't love her back. Poppycock."

Mrs. Watkins cleared her throat. Archer knew well enough not to try to stop someone on a roll. He didn't even move for fear the plastic underneath him would crackle and disturb her.

"My daughter was proud of her work. She was pivotal in everything Backlash accomplished and should have received credit. I told her so. She wouldn't listen even when the last months were especially grueling. Jimmy Burroughs insisted that battery be ready for a test on that exact day. If he hadn't, she wouldn't have been on the road. It was the car, sir, not my daughter who failed."

"What was her relationship with Mr. Burroughs?" Archer asked.

"She was fiercely loyal to him." Mrs. Watkins crinkled her long nose as if she had just smelled something mildly foul. "I was taken aback when I met him at the cemetery. He was not what I expected, given her high praise."

"What was your take?"

Archer reached for his tea cup, and the plastic-wrapped couch made a strange sucking noise. He didn't particularly like tea, but the house felt like a tomb, and he moved just to make sure he was still alive.

"He seemed disingenuous, to put it politely."

"How so?" The tea was cold. Archer put the cup back on the saucer.

"He thought that if he touched me, took my hand, that I would believe he was sincere in his condolences. He thought his empty words showed concern for Mary Margaret's state of mind," she said. "If nothing else, they did just the opposite. He was like a leech. That's my take, sir. He was an arrogant, stupid little man to think that I couldn't read between the lines. Even then, standing by her grave, looking at her coffin, he was setting me up so that I would believe the fault rested squarely on Mary Margaret's shoulders."

"Why do you think he would want that?"

"Because he was protecting himself," Mrs. Watkins said. "He was prepping me for what was to come. I should be ready to admit that it was my daughter who was flawed when in reality it was his battery. I believe the battery failed when she reached those tracks. Our lawyers tried their hardest to gain access to it or at least the schematics that Mary Margaret worked so hard on, but Mr. Burroughs had better lawyers. We were denied at every turn."

"Was there any evidence that your daughter tried to get the car working again once it stalled?" Archer said. "Do you think she was trying to save the battery, and it was too late by the time she realized that was impossible?"

"Mary Margaret was not a risk taker," Mrs. Watkins said. "Whatever happened, it was out of her control. But the engineers the lawyers brought in to testify—and Mr. Burroughs himself—made convincing arguments that the battery was working perfectly. Therefore, it has to be a command to the operating system that went awry. They looked at those codes and found that, indeed, they had been changed, but there was no way to prove that it made a difference without the battery being in working order. There were so many small things. It's all in here."

Mrs. Watkins placed her hand atop one pile of binders like it was a stack of Bibles.

"Mary Margaret would have saved herself if it was at all possible, but it wasn't. The seat belt never released. The seat belt was flawed. The battery was flawed. Mr. Burroughs pushed that test too early. My girl was murdered by ineptitude and arrogance, pure and simple."

Mrs. Watkins sat back, but it was more of a lean. Archer was reminded of a drawbridge rising to let a massive ship pass. Her spine appeared to be made of concrete, her heart of stone except for the little place where Mary Margaret had burrowed in and rested.

For one moment, Archer got a look into that place when Mrs. Watkins said, "My girl—my baby. I looked at her even though they told me not to, and she was so broken. Not her face, oddly. That was not marred, so I looked at her face mostly. She was my daughter, and I loved her, and my life is empty with her gone."

She sighed. She listed. She gave herself one more moment before the drawbridge went back down and locked in place.

"Then again," Mrs. Watkins said. "Mary Margaret lived the life she chose. Not like the others. Not like those poor children. They never got to decide anything. That was a true tragedy."

━━

Zack, the girl-with-the-green-hair, sat in a small room in the offices of Rusty Gates with a young woman about her own age who looked like a Fans Only model and was named Clarissa. Everything about her sparkled: her hair, her eyes, her voice.

She sparkled so brightly that Zack wondered if she and this woman were even part of the same species. Yet the words she spoke were all business, so Zack tried to focus on what she was saying. Zack had to give Lily credit. That woman had juggled multiple lawsuits for Jimmy. Now it was Zack's job, and it was hard filling Lily's shoes.

"Without specific dates or descriptions of the documents you're seeking to have reverted, it's going to be difficult for us to demand that the estate immediately release anything to Mr. Burroughs."

"I understand that, and I'm trying to get information from Jimmy," Zack said. "But I want to go on record telling you how it was. Lily was the last employee, Jimmy told me she took care of everything, but when she left, he didn't pay her anymore, so she wasn't an employee. Wouldn't she have to give back stuff because he didn't employ her anymore?"

"It depends," Clarissa, the lawyer, said.

"Everything depends." Frustrated, Zack threw up her hands. "Look, I handle things now. He brought me back to do Lily's job, but I can't do it without all the stuff in that garage. Jimmy gave me general descriptions of what's in there, but he doesn't know specific dates and things."

Zack cast around for an answer. She didn't think as quickly as all these people, but finally she lit upon an idea. "Maybe you could just do a general ask. Say something like, Jimmy would like all documents between certain dates that refer to *Distant2* or the battery. What about that?"

"We can try, but the court isn't going to turn over anything just because we say pretty-please. It's the executor who has the power, and unless there is some compelling evidence that Ms. Daye should not have had these things in the first place, we will need to wait for her okay. You realize that they were in Ms. Daye's possession for three years, right? The court will ask what makes it so urgent that they are returned now. Can you help me out with that?"

"Jimmy always wanted them back, but he didn't know where Lily was. He also didn't know how much she had taken because...well..." Zack shrugged. "It's hard to explain how he works. He relies on all of us for the everyday work. I found some information from before Lily joined the company. After she took over, she created her own system and I wasn't around. Anyway, here's what I've got from the time I was there."

Zack pushed a binder across the table. The beautiful attorney took a sip of her coffee and flipped through the folder. The woman made Zack nervous when she went quiet, so Zack narrated.

"Those are copies of the original meeting notes between the military contacts, the investors, and Jimmy. There is an early outline of the *Distant2* project, schematics, and such."

"Where did you get this?"

"I pieced it together from Jimmy's computer, and a few of the things came from my own."

"So, you took things from Mr. Burroughs when you were let go?" the attorney asked.

"No, I mean, I took stuff from my desk," she said. "Jimmy let me keep my computer. None of us thought about down the road. You don't know what it was like."

"So, what's missing?" The woman closed the binder.

"We don't know exactly. Lily might have duplicates of some of these documents, plus correspondence and backup data. It's been seven years of court stuff. I guess she would have files on communications between vendors and the military, internal testing information. I have the location of the storage unit where these files were initially kept and the trucking company that transferred everything to Southern California. Those were paid for out of a Backlash account."

"Well, that's helpful," the attorney said.

"Except when she moved everything again a month later, Lily paid cash to settle the bill. They said it was a private transaction and wouldn't tell me where they moved everything."

"Okay, that's not helpful. The courts are going to stick on the fact that it was years before Mr. Burroughs brought this to light."

"But Lily signed an NDA. I had her do that myself. I can testify to that."

"I'm afraid that's moot at this point," the lawyer said. "Even if Ms. Daye shared information that might be detrimental to Mr. Burroughs, her status as an executive of Backlash would call the NDA into question."

"How could that be?" Zack said.

"It could be argued that if Ms. Daye was given authority over all legal proceedings as well as the bank accounts, and in all other ways acted with the blessing of Mr. Burroughs, then she was relieved of all proprietary restrictions."

Zack crumpled in her chair. She raised a hand and gnawed her nail. She was defeated, and the attorney was not unsympathetic. There was always hope and a little hope went a long way. Not to mention a lot of billable hours built on that little flicker of faith.

"Look, we can do a general ask of the court for a mutual look-see. That way you can determine what it is Ms. Daye's estate has and confirm that the documents were generated by Backlash. If we get that, you're going to have to establish a chain of command where Lily Daye wasn't the final word on disposition of the documents. You won't be able to take them, but at least you might be able to satisfy the court that they are of no value to Ms. Daye's estate."

The beautiful lawyer shrugged, and her pretty silk blouse fluttered over very perfect breasts.

"Okay," Zack said. "Let's do that."

"Frankly, Zack, it sounds like Mr. Burroughs handed her

the keys to the kingdom and said go for it. I'm not as surprised by her access to the business history, but I find the financial arrangement strange. While I realize the money isn't a priority at the moment, Rusty will want us to seek restitution on that too. Ms. Daye did not clean out Mr. Burroughs's bank accounts despite her access. It could be argued that at her level of administration that was back salary. Mr. Gates—"

"Speak of the devil, and here he is." Rusty Gates swooped in, giving his colleague an encouraging chuck on the shoulder and Zack a brilliant smile.

Neither impressed Zack very much, though she could see the benefit of having someone like Rusty Gates speaking for Jimmy.

"What's cooking, ladies?"

"I was just going to say that I don't know why we're paying you anything if you can't get Jimmy what he wants," Zack said.

"And I was explaining that we can't work in a vacuum. I'm going to request a mutual review at the estate's physical holdings," the lady lawyer said.

"Great idea," Rusty said. "It would help if Jimmy gave us something, even if he can identify specific personal correspondence between him and the dead woman. One or two items would open that door, but if not, Judge Alby will probably be reasonable."

"I'll get you something by the end of day," Zack said.

"Well, that all sounds fine," Rusty said.

Seeing Zack's disappointment, he commiserated. "I know the wheels of justice turn slowly, but when we go back into court, we want to make sure there is no wiggle room. I promise, I'll keep the pressure on the executor. We'll make Jimmy happy."

"Do what you can. Jimmy needs to focus on the new project, and right now he's stressed out because of this."

Zack stood up. She didn't know what she was supposed to do now, or how else she could help Jimmy.

"Zack," Rusty said, "we will make this right, and then we hope to help Jimmy with his new venture, but you are his right hand now. From this moment on, I need you to keep meticulous records, write down any memories you have of—"

"Rusty?" Clarissa interrupted him. She was leaning into her desk in such a way that her cleavage instantly doubled. Her brow was furrowed, her peach tinted lips were pursed. "I think there might be a work-around on one thing."

"Beauty and brains, the hallmark of the firm," Rusty said. "Let's hear it?"

"The items in Ms. Daye's possession were moved out of storage, and most were files belonging to the company. We know the argument Josie Bates is making that her client was given full control of everything belonging to the company including bank accounts, but according to Mr. Burroughs, the Backlash battery was inside a private vehicle that belonged to another employee, Mary Margaret Watkins. Lily Daye transported that, too. We could make the case that car should be returned to Ms. Watkins's family. We could make the point that, in essence, Lily Daye stole that car.

"Once that is done, Mr. Burroughs can deal with the Watkins family, and offer to transport or dispose of the vehicle. We could offer a lump sum to the family in honor of the dead woman, remove the battery, and return it to Mr. Burroughs. The patent pending will act as proof of Backlash ownership. This way we removed one item from further scrutiny by Ms. Bates."

"That would be good," Zack said. "If we get that win, it might open the door for other stuff that could be in the boxes. I don't know, things like correspondence between Mary Margaret and Jimmy about the battery. We just chip away until it's more trouble to fight for possession than it is to let it go, right?"

"I like brilliant, beautiful attorneys, but I like beautiful, brilliant clients even better," Rusty said.

Zack blushed, but Rusty needed no proof that his compliment had landed. He gave his associate her marching orders.

"Contact the family and let's get that rolling. Zack, we'll still need your input on the files. Don't let me down." Rusty made to leave, but he had a question. "When would you and Jimmy be available for a look-see at those boxes if we get the court order?"

"We have to be back up north four days from now for a meeting. We could come back the week after that," Zack said.

"Better sooner than later then," Rusty said. "Clarissa, get to work on the ask of Judge Alby. Push it through and see if we can do it day after tomorrow. Nice to see you, Zack, and tell Jimmy if he needs anything to call."

Rusty gave the door frame a little whack as he went on his way, back to his incredibly large office and the reporter from the *Law Daily* who was doing a profile on him. Clarissa gathered her papers and then walked out to the receptionist, who ordered a car, and Zack was packed off.

She gave the address of the hotel to the Uber driver, pressed her forehead against the window, and closed her eyes. She had no desire to see the sad dirty streets of downtown Los Angeles. Jimmy would be in a snit when she got back. He hated not getting what he asked for, but she was coming back with a game plan. That was something. That should make him happy for a while.

Not for the first time, Zack wondered what it was about him that made certain women want to do his bidding. Her, Lily, Mary Margaret—they were all so different, and yet each had found something irresistible about Jimmy Burroughs. She couldn't even define what it was about him that made her want to stay close.

Zack opened her eyes. She sat up. The truth hit her like a sucker punch. Jimmy was like Los Angeles: mysterious, romantic and full of promise in the dark, but in the light of day, he just wasn't all that. Maybe that's why Lily left. Maybe that's why Mary Margaret killed herself—if indeed she did. They couldn't bear the thought that they had given so much to the emperor who had very few clothes.

Zack giggled. That thought was funny and pathetic all at the same time. She had moved into the vacuum those two left without a second thought. What did that say about her? That she was desperate, or that the dark with him just felt so good that she had missed it?

She put her forehead back against the glass and breathed in the scent of pine from the Uber driver's little Christmas-tree air freshener.

Yep, Jimmy's dark was pretty enticing especially when Zack considered she really had nowhere else to go.

CHAPTER 39

THE SIXTH WITNESS
THE FLORIST

Josie watched George work Lily's computer as she lounged in the doorway of the second bedroom. Hunched over, fingers flying, he was determined to hack into that thing and hadn't moved for the last two hours. Twice Josie told him it was time for a break, but he kept begging off. He swore it would just take one more minute to figure it out. The second time he said that, Josie took him at his word, and left him alone.

The first bedroom was clean, bear body parts boxed, and a determination had been made that they held no monetary value except to Jolly, Inc. Jolly, Inc. had no wish to pay the shipping costs to reclaim them and advised that Josie could dispose of them as she wished. The person on the other end offered rote condolences on the death of Lily Daye. Josie found a willing charity on her first call, and the bears would soon be gone.

The only things left in that room were the flower vases, and Josie would donate those, too, once she packed them up. She had dumped the dead flowers and washed that vase. She took the picture of the children to Lily's bedroom to pack it with her personal items. Hopefully, she would pass it all on to a relative one day.

Dax was with her since Archer was gone, and she had left him to roam the Vanderhaven grounds, impressed when he stayed close to the cottage. She had just opened the small refrigerator when she heard George call her from the computer room. Josie took two water bottles and went to see what he had. He leaned back so that the chair wiggled a little as he swiveled toward her.

"Want to see what your lady was up to?" He took the water bottle and uncapped it.

He swiveled back to the screen. Josie stood behind him; she put her hands on the back of the chair and leaned over his shoulder.

"Good grief," Josie said as the home screen populated with a hundred folders and another hundred files. "What is all that?"

George hit a key and pulled up a random file. When he clicked on that the screen populate again, this time with pictures that seemed to span decades of one family. There were couples young and old, weddings, funerals, children playing, picnics, and pets.

"Almost all of these are photo files," he said. "Family pictures. Corporate events. I did find a few manuscripts."

"Like books?" Josie asked.

"Yep. Those were formatted, so it looks like they were scanned from actual books."

"And are the pictures of the same people? Is this some kind of gigantic family album?"

"No, the people are different," he said. "It looks like your lady was running a formatting business. I haven't figured out yet if she was working for herself or a company, but I'll get to it."

"Okay, I'm still not clear." Josie pulled up a chair to sit next to him while he clicked and clicked. "How does this work?"

"People used to keep their pictures in physical albums. When all this optional storage came into play, reformatting businesses popped up. People send their pictures in, the company scans them, and saves them to whatever format the client wants. They charge a fortune for something anyone with patience could do," George said. "So instead of having three big picture albums sitting on a shelf, you've got the family history or your wedding on a little thumb drive."

"But she has floppies, too," Josie said.

"Technology changed. People had their pictures put on a floppy, but then thumb drives were invented. Floppies deteriorate, so they send those back in and your lady does the process all over again. It's a good little side gig."

"And you didn't find anything from Backlash Technologies? Nothing from Jimmy Burroughs?

"Not yet. I'll do a search, but It would take forever for me to go through all of this so you're going to have to decide how much you want to fork over."

Josie took a deep breath and looked at the baskets and boxes. George could spend the next week going through this, and he didn't work cheap.

"How about we split the difference? You search fifty random drives—some thumb drives and some of the discs— and if all you come up with are pictures and books, then we can assume there's nothing earth shattering in the rest of them."

"Sounds good," he said. "So, the key words I'll look for are Backlash, Backlash Technologies, and Jimmy Burrows."

"Add in *Distant2* or battery. Anything like that will be critical. Also, if you find anything referencing a Mr. Murray or Murray," Josie said.

"You got it." He grabbed a thumb drive out of a box. "Any chance I can get you to bring me something to snack on?"

"Sure," Josie said.

George was back to work and Josie was half way to the kitchen when the doorbell rang. She detoured, but before she got to the door, she called back to George.

"Also, if you find anything referencing Carolyn Barnes or personal stuff for Lily Daye, I want that too. Actually, I want that especially."

With that, Josie opened the door to find a young woman on Lily Daye's doorstep holding a huge bouquet of flowers.

"Hey, there," she said. "Is Lily home?"

"No, I'm sorry, she's not," Josie said. "I'm afraid she passed away."

"Wow, really?" The woman was sincerely shocked and sorry. "If I'd known, I would have sent these to the funeral home or something."

"There hasn't been a funeral yet, but maybe you should tell whoever ordered these that Lily didn't receive them."

"Oh, there's no one to tell," she said. "Lily ordered these flowers. For the kids, you know?"

"No, I don't know." Josie opened the door wider. "My name is Josie Bates. Do you have a minute?"

⊏⊐

"YEP, THOSE ARE OURS."

Josie and the florist, whose name was Karen Watson, stood in the bear room looking at the flower vases in the closet. Karen owned a florist shop in Golden Cove, a small shopping area just down the road from the Vanderhaven estate. She had been delivering flowers to Lily for three years like clockwork. All of them paid for, in cash, by Lily Daye.

"I should have gotten those vases sooner. I forget them because most times Lily and I would get to talking on the stoop, and then she'd just say goodbye, and off I'd go," Karen said. "Eventually I would have remembered to come back for them."

Josie turned away and rested an elbow on one stack of boxes.

"What did you and Lily talk about?"

"This and that. The weather. She always asked about my mom, and that was nice," Karen said. "Lily didn't like the heat. She was from England, so I guess that makes sense. Luckily that isn't much of a problem here with the ocean so close. One time, I had someone cancel an order at the last minute. It was in the truck, so I asked Lily if she wanted it. She said no. Can you believe it? I don't know anyone who would turn down free flowers. They aren't cheap, believe me."

Karen put her back up against the wall, happy to take a minute to chat.

"She told me to take them up to the main house, and give them to the lady who lived there. Lily said she was old, and her son was mean, and she deserved something nice. So that's what I did. I handed them to the lady who opened the door, and she said thanks, and that was it."

"Did you tell the lady that Lily sent the flowers?" Josie asked.

"I did," Karen said. "I got nothing, not even a smile. I thought that was rude, and she wasn't that old."

"I have a feeling you gave them to the caregiver. She's not exactly fun," Josie said. "Still, I'm sure she told Mrs. Vanderhaven. She's old and she would have forgotten what she was told ten minutes later."

"Well, it was no big deal. You'd be surprised how many

people just shut the door once I give them the flowers." Karen sighed. She looked in the closet. "Is it okay if I take these? I can recycle them. It would save me a little money."

"You can have those boxes." Josie pointed to the corner. "I'll get some tape for you."

When she came back, Josie had an old newspaper she found in Lily's room and together she and Karen wrapped the vases and packed them in boxes.

"Did Lily ever say why she had all these flowers delivered?" Josie asked as they worked.

"She told me some children had died. It was a remembrance thing. I could tell that It was really hard for her to think about them, so I didn't ask again."

"Were they Lily's children?" Josie asked.

"I don't know, but I don't think so. She showed me a picture once when she was feeling really chatty," Karen said. "There were like four or five of them. Really cute kids. I was glad she didn't want to talk much about them. I like to do flowers for weddings, but funerals suck.

"Anyway, every time she said the flowers were beautiful and it was good the children would be remembered. Personally, I thought the flowers made it worse, but it wasn't for me to say."

Karen sighed as she finished packing her box and reached for the tape to seal it.

"What would you do? I mean if you had something really sad in your life. Would you, like, mark the day? I think it would make the rest of the year miserable 'cause you'd know it was coming around again and again and again."

Josie tore off a piece of tape and tossed the roll to Karen. That innocent question hit her like a ton of bricks, and her heart fell. She had a dark hole that could never be filled with flowers, and she would always remember her worst day. It wasn't something she wanted to talk about, so she circled back.

"Then Lily didn't share any details about how those children died or who they were?"

"She didn't, and I've delivered the big bouquet on this day every year for three years. There were other dates, too, but those bouquets were smaller. That's why there are so many vases."

"Do you know the other dates offhand?"

"Sure," Karen said. "If you have something to write with, I'll put them down."

Josie went back to the computer room, got paper and pen out of the desk, and gave it to Karen when she returned. It took no more than a minute before she handed it back.

"Here you go. Seven dates plus the big one."

"Thanks. I'm trying to run down family and this might help?"

"I hope it does." Karen taped her box and stood up. "I guess that's it. I'm glad you were here. I would have left the flowers and assumed Lily was out. I'm really sorry to hear that she passed. She was quiet, but she was always nice to me."

"Can you hold on for a minute?" Josie asked.

"Just a minute. I've got a few more deliveries," Karen said.

Josie went to Lily's bedroom, got the picture and brought it back.

"Is this the picture Lily showed you? Are these the children?"

"I think so, but I wouldn't swear to it. I just glanced and said I was sorry," Karen said.

"What did she say?"

"That she was sorry, too," Karen said. "She said she was sorrier than anyone would ever know."

"Thanks for all the information. I really appreciate it," Josie said.

"Well, I'm glad someone nice is taking care of Lily's things," Karen said. "And thanks for letting me take the vases."

"Not a problem," Josie said. "One less thing to worry about."

Karen took one box of vases to her car. Josie went back to Lily's bedroom to pack up Dax's bed. She had just stuffed it in a large trash bag when Karen, carrying the second box, poked her head through the door.

"Look, Lily paid up front for next year, so where shall I send the refund?" Karen asked.

"Don't worry about it," Josie said. "It will be Lily's Christmas present to you."

"Okay. Thanks." Karen was about to leave, but she had one more question. "Just so I'm clear about the deliveries. You want me to stop all of them? Even the one to Mr. Murray, right?"

CHAPTER 40

THE SEVENTH WITNESS
MR. MURRAY

Archer changed his flight as soon as Josie called, and bought himself three hours. Luckily Mr. Murray lived in South San Francisco and the airport was right there. That meant he wouldn't have to rush after he gave the guy the good news about his three-million-dollar windfall. Archer found the address easily, but now he sat in the car, engine running, checking one more time to see that he was in the right place.

This house was a decent size and sat on the edge of a worse-for-wear working-class neighborhood. It was wedged between an apartment building and a liquor store. The angle was odd, as if it was built before there were zoning laws. The apartment building looked like a cell block, the liquor store like where you'd get your booze in a brown paper bag and finish it before you got to your flop.

Archer turned the car off, wishing that he didn't have the itchy feeling that something was off. The house was too quiet. Too closed up. The front lawn was almost dead, the driveway cracked, and the windows could use a wash. The front steps going up to the house were wide, and half of them were covered by a ramp. Nothing moved inside or out. In his cop days, Archer would designate this a *hinky* call, and yet he wasn't sensing danger. In fact, the only emotion he could put his finger on was despair.

Since speculation was a waste of time, Archer got out of the car, walked up the stairs, and rang the bell. A middle-aged woman answered. Despite her smile, Archer knew he had been right. He had reached the end of earth's road, right here in South San Francisco.

Inside, a television droned, the smell of rubbing alcohol and detergent wafted out the door, escaping the still, airless interior. From where he stood, Archer saw a lady in a wheel-chair, her hair so white he could see her bright red scalp through it. A man was lying on the couch. Archer knew It was a man because he could see his big feet clad in brightly colored socks on one end and the dome of a bald head on the other.

"Hello?" The woman gave Archer a verbal nudge.

"Sorry. I was expecting someone else." He dug in his pocket and presented his I.D. "I'm a private investigator working for an attorney named Josie Bates. I'm helping settle a probate in Los Angeles, and I'm looking for Mr. Murray."

"Oh, that's lovely," she said as she gave Archer's identification a good look. "Mr. Murray doesn't get any visitors. Come on in. I'm sure he'll be happy to see you."

Archer wiped his feet. The lady chuckled.

"I sometimes forget about things like wiping your feet," she said. "It's not often necessary here."

Archer stepped through the door and then took another step aside so that she could close it.

"I'm Mrs. Newman," she said. "I run this place."

"This isn't Mr. Murray's home?" Archer asked.

"Well, of course it is, but it's not just *his*." Mrs. Newman paused and her smile faded. "You don't know about Mr. Murray at all, do you?"

"I don't, but I'd be much obliged if you could fill me in."

"Perhaps you should see him first," she said, "And then we'll talk."

"As long as it's okay with him," Archer said.

"Oh, I'm sure he won't mind."

———

LOOKING at Mr. Murray was tough; Archer would admit it if anyone bothered to ask. The man was living Archer's worst nightmare: the person gone, the body left behind, capable only of breathing and then only with a tube stuck in his throat.

Mr. Murray sat upright but only because his chair had been manufactured to make that possible. His hair was combed and his clothes were clean because Mrs. Newman, and whoever helped her, made it so. The man was positioned to face the window that looked out onto the parking lot of the liquor store, but his eyes didn't move. He did blink now and again, but Archer knew this to be muscle memory.

"How long has he been here?"

Archer didn't take his eyes off Mr. Murray as he asked the question; Mrs. Newman didn't take her eyes off her charge when she answered.

"He was in various hospitals and rehabs the first year after the accident, but, honestly, there was never any hope. His injuries were catastrophic. So, let's see, he's been with us for, oh, six years maybe. I could get you the exact date if you need it."

"No, that's fine," Archer said. "Would his injuries have been fatal without intervention?"

"Who's to say in situations like this? Personally, I think somewhere deep inside, he knows what's happening to him, that's why I talk to him as if he can hear me." Her head tipped to one side and then the other. "It's a cruel joke, isn't it? I mean, what purpose could the Divine have to keep him like this?"

"I don't know," Archer said. "What about his family? Didn't they make the call on the breathing tube—"

Mrs. Newman put her hand on Archer's arm, a signal that this was not the place to discuss Mr. Murray's situation. Archer stepped back and watched while she tucked in the man's shirt, moved his foot an inch as if that would make him more comfortable, and checked the straps that held him in place.

"There you go, Mr. Murray. I'll be back to sit with you in a bit."

She smiled right at him, moving her head so that he would see her if, as she hoped, he could see.

When she was done, Mrs. Newman wiggled two fingers at Archer, and he followed her into the kitchen. She called out to the two people sitting in the living room, asking if they would like the channel changed. She seemed not to expect a response because she bustled right by.

"I've got a soda pop or ice tea," she said.

"Ice tea," Archer said, knowing he would have his year's ration of tea by the time this day was done.

"You're a man after my own heart."

She poured them both tall glasses, put a lemon wedge on the edge of his, and settled in for a chat, clearly relishing time with someone who talked back.

"We're a long-term care home, as I imagine you figured out," she said. "Our maximum is four residents. Everybody has their own bedroom. We're quite proud of that. Saves a bit of dignity, you know."

"How come there isn't a sign out front?"

"The neighbors aren't thrilled that we're here. I find that funny, really, considering the neighborhood. Maybe they would prefer a halfway house for drug addicts or people on parole. They should count their blessings."

"You don't care for these people on your own, do you?" Archer asked.

"Heavens, no. We have therapists who come in. I'm only on my own a few hours a day. I can't lift our patients, but I feed the residents, talk to them, and keep the house presentable. We're not the most beautiful facility, but we take our work seriously." Mrs. Newman took a sip of her tea. "There's a gentleman on staff at night. It needs to be a man because there might be need of lifting."

"If Mr. Murray's been here that long, his family must be well off." Archer fingered his glass, then took the lemon and squeezed it into his tea. "Even if this isn't the fanciest place, this kind of care doesn't come cheap."

"We do our best to keep costs down, but it's difficult," she said. "Some of our funding comes from The First Street Church, most comes from Medicaid if the resident is eligible, but family is the biggest source of funds."

"Can you give me a contact for Mr. Murray's family?" Archer said. "Or pass along my number so that they can call me."

"Sadly, Mr. Murray's family is estranged. There were law suits after the accident, but as I understand it, many were directed at Mr. Murray himself. Of course, his family sued on his behalf, and there was a small settlement from one of the parties, but he's pretty much on his own." Mrs. Newman sighed. "His wife divorced him. I found that saddest of all after everything that happened."

Mrs. Newman perked up as she tried to cover for any offense her observation caused. "Don't get me wrong. The woman did her best. She bought that wheelchair. She paid for this residence the first year. I often saw her in that room, crying her eyes out, poor thing. I could tell, though, that this wouldn't end well. She never touched him, you see. She didn't kiss him hello or goodbye when she left. She didn't talk to him that I could hear. It was too much for the poor woman, considering what happened."

"What did happen?" Archer asked.

Mrs. Newman's voice lowered to a tone a click above a whisper. It was as if she didn't want anyone overhearing her gossip, though this wasn't gossip at all.

"Mr. Murray was the church's choir director. He had the children's choir at the depot that day. It was just before Christmas, and as a surprise, he arranged for all of them to ride to the next town where his wife and the children's parents would meet them. They were supposed to be in the back cars, but Mr. Murray somehow got them all in the engine as a treat.

"Well, everything was fine until a car stalled on the tracks and the train couldn't stop. It hit the car and everyone in the engine died. The engineer too. Well, everyone except Mr. Murray."

Mrs. Newman looked out the kitchen door as if she could see Mr. Murray.

"It's a blessing he is as he is if it was his fate to survive. His little daughter died that day. She was part of the choir." She looked back at Archer. "I think it would have killed him if she was dead and he recovered. Yes, sometimes there are small blessings even when tragedy strikes."

"Yes, ma'am," Archer said as he took out his phone and pressed record. "I wonder if you could tell me everything you know about that accident."

CHAPTER 41

Josie waited outside Lily Daye's cottage for Rusty and the gang to arrive. It had been two days since Archer came home from his trip up north. Knowing that there had been a catastrophic injury to Mr. Murray involving a car equipped with a Backlash product, that Lily sent flowers to Mr. Murray every year on the day of the accident, that she wanted to provide for his welfare, that she kept a collage of the dead children's photos, and that Jimmy Burroughs was fighting tooth and nail for records in Lily's possession led Josie to one conclusion: there was litigation still pending and whatever Lily had could inform a settlement that might bankrupt Jimmy Burroughs. Worst case scenario, it could leave him criminally culpable.

There were questions of course, the first one being why Lily seemed to harbor a personal guilt about the accident. She had started work the day it happened, so she wasn't personally involved in any aspect of the manufacture or disposition of the battery in that car. Josie also wondered how much Lily really knew about Mr. Murray. Since the money was not left in a trust, the estranged wife could possibly control it when Josie made the distribution. Josie was sure that was not what Lily intended. Knowing about the divorce, Josie would set up the trust herself but appoint a bank trustee. The last thing Josie wanted was to be responsible for Lily Daye's estate in perpetuity. Now there was only one real and present danger to the disposal of estate holdings: Rusty Gates.

Rusty had succeeded in getting the court to agree that there should be a mutual viewing of the items in Lily's garage and house to determine the worth of such and attempt arbitration. In anticipation of the visit, Josie had extended George Handle's contract, and he had worked over-time searching all the discs and drives in Lily's office. Archer and Josie had managed to get through a few boxes in the garage. All of them were looking for anything that appeared to be information critical to the numerous court cases against Jimmy Burroughs. The only thing George found was the name of the conversion company that Lily briefly worked for. They were out of business partially because they could never recover customer files from Lily when she fell off the face of the earth. She didn't respond to emails, phone calls, or letters demanding the return of their client's property. When Josie offered to return what she had in her possession, the man she was talking to hung up on her.

Josie directed George to set aside any of the drives that had identification. She would return them to their owners. It wasn't much, but it was something, considering Lily had a room full of family histories.

Josie rubbed her eyes. She was tired and hoped they would show up so they could get this over sooner than later. A squirrel dive-bombed out of a tree just as the door of the cottage opened, and Archer came out to join her.

"Still a few minutes."

He put a hand on her neck, and pulled her close enough to kiss the side of her head. Dax crossed their path without giving them a second look and disappeared around the back of the house.

Josie shaded her eyes with one hand. She said, "I feel like we're at the O.K. Corral waiting for Wyatt Earp."

"The casting's right considering it's Rusty," Archer said.

"If he shows up with a duster and a six gun, I'm out of here."

Archer gave her a nudge and pointed to the drive below. "Here they are."

Josie looked downhill toward the gate as a big black car squeezed through the side of the gate that opened and drove on toward the hacienda.

"You didn't tell them about the shortcut did you, Jo?" Archer entertained a smile, amused by Josie's minor one-upmanship.

"It'll do Burroughs and Rusty good to take a hike," she said.

Archer snorted. Dax was behind them sniffing around the trunk of a particularly stately tree. He raised his head at the sound of car doors slamming. The dog looked at Josie and Archer, saw no change in their demeanor, and went on his way.

"Show time."

Josie walked down the path, stopping at the end of the blue pavers knowing she would see them before they saw her. When she did, she almost laughed. Rusty had left the fancy suit at home, opting for khakis and a checked shirt, the picture-perfect attorney getting down and dirty in the trenches for his client.

Next to him was Jimmy Burroughs, looking like a scoundrel in his ill-fitting jacket and shirt. Rusty matched Burroughs's pace, which was painfully slow for a man of Rusty's size and energy.

The green-haired girl, Zack, followed the men. Though her head was down, her eyes were moving as if wary of the outdoors.

Pulling up the rear was a young man laden with camera equipment. "Ms. Bates."

Rusty called a hearty hello the minute he saw her. He took Jimmy Burroughs by the elbow to help him make the transition from earth to paver, an incline of two inches if that.

"Mr. Gates," she said as Rusty and Jimmy Burroughs came alongside her. She turned smoothly and accompanied them up the walkway.

"Thanks for meeting us here on short notice," Rusty said.

"Not a problem considering your invitation came by way of a court order."

His mega-watt grin morphed into a less charming tight-lipped smile.

"Mr. Burroughs." Josie nodded at the man and then again at Zack before she looked over their heads. "I see you brought a crew."

"Michael is wonderful. In-house. Nothing fancy. You'll like working with him."

With those words, Rusty raised the specter of her future at Baxter & Baxter.

"I'm sure I would if circumstances warranted, but the order was for Mr. Burroughs to view the contents of the boxes. Your assistant is, of course, welcome." Josie addressed Jimmy Burroughs. "My associate will join us after he shows Michael where he can wait. Nothing will be photographed or filmed."

"I think you're mistaken—" Rusty began.

"The judge's order is clear," Josie said, cutting him off. "You, Mr. Burroughs, and Zack can come with me, or you can all stay here while I call Judge Alby to clarify. I don't think she'll take kindly to the specificity of her order being questioned. It's up to you, of course."

The ultimatum was delivered cordially, but there was no doubt that Josie was digging in. Rusty knew that any delay would upset Jimmy Burroughs. Over the course of their association, Rusty had determined that the man had two modes: pissed off and stoned. Rusty didn't particularly care for either one.

"In the spirit of cooperation, and since this is a preliminary look-see to determine the origin of the items transported by Lily Daye, we'll proceed. I am assuming you won't mind if Zack takes notes."

"Not at all," Josie said.

"Onward and upward, then," Rusty said.

Josie led the group, but Rusty fell back, whispered to Michael who dropped his tripod and case and lifted his camera. When Rusty walked away, Michael focused on the attorney as he turned his head in profile. The photographer got every shot.

"The man's something," Michael said, when Archer walked down the path to collect him.

"That's one way of putting it." Archer pointed at the cottage. "You'll wait there."

When he was sure Michael was settled, Archer headed for the garage, getting there just as Josie was about to put the key in the padlock. Before she could do that, Dax charged around the corner, barking a warning, inserting himself between Josie and Rusty, Jimmy, and Zack.

Zack screamed. Jimmy Burroughs cried out, stumbled and grabbed at Zack. He took her down as he fell. Josie went for the dog, unsure of what command would stop him.

"Dax! No. Down."

He moved forward, sideways, barking to wake the dead. Zack and Jimmy skittered toward one another, Jimmy pushing the girl with the green hair in front of him.

"Stop him. He'll kill us," Jimmy Burroughs cried. "Stop him."

Rusty bellowed at the dog to no avail. Josie's hands were on his collar, but he jerked away. Thankfully, Archer was close enough and got a firm hold on him. He pulled the dog to his side, knelt beside him, and wrapped his arms around him until he quieted.

"Have you got him?" Zack's voice shook, and the color had drained from her face.

"Good God," Rusty said. "I'm going to report you. I can't believe you have an animal like—"

"Stop it, Rusty," Josie said. "That's Lily Daye's dog. He belongs here."

Josie looked at Archer and inclined her head.

"I'll put him in the car," Archer said.

Only when they heard a distant slamming of a door did Zack get up. Rusty rushed to Jimmy and got him on this feet.

"Do you want to go into the house?" Josie asked. "I have water inside. You could rest a minute."

"No, we'll start here if this is where most of the boxes are," Jimmy said.

"Take a breath, and I'll go get some water bottles. It's dusty inside. Just give me a minute."

Josie followed Archer's route, catching him as he was coming back to join the group. She took his hand. "Come with me."

Together, they hurried into the house. Michael was nowhere to be seen, but his equipment was there so Josie assumed he was in the bathroom. Still, when she got the bottles out of the fridge, she kept her voice low as she gave Archer his marching orders. He went one way, and she hurried back to the garage. Josie handed out apologies with the water bottles, unlocked the garage, and pushed back the door.

Rusty went in first, then Zack. Jimmy Burroughs held back, and at first Josie thought it was the sight of Mary Margaret's car that gave him pause. Knowing what she knew now, the car either brought back horrific memories of a colleague's death and the demise of his company, or guilt because, like Mrs.

Watkins thought, Jimmy Burroughs knew his battery was defective and responsible for the accident. Josie was wrong on both counts.

Jimmy Burroughs wasn't thinking about the car, the battery, or Mary Margaret Watkins. He wasn't even thinking about Lily Daye. He was looking at Josie Bates.

"What did you call that dog?"

"Dax," she said.

"Lovely," he responded.

⊏⊐

"HE WORKS for the lady lawyer. The one who came to see you about Lily."

Fran-the-caregiver had one hand on Mrs. Vanderhaven's chair to steady herself and the other on her lower back. Her ample hips were thrown westward while the rest of her went east. Archer stood at the ready if she needed help righting herself. She raised her voice to Mrs. Vanderhaven.

"You remember that tall lady who was here about Lily, don't you?"

"I didn't like Lily Daye, but I remember the other one."

The old lady looked around her caregiver. Fran rotated to give her a clear view of Archer.

"She's the big one, right? Tall. Doesn't look like a lady. Looks too strong for a lady."

"That's the one, ma'am," Archer said.

"She was okay." The woman sat back in her chair and pointed the remote at the T.V. "You can come talk to me then."

Archer went to the old lady's side, phone at the ready.

"We're starting to move things out of Ms. Daye's house—"

"Lily's moving?"

"Well, Ms. Daye's already moved on, so to speak," Archer

281

said. "We're just helping move her things. Ms. Bates has a question for you."

The old woman hit the remote again. Archer raised his brows at Fran. He had no idea if Mrs. Vanderhaven heard him. The old lady made it clear she had.

"Get down here and tell me what you want. I've got arthritis in my neck. I can't be looking up at you all day."

Archer did as he was told and got down on one knee. He held out his phone with the picture of Jimmy Burroughs on it. It was an airbrushed beauty shot, and even though he wore his uniform of t-shirt and jacket, he looked pretty good.

"Ms. Bates said you saw a man going to Lily Daye's cottage a couple of times," Archer said. "Was it this man?"

"Closer."

Mrs. Vanderhaven grabbed for the phone, wrapping her papery, soft fingers around his in a death grip. She took her own good time and Archer's knee was beginning to ache.

Suddenly, she pushed his hand away, raised the remote and said, "Nope. Never seen him before."

CHAPTER 42

Jimmy Burroughs sat in the middle of the garage on the camp chair Josie kept in the Jeep and had brought in just for him. It was odd that he was curious about the dog since they seemed to dislike one another equally, but not strange that he demanded to sit like a little king while the rest of them stood in the dirt and dust. Archer returned just as Jimmy settled himself. He gave Josie a quick shake of his head.

No, Jimmy Burroughs was not the man Mrs. Vanderhaven had seen going into Lily's cottage.

No, Jimmy Burroughs was not the visitor that caused Dax to be chained in the garage.

Josie raised one shoulder, then pulled a face, acknowledging that it had been a long shot. She knew that Frank from the auto dealership had been there once, but Mrs. Vanderhaven had mentioned multiple sightings of a man. The way Dax reacted to Jimmy led Josie to wonder if he had paid Lily a visit at some point. Perhaps lied when he said he read about Lily's death the paper. Maybe he had been with Lily when she died. He hadn't, though, and Josie knew it. The man she was looking at would never go anywhere on his own, much less skulk around in the dark.

They were now an hour and a half into the search for who-knew-what. Zack and Rusty brought boxes, opened them, and handed him files to review. Jimmy flipped through them, discarding them almost as quickly as they were given to him.

Josie had her back up against a post, situated so that she could look over the man's shoulder. The only things big enough to read were the labels on the files, but if Jimmy lingered over something, she made a note to revisit it.

He didn't linger over much.

"No. All of this is a waste of my time." Jimmy was suddenly animated, throwing the file in his hand at no one in particular, scattering the pages. "There has to be something more here. I am missing notebooks, I'm sure of it. I am missing schematics. I know Lily had them. I gave them to her for safe keeping. They are critical to *Distant2*."

With that, the two lawyers' eyes met, and Archer straightened up. Only Zack didn't realize the significance of what Jimmy had said. He knew what he was looking for all along. Unsure of what she wanted to do with that information, Josie walked to the center of the room, picking up papers as she went.

When she was in front of Jimmy Burrows, she said, "Right now, all of this is property of Lily Daye's estate. If I were you, I would treat it respectfully." She tapped the file until all the papers were in order and then put it back in the box. "Now that we know what you're looking for, and the fact that the two hours we scheduled are almost up, would you like to keep going with the boxes or do you want to look in the house?"

"The house."

Jimmy stood up so fast, the camp chair toppled over. As he made for the outside, he looked at the wreck of the car. Josie thought she saw a ghost of a smile. When he spoke, it was to Rusty, who was on the man's heels.

"Is this taken care of?" Jimmy asked.

"It will be by tomorrow," Rusty said.

With that, Jimmy Burroughs was gone into the light, holding an arm up to his eyes, disliking the low hanging sun. Zack was by his side.

Rusty waited for Josie. "What's he going to find in the house?" Rusty said.

Josie gave him the side-eye, delighting in the rip in his confidence. The day had not gone exactly as planned: the client was agitated, the opposing counsel was not, and his khakis were dirty.

"Teddy bears," Josie said, and went on ahead.

Rusty watched her walk away. Archer pulled up next to him.

"You're a helluva man, my friend," Rusty said. "I don't know how you hang on to that one. Gorgeous, but a ball buster."

"Sometimes you get lucky."

Archer moved on, kicking at the leaves, smiling until Rusty caught up with him. When they got to the cottage, Archer held the door for him. They sat on the small plaid sofa that was barely big enough for the both of them. Jimmy and Zack went through the boxes in the bedroom and every drawer in the place. The day was wearing on Rusty Gates. When Michael pointed a camera his way, Rusty waved him off. Josie had followed Jimmy into every room. Now that he was in the kitchen and they could all keep an eye on him, she sat on the rolled arm of the sofa near Rusty.

"Do you have it, Bates?" Rusty asked.

"What he wants isn't here," she said. "He could have saved us all a lot of trouble if he just told us about it in the first place instead of demanding everything be turned over. Greed isn't good, Rusty."

Rusty eyed her. Josie Bates, a colleague and storied lawyer, was a piece of work and he would put nothing past her. Both of them knew honesty was a commodity in their business. Everybody traded on it in their own way. Rusty played a little fast and loose; Bates was a straight shooter. Still, there were always exceptions even for her. Being dishonest was like cheating on your spouse. There's always a first time, and sometimes it really did just happen. For the life of him, he couldn't tell if Josie was fooling around or screwing the truth in earnest.

When Jimmy's muttering started to grate on them, when Zack looked exhausted, when the day was slipping away, Rusty clapped his hands, rubbed them together, and announced the party was over.

"We'll call it a day and make a date to revisit before Zack and Jimmy need to go back up north. Jimmy? You good with that?"

Jimmy nodded.

"Excellent." Rusty stood up and faced Josie and Archer. "Thank you for taking so much time with us. In the spirit of full disclosure, we are asking Judge Alby to release the car as-is to Mr. Burroughs. The Watkins family has no objection, and he has paid them a fair price for it. I had word from my associate that the judge agrees that the car is not part of Lily Daye's estate."

Josie stood up, too, shocking everyone when she didn't put up a fight. "Let me know when the transportation company will be here. Now that we know that Mr. Burroughs has a very clear idea of the items he wants, we'll expect a detailed list."

With that, Archer and Josie saw everyone out, locked up the cottage, the garage, and left the Vanderhaven estate. It wasn't until they were sitting on the patio at Burt's, dinner order in, Dax with a water bowl in front of him, that Archer asked the million-dollar question.

"Do you have what Burroughs is looking for, Jo?"

CHAPTER 43

Dax was bedded down for the night, Josie and Archer were headed for the sack, but she didn't want to go to bed without full disclosure. She put Lily's briefcase on the dining room table, released the latches, and opened it up. Inside was a leather-bound notebook.

"I don't know what this is, but if Burroughs wants it so bad then it must have some value."

Archer picked up the notebook and paged through it. Josie sat down opposite him, comfortable with the fact that she had only told the literal truth. The items Jimmy wanted were not in the garage or Lily's cottage, they were in Josie's home, and she was protecting Lily's interests.

"It's all code, Archer," Josie said. "I don't think you'll be able to make heads or tails of it either. Frankly, I'm not even sure if this is what he wants. It could be Lily's. It could be anyone's."

"Then why not just show it to him, and have him tell you if it's what he's looking for."

"I'll only have Burroughs's explanation. I'd rather have some idea of what we're looking at, so we can know if he's telling the truth," Josie said. "Do we really know if Lily was a glorified administrative assistant? How do we know that she wasn't an engineer? What if she has some stake in the intellectual property of the battery or that other thing?"

"That's why you get the big bucks, Jo," Archer said.

Josie snorted. If she came out of this with a dime it would be amazing. Archer closed the journal and tossed it into the briefcase.

"I don't know what I'm looking at either."

"Then there's this."

Josie took the thumb drive out of the envelope she had found in the safe deposit box. Archer took off the rubber band, and unrolled the paper wrapped around the thumb drive.

"Have you seen what's on here?" he said.

"More of the same, except this one is labeled. It's for *Distant2*," Josie said.

"Which was?"

"The big secret thing that was being shipped the day of the accident, Lily's first day of work. Half the lawsuits are the government suing Jimmy and Jimmy countersuing the government over who really owned that thing. Burroughs says that the internal housing was damaged beyond repair in the wreck. He shut the project down and will not revisit it. The military says he needs to hand over the codes, and they will deal with the damaged hardware to get it up and running. But the actual manufacturing of the unit wasn't part of the deal with Uncle Sam. It's a mess and I'm glad I'm not part of it."

"It's all ancient history," Archer said. "In seven years, the technology has probably surpassed whatever Burroughs made back then. I don't know why he'd be so antsy about it today or why the government would care."

"What if Lily was instrumental in the creation of that thing? Maybe she has some investment in the patent."

"How could that be if it was her first day?" Archer said.

"Although it could be that she didn't want Burroughs to be able to recreate it. Maybe she knew something that convinced her it should stay buried. That could be the reason she disappeared. She was depressed already, and her self-imposed isolation could have pushed her over the edge. From what I've heard, that woman was wound pretty tight."

He paused for a minute, then closed the briefcase.

"So long as we're playing what if…" he went on. "What if Lily Daye was more of a partner than we thought. She and Burroughs disagree on something technical. Burroughs has the money and could strong arm her into submission. Lily doesn't like that, so she takes this stuff."

Archer waved a hand over the briefcase and thumb drive.

"Or, what if the military is involved? We might be looking at something more sinister than an industrial problem. Maybe she was hiding out from Burroughs and the government."

"Or, Lily knows all this stuff could hurt Jimmy in court. She lived with him. She loved him—" Josie said.

"According to him." Archer pointed a finger, making an edit.

"Oh, come on. Stipulate she loved him and she thought she was protecting him by disappearing with information that might hurt him. She gives him plausible deniability. She was going to reappear when the last case was put to bed. You know, wait out the statute of limitations. Part of that could be inferred from Carolyn's letters."

Archer put his hands behind his head and grinned at her.

"That's kind of a romantic spin," he said. "What woman would be that selfless and not let her man know what kind of sacrifice she was making? People disappear because they're afraid of someone or something. It's been three years since she saw the guy, and he only found out because you were on top of things. And why kill herself?"

"I think we can rule out murder," Josie said. "But

Burroughs is a druggie, she lived with him, she's got a pharmacy of anti-depressants, ergo Lily and Burroughs share a bad habit."

"Burroughs is a doper. That's not a fatal habit," Archer said.

"Lily's meds are legal, too," Josie said. "To each his own. All I'm saying is that they probably fed on one another."

Archer rolled his head. He pulled his shoulders back and yawned.

"Look, maybe with all the travel, I'm not on top of my game, but I think I know what's going on."

"You do?" Josie was excited, eager to hear his analysis.

He raised a hand, and then one finger.

"You are a sucker for a woman in distress. There's no bigger distress than being alone with a problem. You want to do right by her."

Another finger went up.

"You were fine taking care of her estate by the book, and now you're ticked that you can't pull it off with one hand tied behind your back."

The third finger went up.

"Three, what this is really about is you're mad at Rusty Gates for existing. He's screwing up things with Faye, he's screwing up things on this simple executorship, and he's part of your history that you don't particularly like."

"Anything else?" Josie asked, her excitement cooling.

"Yeah, that guy Burroughs is really weird, and you don't want anything Lily has to go to him," Archer said.

"Point taken," she said, before giving in completely. "A little bit of all points actually."

"Josie, sometimes good enough is good enough. Burroughs is willing to forego the money, Mr. Murray will be well taken care of, and Dax will stay with you. Give all this crap to Burroughs, shut down the house, and pay the bills."

While Archer spoke, Josie rewrapped the thumb drive. She opened the briefcase and took out the leather-bound notebook, and put the two together.

"You are probably right." She held the little package out like the apple to Adam. "But humor me. See if you can find someone who can tell us what this is before I fold."

━━━

JIMMY BURROUGHS ORDERED room service for two. He sent Zack to have a massage, noting that she looked a bit weary after their ordeal that day. Zack, delighted by the attention, had the massage and ate the dinner. Then, a miracle happened. After she put the room service tray outside the door of the suite, Jimmy rolled her a joint and asked her to smoke with him.

She was so happy, she wanted to cry. Jimmy had never shared his stash, nor had they spent any quality time together. Zack kicked off her shoes. She took off her jeans and got comfy. Her oversized t-shirt covered her up enough—not that she thought Jimmy would have any prurient interest in her. Lily was soft and round, Zack was narrow and small. Jimmy preferred soft and round, and that was fine with Zack because men didn't interest her any more than women did. Belonging was her thing. Being chosen was what rang her chimes. That was why being Jimmy's first employee meant the world to Zack. Her initial anger at being let go at all gave way to gratitude now that she saw what Lily dealt with. All those lawyers would have eaten her alive back then. Zack was better now, older and stronger. Still, today had been stressful, but the attention Jimmy was showering on her made it all worthwhile.

"I wish Backlash would go away," she said, more to herself than Jimmy.

He struck a match and lit her joint. She breathed in and held the first toke.

"I do, too," Jimmy said. "If only we could think of a way to make it happen. Everything gone at once."

The night got long. Zack smoked a second joint. Jimmy did not. She ended up on the floor. Jimmy eventually helped her to her bed.

Zack was so grateful. She thanked him over and over again, telling him that no one in her whole life had sat on the edge of her bed and pulled the covers up to her chin. No one in her whole life had hummed a little song and petted her head to put her to sleep. No one ever had cupped her face with a warm hand and not expected something in return.

When Jimmy stopped humming, and Zack was almost asleep, he hovered over her and whispered. "I think I know how Backlash could go away."

"Okay," Zack mumbled.

"Or maybe it's silly." Jimmy patted her cheek and tucked the covers.

Zack stretched like a cat. She fought to keep her eyes open.

"I bet it's not," she mumbled, knowing that Jimmy could never be silly. "Tell me what it is."

Jimmy told her what he was thinking, and it didn't sound good to Zack at all. It sounded smart, but not good. Still, she wanted Jimmy to be happy.

"Yes. I'll find a way," Zack said, her voice deep and dreamy.

"Lovely," Jimmy answered. "Lovely."

And Zack drifted off. Her last thought was that Jimmy Burroughs was brilliant and kind and she would die for him.

CHAPTER 44

THE EIGHTH WITNESS
THE FRIEND

Josie and Faye were in the conference room presumably talking business but mostly enjoying lunch. Josie had enchiladas and Faye a tostada. In a nod to the Christmas spirit, Josie had brought cookies from the baker. She was holding a Santa cookie and had already munched away his hat and one eye. The courts were as good as shut down and wouldn't reopen until the new year, so the pressure of their daily grind was off.

"Do you have a firm date then?" Josie said.

"My new house closes February first," Faye said. "The movers are lined up for February fifteenth."

"So soon." To Josie the date felt as though it was day after tomorrow.

"I'm not going to disappear, you know," Faye said. "Cutting the cord is going to be hard."

"I'm glad you'll still be around even if it's on the sidelines," Josie said.

"Then you're staying if Rusty takes over?" Faye plucked a

Christmas tree cookie out of the box, broke the top off, ate the icing star.

"I'm still thinking about it," Josie said. "Have you signed on the dotted line?"

"No, but not because anything is wrong," Faye said. "Rusty's offer is generous. The contract is in order."

"But…"

"But it's Christmas, and I'd rather be wrapping presents," Faye said, rousing her good humor. "Besides, I want to see how things play out between you two."

"No matter what happens, I'll be here at least through the first quarter of the new year. I won't leave any of the clients hanging. That being said…" Josie reached into a bag that had been on the floor next to her and brought out two wrapped packages. "I have something for you."

"I thought we didn't do gifts." Faye objected even though it was clear that she was pleased with the gesture.

"Think of it as a housewarming present," Josie said as Faye pulled the ribbon on the first one and carefully unwrapped it.

"Oh, Josie, this is beautiful." Faye turned the frame so they could both look at the candid picture of Hannah, Archer, Josie, Billy, and Max. "Where were you all at the same time and not in trouble?"

"The concert on the pier," Josie said.

"Hannah and Billy are so young," Faye said. "My god, they were just kids."

"Weren't we all?" Josie laughed. "Open the other one."

Faye did as she was told, and this time she looked a long while at the framed picture, clearly touched.

"This is wonderful. Beautiful," she said.

"Hannah painted it before she left." Josie tapped the frame. She didn't have to see it to remember how beautiful the oil painting of the Baxter & Baxter office was. Faye looked from one corner to the other corner, up and down as she took it all in.

"She even painted the sign. It looks so real."

Faye looked a bit longer, surprised to find herself so touched by the gift. She glanced at Josie, and it dawned on her that touched might not be the right word for what she was feeling. The gift was a like a pin in the map of her life, and she was about to pluck it out and pin it somewhere else because she assumed it was time for her to do so. If she did, though, the little hole would remain. She could never put her pin in it; there would be no going back because Rusty would have driven his golden nail right through it.

She smiled and tucked away both her melancholy and the pictures, coiling the ribbon on top. Nothing was set in stone; the ribbon on the deal wasn't tied in a bow.

"We're lucky, aren't we, Josie?" Faye said. "We both have lovely daughters."

Josie gave Faye no argument. Hannah had been Josie's client, then her ward, and now she was an adult with a life of her own. It didn't matter how old she was or that she was not a blood relative. Hannah was the daughter of Josie's heart.

"We do, and Hannah will be back soon," Josie said as she got up to clear the table.

"Where's Archer today?" Faye said.

"He's out at JPL trying to run down some information for me," Josie said.

"That's far afield. I thought you were winding down on the Lily Daye matter."

"I don't want Rusty getting anything more than his client deserves. There is something really weird about Burroughs. I have this gut feeling that he's responsible for…"

Josie paused. She dumped the paper plates in the trash can.

"I don't know what he's responsible for, but I believe he was somehow instrumental in Lily dying somehow. Indirectly, maybe, but still responsible. If he had asked once about her, offered to bury her, shown some concern, I don't think I'd be this dug in."

"Hopefully you'll figure that part of it out soon. I can't think of anything worse than no one wanting to claim me. I hate to think of her alone in that mortuary, Christmas or not."

Before Josie could sit down, the phone in the conference room rang. Josie picked it up and listened, and when she hung up, she said, "From your mouth to God's ear, Faye. Carolyn Barnes just called."

JOSIE PROPPED her computer on a stack of books, tapped the key to let Carolyn Barnes into the Zoom meeting room, and got her first glimpse of the woman who wrote letters to Lily Daye. She was in her forties, attractive, and concerned. Josie thanked her for agreeing to a call and introduced herself.

"Yes? What is it? Our police ran me down. They said a barrister from the United States has been trying to get ahold of me at my old address, but they told me nothing more."

"I am sorry that we have to have this conversation this way, but I am calling on behalf of Lily Daye," Josie said. "Actually, I am calling on behalf of Lily Daye's estate. I am so sorry to bring you the news, but Ms. Daye has passed away."

"THIS IS FASCINATING, Archer, but I don't think I have the time to do it justice now. My mother-in-law is coming for dinner, and Janice will kill me if I'm late."

Ben Luce, star physicist at Nasa's Jet Propulsion Laboratory, had been looking over the leather-bound notebook for almost forty-five minutes. Archer sat patiently, waiting for him to say something earth shattering that would wrap up the equation of Lily Daye, Jimmy Burroughs, and a load of files from a defunct company.

"Is there anything you can tell me just from the once over?" Archer said.

"This isn't like your police television shows where you see the clue buried in a report and instantly solve the crime. You do mean like that, right?"

Ben turned his chair, took his glasses off, and rubbed the bridge of his nose. His smile was impish and his analogy was not far off.

"Yeah, like that," Archer said.

"The short answer is no. It won't work that way." His glasses were back on, but he was not giving up. "Let me keep this for a day or so."

Archer opened his mouth, but before he could beg for a miracle, Ben held up both hands and pushed back such a notion.

"I know. I know what you want, but patience is called for," Ben said. "The good news is that I do know what I am looking at and it's quite remarkable. May I ask where you got this?"

"Josie is executor on an estate. There are boxes of stuff from the company the woman worked for. Josie needs to make sure there is no monetary value to these things. If there is, maybe the book and the drive could be auctioned or something." Archer shrugged. "I don't know, really. She just doesn't want to let it go without fully understanding what she's got."

"Well, it would probably have a great deal of value to certain people, especially the person who wrote it. I am assuming it is not your dead lady."

"All we know is that she worked for a tech company called Backlash and—"

"Hah, Jimmy Burroughs." Ben crinkled his nose and

nodded his head. "The plot thickens. Maybe I won't go home to dinner after all."

"Is Burroughs a friend of yours?" Archer said.

"Hardly." Ben began to laugh. When it wore down to a snicker, he said, "He's smart as they come, but the only friend Jimmy Burroughs has is Jimmy Burroughs."

CHAPTER 45

Josie left the office immediately after the video call with Carolyn Barnes ended.

After the first shock of Josie's news, Carolyn Barnes did her friend's memory justice, painting a picture of a once happy woman brought low by tragedy.

Lily Daye and Carolyn had been childhood friends, both growing up in the countryside where Lily's father taught her to shoot and Carolyn's mother taught her to sew. When they grew up, Carolyn married a man she'd met clubbing; Lily married Carolyn's brother, George Kensington, a grocer. Lily kept the books for the business. She and George had two children. They were happy. Then, a rich man, driving too fast through their village, killed Lily Daye Kensington's children, Patrick and Andy.

The marriage did not survive.

The rich man did not go to jail.

Lily never emotionally recovered. She drank. She smoked. She fell into depression and married a man who took her to the United States. The only good thing to come out of that was that Lily stopped drinking and smoking as far as Carolyn knew. She also quit feeling. Lily was still lovely, but nothing touched her. As hard as Carolyn tried, she could not help her friend.

"Do you know anything about her last job?" Josie asked.

"You mean her last real job? The one with Jimmy?"

Carolyn was off again. Nothing touched Lily until Jimmy. Once she met him, everything changed. Lily was devoted to him. In her letters she sounded happy again, and then suddenly she was not. After that, Lily wrote sporadically. She told Carolyn she no longer lived with Jimmy.

No, Carolyn knew nothing of the work Lily had done for that man, and only a little of the work she did after Jimmy. Carolyn laughed when she told Josie that Lily sewed teddy bears together to make ends meet. She did something with computers. Neither job paid much. She would have been better off teaching people to shoot. As far as Carolyn knew, Lily did not like to go far afield from her house. Josie stayed quiet, letting Carolyn tell her things she already knew, taking to heart the things she didn't. Josie now had context for the threads of Lily's life.

Carolyn couldn't speak to what happened to Lily after she left Jimmy. She had a new address. She asked Carolyn not to speak to anyone about her. Lily stopped answering Carolyn's letters about six months ago. She stopped answering her phone three months ago.

Carolyn knew the depression had taken hold again, but what could she do? It really didn't surprise her that Lily was dead, poor tortured soul. Angry about the death of her children, angry at the death of her marriage, but most of all angry that no one was ever held to account. Lily had, more than likely, given up.

Josie ended the call, grateful that Carolyn would accept Lily's body and lay her to rest with Patrick and Andy. Carolyn would also tell her brother. And, yes, she would like the tea cups sent back, the cups Lily loved because they reminded her of home.

Josie was also grateful because the conversation with Carolyn Barnes put Lily in perspective. She now understood the pictures of the children, including Lily's own, and flowers to commemorate their deaths. Josie understood Lily's desire to help Mr. Murray, a man whose life was ruined in a terrible accident caused, perhaps, by a rich man. Josie understood Lily's gig work. Devastated by what the work of Backlash wrought, she wanted to take no chances on being party to anything like that again. Her one hope had been Frank, a man with grease under his nails and a great admiration for her, but Lily was too far gone to grab the lifeline he offered.

That left one question mark: Jimmy Burroughs. What reason would Lily have to suddenly turn on him? Jimmy Burroughs's life had been destroyed by the accident too.

Then again, Josie knew that mental illness, paranoia, and fantasy, could wreak havoc on a heart after a trauma. She'd had a taste of it and it was an ugly thing. The difference between her and Lily was family.

Josie thought about all of this as she drove to the Vanderhaven estate with Dax by her side. Archer had called asking her to return to the garage and look for any records that referenced the words Digital Analysis Expression. Ben had limited time and it was the one thing he had asked for.

Happy to get out of the office but in no mood to run into any of the Vanderhavens, Josie parked on the bluffs across from the estate, took Dax, and walked the quarter mile to Lily Daye's cottage.

When they arrived, Josie let Dax run free while she opened the garage. The earth had shifted yet again and the door only opened wide enough for her to go through. Josie ran her hand over the car as she passed it. The towing company would come for it soon, and the last reminder of what happened to Mary

Margaret Watkins would be gone. Within the week, Lily would be sent off to England to rest beside her sons. Within the month, Josie would have the trust set up for the benefit of Mr. Murray. Barring any shenanigans, she would have looked at all these files, heard from Ben, and made a decision about all the stuff in the garage before Christmas day. Josie hoped Lily would be pleased that at least some of her business was being taken care of.

Righting the camp chair that Jimmy Burroughs had knocked over, Josie dusted off the seat, dragged it toward the boxes that had not been examined, and set to work looking for three little words in boxes of history that were almost a decade old.

———

"COME ON MRS. V., let's hit the hay."

"Who's staying tonight?" Mrs. Vanderhaven stood in the space between the big window and her big bed, holding onto her walker like a battering ram. "Who's going to be here?"

"I'm here all night. You know that." Fran turned down the old woman's bed.

"What about him?" Mrs. Vanderhaven's eyes narrowed. She trusted no one.

"Him, your son?"

"Yes, him. I don't want him to stay. He's up to something. You can always tell when he's up to something. Never really liked him after he got old," she said. "Don't know how that happened. Him getting old."

"Yeah, well, I don't think you can change him now." Fran waited, shifting from one foot to the other. "So, are you going to let me get you in bed?"

Fran was tired. She wanted to go to her room, kick off her shoes, have a shot from the bottle she kept next to her own bed, and drift off while she watched anything but game shows on the television. When the old woman didn't move, Fran gave up.

"Okay, get yourself in bed when you feel like it," Fran said.

"Damn straight I can. I'm not an invalid, you know. I own this place. I got rights."

Fran rolled her eyes, pulled her sweater tight, and tried very hard not to point out the obvious: Alice Vanderhaven could barely feed herself and only had enough strength to shoot off her mouth. Fran also knew what the son was up to, and pretty soon Alice would be in a home. That was too bad. But there was nothing she could do about it. Fran would be on to her next old girl and go through all this again. She didn't pause as she walked out the door, but she did give a backward wave.

"You knock on the wall if you need a boost," she said.

In her room, Fran looked at the clock and started counting down the minutes. She gave Mrs. V. seven to figure out she couldn't get up on that mattress. Seven minutes, and the old girl would be banging on the wall. Seven minutes was time enough for her first drink, so Fran took out her bottle, poured two fingers, and waited.

Left alone, Alice Vanderhaven turned herself around, reached behind the pillows on the window seat, and found her binoculars. Her caregiver was not a vigilant person, but Alice was. She knew the value of the things in the villa. The stupid woman said that because the compound was on a peninsula that had no freeway access, and behind a wall to boot, so no self-respecting thief and murderer would go to the trouble of breaking in.

Yes, Fran was a stupid and unimaginative while Alice was smart.

She knew that it was exactly because they were behind a wall that bad people would come onto the grounds. Who was there to see them once they were over, skulking around ready to do their worst? Rape and pillage, that's what they would do.

Then they would steal. There was plenty to steal in Casa Alicia.

Mrs. Vanderhaven held the binoculars in one hand. They were heavy and her hand shook. It took two tries for her to get them up to her eyes. Things were still a little wiggly when she swept the land below, but she was old and a little tremor was nothing when it came to protecting her land. From her bedroom Alice could see everything: every tree and cottage, every statue and stone.

She knew it all like the back of her hand. Alice Greely Vanderhaven knew when something was wrong in her universe, and boy something was really wrong.

ONLY FOUR MINUTES passed before Alice Vanderhaven thumped on the wall. Fran snorted. One of these days, the old woman would appreciate her. Just to show her who was boss, Fran decided to finish her drink before she went to put Alice in bed. The glass was halfway to her lips when Fran heard the second thump. And then another and another.

She was faster than lightning, dropping the drink, flinging open the door of her bedroom, and rushing to the old lady's room. She called out for Brian Vanderhaven even though he wouldn't hear because the house was so damn big.

Fran flung open Mrs. V's. bedroom door. It was almost dark now because the winter sun had sunk quickly over the ocean. Still, there was enough light coming through the big window for Fran to make out the silhouettes in the room: the huge bed, the tallboy against the far wall, the overstuffed chair that the lady could not get out of on her own if she sat down. Fran expected to see the old woman prone on the floor, fallen, her hip broken, pounding on the wall, desperate to be saved.

Instead, Alice Vanderhaven was standing on her own two

feet, holding her binoculars with one hand while she pounded on the wall with the other.

"What? What?" Fran cried.

She rushed into the room, but before she got to Alice Vanderhaven's side, the old woman snapped, "Call the tall person. Call her now."

"The lawyer?" Fran said.

"Yes, you stupid girl. Call her now. They've breached the wall."

CHAPTER 46

Josie got through two boxes of Backlash files before the light began to fail. She found internal memos reporting progress or set-backs on *Distant2*, delays in parts shipments, armed services updates, congressional funding, and testing failures. There was communication checking in with various people within the Backlash organization noting timelines, agreeing to changes, questioning whether or not data had been sent, follow ups with said data attached.

The content of each message imprinted itself on Josie's brain briefly before dissolving because she was looking for one phrase and one phrase only: Digital Analysis Expression.

When she finished with a box, she packed everything up and sealed it again. There was, she thought, some merit to Jimmy Burroughs wanting these things back. It also appeared that none of this was valuable to Lily's estate. Perhaps Lily had been both depressed and insane. Josie understood her taking the money for Mr. Murray, but carting all this stuff around seemed ridiculous.

She thought about going home. Archer was probably there by now, and it didn't look like she was going to find what she was looking for. She picked up her phone and looked at the flashlight app. Her second option was to light it up and finish what she started. Archer's friend Ben had taken time to help her out, and the least she could do was make his time worthwhile.

Before she tackled the next box, though, Josie decided she would stretch her legs and check on Dax. She never even got out of the chair because she heard a sound, felt a draft. Something or someone had slipped into the garage, and before Josie could investigate, her phone vibrated.

WITH MRS. VANDERHAVEN keeping watch upstairs, Fran rushed downstairs, found the card for Lily Daye's lawyer, and dialed the number from the kitchen phone. She was so nervous that it took her two tries to get it right. The phone was answered on the first ring. Josie Bates whispered hello.

Fran cupped the receiver, intending to whisper back. Instead, she screamed, "Come quick. Mrs. V. saw the man. He's going into the garage behind Lily's cottage."

JOSIE HUNG up without saying goodbye, slid out of the chair, and got into a crouch: knees bent, fingers resting on the dirt, hunkered down behind Mary Margaret's vehicle.

With her car parked near the bluffs, Josie knew the women inside the hacienda assumed she wasn't on property. They would further assume that Josie would bring the police. But Josie was inside the garage, and the warning call had come too late, and the man was already inside the garage, and Dax was wandering too far afield to have barked a warning.

Against the far wall, Josie hugged the crumpled bumper of

the car, trying to steer clear of the sharp edges of metal and the shards of glass over the headlight. Whoever was in the garage with her would be forced to walk the same path Josie had when she came in. The man would pass the car on the undamaged side. That was the only certainty.

Her breathing slowed. Josie went stone still, waiting for the first glimpse of the man. In the pit of her stomach, there was the tell-tale knot of anxiety. She ignored it. She couldn't afford to let her guard down. She heard a bump and a shuffle before she saw him.

The person was not large like Brian Vanderhaven; he was not small and soft like Jimmy Burroughs. He was lithe, narrow, moving slowly, but not without purpose. He knew where he was going and he was coming her way, using his phone to create a puddle of light in front of him. He stopped at the boxes that Jimmy Burroughs had rejected, opened one and then another.

Josie fell back into the shadows. She heard him unstacking the boxes. Josie tried to see what was going on, but it was impossible without giving herself away. Whatever that man wanted, he could have it, yet he didn't seem to want anything. Instead, he was ripping the tape off the boxes and rooting around. A few pages fluttered to the ground near the car. When the box was empty, he threw it up against the car and opened another and another. More paper, more discarded boxes.

Overcome with curiosity, Josie strained to get a better look hoping he wouldn't notice her now that he was engaged. She saw a jacket that seemed too big for the man, a watch cap pulled low, heavy-soled boots. He wore a cross-body sling that bulged with whatever he was carrying.

He paused, raised his head like a prairie dog, and seemed to sniff the air. He felt her there, she was sure of it. He put his phone against his thigh until he had satisfied himself that whatever had given him pause was only his imagination. Josie fell back, closed her eyes, and held her breath. She willed herself to be invisible.

For a moment, she thought this person might be homeless. It would be so easy to sneak in, shelter for the night, and leave the next morning without being seen. But a homeless man wouldn't have a phone, or a fine jacket, or fancy boots. A homeless man would have no reason to ravage boxes of files. A homeless man would not—

Josie's reasoning clicked off along with the man's light. The garage was plunged into complete darkness. Holding onto the car's fender, she pulled herself up inch by inch. Before she could stand upright and confront the man, she heard the faint sound of metal turning on metal.

Next came the smell of alcohol, the sound of liquid hitting paper, the hiss of a flint like strike, and the acrid smell of sulfur.

CHAPTER 47

In the illumination of the match's flame, Josie saw Zack, the green-haired girl, her face

contorted into an expression of determination, uncertainty, and terror.

In that split-second Josie saw that the girl's eyes were blood-shot and unfocused.

In that split-second Josie understood what Zack was doing, but she couldn't react fast enough to stop her.

Zack dropped the match, and a split second was all it needed to ignite the accelerant she had poured on the papers.

"Oh my god."

The sound of Josie's voice startled the girl. She looked into the shadows, stunned to see Josie but paralyzed by the sight of the fire.

"Stomp on it!" Josie barked. "Use your feet!"

Josie threw out the order as she ran to the back of the garage to look for the packing blanket she had seen there. In the dark, she rooted around, throwing aside tools and trash, finally putting her hands on the dirty, torn fabric. Behind her, the fire surged. She grabbed the blanket, gathering it in her arms. It was heavy and cumbersome, and she half dragged it as she stumbled toward the fire. Horrified by what she saw, Josie hurried. The fire had grown, pushing Zack back up against the wall.

"Stomp on it! Come on, Zack." Josie cried again.

Zack put one foot out, but she was afraid to do what Josie wanted, and her half-hearted effort did nothing more than send sparks and shards of blackened paper up into the eaves.

Josie sprinted forward, doing her best to throw one end of the blanket over the fire to the girl.

"Grab it! Help me!"

Zack shook her head. She backed off, moving down the wall of brittle wood toward the door, leaving Josie behind the fire line and alone. Josie coughed and threw her arm over her nose and mouth. Eyes watering, she held her breath and threw the heavy blanket as best she could. It settled over a three-foot area, and for a moment the flames were quelled. She dragged it back, and tried again, but the smoke was getting thicker, the fire hotter, and the green haired girl was fleeing.

"Help m—" Josie tried again to get Zack's attention, but the words were choked off.

Zack gave no thought to Josie and was leaving her to die. Josie squinted through the smoke. The girl was almost at the door, but she never went through.

Suddenly, Dax was there flying at the girl, sinking his teeth into the sleeve of her big jacket. Zack screamed, but the sound was lost in her own coughing as the smoke filled the building. The struggle was fierce, and as much as Josie wanted to stop it, there was nothing she could do. The fire had created a dividing line and Josie was on the wrong side of it.

Again, she picked up the blanket and tried to throw it on the fire, but her strength was waning. Suddenly, Zack broke away from the dog. Dax shook his head, tossing away the length of fabric he had torn off Zack's jacket. Panicked, the girl ran toward Josie and the flames only to veer toward the car, wrenched open the door, and threw herself inside, terrified of the dog, the dark, and the fire.

Dax jumped and barked, lunged and whined. He ran into the night and back in again, unsure of what he should do. Then he was gone. She heard his barking grow faint as he ran away from the burning building.

The fire skittered up the garage wall to Josie's left, devouring the dry wood. It was burning under the car, leaving Josie with one escape route. She threw the blanket over the flames and stumbled to the other side of the garage where the car was pushed up against the wall. Coughing, hacking, Josie threw herself atop the car, the sharp metal slicing her hand. She ignored the blood and pain as she began to crawl, stopping only when she saw Zack cowering inside the car.

Their eyes met. Josie mouthed the words 'Get out'. She moved on. There was no other choice. The wreck Josie was crawling over was tight against the wall. There was no way to open the doors. Zack had to save herself; Josie had to do the same. Reaching the edge, Josie rolled off the car and onto the cold earth. She stayed down, trying to find a pocket of air to sustain her, but it wasn't to be found. Her lungs were on fire; her eyes were seared. Desperately, she reached for the car, hoping to use it as leverage, hoping it would ground her so that she could get her bearings and figure which way was out, but the smoke was too much.

Josie was human.

She was afraid.

She was suffocating.

She ached with unbearable pain knowing that she would not see Archer or Hannah or Billy again.

Flat on the ground, in one last desperate attempt to save herself, Josie scratched at the earth, trying to pull herself forward.

She failed.

She was dying.

The smoke now filled the garage top to bottom, the flames were advancing. Josie hoped that Zack had found her courage, gotten out of the car, and rushed past her unseen. She prayed that one of them would make it out alive. That was Josie's last thought before she slipped away, tilting on the edge of consciousness.

But then something happened. The devil who didn't fear the flames of hell came for Josie Bates. He took the form of a dog who feared nothing, who had cheated the hand of God as it reached for Josie's soul. What she didn't know was that Dax's lungs labored like hers. His strength was diminished like hers. But his spirit was one bit stronger than hers.

The dog's ferocious teeth dug into her shoulder, and his hot drool streamed down her neck. He dragged her, tugged at her, ignored the stones and glass and metal that littered the ground of the old garage. Dax used every ounce of his strength. He would save Josie or die trying. In a fog, she understood what was happening, and tried to help, pushing the soles of her shoes into the earth.

With one last heroic effort, Dax pulled her through the door, and both of them were expelled in a billow of smoke. Even then, Dax didn't stop. He dragged her, tugged at her, his great teeth puncturing her shoulder. Josie twisted onto her stomach and got to her knees. It was only then he let her go. She crawled away from the garage. Dax followed, unsteady, damaged, valiant.

When she could go no further, Josie rolled on her back and let her tears flow, trying to cool her burning eyes. Each breath was like a knife in her chest. She lay amid eucalyptus leaves under the cool moon of the December sky, unable to move.

Josie heard sirens.

She registered lights on the road below.

Her head lolled.

Dax was there, lying beside her. Dax who had saved her. His broad chest heaved, and his black eyes were steady on her. She tried to smile and reach for him. Instead, she rolled onto her shoulder and retched up cinders and smoke.

The dog raised his paw, touching her as people scrambled up the hill toward them. The sirens had stopped, but lights still flashed, flames grew tall and licked into the oh-so-flammable eucalyptus.

She wanted them to hurry. The men who could put out the fire, save Lily Daye's cottage, save her and the green-haired girl trapped in Mary Margaret Watkins's car.

Suddenly Dax rose up. Josie feared he was going to leave her. Instead, the dog threw himself on top of her: head-to-head, paws over her shoulders, his heavy body making it even more difficult to breathe. Josie tried to push him off, but it was impossible. He wouldn't have it. It was then, with the trees starting to flame, the old garage exploded in a fiery ball that rained down shards of wood and cinders and sorrow.

CHAPTER 48

THE NINTH WITNESS
THE PHONE

Josie sat on the living room floor tending to Dax.

Josie was cut and bruised, her lungs not fully recovered from the fire. One hand was bandaged and stitched, but it was Dax who had taken the brunt of the fallout when the garage exploded. A shard of wood flew into the sky like a kite, and then fell to earth like a spear. If Dax had not been on top of her, Josie would be dead. By some grace, when that piece of wood pierced the dog's back, it missed Dax's vital organs. He seemed more miffed with the fact that his beautiful coat had been shaved to allow the doctor to operate than he did with any pain the wound itself caused.

"How's it looking?"

Archer sat at the dining room table, going through the last of the things they had taken from Lily Daye's desk. More often than not, though, he was looking at Josie as if he feared she would disappear.

"Good." She gave Dax a pat. "You are, aren't you?"

Dax looked up, snuggled against her before going out to the patio. He put his front paws on the low wall and watched. Josie got up off the floor and went to the dining room table. She pulled out a chair, sat down, and poked at the stack of papers Archer was dutifully looking through before shredding them.

"Did Hannah call?" Josie asked.

"She checked in last night after you went to sleep," Archer said. "She's sorry she's been delayed. She says maybe she'll be here Christmas Day."

"I hope so." Josie looked around the house. It seemed too bare now. "We should put a Christmas tree up."

The shredder whirred. Josie crossed her arms on the table, happy to be doing nothing but watching Archer. Funny how looking death in the eye could make living so much better.

"When we finish this, I'll take you to get one." Archer looked sidelong at her. "They'll be cheap, we're so close to the day."

Josie chuckled. She drew a circle on the table and then flexed her fingers. Thankfully there had been no nerve damage. A few weeks and she would be playing volleyball again. Tiring of watching, she reached for Lily's briefcase, the last thing that needed to be cleared out.

"Do you want to send these on, Jo?" He handed over a stack of letters. Josie looked at the envelopes address to Carolyn Barnes; letters Lily had never sent. "I'm not sure what the call is here."

Josie looked out the French doors. Dax was still watching the walkway. A neighbor stopped to pet him. It was a good way to pass the time. She would join him as soon as she was done with Lily Daye.

"Jo?"

"Sorry. Yes, I'll send these along with the teacups." She pulled one leg under her and sat askew on the chair. "Do you think we should read them? I mean they might have something about Jimmy Burroughs."

"And then what?" Archer said.

"I don't know." Josie sighed. She was uncomfortable with so many loose ends. "The man got away with murder. Zack is dead because of him."

Archer stopped shredding and gave Josie his full attention. He'd been waiting for this conversation since she came home.

"Burroughs may have been manipulative, Jo," Archer said. "But he didn't light the match."

"I'm sure Jimmy Burroughs planted the seed. It probably sounded so easy: a fire wipes out all the records of Backlash, and Jimmy is home free. That girl was vulnerable to suggestion."

"So was Lily," Archer said. "Burroughs is a master at using vulnerable women, and he's a coward. But neither of those things is a crime."

"No, but there might have been evidence of wrongdoing in that car battery," Josie said. "I wish that had survived. I wish I could have done something to help Zack."

"I wish the same thing on both counts, but once the fire hit that battery, that was the end. They call it a thermal runaway. Nobody could have stopped it and nobody could put that thing back together once it happened," Archer said. "At least Lily managed to get under that guy's skin. She took his files; she took his money. It drove him nuts that he couldn't control her."

"Doesn't it bother you that we'll never know why he wanted all those records and not the money?"

Josie put her bandaged hand out to Archer. He put the paper he was holding in the shredder before he touched her fingertips.

"I don't care," Archer said. "It's Christmas. Forget Burroughs, and remember that you went over and above for Lily. You may never know whether or not she killed herself.

You may never know why Dax was chained or who the man was that the old lady saw. But you do know Lily had a big heart. She remembered those children, and she took care of Mr. Murray. Whatever guilt she felt, it was hers." He went back to his chore and said, "I'll grant you it's kind of odd it took her years to start feeling guilty."

"Something must have triggered it. Something Burroughs did," Josie said.

"Enough of Burroughs. What do you have in the case?"

Josie picked up a handful of papers. "Past due notices for the electric."

Josie handed them to him and the shredder ate them.

"Past due notices for the gas company."

Again, the shredder whirred. Dax came in and settled beside her.

"Wouldn't you like to know—" Josie said.

"No." Archer didn't let her finish. He held out his hand. Josie gave him a notice to vacate signed by Brian Vanderhaven.

She took the last two pieces of paper from the brief case. The first she handed to Archer. He held out his hand for the last one, but Josie held on to it. He waited while she read it more closely.

When she was done, Josie stood up and said, "Get your keys. We've got to go."

⊏⊐

THE LAST THING Josie found in Lily Daye's briefcase was a receipt for a local storage unit. It was the only bill that was not in arrears, and that, Josie believed, was Lily speaking to her from the grave.

The unit was housed in a large complex behind an electri-fied fence near King Harbor. Lily had written the access code neatly in the upper corner of the rental contract.

"Got it, Jo."

Archer stepped away from the keypad. It glowed green, indicating that the code had been correct. He reached down, grasped the handle, and opened the rolling door. Dax started at the sound. Josie and the dog waited while Archer went in, found the light switch, and gave them the all clear.

Inside was chilly inside and smelled stale as if the door hadn't been opened in a very long while. The unit itself was a small square of concrete. The only thing inside was a table made of polished stone and a wooden box on top of that.

"Want me to see what it is?" Archer asked.

Josie shook her head and she handed him Dax's leash. She walked to the table, a display so stark and odd that she felt as if they had stumbled into a crypt. Yet this would not be strange for the Lily Daye Josie had come to know. Lily, who took on complex problems and boiled them down to neatly typed reports. Lily, who had found Josie and entrusted her with her legacy, a plan months and maybe years in the making. Lily, who had left an intricate trail of clues that told a simple story of pain and regret.

Josie ran a hand across the top of the box, plain hewn and inexpensive. There was a small gold clasp. Josie swung it free, used both hands to open the lid, and considered the contents. The box itself was divided into two sections. In one there was an old phone and a charger. In the second were two bound reports, modest in size, neatly labeled with the title: "The Case Against Jimmy Burroughs." Underneath that was a single sheet of paper.

Archer came to her side. She held it up for him to see.

"An NDA." he said.

"Dated seven years ago."

Josie handed it to him. She knew Zack had made Lily sign it the first day she came to work at Backlash. Lily, who loved a paper trail, who played by every rule, had honored this order all the days of her life. Now, it didn't matter. Now Lily could speak, albeit from the grave. Josie opened one of the reports and began to read.

Ms. Bates,

If you are reading this, I have passed. In your hand is the full transcript of conversations between Mr. Jimmy Burroughs and Ms. Mary Margaret Watkins and his verbal interaction with the onboard battery computer that had been placed in Ms. Watkins's car.

You will find in these pages proof that Mr. Burroughs knowingly reprogrammed Mary Margaret Watkins's car so that it would take a precise route and shut off when it was on the railroad tracks at an unmarked crossing in Emeryville, California on December 13, the day the Southern Pacific train carrying Backlash Technologies' Distant2 hardware crashed into said car.

Mr. Burrows knowingly disabled the car, causing the crash that killed seven souls and injured Mr. John Murray. Mr. Burroughs did this, because Distant2 did not work and would never work. He defrauded the military of their money. He led everyone to believe that it was the train wreck that damaged the hardware beyond repair. He blamed the railroad's negligence, and he put the blame on Mary Margaret Watkins. He said, under oath, that she had taken her own life and changed the battery codes. She did not. He changed those codes. You will see that she complained about the seatbelt and questioned the code change.

The truth is that Mr. Burroughs, and Mr. Burroughs alone, is responsible for all of this. I am ashamed that I had neither the strength nor the courage to do anything about this while I lived; I am ashamed I did not have the will to live with this knowledge any longer. I believe Mr. Burroughs is criminally responsible for lives lost, fraud, and other crimes.

Regarding the money found in an account with Merrill Lynch. I did not use any for personal gain. I took only as much as I believed a jury would award Mr. Murray should Jimmy Burroughs ever be held to account.

While you will not remember me, I spoke to you outside a courtroom in Los Angeles California. I was impressed by your representation of your client that day. Above all, you were kind and assured me of your help when I was ready to seek it. I hope my faith in you was not misplaced.

I further hope that you will proceed with the authorities regarding Mr. Burroughs culpability.

The transcript is notarized. However, should you need further proof, please charge the phone you find in this box. The original recording of Mr. Burroughs changing the code on the battery can be clearly heard. Regarding Distant2, the reason it did not work and could never work is because of a defective code. If the code had been given to the military, they would have discovered that Jimmy Burroughs had perpetrated a hoax and was not going to deliver what he promised and never could. The code is the Digital Analysis Expression. Please give the authorities the leather-bound notebook you found in my briefcase, the thumb drive you found in a safe deposit box, and the DAX code that you will find.

Josie stopped reading aloud. She turned toward Archer. They both looked at the dog, but it was Josie who discarded the report, got down beside him, and removed his heavy collar. She pulled the leather straight so that they could clearly see the letters and numbers burned into the leather. This was not the dog's name; this was the key to everything.

Lily Daye had covered her bases. Worried that Jimmy Burroughs might hunt her down, worried that she might be powerless to fight him, Lily dispersed the evidence, hiding it in so many places he would never find it. Even if he destroyed some of it, as he had with the fire, he could never destroy all of it. Lily's briefcase, her safe deposit box, and finally a dog that Jimmy Burroughs would fear were the blocks Lily used to build a case against the god of Backlash Technologies.

"I wish I'd known Lily," Josie said.

Archer put his hand on the dog's head.

"Are you going to give him a new name?" Archer asked.

Josie shook her head.

"No." She put the collar back on. "But I think it's time for a new leash. Pink isn't his color."

CHAPTER 49

"Don't forget the cinnamon rolls."

Josie got Dax out of the back seat of the Jeep while Archer dutifully picked up the box of rolls.

It was Christmas Day and Josie was downright joyful. She and Archer would celebrate with Faye, both their calendars were clear until after the new year, Lily was on her way back to England, and Jimmy Burroughs was in a mess of trouble.

Josie had shared the phone recording and files with the Feds. Burroughs had been arrested the night before on Christmas Eve. Josie's only disappointment was that he would not be charged with the deaths of Lily Daye and Zack, but the seven counts of murder and a laundry list of other charges the U.S. Attorney had brought would keep him in jail for the rest of his life.

"There you are!"

Josie, Archer, and Dax turned to see Rusty Gates burst out of Faye's house and office, waving at them, hailing them like long lost relatives.

"Oh my god." Josie hung her head and laughed.

Archer put his arm around her, kissed her. and said, "It's

Christmas, Jo. Be nice."

Josie kissed him back and went to give Rusty her best.

"Shouldn't you be home with your gorgeous wife?" she said just before he gave her a bear hug.

"Not until dinner time. That means I can have brunch with you," he said. "I shouldn't even talk to you after what you did to Jimmy. Then again, I'll make a fortune defending him so maybe that wasn't coal I was seeing in my stocking after all."

"I'm happy things worked out for both of you," Josie said.

Rusty reached around Josie to shake Archer's hand.

"Faye invited me because she wanted to have the unveiling today."

Josie lifted her chin and hoped whatever her lips were doing passed for a smile. Josie glanced at the sign on the lawn. It was covered in a painter's cloth. There was a bow on the corner of it. She was surprised that Faye would choose today of all days to announce the new ownership of Baxter & Baxter. She didn't want to be reminded that the new year would bring new management to Baxter & Baxter in the form of Rusty Gates. But it wasn't her call and she had only herself to blame.

"Where is Faye?"

"Coming now."

Rusty hurried back to the house and offered a hand to Faye as she came down the stairs. He passed her off to Josie and Archer. Kisses and hugs were exchanged.

"I can't believe you invited Rusty today," Josie said. "I thought it was family today."

"It is," Faye said.

Archer turned Josie until she faced the front door. In the next second, Hannah and Billy bounded out of the house laughing, delighted with the surprise.

"They've been here a while," Archer said.

Josie wasn't listening. She was hugging Faye, and then rushing to do the same to Hannah and Billy.

"I can't believe it. I just can't," Josie said. "When did you get here?"

"Billy docked yesterday," Hannah said. "I've been here a few days, but I didn't want you bothering me while I worked."

"Where are you working?"

"Get to it, Hannah. Show us the new sign." Rusty gave the order as if he had known Hannah all her life.

Hannah, her long black hair still a riot of gorgeous curls, her green eyes sparkling, took Billy's hand. When they got to the sign, she took hold of one end of the cloth and Billy the other.

"I am unveiling my latest work," Hannah said, just before she counted to three.

On cue, the two young people pulled the cloth away. Josie took a step forward and then another.

Rusty had his arm around her shoulder. He kissed her hair.

"Guess the best man won," he said.

The new driftwood was larger than the last one and darker. It was polished to a mirror-like sheen. Rusty stepped back.

Josie shook her head, and Faye linked arms with her.

"I figure I could work remotely for a while," Faye said.

"I figure you could."

The two women stood there, looking at the sign, admiring Hannah's work and the words she had carved into the beautiful wood.

Baxter, Baxter, & Bates.

***

Turn the page to start reading
SEVERED RELATIONS
Book 1, Finn O'Brien Thrillers

SEVERED RELATIONS

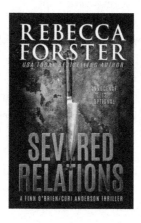

Chapter 1
DAY 1 – MORNING

It was late – or early – depending on one's point of view. Neither Mort, the short redheaded guy, nor the man so unremarkable that Mort had christened him Medium Man, cared about the hour. For them it was just time to go to work.

While they drove, they shot the shit about cars and chicks, the gates, the guard, the price of shoes and booze, and getting into the house. Mort laughed hard and quick and said they would have to quit the business the day they couldn't get in a house. When Medium Man laughed, he huffed and puffed and wiggled like he had to hit the john. Even when he wasn't laughing, Medium Man itched and twitched. But he was reliable and good at his job so Mort didn't mind so much.

They drove the length of Wilshire Boulevard, deserted this time of night, found the side street that would take them to another side street and yet another that would eventually get them where they were going. Mort said getting to this place was like driving through a damn crop circle in the middle of L.A. Medium Man didn't know what that was, and Mort didn't feel like explaining, so they stopped talking until Mort finally pulled over. He parked the car at the curb between two houses. Anyone who looked at it would assume the car belonged to a kid home from college, a maid, or was just the fourth-car-out in the land of three car garages.

Mort and Medium Man walked the wide streets, admiring the houses. Mort put his hands in his pocket and kicked at a pebble. Medium Man yawned. They acted as if they belonged, but if anyone bought that then Mort had a bridge for them. Finally, Mort put his arm out. Medium Man stopped, wiped the back of his hand across his nose, and asked:

"This it?"

"Yep," Mort said and took stock of the property.

One light burned in the back of the impressive Tudor with its peaked roof and leaded windows. In front, the outdoor fixtures were strategically placed for beauty, not safety. The flowerbeds pooled with a soft light that didn't reach the ridiculous sweep of lawn on which they stood. The front door was illuminated but brick arches shadowed the entrance. The houses on either side were set back on lots that were just as big as this one. Between them, beautiful old trees and flowering foliage created a natural sound barrier and screen.

Wordlessly they walked up the driveway, Medium Man cutting off to the side of the house and Mort to the shadows of the entry arches. When Medium Man came around again, Mort tended to the door.

A jab. A touch. A flick. A click and it was done.

Inside, they got the lay of the land. Mort had seen better but not by much. Medium Man, though, stood in the foyer with his mouth hanging open. He looked at the grand staircase, the shiny marble floor in the entry, and the hardwood floors beyond that. He looked at the entry table and all the silver-framed pictures on top of it. Tears welled in his eyes when he saw the picture of a woman caught in a moment of happy surprise. She was so beautiful. Medium Man wished he had a picture of someone like that to put in a frame. He was picking it up, thinking to take it with him, when Mort hissed:

"Don't touch nothin'."

Medium Man wiped the frame clean with his shirt, put it down, and circled back to Mort like a dog returning to the place where the scent was strong. They went up the stairs, Mort first. There wasn't a creak and that impressed Mort. The place was quality all the way.

Upstairs, there were five doors as expected. Three were closed, two ajar. He looked into the first room, stepped back and nodded to Medium Man who reached into his pocket for the gun. It was heavier than the knife he preferred, but Mort said they were there to do a job and not make a statement. Medium Man didn't quite understand that since he never said anything at work. Still, he never argued with Mort so he held the gun and waited for the signal.

When he got it, Medium Man went into the first room and

bee-lined for the brass studio bed. A couch by day, the frilly cover was now folded neatly at the foot of the mattress. The woman in it made little sighing sounds while she dreamed. At first Medium Man's heart sank. She looked pretty and that was too bad. He hated hurting pretty things. When he got a little closer, though, he saw that she wasn't all that pretty so it was okay.

His footfall wasn't even a whisper on the plush carpet, yet as he raised the gun the woman threw back the covers and bolted out of bed. Shorter and stockier than he had imagined her to be, Medium Man was shocked as she lunged for her phone on the night table. He let out a yelp, threw out his arm, and knocked her back. She tumbled to the floor only to roll and push off again. This time, she lowered her head and ran straight for Medium Man. Her skull caught him hard under the ribs.

He doubled over, grunting, the breath pushed out of him. He went down clutching his stomach. The gun dropped out of his hand and fell to the floor. He could feel it against his knee but had no time to grab it up because the woman was everywhere: hands and teeth, arms and knees, hair flying, fighting silently like she was mute, fighting hard like she was an animal. She reached for his face and her nails grazed his cheek. Those nails were short so she didn't draw blood. Her nightdress was long and she tangled in it as she tried to scramble over him. He was mad that she was causing such trouble; he was repulsed by her big breasts, her plump butt, and her woman smell. Still, he was determined not to let her get the best of him so he kept pulling at her. Her foot caught his thigh and she tried to use it for leverage, but she got no traction. In fact, she got nowhere at all because Mort was there.

Yes, there he was, in the room filled with muffled grunts and desperate breathing. He grabbed the woman's arms and twisted her wrists one over the other, flipping her onto her back. Medium Man scampered up at the same time, swiping up the gun just as Mort knelt down hard on the woman's crossed arms.

"I coulda–" Medium Man began, but Mort shot him a look so he shut up.

The woman was gurgling like she was trying to say something, but her lips weren't working. Medium Man watched Mort, the master, as he looked into the woman's wild, terrified eyes. He put one hand on top of her head, and said:

"Hush now."

The woman trembled and then stopped struggling. That's when Medium Man swooped down, put the muzzle against her temple, and pulled the trigger. In the same instant, Mort moved his hand. The small caliber bullet made a clean exit on the other side of her skull. It brought with it bits of her brain, some bone, and a spray of blood.

Mort brushed at the blood spray on his shirt, but it was only a reflex. He knew that you never got all the blood out of anything so it was useless to try to wipe it away. That was too bad since he was especially partial to this shirt. All in all, though, the job went okay. He would have preferred it went perfect, but he blamed himself for not anticipating this woman's reaction and preparing for it.

She was trained to listen for the slightest noise: a call, a moan, a cry in the night. It was her job to protect and she had tried as hard as she could to do it well. Mort admired that in the same way he admired Medium Man for doing his. He would tell that to Medium Man when they were in the car. It wasn't easy to do the kind of work they did. Now they were finished. It was time to go. Yet when he looked at his compadre he saw that something was amiss. Medium Man was looking past him, so Mort turned his head to see what had caught the guy's attention. All he saw was a flash of color like you see when someone is running away to hide.

Before he could do anything, Medium Man was out the door, his beloved knife in hand. Mort hung his head for a second and then picked up the gun his partner had dropped. He pocketed the piece and took a second look at the dead woman. If she were alive, he would have apologized. He would have told her this wasn't part of the plan. He would have explained that there was no stopping Medium Man once he got the fever.

That was a pity.

Not a crying shame.

Just a pity.

CHAPTER 2

Murder behind the gates of Fremont Place was unheard of. A triple homicide, two of the victims children, in the home of a wealthy, young attorney was downright bizarre, and it was Finn O'Brien's bad luck that it was his first call since reporting to Wilshire Division. It was the kind of call that would put his heart crossways, as his mother would say. He would have agreed with her except his Irish heart had been crossways for years already – ever since Alexander died – and he had learned to live with it. He doubted what he found in Fremont Place could do more damage.

Finn made a right off Wilshire Boulevard, drove a hundred feet to the guardhouse and stopped at the waste-of-money fancy iron gates stuck into the high stone walls. Inside the shack, a kid barely out of his teens slumped over the desk. He was dressed in an ill-fitting, puke-beige, polyester shirt with an official looking patch on the shoulder.

When the kid realized someone was waiting on him, he swung his head and eyed the dark car and the man wearing a leather jacket and aviator sunglasses. It took a minute, but eventually he figured out who Finn was and dragged himself off his chair. He stood in the doorway of the faux house, arms hanging, his face so long he would have asphalt burns on his chin by the time his shift ended. Finn showed his badge and then started the conversation while he slipped it back in his pocket.

"Been here long, have you?"

"Since midnight."

"Good boy to hang in." Finn swung his head in sympathy. "Tough times. I know how it is. Very rough for you, don't let anyone tell you different."

A little sympathy was all it took for the kid's mouth to run away with him. He stepped down, lowered his voice, and grabbed onto Finn's open window.

"The only people that came through belonged here. I logged every single car and called up to the houses to confirm visitors. I swear I did. Nobody walked through. I would have done something if somebody tried to walk through. I have a good sense for stuff. If somebody tried to come in who shouldn't have been here, I would have known. If they had tried to talk their way in, I wouldn't have let them. I would have called someone... I would have called... I..."

Finn winced as he listened to the boy. He had made those same declarations to anyone who would listen after his brother's death. If he had only known, Finn swore, he would have done heroic things. But he hadn't known because Finn had been seventeen and full of hisself as his mother told anyone who would listen. That day he was behind the bleachers, so lost in the deep wet kisses of a cheerleader that he forgot to pick the little boy up from school. The next time Finn saw Alexander he was in a coffin, dressed in a stiff shirt and dark suit bought especially for the occasion of his burial. Still, if he had known what was going to happen, Finn swore that he would have been brave and he would have saved Alexander — or died trying. Finn's father had nodded as if he knew that to be true, his mother had held her oldest son to her and said she believed the same. It was bull but people were kind all those years ago, so Finn was kind now.

"There's no stopping the devil from his rounds. There's nothing you could have done," he said. "And if there had been, I know you would have done it. I can tell you're a brave sort by looking at you."

With that, the young man actually focused on Finn and the detective saw that he had eyes the color of caramel and a heart that was just as soft. He wouldn't have known a liar if he saw one. Finn lifted the edge of his lips and gave him the slightest nod. The boy's chest caved with relief. His relief proved Finn right; the boy didn't know a liar when he saw one.

"We're going to be needing to talk to you, so don't go upsetting yourself when someone calls. It will probably be me; might be my partner. Can't give you a name on that yet, but they'll identify themselves as working with Detective O'Brien. You being in law enforcement yourself, you know how an investigation goes. We'll want to be thorough. You understand?"

The kid nodded, and licked his lips, and nodded some more. He looked like a bobble-head doll.

"Rest up when you get home," Finn went on. "Calm yourself. Don't think too hard about what happened last night. Sometimes you remember more things when you don't think too hard."

"Yeah, okay. Okay." The young man swallowed hard. Color was coming back to his cheeks, but it wasn't the right color for a healthy person. He straightened up. His voice was more measured when he said:

"The last car came in at one-thirteen. By the book."

"Good man." Finn handed him a card. "Hang on to that log of yours and give it over to your supervisor, not your replacement. If you think of anything, call me. If you just find yourself needing someone to talk to, I can manage some time for that too."

If the boy answered, Finn didn't hear him. The detective's eyes were on the gate. The boy with the caramel eyes now knew what was what, and they both had to get on with this terrible day. The kid stepped back, punched whatever button raised the gate, and by the time the arm lowered again he was slumped back in his chair. Now he was holding tight to the card with the name Finn O'Brien, Detective printed neatly under the logo of the LAPD.

As Finn drove on, he took note of his surroundings in the same way a boyo at the pub might admire a beautiful girl who was out of his league. Fremont Place was an impressive enclave: wide streets, big, beautiful houses, setbacks the size of small parks, and garages bigger than most people's apartments. These stately homes were built of brick and stucco, leaded windows faced tree-lined streets, and inside the walls were crafted of real lathe and plaster. New money owned them, but old money had built them in the thirties. There were two elite schools and a tennis club within the boundaries.

Just beyond the wall surrounding Fremont Place, the real world was a mash-up. Wilshire high rises, bustling during the day, were deserted after seven. A few blocks over were neighborhoods that had no names where people of color owned houses with bars on the windows. A little further to the east was downtown Los Angeles. Hollywood spread north into the hills. Koreatown, Little Tokyo, and Chinatown were all within spitting distance. Fremont Place was a suburb held hostage in the heart of a big, ugly city and it just got a reminder of that in spades.

When he arrived at his destination, Finn parked his car behind a black and white and two panel vans. There were two more black and whites parked a half a block down. A uniformed officer watched the perimeter of the house while one stood on the porch, eyes forward.

Finn took note of the time and of the well-kept women huddled together in the street. They swayed like tall grass every time a whispered speculation or murmur of disbelief passed from one to the other. When Alexander was killed the women came to Finn's mother, too. They had casseroles and arms to wrap around her while the men lamented the horrible crime over their whiskey. These women would not bring casseroles to whoever was inside and there was no doubt someone was in the house from the looks of the Jaguar in the driveway. The car was bronze-colored, top-of-the-line, and new. The trunk yawned. There was a suitcase still inside and two on the ground. One had burst open, and the contents had spilled over the concrete and brick. A wrought-iron gate stood open in front of the car and past that, deep into the property and hardly visible from where Finn stood, was a large garage. The folks of Fremont Place seemed to be fond of fancy, useless gates.

When Finn got out of his car, it was a lady with red hair who saw him first. She did a double take, touched the woman next to her, and said something. That woman looked at Finn and then another and another. It had been that way since he was thirteen and puberty ambushed his childhood. Overnight he had become a strapping man with a swagger. Of course, that was God's doing and not his. Kicking a soccer ball half his life had made him quick and graceful on the run but the swagger left no doubt he was not meant to fly. He did not regret that he looked like a tough – it was good for the job – but Finn regretted that, at times, the good people feared him because of it.

He went past the gaggle of neighbor ladies, acknowledged no one, and looked for anyone who didn't seem overly curious, stunned, or horrified. That would be the person to talk to. Finn saw no one who fit the bill, so he didn't break his stride. When a news van pulled up Finn O'Brien gave it the evil eye for good measure, picked up the pace, and was past the cop on the porch before the van doors opened and the fools with microphones saw him.

You can find SEVERED RELATIONS at your favorite online bookstore now

Also by Rebecca Forster

THE WITNESS SERIES
JOSIE BATES THRILLERS

HOSTILE WITNESS Book #1

Includes **HANNAH'S DIARY**, a bonus novella

Some secrets aren't uncovered, they're unleashed

A prominent judge is brutally murdered. The accused killer is a 16-year-old girl with shocking secrets. Josie Bates takes her case, a decision that will change both their lives forever.

SILENT WITNESS Book #2

Nothing speaks louder than the truth

Josie Bates is blindsided when Archer is accused of murder. Reluctant to come clean about his stepson's suspicious death years ago, Josie finds her faith tested as she defends the man she loves.

PRIVILEGED WITNESS Book #3

An old flame; a new fear

The beautiful wife of a senate candidate falls to her death, his disturbed sister is accused and a critical election is at risk. Josie Bates must face her ex-lover to fight for justice in a world corrupted by lies, power, and abuse.

EXPERT WITNESS Book #4

Some things you don't want to know

When Josie Bates disappears without a trace, Hannah and Archer must pull together to connect the dots between the woman they love, the ruthless attorney she used to be, and the people who want her gone for good.

EYEWITNESS, Book #5

Blame is in the eye of the beholder

Three people are massacred in a California beach house; a latchkey kid Josie cares about is accused. The justice she seeks is brutal, barbaric and buried in a blood soaked past half a world away.

FORGOTTEN WITNESS Book #6

When death is slow, the fight is fierce

A madman's ramblings put Josie Bates on the road to find the teenage runaway she loves. But Josie's journey puts her on a collision course with the United States government that wants to keep the truth top secret at any cost.

DARK WITNESS Book #7

The final flight; the darkest fight

In a remote wilderness, Hannah's life hangs in the balance. To save her, Josie Bates invokes the fierce, primal law that she knows the girl's captors will understand: survival of the fittest.

LOST WITNESS Book #8

A hidden past, a deadly future

In the hold of a cargo ship off the Port of L.A., a powerful man is dead and the woman who killed him is mortally wounded. On shore a man staggers from the surf, a man whose plea for help Josie Bates will not be able refuse even if it means hers might be the next life lost.

THE 9TH WITNESS Book#9

Josie Bates's personal and professional life is headed for a sea change when Lily Daye, a woman Josie has never heard of, names her executor of her estate. Seemingly meager, the estate hides secrets that put Josie in the sights of a man with more money than God and a reason for wanting the dead to stay silent.

FINN O'BRIEN/CORI ANDERSON

CRIME THRILLERS

SEVERED RELATIONS Book #1

Two children and their nanny are slaughtered. A shunned cop catches the call.

Two children and their nanny are slaughtered in the home of a rich young attorney and his beautiful wife. Detective Finn O'Brien follows a trail of bodies and shattered relationships that ends with a choice that is both personal and deadly.

FOREIGN RELATIONS Book #2

A Foreign Woman is dead. Two countries want the truth buried along with the body.

When a woman hurtles from a freeway overpass, Finn O'Brien discovers she is not what she seems. More than one person wanted her dead, two countries want her forgotten, and Finn O'Brien won't rest until he knows why.

SECRET RELATIONS Book #3

They're illegal. They're undocumented. They're disappearing.

Finn is drawn into the crosshairs of controversy when his partner's daughter asks him to find her boyfriend - an illegal immigrant. Soon Finn is tracking a killer with a gruesome secret that has been buried under decades of shame; a killer the world has forgotten about until now.

INTIMATE RELATIONS- Book #4

Desire is an art; death is a craft.

A domestic disturbance brings Finn O'Brien to an artists' colony on the frayed edges of the city. There he finds a bizarre gathering of Los Angeles elites, a man in a rage, and a young woman beaten to death. As he hunts a killer, Finn finds himself in a surreal world where art and science create strange bedfellows, money and desire birth shameful descendants, and the deadliest relationships of all are the most intimate.

DISTANT RELATIONS - Book #5

Sometimes distance can be deadly.

A private plane explodes killing Finn's estranged uncle and his childhood love. Coming to grips with the tragedy, Finn O'Brien puts the accident behind him until a misdirected insurance settlement, a federal investigation, and an arrogant ATF agent pique his curiosity and provoke his anger. Finn goes rogue, only to discover that his life, and the lives of those he loves, are in the hands of a distant and deadly relation.

MORE THRILLING READS

BEFORE HER EYES

She runs; death follows

A mountain grocer is executed and a fading model is missing. Sheriff Dove Connelly embarks on an investigation that drags him into a twilight world where nothing is at it seems, life and death hang in a delicate balance and his very thoughts could tip the scales toward hell.

THE MENTOR

When justice is an illusion, the verdict is deadly

When homegrown terrorists bomb an IRS building, fledgling US Attorney Lauren Kingsley looks to her mentor to guide her through a prosecution fraught with peril. Little does she know that those closest to her, are the most dangerous people of all.

BEYOND MALICE

Some lawyers will do anything for the firm

When beautiful, arrogant Nora Royce is accused of murder, her sister, Amanda Cross, is the only one willing to defend her. Outgunned and outmanned, Amanda peels away the layers of entitlement and political protection surrounding L.A.'s legal elites to uncover a truth that could end Amanda's career and both their lives.

KEEPING COUNSEL

Take an oath, give up your life

Attorney Tara Linley takes on her best friend's lover as a client and gets more than she bargained for. A killer smile and smooth-talking ways can't hide this psychopath's insanity as he pushes the boundaries of client privilege, sexual desire and the limits of friendship.

<u>CHARACTER WITNESS</u>

When opportunity knocks, run

(NOT a Josie Bates thriller)

Kathleen Cotter, junior partner at a past-its-prime Beverly Hills law firm gets a doozy of a first case. A dead man's ex-wife says it's murder; the insurance company says suicide. Kathleen thinks everyone is nuts until she uncovers a trail of lies and corruption that threaten to make her first case her last.

⊏⊐

About the Author

Rebecca Forster started writing on a crazy dare. Now with almost forty books to her name, she is a USA Today and Amazon best-selling author. She lives in Southern California, is married to a superior court judge and is the proud mother of two sons.

FIND OUT MORE ABOUT REBECCA
or follow her on any of these sites

Made in the USA
Middletown, DE
18 October 2024

62681829R00199